W9-BFT-123

COURAGE AT
THE CROSSROADS

Wolf of Foix had known so much of all there was to know of life—the intoxication of bloodlust and the heady thrust and parry of battle . . . the thrill of victory and the bitterness of defeat . . . the celebration of homecoming and the emptiness of exile . . . the love of a wife and the passion of a woman who was everything that a wife could never be . . .

But now Wolf of Foix was for the first time tempted to lay down his sword . . . to admit defeat . . . to surrender to those he had fought since his first coming into manhood . . .

. . . and neither the hatred burning in his soul nor the pleading woman at his side could help him make the agonizing choice that was his alone. . . .

"A rich tapestry . . . a well-written novel"

—*Best Sellers*

"Epic drama . . . wonderful . . . gripping . . . thoughtful . . . great!" —*New York Herald Tribune*

Popular Library is proud to present Hannah Closs's
THE TARN TRILOGY in paperback:

HIGH ARE THE MOUNTAINS (#1) 04219-2 $1.95
DEEP ARE THE VALLEYS (#2) 04250-8 $1.95
THE SILENT TARN (#3) 04275-3 $1.95

The Tarn Trilogy · III
THE SILENT TARN
by Hannah Closs

POPULAR LIBRARY • NEW YORK

THE SILENT TARN (THE TARN TRILOGY #3)

Published by Popular Library, a unit of CBS Publications, the Consumer Publishing Division of CBS Inc., by arrangement with The Vanguard Press, Inc.

Copyright © 1963 by The Vanguard Press, Inc.

All rights reserved. No portion of this book may be reproduced in any form without the written permission of the publisher, except by a reviewer who may wish to quote brief passages in connection with a review for a newspaper or magazine.

ISBN: 0-445-04275-3

Printed in the United States of America

10 9 8 7 6 5 4 3 2 1

LIST OF CHARACTERS

RAYMOND VI, *Count of Toulouse*
RAMONET, *his son*
RAMÒN-ROGER, *Count of Foix*
ROGER, *his legitimate son*
WOLF, *his bastard*
ESCLARMONDE OF FOIX, *sister to Ramon-Roger*
JORDAN OF THE ISLE, *her son*
RAIMON-ROGER, *son of Raimon-Roger* TRENCAVEL
   of Carcassone and AGNES OF MONTPELLIER
MIRIAM CARAVITA, *daughter of a Jewish financier*
COUNT THIBAUT IV OF CHAMPAGNE
SICARD OF DURBAN
HONORIA, *his sister and the wife of Wolf*
PEIRE-ROGER OF MIREPOIX
RAMON OF PÉRELHA IN ROCCAFISSADA (ROQUE-
   FIXADE)
CORBA, *his wife*
PHILIPPA *and* ESCLARMONDE OF PÉRELHA, *his
   daughters*
HUGO D'ALFARO, *a student of noble Spanish descent
   but nihilist inclination*
A HERMIT, *in the Sabarthez caverns of the Ariège valley*
SIMON DE MONTFORT
ALYS DE MONTMORENCY, *his wife*
AMAURY DE MONTFORT, *their son*
YOLANDE, *their daughter*
GUY DE LÉVIS, *King Louis's maréchal*
FRIAR GUILLAUME ARNAUD
FULK, *Bishop of Toulouse, formerly a troubadour of
   Marseilles*
ARNAUD-AMALRIC, *Bishop of Citeaux*
DOMINGO DI GUZMAN (*St. Dominic*)

THE SILENT TARN

MAGIC LANDSCAPE

Charm'd magic casements, opening on the foam
Of perilous seas, in faery lands forlorn.

(KEATS: *Ode to a Nightingale*)

AND ONE MORE STONE AND YET ANOTHER, BOULDER ON boulder piled to the bald, blunt crown of that petrified and Cyclopean head. . . .

Sitting back on her heels, Esclarmonde of Pérelha paused in her labors and gazed critically on the image fashioned by her hands.

The jutting jaws, the cavern of the mouth ravenous with shadow, fanged teeth—scabrous with lichen, perilous as a giddy crag; and last, set deep beneath the gashed and beetling brows, a glassy pebble, clear and impenetrable as a mountain tarn.

Raising herself on her knees and sweeping together the pine needles littering the ground, the child gathered them to an ocean round the rocky pile. For a moment she hesitated, then, dragging toward her a stone she had set apart, thrust it into the midst of the encircling tide. Towered and turreted, crested with gleaming quartz, it rose above those dark unnavigable seas, an unreachable island, jealously guarded by its giant custodian, unceasingly watched over by that lidless and unwinking eye.

For some little time longer she continued rapt in contemplation, then, apparently satisfied, rose to her feet. Taking a long twig of hazel, she prodded the tip into the ground and, pushing it before her, proceeded to walk in a circle round the miniature landscape spread at her feet.

She moved slowly and with a grave intention, as one who performs a solemn rite, her eyes fixed on the ground so that no unevenness in the surface should cause her hand to waver or the line of her circuit to break. And then, half muttering, half singing, she began to chant under her breath.

Imprisoned in its magic ring, the landscape, a world apart, lay bound by a law unfathomable, apprehensible only in sign and symbol, the dark utterance of that secret tongue.

Oblivious of all but her task, she scarcely heard the long winding blast of a horn rise on the air, till, fading, it rose once more and, dying, echoed among the hills.

Now, as if suddenly waking, she raised her head, listening, then, dropping the wand, pushed her way through the bushes that hemmed in her secret grove and, as fast as her hands and feet would carry her, scrambled up the scarp beyond.

Arrived at the top, she halted and, shading her eyes against the setting sun, gazed down into the valley that spread on two sides of the cliff-like promontory on which she stood.

Beneath her the land, blotched with dark masses of forest, broken here and there by umber patches of fresh-tilled soil, rose undulating toward the wall of mountain that barred the horizon and, bulging forward, swelled to a menacing head. Wreathed in clouds, the summit was invisible, but between it and the ridges of hills that rose on the left a rocky peak crowned by the lighter gleam of masonry jutted, even as in that miniature landscape, out of the impenetrable ocean of the woods.

It was not on these, however, that the child's gaze was fixed but on the long ribbon of road winding between the ruddy trunks of the trees. Bathed in liquid light, the cavalcade approaching far off along that sun-gilded track seemed so minute that it seemed almost the procession of some strange and iridescent species of ant.

Breathless, she watched till the long antennae, the scintillating caparison of the approaching host, had resolved themselves into the bristling shafts, the glitter of lance and hunting gear. Even then she waited till with certainty she could make out, against a foil of emerald and gold, the triple bearings—turret, fish, and crescent moon—arms of

Peire-Roger of Mirepoix, head of the house of Luna. Not, however, until the last of the horsemen had been swallowed up by a bend in the road did she leave her post and without apparent haste retrace her steps. In the grove she paused and slowly but resolutely began to efface all vestiges of her work. Then, as though lost in thought, she made her way back to the manor, half hidden behind the trees.

"Esclarmonde—child, where have you been?"

Turning to reach for another nail with which she was hurriedly trying to attach a strip of tapestry to a protruding beam, Corba of Pérelha paused, seeing her younger daughter standing in the middle of the hall staring in amazement at the transformation taking place around her. Unbelieving, the child's eyes roamed past the excited maids struggling to obey their mistress's distraught behests, the ungroomed yokels dragging in trestles and boards toward where, behind the improvised high seat, her mother, perched high upon a stool, was stretching a length of frayed and faded arras across the fire-scarred walls.

Bemused, still half enwoven in her recent rites, the child moved forward, gingerly treading the fresh-strewn rushes on the floor, her eyes fixed unwavering on the dim web of tapestry.

Dark forests, leaf-enmeshed and out of the tangled gloom, the white beast prancing in his blind career, trampling on flower and leaf—pursuing or pursued?

As if in answer, the horns rang out, shattering the greenness, echoing through the fastness of her grove, then, suddenly close at hand, burst in a fierce flourish through the walls.

In a flutter of dismay Corba of Pérelha alighted from her stool.

"Another moment and he'll be here. Child, where have you been?" she repeated, staring at her daughter's crumpled dress, the disheveled strands of long, bright coppery hair.

Roused at last, Esclarmonde glanced at her mud-stained frock and grubby hands.

11

"There isn't even time to change. Do you imagine," her mother asked angrily, "you can appear like that?"

"She won't appear in any case."

It was the terrible finality of her father's voice that tore her from her trance.

Ramon of Pérelha stood in the center of the hall. He had just come in, and, indeed, his appearance resembled far more closely that of a man who would be returning forthwith to the fields or byres than one who was preparing to receive a guest. As he spoke, his eyes wandered around the room while his high broad forehead contracted as he viewed the attempts at improvised festivity, which his wife, despite his explicit injunctions to the contrary, appeared to have made.

"Did I not say I would have no preparations?" he thundered. "One would think we were staging a royal reception."

"But I thought——" Corba remonstrated nervously, while with restless, bird-like movements she still attempted to put a final touch to the festive board——"I thought we ought to do our best. After all, he warned us he might come."

"Warned!" Her husband's stern yet usually restrained voice broke out once more in unaccustomed vehemence. "Since when does Peire-Roger of Mirepoix presume to warn me of the possible materialization of his whims?" Striding to the end of the hall, he rudely thrust aside the elongated board and, reaching up, tore the tapestry from its nails. "What is good enough for us will suffice for him."

How was it possible that Corba, always so meekly subservient to his authority, had today flagrantly opposed his will? Only this morning, when the messenger had arrived with the news that Peire-Roger of Mirepoix was hunting in the district and intimated the possibility of passing the night at Lavelanet, Ramon had impressed on his wife that there should be no preparations. "If Mirepoix chooses to turn up," he had grumbled, "he will find a meal and a bed in which to sleep. But he will take the place as he finds it."

"He'll think he's landed in a peasant's cot," his elder

12

daughter Philippa had complained, gazing in disgust at the blotched and scabrous stone grinning naked between the medley of charred and crude unseasoned timbers.

"He may thank his stars that his host can provide a roof over his head," had been her father's retort. "It's more than he himself could have boasted of till lately."

"He has won back Mirepoix," Philippa had protested.

"Thanks to the Count of Foix." The anger on her father's face had hardened to a painful bitterness. "It's likely he scarce reckons the debt he will never pay."

He could never pay it even if he wished, Pérelha brooded continually, for Ramon-Roger of Foix had died, three months before, of wounds received at that very siege, in the hour that had marked one of the decisive steps on the way to victory and the liberation of Languedoc. Perhaps no end could have been more fitting for the man who for years, through thick and thin, had resisted the double onslaught of French aggression and the machinations of the Roman Church. Yet must it have occurred at that particular siege, in order that Peire-Roger, that swaggering peacock of a youth, should regain the property he had scarcely taken the trouble to defend? True, an inborn sense of justice prompted Pérelha to admit there had been little or no chance of defending Mirepoix in those early days while fortress on fortress, town on town, fell beneath the sword of Simon de Montfort, the perfidy of the legates, or the brute onslaught of the Northern hordes. Since then, indeed, it might be admitted that at moments Peire-Roger had played an effective though sensational enough part in outwitting the strategy of the foe. Still he could see him, striking terror into the hearts of the French pioneers while at nightfall they attempted to scale the precipices of Montségur.

But his heroics, Ramon considered impatiently, were as evanescent as the freaks and fantasies of his novelty-craving brain, the fickleness of his famed *amours*. During his exile in Spain, he was said to have dabbled in alchemy. Heaven alone knew what field he would choose for the enaction of his latest *bizarreries*. He had best betake himself to the court of young Ramonet at Toulouse.

At any rate, Pérelha pondered, he would see that his activities were well removed from the pale of his own lands. One thing, however, was certain. There would be no more excuse for him to meddle in the affairs of Montségur. The Cathars, even if Ramonet kept his pledge to the Catholic Church and refused their reinstallment in Toulouse, would have no need for a mountain citadel. In any case, Bishop Guihalbert had had enough of Peire-Roger's vagaries, as he had himself. Did the young coxcómb imagine he had time to waste on his whims and caprices, just now of all times when every moment was occupied in trying to repair his war-scathed lands?

And to crown his annoyance, so sensible a woman as his own wife had evidently had her brain turned by the thought of Mirepoix's visit, as though it were that of her liege. In a renewed fit of exasperation, Ramon of Pérelha's eyes swept over the board, marking with growing fury the silver platters, the aquaemanales, the goblets that had been raked out from God knows where. But even as he raised his hand to sweep them from the board, it was not the many indications of an improvised banquet that caused it to fall clenched to his side and his body stiffen in sheer incredulity but the figure of the girl standing framed in the arch of a small doorway.

"Philippa—"

During those long years of war in which, twice over, the estates of the Pérelhas had been ravaged by fire and sword, nearly everything that their somewhat puritanically restricted ménage could boast of finery had been utterly destroyed. What use, in any case, would silk and velvet, satin and brocade have had for women subjected to a life of protracted sieges, rustic hardship, and toil? So Ramon's children had grown up with little more luxury than their own serfs. Only the elder daughter Philippa, dispatched after prolonged sickness to her uncle's estates in Catalonia, had enjoyed a glimpse of a more glamourous world. As from a visit to fairyland she had brought back into a world of devastation and ruin not only an abiding discontent but a tangible proof that, after all, that enchanted sphere belonged to more than a world of make-believe and dream. A dress of crimson damask bordered and

14

girdled with jewel-encrusted gold—the cherished souvenir of her uncle's generosity—had lain for the last year locked in the great oak chest in her room, unworn but gazed at periodically with the humble adoration others might render the relics of a saint, while tentatively, hungrily, her fingers would linger on the web of golden tissue and silk.

But today it had been lifted from its hiding place. Trembling, her hands had smoothed the folds down her tensed limbs, hooked the clasp across her breasts. And now she stood sheathed in its splendor, as if all the days of her seventeen years had existed but for this end, to step forth in her glory as a bride, oblivious of the fact that the deep vinous silk exaggerated the sallowness of her skin and that beneath the enameled coronet her homely features looked blurred and insignificant. Rapt in exaltation, expectant of heaven knew what marvels through which her mother had promised to transform the ruined hall, a moment passed before she took in the new-wrought damage. Even as her eyes lit uncomprehending and aghast upon Corba's distraught countenance, the agitated servants, and the tapestry crumpled on the floor, her ears, almost unable to understand the meaning, became aware of her father's words.

"Has the world gone mad, has victory turned your heads, that I should see my wife disobey my injunctions, my daughter parade before this coxcomb like a courtesan?"

The rest was lost in the avalanche closing in upon her, thrusting her back, step by step up the narrow winding stair into the confines of her room. She was so stunned that during the next ten minutes she scarcely realized the full significance of what was taking place even when the door fell to behind her and the bolts were rammed fast. It was the sound of the horn mounting now from the foot of the very walls that roused her from her stupor. Rushing to the window, she pressed herself against the narrow lattice, almost forgetting it opened not on the courtyard but on the fields.

From round the angle of the wall she could hear the clatter of hoofs on cobbles, and between them shouts and

15

a babble of voices. Straining her ears, she thought for a moment she detected, rising above them, one that, familiar and strangely magnetic, caused her pulses to leap. But once again all faded into a confused jumble of bustling grooms, of horses being led away.

He must be in the hall now. As if suddenly convinced that after all, she was dreaming, she rushed back to the door and shook violently at the latch. But the bolts did not give way. And still she rattled at the lock, tearing her nails and fingers as she clawed at the wood, while convulsively her lips framed her mother's and her sister's name.

"Esclarmonde—"

There was no answer. A sense of utter desertion annihilaged her more completely even than disappointment and rage. Her efforts became even feebler. And then suddenly, as though all the pent-up emotions of the last hours had reached the boiling point, they broke from her in a torrent of despair. Catching the clasps that hooked her bodice, she tore the dress from her shoulders and sank upon the bed.

For the outburst of apparent vanity that had aroused the wrath of her father was in reality but the culmination of that ever-tightening web of fantasy in which she had entangled herself since, one evening during that unforgettable sojourn in Catalonia, she had set eyes on Peire-Roger of Mirepox while he paid a brief visit at her uncle's house on his way back from exile in Spain. Never had she dared admit to her father, even to her mother, anything of the true impression made on her by that casual meeting. Only to her small sister Esclarmonde had Philippa, at moments when her anguish threatened to overcome her, confessed, in terms whose import the child apprehended but could not understand, the havoc Peire-Roger of Mirepoix had wrought in her heart.

So through the weeks and months, from tales gathered from hearsay, from the yearnings of a maidenhood frustrated by the limitations of a war-scourged land, Philippa had spun around his name a mesh of fantasies, till gradually she had come to identify herself with the heroine of each tale, and in Peire-Roger's casually suggested visit she had seen but an inevitable fulfillment, in which the paladin, the prince of fairy tale, had come for no other purpose than to redeem the promise of one short hour.

An hour must have passed. In the window the last glow of the setting sun had faded, while, stealthy and implacable, the fading light drained the life from the rude furnishings, the disheveled, abandoned figure on the bed. Only the dress, a deepening blotch of inexhaustible crimson, seemed yet to preserve, in the piled heap of its metallic folds, a strange intactness amid disintegration, as if in the secret ritual of those months it had absorbed into itself the heartblood of a girl's adolescent dreams.

THE LOVE CASKET

What's in a name? That which we call a rose,
By any other name would smell as sweet.

(SHAKESPEARE: *Romeo and Juliet*)

For did I find that which I seek, I would cease becoming.
We must be limited in order to become.

IT WAS DEEP NIGHT WHEN AT LAST THE BOLTS WERE
pushed back, but she was almost oblivious of the door
opening, the footsteps approaching the bed.

"Philippa!"

Only at the sound of her sister's voice did she stir a
little, but she made no attempt to rise.

"I brought you this."

The child was crouching at her side. She could feel
something sweet and sticky crushed against her mouth.

"Aren't you hungry?" Esclarmonde asked as Philippa
thrust it aside.

"Was it you who told father—?" the elder girl
muttered, overwhelmed by bitterness.

"Told him—what?"

"About me—and him?"

"Why should I?" There was such simplicity in the answer that Philippa began to weep.

Tentatively the child's hand stretched through the dark,
stroking the naked shoulder.

"How cold you are—" she murmured, and attempted
to pull the coverlet over her.

"Shall I go?" she whispered at last as still there was no
response.

But the thought of being left alone once more suddenly
filled Philippa with such fear that she thrust out her hands
to hold her.

Almost indifferently she allowed Esclarmonde to draw

18

her farther onto the bed. Then, pulling off her own frock, the child lay down beside her. After a little time, seeing all her attempts at consolation were hopeless, she began to consume the sweet herself.

"Why didn't you come before?" Philippa asked, bitterly injured afresh at such apparent callousness.

"I couldn't. I would have been discovered."

"Father didn't try to lock you in, too, did he?"

"No." Esclarmonde gave a little laugh. "He thought I'd gone to bed. Mother kept quiet because she guessed I'd probably slipped along to you. And by then he had so much to do, nothing mattered, I suppose, so long as I kept out of the way. But I was there all the time," she whispered, triumphant, "and they never knew."

"There?" Philippa echoed incredulously. "What do you mean?"

"I made myself invisible. I hid up in the gallery just above them behind the unfinished beams. If I'd bent down I almost could have pulled his hair.

"Whose—?" Philippa caught her breath.

"Peire-Roger of Mirepoix's—your wonderful cavalier's. I'm sure he scents it. The perfume tickled my nose. I was terrified I'd sneeze."

Philippa, wounded by the insouciant commentary, turned her face to the wall, but in the end her thirst for information conquered even her chagrin.

"What did he look like?" she asked with bated breath.

"Dazzling—like a knight of the Round Table," the child added, trying to hunt for an adequate description.

"Like Lancelot?"

"Oh, no! He's far too easy-going. Besides, his hair's chestnut and Lancelot's was raven black. But he's frightfully fashionable," she went on. "His tunic's all scalloped, and the sleeves reach to his knees. And then his hunting knife—he pulled it out to cut the meat. The hilt is of ivory, all carved and banded with gold. He must be awfully rich," she added meditatively.

Supposing he ran into debt, Philippa pondered with a tremor of fear, but the description had heightened her excitement to an unbearable degree. Had he spoken of her? She dared not ask.

19

"What did he talk about?" she asked instead.

"Oh—everything. He never stopped." Esclarmonde gave a little yawn. "His voice is so strange. It clings—like dark ivy."

"But of what did he talk?" Philippa persisted, impatient, yet afraid.

Of what? the child thought drowsily. How disentangle the sense from those sinuous, twining branches of sound? One might gather leaves, deep green and glossy, heavy with sap, not words.

"The war, I suppose," she murmured, "and the French and Toulouse. And then, of course, the death of the Count of Foix."

"What else?" Philippa persisted.

Esclarmonde made a desperate effort to remember. "Mostly about Roger of Foix's succession. There's probably to be a grand assembly of the barons—and a feast. And then about the division of the lands. He said something about Montségur."

"Montségur?" Philippa echoed with awakening curiosity. "It's our fief."

"Wasn't it half my godmother's? He was talking about her—Esclarmonde of Foix."

"While she lived. Since then the old Count let us keep it," Philippa's voice trailed away in bored disappointment. It was the child's that kindled to interest now.

"But Mirepoix thinks that Count Roger may feel differently. It may all have to go back to Foix."

"How can it?" Philippa murmured impatiently. "She left it to us. Jordan of the Isle, her son, hated her for her heresy. He wouldn't have anything to do with Montségur."

The child shrugged. "He said something about there being no real will and offering to strengthen our claim. But Father got furious and said he would have no such discussions behind Count Roger's back."

Philippa started up in dismay. "Wasn't he terribly offended?"

"He didn't seem to be. He just shrugged and said it would probably turn out all right when it came to it. Count Roger wouldn't care so much about it and the

20

Bastard would hardly have a claim. Who is the Bastard?" she asked sleepily.

"The Count's half brother," Philippa muttered, indifferent. "He and his wife keep a Cathar hostel at Durban. I believe his name is Wolf."

"Wolf—?" the child echoed, startled, and then almost laughed, for of course it couldn't be the same. Why, she had made that very mistake before. Nevertheless she couldn't help thinking of him now, the man she had met so unexpectedly down in the valley of the Sabarthez. It must be over a year ago now. Her father had left her playing by the lake while he was talking to the Cathar elders. Such a curious man, she went on thinking, all haggard and unshaven, and with that useless arm. And she had taken him at first for a hermit and then for poor mad Peire Vidal, who had run wild in a wolfskin for love of the Loba. It had all happened just because he had said his name was Wolf. She'd better not get it mixed up again.

But to Philippa the uncertainty was becoming unendurable. "Didn't he ask for me?" she forced out the question at last.

"Who?" Esclarmonde murmured vacantly, dragged from her own thoughts. "Peire-Roger of Mirepoix?"

"Who else? What can you understand?" her sister retorted bitterly. "A child of eleven—"

"I expect he asked for you at first," Esclarmonde attempted to console her, "I didn't hear half of what they said, especially when he arrived. Father may have stopped him."

Why, she went on thinking, had she never tried to find out who the stranger was? Her father, she remembered, had been preoccupied that day, and she had long learned the folly of pestering him with questions during those moods. But afterward—? By then, perhaps, she had relegated the whole adventure to her secret world—a world that others scorned as a realm of make-believe and lies, a world across whose shifting boundaries she alone had entry. Whoever trespassed there was caught inevitably in her spell.

I magicked him, she thought. He cannot escape. But it was I who saved him. Once more she seemed to see him

21

staring into the dark mirror of the lake, bowed forward a little, like a lopping tree. In another moment he would have fallen in—the kelpies would have got him if she hadn't thrown the stone. But at first he'd been almost cross. And afterward she really believed he was frightened, though he didn't want to admit it—frightened of the snakes. Yet, as he said, he'd climbed the mountain as a boy—right to the very top of the giant's head. Perhaps he had even gazed into that glazed and unwinking eye. One day he will take me. He promised, she whispered to herself. And if he forgot? "You can remind me," he had said.

"He has forgotten," Philippa was sighing out of the dark.

"You can remind him," answered the child, "if he promised."

Philippa bit her lip. Promised—what? If she could only remember, but the figments and fantasies on which she had nourished herself through the months dissolved into the fluid, velvet accents of Peire-Roger's voice. She held nothing but a wraith. In despair she threw herself on her side and buried her face in the pillows.

Esclarmonde's hand touched her hair. "You must send him something, a token."

"But what?" Philippa's sobs only grew more convulsive.

"The rose." It came after a long silence, tentative and awed, as if in uttering the word the child once more conjured up the mystery and excitement of the day on which, unable to bear any longer the burden of her secret infatuation, Philippa had beckoned her and amid hesitations and exhortations of silence had crossed over to the chest and, lifting out a casket, unlocked the lid.

"The rose?" Philippa echoed, incredulous.

"You must show it him—and how you've kept it faithfully."

"Show it, but how?"

The very impossibility only increased Philippa's misery. Never would her father let her see her lover, let alone speak with him.

"How can I?" she moaned.

22

There was a little pause.

"You must go now."

"Now?" Philippa trembled.

"Why not? He's sleeping in the small guest chamber up the turret stair. His squires are all in the hall. They've drunk so much they'll never wake. You can slip along the gallery and lay the casket on his bed. When he wakes he'll find it."

"But if he wakes before?"

"Why, then you can show it to him yourself."

But the thought was too preposterous for Philippa to countenance. Did even her little sister imagine her as brazen as their father had inferred? "Never—never—" she whispered, appalled.

"If you love him," said the child.

Philippa did not answer. She lay outstretched, rigid, staring into the dark. Esclarmonde could feel the trembling of her limbs, but when she stretched out her hand in attempted comfort, her sister's body shook with such convulsive spasms that she drew it back, terrified by her utter helplessness before that onslaught of despair. At last the sobs grew quieter; the anguished breath, but for an intermittent shudder, calmed. Worn out, Philippa slept. But Esclarmonde could find no rest.

What was this terrible and secret power that bound her sister by the token of a withered flower?

Out of the darkness the rose glowed vinous, burning like a jewel. On the day Philippa, fetching the casket, had unlocked the lid, Esclarmonde had expected to see it lying there, deep crimson, velvet-petaled, glowing with the fullness of its life, and instead she had found herself gazing on a withered stalk, a wisp of shriveled petals, faded and sere. Yet at the time the shock had almost augmented her awe, as if that sudden realization of transitoriness only revealed more strongly the mysterious potency inherent in all things. A withered flower, symbol of God knows what word, what oath, what promise unredeemed.

What if it were never fulfilled, she thought with sudden terror; would the burden of that secret shared weigh on her forever, heavy with a mystery she apprehended but could not comprehend?

23

Unable to bear the thought any longer, she slipped from the bed.

The moon had risen, but as yet its beams did not directly illumine the room, though they sufficed for her to see the outlines of the huge oak chest. Kneeling beside it, carefully, fearing that the creak of the hinge might rouse her sister, she raised the lid, then tentatively groped among the layers of silk and linen till at last her hand encountered a hard rectangular edge. The casket. . . . She knew it by the feel of those crisp-cut edges of ivory, encompassing their tendriled labyrinth of men and trees and beasts. But the key . . . ? For a moment her heart misgave her, and then she remembered. Groping once more, her fingers dived to the center of a close ball of wool and extracted a tiny key.

Then, closing the chest, she rose to her feet, listening for any sound from the bed. But Philippa made no stir. Clasping the casket, Esclarmonde slipped noiselessly from the room.

He must have been dreaming. Incredulous, Peire-Roger of Mirepoix, raising himself on his elbow, gazed at the empty floor.

A child—she had stood there in the middle of the moonbeam, her bare feet protruding from under the straight white shift. Above it, between long clinging strands of hair, a pointed elfin face had regarded him in mingled curiosity and awe.

He lay back on the pillow, already half immersed in sleep. As he rolled over, his arm encountered something hard. Groping, his fingers discovered a rectangular object, notched and carved. Fully awake now, he sprang from the bed and crossed to the window. The moonlight pouring through the deep embrasure fell full on the box in his hand, tracing the contours and chiseling a shadowy pattern out of the pale ivory. Dimly he distinguished two figures, the crisp, cusped foliage of a tree. Tristan and Iseult? A love casket, Peire-Roger softly laughed.

So, after all, the nocturnal mystery was to resolve itself into one of his innumerable adventures in Eros' realm. Curious, and prolonging the relish of expectation, his fingers toyed with the key; then, turning it, he lifted the lid—and forthwith closed it again.

How many other withered tokens of an hour's idle dalliance, he pondered, might not be as fondly cherished by their recipient's hand? But in this case, whose? Not the child's, if child indeed she was and not a changeling. Had Pérelha other daughters then? Faintly there stirred in him a vague memory, till gradually there crystallized in his mind the image of a brown-haired, sallow girl in an absurd, incongruously opulent dress.

But where on earth had he encountered her? And then suddenly he knew. One evening spent at the Lantars' in Catalonia, on his return from Spain. The girl, as far as he remembered, had been Bertran's niece—Pérelha's daughter, then? A little stroll, a few sweet, airy nothings whispered out on the ramparts under the stars. Had she taken them to heart, confessed them to her father? Perhaps that was why Ramon of Pérelha had proved so intransigent, though the old man had always looked askance at his imaginative flights.

Leaning against the casement, Peire-Roger gazed out on the moon-flooded landscape beyond. Beneath him, the undulating earth seemed to flow and ebb in fluctuating waves. Beyond, flanked by a massive bulwark of shadow, a cone of rock thrust up out of that uncertain sea—Montségur . . . Montsalvat.

Never, it struck him ironically, had it so closely resembled the fantasies that in hours of languor and idleness he had spun around its heights. During the unending tedium of siege-warfare, when it had stood firm as a Cathar refuge while Languedoc was systematically laid waste, he had acted sporadically as one of its guards and played no small part in the defeat of the besiegers; he smiled to himself, recalling with what speed the enemy had hurtled down the abyss at the sight of his tall figure, clad in radiant armor, conjured up suddenly from the dark. But for the scruples of its Cathar bishop, with what a mystic halo he might have encompassed those gaunt and naked walls, till they would have made a fit setting for its high priestess—Esclarmonde of Foix, Countess of Gimoez and the Isle.

25

God, if there had ever been a woman on this earth for whom he had felt more than a passing whim, it was she. As often he had done during her life, he speculated on what she must have been like during her youth. But strangely enough, all the allures of feminine radiance that his experience—and it was wide—evoked failed to supplant that incalculable aura, the breath as of some divine essence that had seemed to envelope the aging woman he had known. In love with a woman of sixty! He laughed, mocking his own caprice. Yet why not? After all, feasting on youthful loveliness, some almost invisible flaw of texture, some unexpected harshness in timbre of voice or glint of eye always intruded to mar perfection, while in her presence the imagination, untrammeled by illusion, had been able to wander, free to endow her with a beauty almost divine. Had he not therein even outrivaled the troubadours and glimpsed a vision of the absolute for which they vainly strove?

Was that really, he asked with amused skepticism, the root of the incalculable urge that had impelled him, with what was for him a strangely constant devotion, to worship almost objectively at her shrine, bearing with him as tributes of his adoration his latest essay in verse, or some article of exquisite craftsmanship that only his infallible taste could be depended upon to supply? Or was it only his insatiable curiosity to sound to the very depths the mysteries of love and solve the tragic secret that had led her to exchange the resplendent images of a dead poet's vision for the dim phantoms of the Cathar faith? Montsalvat—temple of the Grail—dwindled to the earthly proportions of an heretic refuge. Nostalgically his eyes lingered on the pale, moon-flooded peak. Would he not, with his outspoken flair for the appropriate setting, have been able to create a recompensing mystique more convincingly than Wolf of Foix, with his naïve ideals and helpless gaucheries? Yet it was not he but the young Bastard lost among the Pyrenean heights who had reawakened in her heart the dream of that lost citadel. Even when Wolf, caught in the throes of war and vowed to avenge his shattered ties of a more earthly fealty, had long forsaken those more tenuous altitudes of the spirit, she had repudiated the help he, Peire-Roger, was only too eager to give.

Mirepoix sighed. Was it his fate never to be taken seriously? It was not in his nature to feel envy. (Leave that to Jordan, her benighted son, craven with his horror of heresy and his jealousy of a ghost!) What sense was there anyhow in weeping for the irretrievable when who knew but that each new moment offered an equally acceptable alternative? The light of Montségur had faded. With the years it would crumble once more to a heap of ruined stones. And yet. . . . Even as he gazed, the irrepressible mercurial force of his being welled up in a fountainhead of fantasies—"Montségur, a monument to the memory." Wasn't it Hugo d'Alfaro who had suggested the name, down there in Toledo a couple of years ago—a name, incidentally, so apt that after all he was not sure whether he hadn't coined it himself?

And why, after all shouldn't the dream he realized and the abandoned fort rise up anew in the glory with which imagination had invested it: Citadel of the Loftier Vision, Refuge of the Love-Enwrought Heart, Temple of the Grail? Thoughts with which in those earlier days he had skeptically toyed grew, under the web of moonlight or whatever influence brooded over this incalculable spellbound night, to intense and burning realities. It was as though, beneath the supercilious, unappeasable craving for novelty that characterized his nature, there surged up that one enduring passion of which he was capable, a tireless, unslakable thirst for beauty that after all was but an expression for the absolute, liberating, as it had once in the presence of Esclarmonde of Foix, some finer essence in his being of which he himself was scarcely aware. By tomorrow, the cynic within him prompted, the glorious vision would probably have dwindled and would toss amid the flotsam and jetsam, the wrack of whims and fancies that strewed the shimmering foam of his existence, but so strong was the momentary impulse that already it was creating the necessary medium for its materialization.

Had not providence, it flashed through his mind, directed his path? His whim to visit Lavelanet, Ramon of Pérelha's fears, whatever he might probably pretend,

27

concerning Montségur. And then, with a little laugh already tinged with the old ribaldry, his eyes drew back from that spectral moonscape to the object in his hand. Did he not hold the very key?

Leaning back against the wall, he smiled to himself as imagination carried him from stage to stage of that amorous art, in which he was a consummate master, toward the envisaged goal. At last, sure already of ultimate success, he stretched his languorous height and, with one last glance at the rocky pinnacle rising out of the shimmering haze, returned to the bed, placing the casket at his side.

A pity, he smiled to himself, as his fingers, reassuring themselves once more of its presence, glided over the carved rim, that the faithful treasurer of its contents could not realize to what an exalted place she had been raised at this hour in his imagination—she was so unlikely ever to reach there again.

In the room at the other end of the gallery, Philippa of Pérelha moaned while she dreamed. Beside her the child, nestling deeper into the pillows, gave a little sigh of relief. I was right, his hair is scented, she thought to herself as she drowsed into sleep. But with a twig of hazel she was drawing a path round a landscape of rocks and precipices. "And then," she said to herself, "they came to fairyland, but first they had to conquer the mountain giant."

THE CATHAR HOSTEL

Ordo renascendi est crescere posse malis.

(RUTILIUS NAMANTIANUS)

VICTORY AND THE PROMISE OF A LASTING PEACE HAD brought to Languedoc not only the first hope of recovery and restoration of her ravaged lands but renewed desire to consolidate her feudal bonds by strengthened alliances and marriage ties. For that reason the betrothal of Ramon of Pérelha's elder daughter to Peire-Roger of Mirepoix, drowned in the spate of matrimonial celebrations that swept the land during the course of the next three months, failed on the whole to rouse the surprise and curiosity that it might otherwise have done. All private jubilations were indeed threatening to pale before those which, as Esclarmonde had confided in her sister, were to be held in the castle of Foix. Rumors concerning the grand festivities likely to attend Count Roger's installation as liege lord of his restored lands had indeed plunged the whole region into a state of hilarious excitement unknown since the outbreak of war. Only into the remote seclusion of the Cathar settlement by the Mas d'Azil did the restless expectation of gala and revelry, of which the South had been deprived so long, lack power, it seemed, to penetrate.

The day was drawing to a close. In the valley below Durban the meadows sloping from the river bed were already half engulfed in shadow, but up in the woods, the slanting rays of the sun still shot through the clearing, streaking the trees with a sanguineous glow so that, as if

29

branded, they seemed to stand in tense and pillared expectation of their fate before the hatchet's edge had even gashed their bark.

Hacking at a prostrate bough, Wolf of Foix threw a last log into the sledge cart down on the track.

Soon it would be dark, and he still did not have the full load. Half an hour ago or more, perhaps, he had heard the distant tinkle of the bell that called the men to the breaking of the bread. But he had resented the thought of returning with a half-empty cart. Maybe he was slow. He could only get a proper swing on the ax left-handed, and the logs he threw with his right often fell short of the goal, yet he had never dreamed, little more than a year ago, of achieving that much again. There was something else that held him, too, something he had not been able or even tried to explain to himself—a sudden reluctance, almost a fear, to leave behind the magic security that seemed to brood over the place. Perhaps, too, it was mixed with a sudden craving for solitude this afternoon that had made him snatch at an excuse for leaving the work in the fields.

Collecting the scattered logs, he thrust the ax in his belt; then, adjusting the yoke of the oxen, he steered them between the maze of fallen timbers and branches that covered the ground.

Where, widening to a regular track, it began to descend, he halted, stooping to fix the brake to the hub. Lifting his head, he looked back once more at the ravaged circle of earth. Strewn with the pallid dust of wood chips, a litter of splintered bark and bruised and broken weed, it lay as though covered by a glimmering sheen from which the truncated stumps of the trees thrust up, like relics of some primordial forest washed by translucent seas. Upon their verge streaks of mist rose, wraith-like, swathing the boles of the pines. Above, the slanting masts of half-severed trunks loomed like some derelict barque trailing fringes of submarine weed.

As though held once more by a mysterious compulsion, he remained gazing at the scene; then with an effort tore himself free and, goading on the beasts, plunged into the gorge of the trees.

At once blue shadow flowed forward, engulfing him in the darkness of bracken, the scent of fungus, the rotting carcass of beast and bird. He was emptied of himself, disintegrated and gathered again into the mesh of incessant processes woven around him, gripped fast in the beaked hammer of the woodpecker, disseminated in the crumbling atoms of moldering wood.

Lumbering, the beasts lurched on. At the bend of the track, the foliage, thinning once more, gave a momentary glimpse of the valley beneath—tree scarp on tree scarp falling to the blackness of the river bed.

Only beyond, on the gray promontory of rock, the walls of the castle glimmered in a last reflection of light. Disembodied, they had about them something spectral, as though not merely for a couple of years but for centuries they had stood dismantled, the phantom ramparts of a world that was dead. And once more he had the feeling he was moving through a territory submerged.

By the time he had reached the valley it was nearly dusk. Immersed in his trance-like state, he had trudged on, hardly aware he had reached the level ground till, relentless, the angularity of new-built masonry cut through the dusk—the half-built walls of the hostel and, beyond, the steep, sloping roofs, the checkerboard of the manor's façade. He registered them mechanically, almost as incoherent features in a dream. Lights already glimmered through the slit windows of the barnlike structure at its side. As he brought the cart into the courtyard, a figure emerged from the door. Its tall, almost rigid stature told him at once it was that of his wife. Still hardly roused from his torpor, he reflected with vague surprise that she must have left her place at the gathering.

"You're late," she greeted him coldly as he brought the oxen to a halt.

"I know." With an effort he reorientated himself to the familiar scene: the paved yard flanked by the open byre, the great rounded tower of the dovecot almost blotting the view of the manor beyond. To cover his confusion, he gave a little laugh. "I heard you needed the wood. The men were busy in the fields and once I got the cart up there, it seemed a pity not to finish the load."

31

"We had to break bread without you. It's bad for the men. They're laggard enough already. Arnaud will see to the beasts," she added with impatience as he began to busy himself with the oxen. "He'll be out in a minute. Sister Agnes will be saying grace."

Again he felt surprise, acuter now. Had she been waiting for him? It was unlike her to abandon her post of authority at the meal. A little guiltily he reflected that the excuse he had given for his lateness had after all but covered half the truth. Had he not willfully loitered, held fast by the strange aura of the evening as by a spell?

"I'll only loosen the shafts," he promised.

She stood waiting, stark and erect in her long gown, a pillar of shadow in the fast-fading light, planted at a little distance as though anxious to keep a space between her and the rank earthiness of animal existence.

How his preoccupation with the beasts, like all his work on the farm, always goaded her to irritation! And yet, she realized, while the restlessness that had tormented her for the last hours grew to fever point, it might prove her best ally today. Involuntarily her fingers tightened on the letter hidden in the folds of her long loose sleeves.

"I shan't be a moment," he repeated.

As he moved round the head of the oxen, she caught the glint of steel from the hatchet at his belt. In the dusk it might have been a battle-ax. The blade seemed to cut to her nerves.

"You might at least leave the tree-felling to others," she remarked bitterly. "It's the last job you're fit to tackle."

"I was only chopping," he retorted. "I can manage it as well as anything else."

She bit her lip. Was that what he craved for again—it flashed through her mind—the feel of the sword hilt hard in his palm, the cold sharp edge of the steel? The fears that had haunted her all afternoon grew to palpable shape. As though she herself had stood up there in the forest, she seemed to see him hacking with the frustrated fierceness of impaired strength at the unyielding wood. With a rending of torn and lacerated fibers, the giant

32

bough swayed and shuddered, then, heeling sideways, crashed to the ground. . . .

But it was only the thud of the shafts as they fell on the paved stone. The image faded, melting into that of the man who stood before her in the act of knotting the halter to the heavy yoke. His movements, but for a certain awkwardness of his right arm, had a quiet surety and deliberation. He might have been farming all his life, she thought with mingled resentment and relief.

"I'll have your supper served in the parlor," she remarked as, tying the cord to a post by the byre, he crossed to her side. "Surely you needn't bring in your weapons," she added querulously, her eyes fastened once more on the ax. Perplexed, he followed her gaze, then, with a little laugh, he drew the hatchet from his belt and laid it on a bench by the wall. But he had noticed the unaccustomed quiver in her voice. Once more he had the feeling that something was amiss.

"Is anything wrong, Honoria?" he asked, troubled.

Without replying, she turned in the direction of the long barnlike building skirting the farther side of the yard. Uneasy, he followed.

Through the open door came an inarticulate mutter. Giving place for a moment to a female voice, it rose again in a gruff chorus. Involuntarily he paused on the threshold, but at the same moment a bustle and a scramble of feet announced that thanksgiving was over. A second later a couple of peasants issued head foremost through the door.

Honoria stiffened. "They can't even wait till the last words are spoken," she remarked acridly.

"They're anxious to get back to the threshing," he placated.

"They'll use any excuse." Her voice was raised purposely so that they should hear. Then, urging him not to linger, she crossed the courtyard in the direction of the manor house.

Wolf of Foix had beckoned to one of the men. Aware of his mistress's rebuke, the peasant stood shuffling sheepishly, but, receiving only instructions to empty the load, he was soon put at his ease and readily answered questions about the day's farming.

"I'll be joining you later," Wolf concluded. Abstractedly he returned the greeting of a file of old cronies and veterans who were just hobbling out of the door. Through the opening he could see the two Cathar sisters already clearing the refectory table. Within an hour that soiled and littered board would wear, he knew, a hieratic precision that preached a silent reprimand to gastronomic lust.

"Give us this day our heavenly bread!" Those serried rows of pewter bowls would not fail to remind all who partook of their contents that a sustenance greater than that which they provided should be the goal of man's thanksgiving.

Why did it strike him so forcibly only today, and almost with a sense of chill? When he was inside, one of the community, that uniformity and order had often filled him with a sense of harboring peace. He had been late before. Only today he had a sudden feeling he had willfully been playing truant. Yet why? The excuse he had used seemed even less valid than before. As though to shake himself free of a half-forgotten dream, he strode across the courtyard to the pump and, stooping, bathed his face under the cold jet.

The parlor was a long low room in the old manor, the only one that, at any rate until the hostel was completed, could boast any measure of privacy. Even Honoria's ascetic rigor had not been able to purge from those blackened beams and bulging walls a sense of arbitrary lawlessness. It was almost as if those shadowy, recondite nooks and the notched, gnarled furniture mocked every attempt at order. Perhaps on that very account or because of its proximity to the farm buildings, she was seldom found in it. In any case, most of her time was spent in the refectory or tending the aged and sick in a farther barn that served as temporary ward. Tonight, however, she had brought in a great pile of sewing, as though to spend the evening there.

Now she sat by the table, her chair drawn close to the single sconce that illumined the room. In daytime the

34

small windows afforded a view of the deep meadows sloping down to the river in the direction of the Mas d'Azil, and on summer evenings the light would linger long on the meandering coil of water shimmering between the fast-fading outline of cliff and tree. But already the shutters had been closed, as though to shut out any possible beguilement of nature.

As Wolf entered, she scarcely looked up, indicating a steaming tureen at the other end of the board. Only one bowl stood before it.

"Have you eaten?" he inquired, concerned, remembering she had evidently not partaken of the communal meal.

"No." She shook her head. The gesture, the unconscious tightening of cheek and lip, had almost the nature of a reproof, as if even though her husband's life of muscular activity might necessitate the nourishment of the natural man, he might yet have remembered that her spirit had power to conquer the recreant flesh. Only then did it enter his mind that she might be indulging in one of her strict fasts.

"It will get cold if you don't begin," she insisted. Reluctantly he took up the spoon, but in spite of his hesitance his appetite asserted itself and he began to consume the food at full speed. Whether during such spells of abnegation she was making a heroic attempt to conquer temptation or revulsion, or whether she was submitting herself to a form of self-torture or gratification, he was never sure. As if he might yet find out, he regarded her countenance, troubled. But her face, closed by the white starched wimple, wore as usual an almost stony calm that even the candlelight quivering over the long hollowed plane of cheek and forehead failed to soften. Only her eyes would at times dilate and darken to a degree that betrayed an excess of emotion beneath.

At present, however, they were veiled and fixed on her work. And indeed, now that Wolf was safe within the hostel's walls, the fears that had tormented her all afternoon were beginning to abate. After all, she persuaded herself, the rumors that had been circulating for the last month had perhaps gradually worked on her nerves. When all was said and done, Wolf had betrayed no interest whatsoever in his brother's victory celebrations and had never proposed attending the feudal assembly at Foix. Indeed, what signs had he ever shown since his return to Durban of wanting to mix in affairs of state? Even when he had been called to Foix, to his father's deathbed, he had returned, his resolve to withdraw from public life apparently only strengthened. He had learned at last to his cost where arms and violence led. Why, then, she again reflected, should today's news have awakened in her such tormenting fears? Feeling them already half senseless, she looked up, seeking a final reassurance.

Seated at the farther end of the table, his spare body in a coarse dun tunic seemed swallowed up by the shadows, but where the light fell in patches she could detect, on the rim of the sleeve, stains of sweat and resin, the wisps of bark and sawdust caught in his hair. Emerging from the uncertain gloom into the radiance of the candle, his features had a mute and blunted look, as though the once too-vulnerable contour had been blurred over by an invisible thickening of nerve and skin. With a little shock she recalled how once, even in the days of bitterness and defeat, its hard constraint would flash open like a gaping wound, laying bare a boy's sharp ardor and pain. It was sealed over now, though the scars were still there, graven indelibly in eye and lip. But what if the cicatrix break open? What if he was dragged back into the vortex of worldly ambitions and desires? As if the thought were unendurable, she challenged certitude.

"A messenger," she made the effort, "came from Roger today."

He glanced up slightly from the bowl, but his voice was almost indifferent. "What did he want?"

Involuntarily, at his reaction, she gave a little sigh of relief. "I sent down to the fields to fetch you—" she circumlocuted; "I never dreamed you were up in the woods. When I heard, I thought it wasn't worth while his going right up. He was in a great hurry, ranging the whole district."

"But what about?" A sharper note had crept into his voice. Was that, after all, it flashed through his mind, what had been troubling her?

36

"Nothing special. Just the assembly." She forced her voice to casualness while her eyes remained fixed on her work. "It doesn't affect us really. In any case—" Her hands, interrupting their rhythmic task with an almost convulsive effort, drew a scroll of parchment from her sleeve—"he left this letter."

He made no haste to take it. For what seemed to her an eternity it lay between them on the board, a small sealed scroll no different from a score of others doubtless delivered that very day throughout the lands of Foix. Yet in spite of the reassurance she had felt a moment ago, the tight-curled parchment seemed suddenly pregnant with fate.

And still the minutes seemed to lengthen into hours as, under lowered lids, she watched him break the seal and scan the lines.

For a moment his brows narrowed; then, as if the news were of no importance, he continued his meal. "So it's coming off at last," he remarked between two mouthfuls. "Roger's evidently set on making it a grand display."

"Is this the time to hold fetes and galas?" she challenged, seizing her chance. "Aren't there enough good causes on which he could lavish his wealth?"

Wolf thrust aside the bowl. "There isn't much wealth left to lavish in Foix."

"He'll manage to raise it somehow," she retorted, "out of the peasants or the prisoners' ransoms, if it comes to it."

She had scored a point, she knew, noticing the sudden contraction of his eye and lip.

"Wouldn't a simple convocation of the vassals have been sufficient?" she persisted.

"One might have thought so." He had taken a bit of bread and started kneading it to a hard dough. "Still," he added after a little pause, "it's Roger's grand installation as head of the land, and all these years Ermessenda's had to stay among the wilds of Castellbo."

Her lips tightened. "I didn't think she cared so much for fashionable life."

"She may not," he shrugged. "But, as his wife, she's got to be present and play a part."

37

"How? Amid feasts and flattery and courts of love!" She prodded the stiff linen with such protest that the needle ran into her thumb, but the pain seemed almost a satisfaction. "She seemed to have other interests down there in Andorra," she added stringently.

"She may have still. If so, you'll be able to foster them."

"When?" Honoria gave a bitter laugh. "She's already too immersed in court affairs to come down here."

"She probably will some time," he placated. "Anyhow, you'll have a chance of discussing it at the assembly."

"The assembly?" She had dropped her sewing, staring at him as though unable to comprehend that the dread she had overcome had, after all, come to life again. "You don't mean you intend to go?"

"I suppose we'll have to."

"Why?" Her eyes, unrelenting, held his. "You don't have to swear fealty. You're exempt from fighting."

"We owe Roger homage for Durban," he replied.

Her face hardened. "The hostel cannot owe allegiance to any temporal power."

"Not the hostel itself, but the land on which it stands."

"You can go and do homage for that any time. It will be in the middle of the vintage," she insisted, resorting even to the farm as an excuse.

"We can trust Arnaud. In any case, it need only be a couple of days. If the hostel's to be recognized," he added more incisively, "I suppose we'll have to give Roger his due. After all, we owe it to him."

"Roger?" she echoed scathingly. "What does he care about the Faith?"

"All this time Wolf had continued to knead the bread pellet. Now, giving it a sudden twist, he let it fall on the board. "Who else would support us?" he shrugged. "Ramonet? He's been drawing up new edicts against heresy at Toulouse."

"It's only Roger's hardheadedness that makes him help us," she murmured grudgingly.

"Then there's all the more reason not to aggravate him."

38

"But what does he care whether we appear or not? I should have thought he'd almost prefer us to keep away."

"Evidently not." Drawing the letter toward him, his eyes once more deciphered the lines the scribe had so carefully traced across the page. Yet behind the meticulously formed characters he almost seemed to hear the half-bantering, half-threatening tone in which Roger commanded his illegitimate brother to attend with his wife the vassals' assembly at Foix. "He's very insistent. He doesn't want us to keep out of it." He gave a short unnatural laugh.

"You mean," she retorted bitingly, "he doesn't want it said that any brother or half brother of his refuses to support his policy of violence and force."

He did not answer. Thrusting back his chair, he rose to his feet, pushing the letter toward her, but she scarcely needed to take in the words. Hadn't she known all along that sooner or later Roger would do his best to drag Wolf back into the net? Victory and the liberation of the Ariège, even of all Languedoc, were far from meaning freedom for the Cathar faith. For that matter, Carcassonne was not yet retaken and, though Wolf never spoke of it, could she be sure that the old allegiance of his squirehood might not yet, if it came to it, sway his heart? Even if those fears proved unwarranted and he took no part, their position as Cathars was, as Wolf himself insisted, risky. Though young Ramonet of Toulouse had reconquered his possessions from the French, he was still in the hands of the Church. She knew well enough that only Roger's obstinate will to assert Foix's independence had caused him to sanction the erection of a new Cathar hostel, in defiance of the ban proscribing the foundation or renewal of any heretic center in Languedoc. She had realized, moreover, that even if, urged by his wife, Roger might be ready to tolerate what he called his half brother's religious foibles, he would never put up with any hint of what he termed sedition. Wolf should not fail to attend the assembly, to prove himself, in sight of all, a loyal supporter of the land. And once he was brought so far—fear mastered her again—what might not happen next? It was one thing to follow the Gospel of Peace amid the pastoral glades of

Durban, another to uphold it amid the sword-rattling splendors of a feudal court. The thought conjured up so palpable a vision that she broke out in desperation:

"Don't you see that Roger will try to force you to follow his lead? Are you going to sit mum while he mouths his patriotic speeches and gives vent to his lust for vengeance and blood?"

Wolf had taken a few paces up and down the room, but now, coming close to her side, he confronted her. His voice was almost unnaturally calm.

"I think Roger knows my views on the subject well enough."

But she was worked up now to a pitch that knew no restraint.

"It's not only Roger, but the others. Do you realize how they'll interpret your feelings after what happened?"

"I have no mind to ask them." The words came low, yet almost in careless defiance. Nevertheless the twitching of his lips told her she had struck home. He was suffering and she knew it.

Yet was not all his torment the inevitable outcome of his own wrongheadedness? she persuaded herself, returning her attention to her work. Was it not the result of his unappeasable lust for vengeance that even Montfort's death and his own disablement had not cured? She had only to recall how he had returned from the siege of Toulouse, broken in body but inwardly unregenerate. If only he had been content to stay at Durban then and turned his mind from thoughts of the castle's military defenses to the foundation of the hostel instead of riding off in accursed pride to guard that desolate fort in the Sabarthez, what might he not have been saved? She had never plumbed to the depths of his experiences there—tales of a prisoner in his care—a mere boy, by all she'd heard. And on Wolf's shoulders lay heaped the guilt not only of the boy's escape but indirectly that of his mutilation and death. It would haunt him always—a horror of which he would not speak. But she had learned enough from the brethren at Ornolac who had rescued him from the brink of madness and despair. So, after all, he had been converted to the Faith. If her triumph had been mingled with a shade of bitterness that she had failed to lead him there herself, she had not admitted it. Was not the Goal everything, and was she not still God's chosen instrument? Nor had she ever confessed to her secret gratification that, after all, Wolf had not taken the last step and retired from the world but had returned to her.

Enough that one day he had appeared at Durban, not as he had come back that time from Toulouse, but with a strong and silent purposiveness to support her in her work. Even the fact that Roger had exonerated him from any willful complicity in the boy's escape had not swayed his resolution, and though she realized almost with a shock that to a good extent he had recovered the use of his right arm, she was soon persuaded he had no thought of returning to the chivalric career. Almost with relief, though with innate distaste, she had acquiesced in his determination to reorganize the farm. What better proof had she, for that matter, of his conversion than his apparent eagerness to abandon those very walls that once had been the bitterest cause of discussion between them? So the castle on the height had remained deserted, and he had taken his place at her side in the manor till the hostel was complete. He had been returned to her, won for the Faith when she had thought him irrevocably lost. Was he to be torn from her again? In an anguish of pride and fear she lifted her eyes from her sewing.

"It's madness," she insisted.

He had not moved. Turned away from her a little, he stood blindly fingering the parchment's edge. He did not speak, but suddenly something in the mute solitariness of his bearing reminded her of a far-off day.

Deep winter—and in one night the fields sloping to the river bed had been obliterated in an endless monotony of snow. She had gone to wait for him not knowing even whether he would return. He had ridden out, they'd said, in spite of the threatening storm, though it had been the very day after their betrothal.

Still, he had come, perhaps aware himself of the nightmare impossibility of their union. Yet when he would have set her free, she had not let him, compelled by a passion of self-immolation and pride, apprehending that her sacrifice was God-willed, the price of his salvation. And instead she had broken to him the news of Languedoc's ruin and betrayal.

He had stood there motionless, rooted in the white annulling blanket of snow, turned away from her a little, as now—an exile, hardly more than a boy, driven by his country's shame and the death of his friend.

And today? An outcast, haunted by guilt, scorned as a traitor, jeered at for his shattered ideals. The years were spanned between—years of misery and war. But in the end the promise of that hour had found fulfillment. For him there was nothing left but the one Way for which God, through her, had chosen him.

"Wolf—even if they destroy our bodies, they cannot touch the spirit—" The words she had spoken that day echoed somewhere in her brain, while the dark, secret craving for possession that, unknown to herself, had motivated her action rose in her once again in an upsurge of desire more consuming than fleshly lust. Now that she held him secure, not for herself but for God, she persuaded herself consciously, was she to let him go, let him be ensnared once more in the machinations of Satan?

"Wolf—you cannot—" Involuntarily, as though re-enacting in trance her gesture of that former hour, she stretched out her hand and touched his sleeve.

Slowly he turned, mazed, baffled at first by the burning intensity of her gaze that seemed suddenly to have ripped through her customary mask of cold sufferance and reproof, laying naked her own hidden need. Half unbelieving, he felt it sweep in upon the desolate shore of his own hunger.

"Do you think, Honoria, I *want* to go?"

She had, she knew, only to draw down his head, to hold him fast, to blind him against all that lay without. But even as he made a first dumb, wondering movement toward her, the vibrancy in his voice had startled her back to a horrified awareness of his physical presence. Suddenly her fevered senses recorded with overwhelming intensity the mingled odor of sweat and resin rising from his clothes and hair, and, as though stung by the impingement of warm pulsating flesh, her hand loosened in recoil.

Yet still she strained every fiber to hold him in a supreme effort of sheer annihilating will. She was unaware that her fingers, shrinking from the firm encounter of sound flesh and bone, had wandered to his right shoulder as if, irresistibly compelled, they must explore, even through the thickness of the rough homespun, each notch and corruscation in the guarded and pitted tegument beneath.

But with an abrupt movement he pulled himself upright, conscious less of her action than of the fading of that momentary illusion of warmth, while remorselessly there closed in on him the numbing sense of odd, inevitable desolation.

"It's only for the sake of the hostel. We can discuss it later." His voice was faintly bitter but dead. "They're expecting me at the threshing."

Leaving the letter on the table before her, he crossed to the door.

Outside in the courtyard it was by now quite dark. By the light of the torch that had been thrust in a bracket at the corner of the byre he could see that the cart and oxen had been removed, but as he passed under the refectory wall he caught the glint of the ax still lying on the bench.

He picked it up. The steel was clammy with dew. Wiping it on his tunic, he swung it mechanically in his hand.

How overwrought Honoria must be, he thought, recalling her reaction, that the mere sight of steel should rouse her to such bitterness. Did she really grudge him his recovered strength? Maybe. He had known before he returned to Durban, before, in fact, he set out in pride and defiance for the Sabarthez, that in her eyes his disablement had appeared as the visitation of God.

In that doom-haunted valley he had learned that she had been right. Why need she fear, even now that he could swing a sword well enough left-handed and bear the shield's weight on his right, that he would be drawn again into the brute madness of the massacre in which for a blind and futile vengeance he had wasted the best years of

43

his youth? Did she still not believe that all he asked was to learn the detachment of spirit and understanding that could alone merit the name of peace?

"The peace that passeth all understanding," something whispered in his mind. Gradually during the past year he had begun to believe he might one day learn to know the meaning of these words.

He crossed the yard and, pushing open a door, entered a small shed. It contained a collection of tools and objects so familiar that even in the darkness he could have defined each one's place. But as he reached out to hang the ax in its accustomed quarters his fingers fumbled, bruising themselves against the nail. Mechanically he put them to his mouth, sucking at the torn cuticle.

Suddenly, with the taste of blood, the smell was there, not merely on his fingers but filling the whole shed, sickly-sweet and mingled with those other scents, not now or here but unforgotten, the unmistakable tang of tarred netting, fibrous dust of rope and cord, tackle greasy with oil. And between, the faint stale reek of brackish water lapping against the planks.

But even as he recoiled in horror his foot dislodged a familiar spade, grazed against the sharp edge of sickle or scythe. Nothing—he was only imagining, he reassured himself. Yet still the Other was there, imminent in the darkness, drawing in on him on every side. And while part of his brain still told him his groping fingers would encounter only the tools of garden and field, he knew they were even now taking on another identity and that the walls closing around him were no longer those of the tool shed at Durban but the boat hut in the Sabarthez. With a last despairing attempt to save his reason, he made a violent effort to move and staggered backward into the open, dragging the door to behind him.

Outside he stumbled, half reeling, against the dovecot wall. Convulsively, as one suddenly freed from suffocation, he drew in the air and with it the familiar reassuring scents of the farm: the dry, straw-strewn dust of the courtyard, the droppings of the pigeons, the ammoniac pungency of urine from the byre. From afar, between

44

muffled intermittent shouts, sounded unbroken the rhythmic thrashing of the flail.

These, after all, were the reality, he thought with relief, these and the scent of wood and resin, the swish of the sickle, the bite of the ax reiterating into eternity, cutting out time, all that might come, all that had been. Lately he had almost come to believe that those ghosts might be laid. Yet they were there, between a span of a few planks, behind any four walls in the darkness. There was no need, it flashed upon him, to go to Roger's feasts to waken the memories latent in every baleful, every suspicious glance. They might show him scorn—even worse, as Honoria had inferred. In the eyes of some he might even now be guilty of treason—fraternization with a prisoner—responsibility for his escape. But for that deeper crime—the boy's death—who would blame him, or for that matter who would blame the murderer himself?

Jordan of the Isle. . . . Once again the air of the hut seemed to close in on him, stifling. He fought himself free. Had he not yet, he reflected as he grew calmer, in all these months, learned detachment? As though struggling to control his will, he drank in long deep breaths of the night air, trying to concentrate on the exercises of the spirit in which the visiting Cathar elders would sometimes instruct him, till gradually he felt the calm of strength return. After all, what significance did the past year have if it had not achieved that end? He had returned from the Sabarthez hardly knowing in what could lay his aim. He had found it in dedicating himself to the community at Durban.

The hostel—perhaps Honoria was right in often suspecting his heart lay rather in the work of the farm. Yet now, by a stroke of irony, was it not he who was proving its champion? Why had she been filled with those crazy fears? Wasn't the foundation of the hostel the one goal for which she strove, the one fulfillment that, she dreamed, the madness of their marriage might give her? Why, he thought wearily, had he deluded himself once more even for an instant tonight that after all it might bring them more? The initial fault had been his, and in this, at least,

45

he would make good. He had promised himself that, whatever it cost.

Must not any bitterness he felt toward her inevitably spring from himself? What he had done could not be undone. The past was irretrievable. There was no evading it, least of all by remorse. Might not remorse even prove his greatest temptation—a self-indulgence on which he might waste years as once he had wasted them on a fruitless revenge? "Self-hatred," the hermit had said, "is the worst of all destroyers." Could he, Wolf wondered, face the old man today and show he had profited by his teaching? Reluctant to stand before him until he could show some positive proof, dreading the thought of that doom-haunted valley, he had never again revisited the Sabarthez. And then one day one of the Cathar brethren from Ornolac calling at Durban had told him the recluse had departed—as mysteriously, it seemed, as he had come. There were moments, indeed, when Wolf had almost begun to doubt his reality and wonder whether, after all, the old man had been more than a figment of his madness: the voice of his own conscience—or merely, it would flash over him bitterly at moments, of the blind unconquerable urge to existence. And yet was it not he himself who had desired annihilation? Was it not the hermit who had bidden him live—he or a child?

A child? A green-eyed, auburn-headed elfin creature risen suddenly from the shadows of the lake, the very waters in which he had sought oblivion. He wondered at times, had she really existed? He knew no more than her Christian name and even that, he would tell himself skeptically, was perhaps but an echo of another—that of his own aunt, Esclarmonde of Foix, the woman who, once upon a time, years ago in the hospice of Pamiers, had shared with him, a bewildered truant boy fleeing from a monastery, the magic of an adolescent dream: Montségur.

The symbol of man's regeneration. Yet it was into the world she had sent him—to Trencavel and Carcassonne.

The magic had proved an illusion. The world had betrayed him, or he it. Yet when he would have renounced it, he had been sent back. Sent—or had it been by his

46

own will? Even now, he was often not sure. "To escape life is not to transcend it," the hermit had said.

But, having chosen, there was no returning. He had scarcely believed that life could be born anew—had known no more perhaps than that somehow he must find an aim. He had found it, or set himself to find it, in the farm and hostel. There was still in him enough of that odd mixture of obstinacy and idealism to make him determine to defend them stubbornly, as once he had defended Languedoc with his sword.

They must go to Foix. Little except scorn and jeers and worse would await him at the assembly. But he could face them. Tomorrow he would make Honoria see reason.

They would go to Foix and for a moment the jibberings and macawings of a flock of plumed and predatory birds would break in on their seclusion, but it would fail to shatter it. They would return as they had come, but with another step in their purpose achieved. And once more the day would repeat its ordered round, closed in by that deeper intangible security he had felt in the woods. Suddenly he remembered his strange reluctance to leave their shelter. Had he perhaps, unknowing, apprehended that they were trying to utter a warning before even Honoria voiced her senseless fears? He checked himself and, mocking his superstition, his eyes as if in challenge tried to pierce the darkness in the direction of the hill. They could discern only a huge and shapeless hummock heaped against the luminosity of the sky, yet palpably, between him and their impending height, he felt the brooding stillness of the woods. But now they seemed indifferent, almost inimical, remote.

He shivered. Had he after all duped himself as to their promise of peace? Yes, even this very day had he not almost been caught in the toils of a power more incalculable than that whose dangers Honoria envisaged at Foix? He gave a little laugh and, bracing his shoulders, struck out into the darkness across the stretch of trampled grass that led to the threshing floor.

BANQUETING AT FOIX

There was a sound of revelry by night

  (BYRON: *Childe Harold's Pilgrimage*)

Increscunt animi, virescit vulnere virtus.

THE BANQUETING HALL AT FOIX WAS STRONG, SOLID, hewn out of the local rock, as though out of the adjacent mountain itself, but it was not large. Its walls, pierced by the deep-splayed windows, could boast two arms' length in thickness, but no attempt had ever been made to screen them with the exotic traceries that converted the old Gothic castle at Toulouse into some fairy palace of the East, nor had even the hand of any Aladais of Burlats drawn over their harsh contours the veil of feminine allure that rendered the great hall at Carcassonne a perfect setting for her Courts of Love.

True, it had known love-making in its time—the deep recondite recesses of its windows were cut out for that— and long ago, on winter nights when the storms buffeted in vain against its impenetrable masonry, Ramon-Roger, its late owner, returning from the hunt, would often spring up from the board and, his arrogantly handsome features flushed with wine and his recent ride, burst into some passionate aubade of his own making. Still, for the most part it was hunting and battle songs that resounded beneath its rafters. In short, it remained stubbornly and uncompromisingly male, the cradle of a fearless undaunted race, warlike, predatory, and mountain-bred.

For that reason, it might have been argued with some justice that the barbarian French garrison that had been stationed here for the last years might have looked more in place within its walls than the mixed company of Languedocian nobility who crammed the hall to overflowing at the present moment.

For, as Wolf had surmised, Roger was determined to make his installation as Count of Foix an occasion the memory of which should echo beyond the borders of his own lands, with the result that among the rude and stalwart Pyrenean barons who had come, as for generations their forefathers had done, to pay homage and fealty to their new liege lord, a good few of the company represented what the inhabitants of these Pyrenean eyries scathingly termed the effete denizens of the plains. If it hadn't been for their spineless languors, their fads and fatuities, the late Ramon-Roger had mocked, Languedoc would never have been reduced to ruin. And if, Simon de Montfort and the French would growl in turn, the Devil hadn't invented that cursed breed of Foix, Bearn, or Comminges, the God-blasted South would long since have been clasped forever in the embrace of fair France and Holy Church.

If Ramon-Roger of Foix had proved the chief stumbling block in what had at first promised to be a walkover victory for the aggressor, young Roger had proved hardly less formidable. Yet there lay a world of difference between the two. For all his arrogant height and phenomenal strength, the sinewy, thoroughbred raciness of the father had almost vanished in the massive muscularity of his son, while the voice whose ringing tones and incalculable modulations had roused an almost beaten army to new resistance or caused the surrender of a hundred female hearts had given place to a booming guttural heartiness in Roger's throat.

It could be heard even now resounding through the shrill clamor of the feast that had followed the ceremonies of allegiance, and though its accents, as more than one guest had quietly mocked, were scarcely distinguishable from those of his Andorran peasants, they at any rate possessed an indigenous earthiness that chased away forever the last lingering echoes of the hated French.

Roger of Foix was a true child of the wars. The best part of his youth had been spent at the head of his troops and harrying the enemy with his crude uncultivated vassals, but even when he had had the chance, he had chosen to squire a lesser Catalan baron rather than the nobility of Carcassonne and Toulouse.

He had risen now in the high seat to make the oration that should at once pay tribute to his father's memory and recall the glory of the counts of Foix, but as he fell to relating one exploit or another in his boisterous campfire manner, those present inevitably compared with to the grandiloquence of Ramon-Roger's speeches.

"He wouldn't have managed to beat Fulk's calumnies with that jargon," Peire-Roger of Mirepoix remarked to his neighbor, recalling how at the Lateran Council the Count of Foix's rhetoric had induced Pope Innocent, despite the assembled bishops' wrath, to mitigate the sentence pronounced on the exiles of Languedoc. Leaning one elbow on the long trestle table while with the other hand he twirled his goblet till the crimson dregs formed a ruby in the heart of the spinning gold, Mirepoix threw a casual glance toward the dais.

Towering above the board, Roger had paused in his eulogy, shoulders squared, his great tawny head thrust back as though eager to throw off the encumbering robes of state, whose jeweled and metaled borders chafed his ruddy skin so much more sharply than any coat of mail. Looping his thumbs in the broad steel-bossed belt that knit his ample girth, he prepared to embark on what was evidently intended as the grand finale, and now he made an obvious attempt to curb his heartiness to a solemn and pompously oracular tone.

"May the glorious work for which my father strove never be forgotten. May the victory we are gathered here to celebrate in this memorable hour be upheld by sword and steel to the end of our days so that henceforward no Northern upstart may dare to desecrate the sacred soil of the South."

He raised his goblet, and on every side cups were lifted and men sprang to their feet to join in a thundering applause.

"Long live Roger—Victory to Foix and Languedoc! Down with the Capet—Hell and perdition to the French!"

"*He* won't sit chewing the cud," Mirepoix's neighbor commented, reseating himself with an air of studied arrogance. "Should think he'd hold his own against the toughest Norman beefeater in England or France. Bit of a contrast to the Bastard, eh?" His glance, straying along the board, rested a moment on the figure of Wolf, seated at Roger's side. "Christ, if he isn't more of a monkling than ever! Remember him at Carcassonne trying to better the world? I suppose his hopes went under with Trencavel. That seemed to have shaken him up at last. I heard he had a pretty bad time at Toulouse. Looks pretty harrowed anyway."

Shrugging, Peire-Roger gave a short laugh. "He spent six years trying to wreak vengeance on Montfort and ended by getting fairly hacked to pieces himself instead. Couldn't use his right arm for a twelvemonth."

"It still appears somewhat hampered," suggested a voice at Mirepoix's left. The speaker, who had entered the hall only during the toast, had taken advantage of the general commotion and shifting of places to slip in at Peire-Roger's side.

Recognizing the voice, Mirepoix glanced around. As he did so, a look of mingled surprise and distaste flitted over his face. Was Jordan of the Isle making a claim on Montségur after all? But that little matter, he reassured himself quickly, had been satisfactorily settled; thanks to him, he smiled secretly, Pérelha had nothing to fear. Affecting an air of nonchalance, he attempted somewhat perfunctorily to make room on the bench.

"What on earth brings you here, Jordan? Is Roger reviving a due on your fealty through your maternal blood?" The thrust, aimed at Jordan's repudiation of Esclarmonde of Foix for her heresy, struck home and he knew it, though the sallow mask of the newcomer's face betrayed no more than a slight twitching of the muscles around nose and lip. His gaze, however, continued so absorbed in Wolf that he ignored Mirepoix's words.

"I understood," he continued, preoccupied, "that the cure had been almost miraculous. It appears in any case to have been an exaggeration. Evidently he can hardly even bear the weight of his goblet."

51

The curious insistence with which the words were spoken caused Peire-Roger and his companion to fix their attention more fully on the object of Jordan of the Isle's
interest.

Wolf of Foix had sunk back in his seat. Still clasped in
his right hand, the goblet lay heeled over on the table.
The wine trickling over the edge darkened the white linen
with a crimson stain. The face above it looked wan and
distraught.

"Or possibly," Jordan continued with a little smile, "he
may merely have felt disinclined, for some private reason,
to join in the toast."

"Possibly," Peire-Roger passed over the insinuation
with a laugh, "he didn't dare. He's a confirmed Cathar.
No oaths, let alone adjurations of vengeance. Honoria
doubtless keeps him up to the mark. Lucky for you, Jordan." His emerald eyes narrowed, amused, as the
mounting blood traced a dark shadow even under that
opaque olive skin. Turning his back on him, Mirepoix
readdressed his former companion. "I reckon she gives
him hell all right. No wonder the Cathars hold that the
only Inferno's this blessed existence. The woman sits
watching him like a bird of prey."

"She looks pretty cadaverous, whatever she is," the
other admitted, "if you mean the creature sitting at his
side." Narrowing his lids, he scrutinized with evident lack
of appreciation the closely wimpled face staring out over
the entire gathering with the severity of a nun. "Still, all
said and done, one would expect her to be more in his
line than his first passion—that exotic Jewess. Heavens,
how we used to give it him! But now I come to think of
it," his lips curled derisively, "weren't you adorers at the
same shrine?"

Mirepoix yawned. "What centuries ago it seems. Poor
Wolf! He's probably never forgiven me for it, in spite of
Catharism and Honoria and the fact that I'm becoming a
reformed character. Did I tell you, Arnaud, that I'll soon
be entering the matrimonial state?" And, as his
companion regarded him with amused skepticism, "The
girl should prove such a paragon of virtue that there'll be
a surplus for me. Can you guess who it is? Sound
52

mountain stock—good as Cathar." He laughed and, swallowing the last dregs of wine, glanced round him.

The tables seemed to be breaking up. Roving down the long trestle boards, his gaze settled on the farthest corner, but the crowd of rising figures blocked his view. "Alas, even her radiance hasn't power to penetrate all those fat carcasses." He laughed and, lifting the empty goblet, put it as if in salutation to his lips. Then, stretching himself with indolent grace, he rose to his feet and, smoothing the folds of peacock-colored silk that fell to his ankles, readjusted the jeweled belt over his hips. Stooping from his slender height, he bent over his companion. "Coming, Arnaud? I really ought to be paying attention to my prospective bride. I'll introduce you. Maybe your patrician grandezza will ameliorate the old man a little. He still looks on me as if I were some sort of male huri pressing a feudal alliance. If it hadn't been for Roger, I wouldn't have had a chance."

Arnaud of Villemur shot him a supercilious glance.

"One can hardly blame him. From what I know of you, Peire, I should have thought that marriage was scarcely in your line." Stroking back his crisp brown locks, he, too, got to his feet. But the crush was already so great that he was almost immediately separated from his companion, and pride would not allow him to elbow his way through the crowd. Mirepoix's quip had indeed not been without justice. Even as a squire at Carcassonne, Arnaud had been a snob, but his conceit had been mitigated by a highhanded recklessness. The tribulations of war, coupled with the loss and recent restoration of his estates, had, however, successfully rid him of the more incalculable traits in his character and generated an air of overweening dignity and pride.

In the meantime, upon the dais a little crowd was fast gathering around the young count. His progress being checked for a minute, Villemur's gaze was once more arrested by Wolf of Foix.

He had risen. Isolated between the crowd surrounding his legitimate brother and a group of women who were paying attendance on the countess, he was standing hesitant and distraught, but, seeing even his own wife occupied in conversation, he appeared about to turn and slip into the crowd when his path was barred by Jordan of the Isle. For a second the two stood facing each other. Wolf, Villemur noticed, had gone horribly white. He seemed almost to sway on his feet.

But at the same moment the pressure eased. Halfway across the room, Villemur caught sight of Mirepoix glancing back over his shoulder.

Something was definitely wrong between the Bastard and Jordan of the Isle, he thought, but Peire-Roger was beckoning him urgently to follow. A moment or two later he was being introduced to a bearded, plainly dressed man of staid and solid appearance—superior farmer-*cum*-warrior, by the look of him, Arnaud summed him up derisively—at whose side stood a sallow, brown-haired girl nervously fingering the folds of her crimson dress.

"Christ, but she's plain. What on earth's Peire after?" Villemur thought to himself.

Blind to everyone around, Wolf of Foix struggled to push his way through the crowd.

At last, reaching the doorway, he stood still a moment as though to gather strength, then, reviving a little, stumbled down the steps and, crossing the courtyard, thrust open the postern gate. Continuing along the rampart, he rounded the farther tower and, descending another and narrower flight, reached a small crenelated platform overhanging the slope that fell almost precipitously to the river beneath.

Reeling against the parapet, he buried his head on his arms. He was still trembling. His pulses throbbed so violently they seemed to pound out of the stone itself.

Jordan. . . . What on earth was he doing here, turning up at this moment as though to give a horrible reality to the callous ribaldry of that toast? Had he perhaps been there all along, waiting, watching like a beast for its prey, to brand him in sight of all? Was it Roger's doing? But that would go beyond even his customary jests. Perhaps, after all, it was a hallucination, part of the nightmare-confusion into which he had suddenly been plunged. What was he, Wolf, doing here at Foix—the ancestral

54

halls to which he had always come, even to his father's deathbed, with a sense of reluctance and shame? If any place had been his home, it had been Carcassonne. But even that had become a dream whose validity he doubted, a boy's fantasy woven to spite his own sense of inferiority amid a world of feudal prejudice and effete mannerisms, a dream that had landed his friend in death and himself ultimately in crimes worse than those against which he had raged.

He had said good-by to all that. What, then, was he doing amid this crowd of jackals, echoing and applauding the florid bravado of Roger's speech? Was he fevered? Was he perhaps still at Durban? Had he climbed for some forgotten reason to the ramparts of the old castle above the Arise?

He raised his head. From behind him, broken by the tiers of wall, came the sounds of the feast. The crowds, the scornful glances, the tolerant smiles—after all, what did they matter? But Jordan . . . he was real, real as that horror in the Sabarthez, the horror still waiting out there in the hidden valley where the rocks barred the last spiral of the Ariège. It was there, even now flowing toward him, borne on the dark foaming current, hurtling over the boulders, foaming and clattering under the ramparts beneath. . . . Unconsciously he leaned forward. The water was little more than a streamlet shrunk by the summer's drought, but in his ears it seemed to gather to the swirling roar of the river in spate, and on it the white smudged mask of the face, featureless between the floating hair. Not Jordan's only but his, his was the crime . . .

Not willfully, God knows; and yet could even his foolhardiness excuse him? Potentially was he not capable of the same—in the cave, the chapel, among the phantoms, was it really himself he had seen—himself? "In our depths," the hermit had said, "as in our heights, we are, in a sense, one."

He had tried to train himself to that knowledge in the course of a long war. At times he had almost thought he had succeeded. Shouldn't his experience that evening in the tool shed have been warning enough? Yet he had come to Foix to vaunt the quiet and strength of spirit he had imagined he had won.

And now, he realized dimly, as his senses slowly began to calm, added to everything else he had probably forfeited the right he had gained for Durban only a few hours ago. Roger would scarcely forgive him for not joining in the toast. They'd probably be talking already. He hadn't been blind to Mirepoix's mocking glances or Vilemur's scornful stare. Yet even toward Peire-Roger, it dawned on him suddenly, his pretended detachment had failed. Had he not felt stir within him the old grudge against his one-time rival, as if the theft, even though today it meant nothing to him, were a thing he could not forgive?

So Honoria, after all, he thought with shame and bitterness, had proved right. "For the sake of the hostel. . . ."

He could feel her voice freeze him with its edge of cold blank scorn. He seemed almost to hear it now, carried down toward him from the wall above. Perhaps, it flashed through his mind, she was looking for him, that they could return forthwith to Durban. In mingled relief and weariness he roused himself to respond when he seemed to hear her voice more clearly, raised in protest. He almost distinguished the words "evil" and "untruth." Even while he hesitated, reluctant to entangle himself in further controversy, a sharp patter of feet sounded along the upper rampart, grew fainter, and then louder again as they turned the bend. Before he could decide on his next action, a child rushed headlong round the corner, bore down the steps toward him, and, tripping over her long dress, would have fallen, had he not stretched out his hand to save her.

In an instant she had recovered her balance and without glancing up was dashing on, when, realizing that the rampart came to a dead end, she halted and, half turning, stood like a wild, hunted creature at bay. Even then she seemed about to run back the way she had come, when, taking in his presence, she suddenly stopped short, rooted to the spot in dismay.

But he, too, was staring at her in amazement. Framed by the loosened strands of coppery hair, it was the same

56

white elfin face that once, out there in the valley of Sabarthez in the hour when life and hope had lost all meaning, had stared up at him out of the dark mirror of the pool.

Panting, she had backed against the parapet, her hands clasped behind her disheveled dress.

"What's wrong?" he attempted, shaken by his own confusion, but she was dumb, her great deep leaf-green eyes fixed in wondering doubt upon the smooth-skinned, sleek-haired figure in the plain but finely textured tunic of gray-blue wool. Could he really be the same as the wild unshaven creature she had found that day by the lake?

"Then you are the Wolf Philippa talked about—the Wolf of Foix?"

The color rose to his cheeks. So they had discussed him, he realized bitterly, even in front of this child. But to Esclarmonde, the sight of his apparent annoyance only recalled the gravity of her transgression, which the shock of their meeting had for the moment eclipsed. And now the implications appeared almost disastrous, for since he was the Wolf of Foix, the woman she had quarreled with a moment ago must be his wife.

"I'm sorry," she muttered as if he knew all about it, "I suppose I was rude and impertinent and said—oh, I don't know. . . . But I wasn't lying," All at once her eyes kindled to fierce rebellion. "It was true." Suddenly she made as if to spring past him in another attempt to escape but he was blocking her path as once in the Sabarthez she had blocked for him the way to self-destruction.

"What happened? Won't you tell me?" he urged. "After all, since we know each other—"

She waited a moment, struggling against her mingled anger and shame.

"It was the serpents," she blurted out at last.

"The serpents—?"

And then suddenly an image rose before him—the glistening, silver-bellied coils twining against the emerald folds of her frock, till, slithering from her hands they glided into the gaping shadows of the crevasse.

"The snake," he murmured half to himself. She had brought her hands from behind her back and was fingering nervously at a circlet of gold that widened in the center to two jewel-eyed serpents' heads.

"She said they were evil," she stammered. "It was your wife, wasn't it?—and that it was sinful and wicked to wear them in my hair. But they aren't—they weren't once upon a time, at any rate. People used to worship them, because they had a magic power to heal and brought good to them and the land."

"Who told you?" he asked, half wondering, half skeptical.

"My old nurse." Her eyes, flecked with shadow, regarded him stubbornly as though she sensed his unbelief.

But he continued to gaze abstracted at the glistening scaly heads. They were cold, metallic, petrified like their jeweled and scintillating eyes. But in her hand that day the snake had flickered like a living flame. At once repelled and fascinated, he had felt its secret power.

"Aren't they beautiful?" Her fingers traced the sinuous, tortuous coils. He recognized the workmanship of a consummate craftsman, the cold sterile beauty of great artifice.

"How did you get it?" he evaded.

"From Peire-Roger of Mirepoix." She gave a little laugh, gleeful and almost proud. "He's marrying my sister Philippa, and he brought us all presents at the betrothal feast—wonderful ones. . . ."

Peire-Roger! How often in his life had Mirepoix not managed to trespass on what he held most sacred.

"And I got these," she continued while triumphantly she fixed the circlet around her head, "because I'm not afraid of snakes."

"How did he know?" It shot through him with a pang of irrepressible envy, followed at once by unspeakable shame. Had he conquered his passions so little that he could feel jealous of a golden bauble, a child?

"Oh, Philippa told him, I suppose. She can't understand how I play with them." She rippled on in pride and delight, oblivious of his distress, till suddenly she caught sight of his face. All at once chagrin and disappointment snatched the light from her own.

"So you hate them too," she broke out vehemently,

58

"and I thought. . . . But I might have known it—you couldn't bear them even then, that day by the lake." She had turned away, her small shoulders trembling, her hands clenched. Suddenly she tore the circlet off her hair and flung it across the parapet. For a moment it spun, flashing over the gray stone, then, leaping, vanished over the edge. But she, too, had thrown herself against the hard square blocks of masonry and, sinking down in one of the crenelations, buried her face in her hands.

She had completely lost count of time. When she looked up, the rampart was empty. I've made him furious, she thought. And now he's gone. But even her immediate regret could not annul a deeper sense of disillusion. Overcome by a new wave of misery, she pressed herself deeper into the recess.

It was then she became aware of a sound below her. Wrapped in her misery, it was a little time before she roused herself to discover its cause and, almost too wretched to care, leaned forward over the rampart's edge.

Below, the ground, except for some outjutting rocks and shrubs, seemed to fall away almost vertically to the river hurtling beneath. Suddenly, a little way down on her left, she caught sight of a shoulder and the back of a man's head. She could not mistake the gray-blue sleeve, the fluttering strands of light brown, wind-blown hair.

"Wolf—" She caught her breath in fear. From where she crouched he seemed to be suspended from nothingness. She could not see that his left hand held fast to an iron ring in the wall and that one foot was jammed in a crevice of the rock.

"What are you doing?" But even as she tried to cry to him, almost voiceless with terror, his right hand stretched out toward the circlet that glittered suspended from the branches of a protruding bush.

Suddenly the rushing of the river grew to a roaring, deafening clamor in her ears. As if she herself must fall, she clung to the parapet, digging her fingers into the mortar between the stone.

She was still crouching there when, swinging himself over the battlement, he held the circlet toward her.

She did not move.

"Don't you want it?"

Almost unaware, she let it drop onto her knees, slide into her lap. She did not speak. Slowly she raised her head, regarding him with a strange, searching gaze.

"You *are* the same," she murmured at last.

"The same as what?"

"As then—down by the lake."

He took it she referred to his physical appearance. It must have baffled her quite a bit. "I hoped," he laughed a little wryly, "I'd changed a little since then." But the gravity of her expression did not alter.

"Why should you?" she said.

Why should he? If she knew how much in him needed to change, how much until today he had imagined had. With a redoubled sense of shame he thought of his own violent reactions, his lack of control, his jealousy only a few moments before.

How strange he is, she was thinking. He dared to do that—he might have been killed. And he climbed the mountain. And yet . . .

"That day—you *were* afraid of the snake?"

Under the sudden impact of that accusation he was taken unawares.

"I suppose I was," he muttered.

"You pretended it was your arm that made you clumsy. But that was only an excuse." Her eyes rested on his right hand. "Anyhow, it got well, didn't it?"

"It does for most things. Actually"—a smile, faintly mocking, hid his self-consciousness—"I believe it started getting better from that day."

"Then I did magick you."

He gave a little laugh. "Perhaps it was the snake."

She nodded gravely. "You wouldn't believe me when I told you. . . . What is it like at Durban?" she inquired suddenly after a pause.

"There's the valley, with the manor," he began, as if hunting for an adequte description, "down by the banks of the Arise. And then there's the castle—no one lives there now—buried among the woods. The trees are everywhere. One cuts them down, but still—" As he spoke

60

they seemed to encroach on him, silent and warning as on the day in the clearing.

"Trees . . ." she echoed. "There are heaps of them, too, at Lavelanet: oaks and beeches with giant arms. But up in the gorges they're mostly pines. Everything's black or mossy except for the foam frothing over the boulders. It's only a stream up there. But it's strong. It has to turn the water mills lower down for the weaving sheds in the valley. They were smashed in the war. But Father's having them built up again."

Lavelanet . . . he was pondering.

"Is your father a Pérelha?" he asked, suddenly realizing he had known only her Christian name.

"Yes. We own Lavelanet and Pérelha and Roccafissada up on the hills. But most of it's burned down. And through my godmother, Father had a sort of share in Montségur." Her eyes, straying across the ramparts toward the chain of ever-rising hills, missed the sudden tightening of his lips. "You keep a Cathar hostel at Durban, don't you?" she continued, remembering Philippa's words.

"Honoria looks after that. I'm mostly on the farm. There's a lot to do looking after the vineyards and the beasts."

"I know. Father's always busy. We hardly see him during the day." Abstracted, her eyes roved to the far distance, following the wandering river to the bastion of black wooded slopes and rocky peaks.

"Are there mountains at Durban?" she murmured.

"Not as high as those. The castle's built on a precipice. It's all a tangle of bramble and thorn, and down by the Mas d'Azil the river's bored a tunnel right through the hill. It's so dark in there you can hardly see the road, and the water goes thundering over the rocks."

She turned to him, her gaze quickening with excitement. "Was that where you waylaid the French—hiding in the crevasses and jumping out on them in the dark? I've often heard the story, but I never knew it was you. It was, wasn't it, since you're Wolf of Foix?"

His face had darkened at the memory of that slaughter.

He was angry, she imagined, remembering how that

61

day in the Sabarthez she had taken him first for a hermit and then for poor mad Peire Vidal in the story, because he looked so wild and his name was Wolf. And all the time he was a Foix who'd killed so many French and fought against Montfort himself. How explain that, even then, she had thought him very wonderful, since he'd told her he had climbed the Tabor as a boy. He'd promised to take her up. And now she'd spoiled everything.

From the castle the monotonous drone of revelry had become hushed. Instead came the sound of viols and of a man's voice singing. Suddenly he roused to memory of the present.

"I'll have to be going," he said hastily, and then he became aware of the dismay on her face.

"I'm sorry. If I'd known . . ." she began, still thinking him offended, and could get no further. How could she ever explain? She compressed her lips, trying not to cry.

"Why, do you want to hear the singing?" he asked, perplexed.

She shook her head. "They're sure to be nothing but those long love plaints. All about sighing and dying. They never end—or else political satires. In any case I'm not allowed in," she added, her anger with herself making her truculent and defiant. "I'm too young."

"Then we're both outlaws," he laughed wryly.

She looked at him uncomprehending, but at any rate it seemed he wasn't angry any longer.

"I managed to peep in all the same," she confided with a return of her sense of fun. "It was like the banquet in 'Huon de Bordeaux.' "

"Huon—" he echoed, "do you like the story?"

She nodded. "About Oberon and the magic wood. But it ends before the best part."

"Which?" he asked curiously.

"How Huon and Esclarmonde kept their promise to set out in search of fairyland and Monmur."

She was gazing past him, strangely rapt, her eyes fixed on the summits rising beyond the woody slopes.

"Do you think they ever got there?" he asked. And then once more he gave his strange, faint, mocking laugh. "You ought to know. After all, you have the heroine's

62

name. Do you still dislike it? Come!" he continued as she made no reply, "I'm going to the stables. I have to see to the horses. We've got to get back to Durban by dark."

"Aren't you staying?"

He shook his head. "Too much to do on the farm."

Pulling her to her feet, he almost ran up the steps. Neither was aware that the circlet had slipped from her knees and lay forgotten in the shadow of the wall.

THE CHALLENGE

"The Sun hides not the Ocean, which is the dark side of the Earth and which is two-thirds of this Earth. So, therefore, that mortal man who hath more of joy than sorrow in him, that mortal man cannot be true—"

(MELVILLE: *Moby Dick*)

CHRIST, LET'S ESCAPE TILL THEY'VE FINISHED THEIR caterwaulling," Arnaud of Villemur muttered as, the song ended, Mirepoix yawned behind a slender hand.

Seeing his betrothed safely ensconced between a circle of admiring and envious friends, Peire-Roger rose and followed his companion to the door. "Thank heaven for a breath of air. Since our ears must be ruined, we may as well try and spare our lungs. God knows, Roger may have the ears of a mule himself, but he might at least have the kindness to preserve the oral appendages of his human guests."

"Jongleurs and tumblers would be more in his line, I fancy," Villemur retorted. "Though probably he's most at home with his hounds."

"He promised Ermessenda a treat after years in the Andorran wilderness," Mirepoix jested. "Moreover, we have to be reminded that the South is still civilized, in spite of the ravages of the Northern hordes."

Conversing lightly, they sauntered across the courtyard. Both moved with an air of innate self-assurance, but Mirepoix's gait possessed a careless ease that made that of his companion seem, by comparison, almost pompous in its arrogance.

"Well, what do you think of Philippa?" Peire-Roger inquired as they stepped out on the rampart.

For a moment Villemur did not answer; then he turned on him a look of cynical superiority.

"What are you really driving at, Peire?"

Leaning back against the parapet, Mirepoix returned his look with smiling composure. "Nor brains, nor beauty, nor wealth—a little mystery too deep for your supremely ambitious but ever reasonable mind to unravel, Arnaud. But admit, I was always a romantic and possessed a sense for fantasy."

"All very well in the imagination, but when it comes to the flesh—rather you than me." A look of distaste settled on Villemur's well-molded but already slightly thickening features.

Peire-Roger was gazing out on the bastion of hills. "You don't credit me with ideals, do you, Arnaud?" Leaning on his elbow, he regarded his companion with a quizzical lift of one brow. "The higher, the more invisible." He made a gesture in the direction of the distant peaks.

"I'd rather choose my bed well on earth," Villemur scoffed.

"Even dreams will hardly prevent that. Poor little Philippa." Peire-Roger gave a mock sigh. Picking up a bit of rubble, he tossed it on his palm. Suddenly his hand paused half-arrested, as the figures of Wolf and Esclarmonde, mounting from the lower rampart, rounded the farther corner and disappeared through the postern.

"Who on earth is the child?" Villemur asked.

Peire-Roger laughed.

"Philippa's little sister. Do you think I was in too much of a hurry and would have done better to wait for the young one to grow up? Take your luck while you have it. In any case, I'm afraid she might prove even too much for me—the child is fey."

"Doesn't appear too much for the Bastard to tackle. Anyway, her spells seem pretty innocuous. He looks less deathly now than he just did. Did you catch sight of him face to face with Jordan? Thought the monkling was going to faint. What's wrong between them? Jordan seems to have his knife into him all right."

"Always did have." Spinning the stone off the parapet, Peire-Roger let his gaze wander to the hills. "Can't get it out of his mind young Wolf was the dream champion of his mother's Montsalvat—Montségur, alias the symbol of her iniquitous passion for the singer of the Grail. As he couldn't get hold of the original, he persecutes the substitute instead."

"Who *was* the original?" Villemur inquired cynically. "I never imagined the saintly Esclarmonde of Foix ever came down to earth."

"She probably didn't except in Jordan's imagining. The love of the soul can inflame a jealousy worse than that of the flesh, as Roger's prize minstrels are doubtless demonstrating this second." He paused, listening to the lachrymose wailings of a tenor that floated down uncertainly to the strains of a viol. "At least it sounds less intolerable down here. If that's what the South has come to, the French can spare their envious gibes at us poetizing dastards."

But Villemur's interest was too sharply focused on Wolf and Jordan to allow for concern about the aesthetic reputation of Languedoc.

"I'm afraid I don't quite follow your argument. If, as you say, the Bastard was really Esclarmonde's dream-champion, it's strange we never heard of him staking his life for Montségur. I thought, in fact, it was you who played the part of angelic deliverer."

Mirepoix laughed. "In phosphorescent armor. It gave the Frenchies quite a fright. Alas, Bishop Guihalbert failed to appreciate my loftier strivings. I could have turned the place into a regular Temple of the Grail."

"As far as the trappings are concerned," Villemur grimaced. "For the rest, I should have thought the monkling was better cut out for the job. Well, it's too late in the day anyhow. Montségur will soon be crumbling to ruins again."

"It seems so," Peire-Roger shrugged, but a little smile curled his lips. "As usual, the Wolfling missed his chance. Too obsessed at the time by his homicidal hatred of Montfort."

"He seems at present to be demonstrating the other extremes," Arnaud commented dryly.

"Exactly, and now the reaction's set in in full force as with most converts. Even Montségur would be a snare of the Devil and tempt him to brandish the delivering sword. Well, at any rate Jordan can pride himself on getting him where Honoria didn't, for all her prayers."

Villemur kicked at a stone with his foot. "How did he manage it?" he asked, curious.

Peire-Roger yawned. "Some trouble about an escaped prisoner. It seems that in spite of his vengeful obsessions, the Wolfling had become quite fond of him. Then, somehow or other, during the Bastard's absence, the boy managed to escape. Jordan caught him and pushed the blame on to Wolf. A nice little change of appeasing his lifelong grudge, added to which he'd had his game with the lad. A pretty foul business, I reckon. I'd as soon choose the torture chambers of Carcassonne as be at Jordon's mercy. It drove the Wolfling nearly out of his mind. Hardly surprising he landed in the Cathar fold."

Villemur had stiffened visibly. "So that's it." He gave a low whistle. "The Bastard was always a green fool, but it seems he's going rather far. Since he took the matter so much to heart, it's unlikely he's altogether blameless. Fraternizing with his prisoners and then letting them escape! He might at least keep his feelings to himself instead of airing them in public. It's a bit hard on Roger."

"Hm," Mirepoix laughed lightly. "He must have his time cut out keeping him in order. Brother Parzival—the guileless fool."

Arnaud of Villemur cleared his throat. "The Bastard was never in his right wits. Think of all those stunts he tried with Trencavel. 'Join with the citizens' and the rest of it. Still, there's a limit. I wonder Roger stomachs his presence. People will talk—Jordan will doubtless see to that."

"He'd better see that they don't tar him with the same brush," Peire-Roger retorted. "Playing the archpatriot to mask his own treachery. No one is likely to forget the part *he* played. If things had gone badly, he probably would have changed sides again. He may carry it off at Toulouse. Ramonet got inured early to the sight of his own father being feted in the enemy camp, but Jordan had better steer clear of Roger . . ."

No, he went on pondering, there was little chance of

Jordan endearing himself in that quarter. Surprised as he had been to see him at Foix at all, he had already drawn the conclusion that he had come uninvited. To what purpose, God alone knew. If it was to lay a claim to Montségur, he'd find his way barred. Roger had agreed to Pérelha's maintaining the tenure of his old fief—at a price, Mirepoix smiled to himself triumphantly. Feudalism had great advantages if one turned its constrictions to one's own account. The thought of two feudatories' lands consolidated (an unbroken rampart from the Olmes to Montségur) had suited Foix down to the ground, and he had willingly brought pressure to bear. For all his truculence, Pérelha had not been above selling his daughter for a plot of land. He had obtained Montségur; the price, his debt to a son-in-law who hadn't even made a claim on the peak—not yet. The day would come for that, Peire-Roger reflected confidently. He had learned how to handle good Ramon. Altogether, things had developed in his favor with even more than their accustomed luck. Gratified, his mind began speculating on his further success, while he desultorily answered his companion's questions as to life in Toulouse.

"You'd be more at home at Ramonet's court than tied in matrimonial chains," Villemur remarked as, a little later, they sauntered back to the hall.

"Probably," Peire-Roger laughed. "I'll see to it that one of the links is sufficiently weak."

As they crossed the courtyard, Jordan of the Isle came slowly down the steps. He moved with his customary apathetic, almost automatic gait, yet there was something of tension and expectation in the way in which he looked about him.

"Hunting for prey?" Mirepoix jested as they reached his side.

For a second Jordan hesitated under that impudently mocking gaze, then gave a little shrug of indifference. "Roger was wondering what had become of his bastard brother."

"Indeed!" Mirepoix raised his eyebrows in mock surprise. "Does he need his advice? Or maybe he wants him to draw up a report on heretical procedure in the Court of

Foix, addressed to your most holy friend, the Bishop of Toulouse? Is that perhaps what you came for, Jordan?" And as the other's face darkened, he glanced around him as if to assist in the search. "What a pity if he can't be found. After all, he doubtless still writes the pretty hand he learned as a novice. But wait," he continued, As Jordan made to move on, "now I come to think of it, I thought I caught sight of him just now down on the lower rampart." He waved a hand in the direction of the postern. "Evidently he found the merrymaking too much for his Cathar sensibilities and has gone to indulge in a few spiritual exercises. I shouldn't disturb him, Jordan, if I were you," he called over his shoulder, moving on. "The Holy Ghost possesses weapons stronger than those of the flesh."

"That'll send him on a nice goose chase and give the poor Wolfling a moment's respite. The hounds are evidently already on his traces," he remarked to his companion as they mounted the steps, but his good humor met with no response. In the mind of Arnaud of Villemur there was, after all, not much to choose between Jordan's political opportunism and the conscientious objections of Wolf of Foix.

For a moment after they had gone, Jordan of the Isle stood hesitant, smarting under the sting of Mirepoix's thrusts, but, impelled by a force stronger even than that of his rancor, his feet began to move in the direction Peire-Roger had indicated. Passing through the postern and a little way along the rampart, he halted. No one was in sight. He peered over the battlements. Even the lower slopes appeared deserted. Had Mirepoix been gulling him? But the rampart beneath evidently continued in a flight of winding steps. Not far—the walls, on that side, he remembered, ended in a precipice. Had the Bastard, as Peire-Roger suggested, really sought a refuge down there? He moved on, warily, still unable to see beyond the farthest bend.

It was strangely quiet. Or perhaps, in contrast to the noise and confusion he had recently left, the stillness seemed to encompass him with an almost eerie force. Had it even the power to restore the Bastard's shattered equilibrium? Let him find peace while he could! There was no hurry. The longer he had to collect himself, the more shattering would be the effect of his tidings. Besides, he had almost decided to sacrifice the luxury of delivering them himself. The renewed shock of their meeting would rob the news itself of its full effect. He would leave that to Roger. By the time he had recalled the mind of his renegade brother to certain seemingly forgotten loyalties, there would be little peace left for Wolf among his vineyards and fields. Or would there? Were Wolf's defenses stronger than he, Jordan, supposed? Was it only their meeting that had unnerved Wolf? But no, he smiled to himself. Even if the blow failed in its immediate effect, the poison would linger on in secret, eating at the foundations of his Cathar refuge, the green fastness of his blessed pastoral retreat, till the shepherd's crook in his hand trembled as though it were shivering steel.

Heretic hospice or citadel—he would shatter its spurious peace. His lips tightened as he remembered how he had worked to undermine the walls of that other stronghold of faith in which his own mother had sought no less tenuous a refuge from her despair, till when he thought he held her defenseless and exposed, at last she had escaped him again, irrevocably, into death. Yet was it he who had sent her there, he asked himself, he who in the very hour of his triumph and vengeance had felt rise through the accumulated bitterness of years an almost inexplicable tenderness? No, not he but the Bastard—the boy who had won the love she had denied him, Jordan, her own son, the youth who had deserted from the office to which her fantasies had raised him as champion of the citadel of her dreams. Let Pérelha have it. A weed-grown ruin—pasture for the sheep of a prosaic and land-greedy squire—Montségur! He had shattered the image, but the living blood remained. How many years had he spent in pursuing it, how many years would he still spend?

Involuntarily his footsteps had quickened. Without knowing it he had descended the first flight of steps. Now he stopped short. Had he not learned long ago that Wolf of Foix's death would only remove him irretrievably out of his reach? There were other means and so far he had used them with success. If he had patience! Patience for what? He hardly knew. Time had stood still. For Jordan of the Isle, at that moment, the whole of life had but one single purpose: to see once more the horror dawn and slowly deepen on Wolf of Foix's face. But strangely enough, what he visualized was not the wan, scathed countenance he had met an hour ago in the hall, nor that of the youth half demented with apprehension in the bleak fort of the Sabarthez, but the face of a boy with dreamy eyes and vulnerable lips half lifted from the dark mirror of a mountain tarn. It hung there now beyond the rampart, as though suspended on some invisible intangible film of mist. As if, indeed, that image were the pursuer and he himself the pursued, he was drawn forward round the bend.

Fixed in his obsession, a moment passed before, recalling himself to the present and the object of his search, he realized that the platform in which the rampart ended was bare.

So Mirepoix had tricked him after all! In the wave of anger that swept over him, the image shattered. From far away the noise of feast and revelry flowed back as from another world. The singing seemed to have ended. How many minutes had passed, he wondered suddenly, how many hours? By now Roger had probably sent his messengers to scour the place for Wolf. Well and good! A curious indifference filled him, a sense of nullity, as if concentration on the phantasmal image had drained him of all strength. With an effort he braced himself to remount the steps, when he caught the gleam of some object in the shadow of the parapet below. Descending the steps, he stooped and picked it up—a golden circlet curved to two serpents' heads. Four wine-deep garnets flashed from the sockets of their eyes. Curious, he turned it in his hand. Unlikely the Cathar austerities of the Bastard would sanction such baubles. Besides, the circumference was too small. Shrugging, he began to ascend the steps. He had reached the bend when a child came running down the upper flight and, shooting past him, made for the platform below. Halting, he watched

71

her as, evidently in search of some lost article, her eyes roved over floor and crenelation, peered over the parapet, hunted frantically in each recess.

"Are you looking for something?" Slowly he moved toward her, the circlet hidden behind his back.

"My fillet—" For a moment she regarded him hopefully, then, uncertain, a shadow of recoil passed across her face.

"What was it like?"

"A golden serpent—with two heads."

"A costly thing to lose. I suppose you'll be getting into trouble. Was it to bind up that mop of pretty hair?"

He had halted on the step above and rigid in his somber garments, a little smile on his pallid face.

Without answering, she resumed her frantic search. At first his only intention had been to tease her but, apprehending her instinctive repulsion, he was goaded to perpetuate her distress.

"Perhaps someone stole it," he suggested. She shook her head. "There was no one there. It was only a little time ago."

Still she went on hunting. There was something proud, almost defiant, about her dejection, as if she would not let him see her despair.

"No one—" he echoed.

"They were all busy feasting," she retorted as if he disbelieved her. "Everyone except me and Wolf."

"Wolf—?"

His voice was hardly audible, but so harsh that she was taken aback.

"Wolf. . . ?" he repeated as though testing the name.

Suddenly it struck her that he was outraged at the apparent familiarity of tone with which she had pronounced it. "Senhor . . . Cavalier . . ." she attempted, sullen and abashed. Somehow it sounded wrong and then she realized she didn't even know what it should be.

"You needn't worry," Jordan gave a little laugh. "I fancy the Bastard of Foix has ceased to set store by his military titles. In any case, you seem to know him well enough to dispense with them."

Something in his voice was so intolerable that she tried

to go, but his eyes were fixed on her strangely, nailing her to the spot. Suddenly with an effort she tore herself free and fled, stumbling up the slope. Dashing across the courtyard she reached the stables where a few moments ago the messenger had come in search of Wolf. The stalls were crowded with horses, but remembering there'd been a loft above the box in which his was standing she slipped in through the half-open door and, climbing the ladder, threw herself on the pile of hay.

What had she said? What could it matter to the stranger with whom she'd been talking? What did he mean with his black ferreting gaze? At last, in violent reaction, she burst into angry tears. It was all the fault of the wretched circlet. From the first it had only brought her ill luck—her father's anger at the extravagance of Mirepoix's gifts; Honoria of Durban's chiding. And Wolf—oh, she had seen it—he had hated it. And because she had behaved like a spoiled, truculent child, he had risked his life to save it. Once more she knew that moment of annihilating fear as she saw his body suspended across the abyss. And it was all for nothing. Suddenly it seemed to her that now, although she hated the circlet, its loss could never be made good. In a transport of despair she buried her face in the deep acrid hay.

At the far end of the courtyard, Jordan of the Isle called for his horse and she never knew that, as he rode preoccupied along the road to Toulouse, his fingers sometimes strayed mechanically to his side to reassure himself of the circlet buried in the folds of his cloak.

In the meantime Wolf, following in the wake of a young squire, had made his way reluctantly back to the hall. He had little doubt as to what Roger might want with him. The only question seemed to be whether his legitimate brother intended to upbraid him in private or whether, in a characteristic vein of inebriated hilarity, he would choose, in a mingled tone of bullying and jocularity, to make a buffoon of him in front of the assembled guests. The latter, he thought bitterly, was the more likely. Yet since the happenings of the last hour the whole of his experiences at Foix seemed to wear an air of unreality, and as he entered the crowded hall, prepared for all eyes to be focused upon him, he almost felt something of that indifference which, a few weeks ago, he had vaunted to Honoria. Everyone present, however, seemed engrossed in renewed revelry or in discussion of the recent songs, and as he followed the boy through the throng toward the farther door, he guessed, with a growing sense of reality, that Roger intended to see him alone or hold court over him with a few of the outstanding vassals.

His chances were gone, he told himself, as the disastrous absurdity of his visit to Foix flashed in upon him again.

Rather to his surprise, Roger was alone. He was standing with his back toward him, feet planted apart, his hands clasped, gazing with lowered head at the empty hearth. As he turned to see his half brother pause on the threshold, Wolf for a second had the impression of a bull ready to charge. But his expression suggested as did his first words, that he was going to launch his attack in the semijocular tone that always jarred on Wolf worse than rage.

"Still as evasive as ever," Roger's gruff bass rang with impatience. "Suppose the boy had to scour the whole place to find you."

"I was down by the stables."

"Saddling your horse?" Roger laughed through the short red beard he had cultivated since his father's death, though it failed to give him anything of the late Ramon-Roger's elegant imperiousness. "You seem for once to have a flair for what's wanted of you, or has the Cathar woman perhaps endowed you with second sight?"

Wolf stiffened, stung by the gibe.

"She warned me not to come, if that's what you're inferring. It seems she was right."

"Events will prove that."

Leaning back against the chimney piece, Roger regarded his illegitimate brother with a mixture of scorn and derisive amusement that, for all his anger, suggested he was enjoying some private joke.

"Whatever they prove," Wolf muttered, wishing only

74

that Roger would at last come to the point, "it's pretty evident I don't belong here."

"Where then? Among your byres and cowsheds? It's high time you mixed again with other than shepherds and oxen and remembered how to behave at court."

"I'm afraid I'm more at home in the fields."

"At home! And who provides them? Don't you know that if I wished, there would be no sod across which you'd have the right to run your blessed plowshare?"

"I know well enough."

"Then why behave like a demented fool? You seemed to have your wits about you well enough this morning. But at the feast—do you think you haven't caused me enough work shutting their mouths already, that you're set on starting their tongues wagging again?"

Wolf drew a deep breath. Then quietly he faced his half brother.

"Did you expect me, Roger, to drink to that toast?"

"Why not? Do victory and liberation mean nothing to you or that the French are driven at last from the land?"

"There's no reason because of it to damn them wholesale as swine to the slaughter. For that matter, your liberation is only relative. There are still a good many French in Languedoc."

"There won't be for long." Roger burst into a deep laugh. Suddenly, his hands still clasped behind him, he took a step forward. "It might interest you to know that Amaury is evacuating Carcassonne."

"Carcassonne. . . ." The name echoed from Wolf's lips unbelievingly, like something half remembered from a forgotten world.

"Well," grunted Roger at last as Wolf remained motionless, "I thought the news would be specially gratifying to you."

"Who brought it?" The words seemed dragged out as if by an effort.

"Jordan of the Isle. He had it from the most venerable Abbott Arnaud Amalric of Citeaux, now Bishop of Narbonne himself. Old Arnaud's having to supply Amaury with the cash for safely withdrawing his troops to France.

75

I reckon he isn't proving so forthcoming as he was when he brought Simon south."

But Wolf, white and distraught, was staring at Roger. "Jordan—was that why he came?"

"Evidently, as he was leaving forthwith. God knows, he wasn't invited. I'd no wish to see you make a fool of yourself before my vassals. I suppose it was the sight of him drove you mad," he grunted, as though condescending to exonerate his half brother's sin.

"How do you know he wasn't lying?" Wolf persisted, oblivious to everything else.

"Why should he be? No doubt he saw in it a good chance of ingratiating himself. After the Church, the Fatherland, and when there's no heresy in the game, he's glad enough to play the patriotic part. Young Trencavel's been brought up an adamant Catholic in exile. His mother and the Spaniards saw to that."

He paused, taking a step still nearer.

"I'm asking Bernard of Comminges to ride to Catalonia to fetch him." He waited again, as though withholding the prize in order to be able to confer it as a greater boon. "I take it you would like to accompany him."

"Christ, aren't you glad?" he broke out vehemently as Wolf remained dumb. Was this confounded half brother of his really as insensate as he pretended? After that affair in the Sabarthez one might excuse his losing his head for the time and burying himself among his beasts and vineyards to the threnody of Honoria's prayers. But Roger had never doubted that this news would shake Wolf out of his stupor. "You will take only a couple of men, to avoid suspicion." He delivered his commands like a master conveying a special favor on some eager, adventure-loving squire. "In the meantime I'll have gathered a small force. With them we'll take Carcassonne in a trice."

The face that Wolf turned toward him was inscrutable. "Why, Roger, are you asking me this?"

"Why? Because naturally I thought it would bring you to your senses."

"Which means. . . ?" A faint, tired smile seemed almost to pass over Wolf's lips. "You know my attitude toward violence."

"Violence—no one's asking you to hack off the Frenchies' pates if you don't want to, though they'd make pretty pennons to hang from the towers of Carcassonne. There's little likelihood anyway; all they're concerned with is saving their own necks."

"And so by rattling a symbolic sword at the open gates of the city you think I'll redeem my name in your sight and set a good example to your vassals." There was a jarring note in Wolf's voice, but Roger was at the end of his patience.

"If you want to be styled a Cathar anchorite, you can, for all I care, but don't say I didn't give you a chance of getting out of it. Christ, but I thought you'd been waiting for this day for years."

"Perhaps I had." Wolf's face had gone deadly pale. As if unconsciously seeking support, he had half leaned against a chest.

Roger's voice seemed to be coming, like the sound of water infinitely far away, from beyond the years he could not reach. What, he thought as though in a dream, would have been his reaction if the news had reached him a couple of years ago, perhaps even on his return from the Sabarthez before he had found in his rural fastness something that he had imagined security and peace? Was this what Honoria had feared, this latent, ever-present force that after all would try to drag him back into its toils? Was this what he himself had apprehended that day amid the refuge of the woods?

"So," Roger continued his merciless tirade, "it seems you've buried the days of your squirehood for good. There was a time when you never ceased singing the glory of Trencavel."

Was it Roger speaking, Wolf thought dimly, or their father when with biting scorn he used to lash out at the idealism of the Viscount of Carcassonne? Suddenly that past image crowded back on his mind with such vehemence that he caught his breath in pain.

"You can spare your mockery, Roger. If it is a matter of loyalty toward Trencavel, I shall ride to Catalonia and bring back the boy. But after that . . ."

Roger shrugged. The future, he considered, would

settle itself. He had few fears about that. Once the panoply of Wolf's moral conscience was cracked, events would take their natural course and he'd soon be playing a normal role in the world. For that matter he had no special wish for him to play much part at Carcassonne. The old rivalry between Foix and that city was ingrained in his bones. Besides which, it would be foolish to let Wolf get too much of a grip on the boy. He might even think of imbuing him with a flair for his father's reforms, though there wasn't much fear of that. Young Trencavel had been brought up among Spanish hidalgos.

He gave a short laugh. "You can please yourself. We were never vassals of Carcassonne."

Once again for Wolf it might have been their father speaking. What would either Roger have understood of that New Order, the world of which he and Trencavel had dreamed, for which they had fought in vain? Without knowing it he had picked up a hunting knife from the chest and was toying with the hilt.

Gratified and skeptically amused, Roger followed the movement of his hand. "I suppose, since you can wield a scythe left-handed, you can manage a weapon. You still have Trencavel's sword?"

"Trencavel's . . . ?" Wolf gave a little start. "You know yourself it was broken at Muret. It was never mended," he continued abstracted. He was riding at Trencavel's side, at the head of the New City Guard, tilting on the plain below Carcassonne.

"Still, I fancy you kept it," Roger gave a gruff laugh. "I'll fix you up with arms."

Suddenly, as if waking, Wolf became aware of the object in his hand. With a curt, brusque movement he threw it back on the chest; then, in quiet challenge met his half brother's eyes. "I have said I'll go, but it will be unarmed!"

Roger merely shrugged. "As you will. There was a time," he scoffed lightly, "when you thought of treading something meatier than grapes underfoot. You'd better leave at once for Comminges," he added.

With an effort Wolf took in the reality of the situation. "And Honoria?" he queried.

"Leave her to me. I'll get Ermessenda to occupy her. She's already engrossed in some scheme about homes for the orphans of the Ariège." Striding up and down the room, Roger proceeded to give Wolf messages for Bernard of Comminges and injunctions as to their embassy to Catalonia and fetching the boy.

Wolf listened, his brain registering Roger's commands with the precision but impersonality of some mechanism.

It was only as he turned to go that he remembered, as if they belonged to some quite separate world, the misgivings with which he had entered this door, and the whole reason of his visit to Foix. The hostel . . .

Roger was in a mood to grant anything, but with a sense of shame it struck Wolf that the bargain he would be striking was no better than a blasphemy.

At least, he tried to convince himself as a few minutes later he threw himself into the saddle, there was no likelihood of Roger renouncing this morning's ratification of the Durban fief. And with the return of Carcassonne as symbol of the ultimate liberation of the South, even though the Church was bound to continue exerting its stranglehold over Ramonet of Toulouse and young Trencavel, Roger would not fail to take every advantage of underlining the freedom of the Ariège. Freedom—he went on thinking as the horse's hoofs settled to the regular beat of the gallop beneath him—it had another ring when he and Trencavel had spurred their Arabs across the wintry plain. Delusion—one like the other, and was he even now on his way to call yet another into being? No, he assured himself, it was without any illusory dreams that he would restore the boy to his ancestral home.

He was unaware that from the narrow window of a stable loft, a wild-haired, tear-stained child was straining her eyes after the figure of the rider fast diminishing along the road and waving, waving even after it disappeared around the bend.

KINGS MUST DIE FOR
THE PEOPLE

*You must die to yourself . . . for you are but a
bridge, a passage, and your life's reality lies in that
which you transform.*

THREE WEEKS LATER, AT NOON, WOLF ARRIVED BACK AT
Durban.

In the village he heard that Honoria had gone that
morning to visit a dying woman farther down toward the
Mas d'Azil. It was unlikely, he thought to himself, that
she would be home yet. He rode on to the farm. No one
seemed about. The Cathar sisters at this hour were
probably tending their bedridden patients in the dormi-
tory, the veterans enjoying their siesta. As he rode into
the courtyard, the empty square, bleached by the late autumn sun, had the air of a place abandoned, a place from
which life had suddenly died out. Only in the shadow of
the byres, a bent, disheveled figure sat on the floor, cross-
legged, picking over a pile of sunflower seeds.

As Wolf dismounted, the man glanced up, but the
bleared swollen eyes showed no sign of emotion beyond
that of a dull animal stare. Yet, as always, the sight of the
mute filled Wolf against his will with a sense of repug-
nance and uneasiness, as if behind that vacant look there
yet functioned a mode of sense and recognition that registered hidden processes and feelings lying dormant within
himself.

With a slight nod, he led his horse across to the stable
and, unsaddling it, tied the bag of fodder round its neck.
When he came out there was still no one else in sight. For
a moment he stood still, then crossed the yard in the
direction of a small gate that opened on the fields rising

toward the barrier of forest crowned by the castle rock. Mechanically and without haste, as he had carried out all his movements hitherto, he unlatched the wicket.

Blinking between their humid lids, the eyes of the mute watched him as slowly he began to climb the hill.

For a little while the path ran along the slope of the meadows, then it was lost in the trees that rose on either side, growing denser as he mounted toward the height. Many already were bare, except for a last yellowing leaf, but the soaring trunks of beech and elm reared themselves so high that the network of branches blotted out all view of the summit. The undergrowth was an impenetrable thicket. Already during the occupation of the French it had grown rank. Since then a couple of years, the fall of two summers' leaves, had sufficed to blot out the path. He wondered how long it was since he himself had come this way.

The barbican stood open. As he passed beneath, he noticed that the spikes of the portcullis were already red with rust. Beyond, the keep stood massive and silent, the ravages it had suffered during the Crusade already merged with the scars of centuries, while the idyllic interlude of peaceful domesticity it had known under the late chatelaine's care had run riot in a ragged wilderness of brier. But still the crenelated towers, weathered by wind and rain, looked down from their rugged height on the valley, as indifferent to Mabilia's indulgence as to her daughter Honoria's aversion and hate.

Skirting the wall of the keep, Wolf reached a low doorway in one of the farther towers and, drawing out a key, inserted it in the lock. In the silence, the grinding of its hinges sounded as though it must wake the castle from its sleep. But the echo died, rousing no answering sound but the crumbling of loose mortar on the lintel and the sudden flight of a bird. Pushing the door to behind him without locking it, he groped his way up the dark spiral of the stairs. The single door at the top opened on a small circular room empty but for the crude hearth and a long heavy chest. Only a faint light filtered through the narrow slits of the windows in the crude thick walls, but it sufficed for his needs. Stooping over the chest, he pulled out a second key and, fitting it into the lock, lifted the lid.

The sword lay there, sheathed and straight upon its shadowy bed. Yet without seeing or touching it he could still have traced each knot, each spiral twist of the golden coils encasing the blood-red stones. For how many years had it hung or lain at his side day and night while his fingers traced its shape, hungry for vengeance? And even after the disaster at Muret, though he had held it too sacrosanct to have it mended, it had continued to be the symbol of his life's goal.

He bent forward. Slowly, almost fearfully, he lifted it from its place.

"To go on like the riders . . ."

Shutting the chest, he sank upon it, the sword across his knees.

Had he, after all, believed that the past could be reborn, the dream be continued where it was broken off?

Had he really deluded himself into thinking it was only feudal loyalty that had urged him to agree to Roger's plan, loyalty to this boy who had never known his own father, let alone the ideals for which he had died?

"That a golden race spring up throughout the earth . . ."

How should the boy have understood? Bound round with feudal prejudices, reared with the one object of winning back his lost privileges, what should he care for a dream that the world at large had regarded as a mad whim, if not as a treasonable blow against society and the betrayal of his class?

He must have known right from the first how it would end, before he had set out for Catalonia, before heaven alone knew what hidden hopes had urged him to ride on to Carcassonne. All the way he had told himself that the present was an illusion, that the city had ceased to exist. Or if it did exist, what had it to do with him? The past was dead.

But they had ridden on, and at each bend of the road some tree, some peasant's cot, the very slant of a roof, had grown familiar as though seen only yesterday.

"Trencavel . . . Trencavel . . ." The name had re-echoed around him. But it fell from Spanish lips, Catalonian, Aragonese.

And suddenly he had remembered with a start. Might it not have been just like this that long ago Roger Taillefer, the boy's grandfather, surrounded by Aragonese hidalgos, had ridden back to Languedoc from exile to avenge the blow by which a wronged burgher had felled his father on the altar steps? And in one night a whole city lay massacred for the sake of a single noble. Vengeance for vengeance, wrong for wrong, till the guilt had been wiped clean in Trencavel's blood. So the past had claimed its due.

But was it not the future *they* had been creating—he and Trencavel—as they rode along that very road, galloped across those hills, weaving a dream of justice and freedom embracing all mankind?

Ahead the cavalcade had halted. They were gesticulating, clustering around the boy.

"The seat of your fathers, the scions of the house of Asnar—the ancient lineage of the Viscounts of Béziers and Carcassonne."

He had caught the disjointed phrases, had known their thoughts: "if Trencavel had not sacrificed himself for the citizens, if . . ."

He had shut his eyes. They were moving on again before he had braced himself to look . . . if at least something had changed. But there were the towers untouched, unchangeable, welded immovable against the sky—the same as when in those far-off days, returning from the hunt or from some breathless race across the plain, they had borne down toward the bridge, nobles' and burghers' sons side by side, and, at their head, their leader but no less for that their comrade, Trencavel, in his plain belted tunic, bareheaded, with that blue, far-horizoned gaze of his, his bright hair blown on the wind. . . .

The same. Had time stopped still with those unchanging towers to begin again here and now?

Down there by the river bed, behind that clump of tufted pines, the steep-tiled roof of the mill . . . and between them, as they lay, dappled with reed-flecked light, Pan-haunted, the open pages of Vergil:

"That a golden race . . ."

The minutes passed. Slowly the thin shaft of light shifted across the floor.

From the day of his arrival as Roger's ambassador in Catalonia an invisible barrier had thrust itself between him and the boy.

"Are you really a Cathar?" young Trencavel had asked, incredulous, as if, reared between the conventional bigotry of his mother, Agnes of Montpellier, and the zealous guardianship of the priests, the very name filled him with terror.

A Cathar! What would he then have thought of the memories that, even as they rode, were fast resurging in Wolf's mind?

And what, for that matter, Wolf had asked himself repeatedly in the course of the following days, had he himself to do with those lost dreams? Had he not rejected them with all else that belonged to his former life?

But if he had, he brooded now, shut in the musty twilight of the tower, why had he not left the boy in Roger's keeping at Foix, why had he ridden on with them to Carcassonne? Even at the gates, knowing already what must be coming, he could have turned back. Yet, almost unconscious of what he did, he had heard the portcullis fall to behind him and, as though awakening with a sudden shock to the present, found himself confronted by the boy's forget-me-not blue stare.

That stare had haunted him the greater part of the next day when, at Roger's command, he had attempted to initiate young Trencavel into the ins and outs of his father's castle.

With the assurance that, after all, Wolf wasn't quite so mad as he seemed, that, in fact, he had so many Frenchmen's corpses to his credit it wouldn't hurt him for a while to change his wolfskin for sheep's clothing, Roger had managed, up to a point, to overcome the boy's misgivings and make him accept as guide his father's one-time squire and reputed friend.

Perched in the high seat, his hands grasping the two griffons' heads, the boy had plied him with questions regarding the procedure of Trencavel's court; to satisfy him, he had struggled to conjure up the cavalcade of princes, nobles, and hidalgos who in their time had feasted and caroused as guests of the Viscounts of Béziers and Carcassonne. How to convince the young heir, till now starved of his rights and privileges, that to his father the very pomp and etiquette for which he craved had been anathema, that he whose first thought had been to escape into the freedom of wood and field had dispensed wherever he could with any form of retinue?

"But my mother . . . ?" Young Raimon-Roger presumably not satisfied, had leaned back, affecting an air of nonchalance and languid *savoir-faire*. "Was it here she held her Court of Love?"

How conjure up the third-rate poetasters, the perfumed sycophants who, while Trencavel had ridden out to train the new-formed City-Guard, had laid at Agnes' tiny feet their tributes of a questionably soulful rapture?

And once again the music had played, a troubadour had sung. From God knows what ravaged corner of the Carcassès vassal on vassal had flocked, paying homage, pressing his suit. The boy held audience, Roger of Foix or Bernard of Comminges advised. Yet there in the high seat, was it really the small, fair, treble-voiced figure of a child bending forward to receive the feudatories' pledge? Even Montfort, square-shouldered, shaggy-browed, or Raymond of Toulouse, the traitor, picking with bejeweled fingers at the gold tissue of his brocaded cloak, would have had more reality.

With a growing sense that he was moving in a world of ghosts, he had escorted Raimon-Roger from room to room—till they were leaving the state chamber where Agnes of Montpellier had lain in the great bed, the insufferable lap dog at her feet. And then the boy, running on ahead, had turned by chance down a passage to the right and, loitering in idle curiosity, had pointed to the single door that terminated the corridor.

"Where does that lead?"

He had not answered, and suddenly the question repeated, impatient, querulous, had sounded like an ultimatum, reaching him from another world, the challenge, the supreme test. As in a trance, he had moved forward. Still, for a moment he had stood motionless, his hand upon the latch.

Just so he had stood on that very spot the night before while the others slept, had stood so long that when he turned away, his feet were numb. Why had he not opened then? Because there was no need? Could he not see every inch of it still—the square small space between the walls, no more than the tower's breadth; the rough crude masonry of the old fort mocking even the arras of deep-green silk, the only decoration the fan of gleaming spear heads over the door? And there in the corner the low couch, the chest littered with books. He could have entered even in the dark and still known how many paces he must take to reach the hearth, had only to stretch out his hand and draw the sconce toward him to see it all flare up into its place.

Had he needed the protection of the boy against the past or against himself?

The youngster was prodding him impatiently. Suddenly, with a sharp movement, Wolf thrust open the door. And then very slowly it began to dawn on him that he must have known long ago the room would be empty, swept bare.

His expectations thwarted, bored, almost angry, young Raimon-Roger had stood gauging the narrow limits of the barren walls, and then, as if the silence had pierced at last even his callous indifference, he had faced him irresolute.

"Was it here . . . they imprisoned him . . . my father? I thought it was in the dungeons." Almost, there had been a tinge of disappointment in his voice.

"No . . . it was here we used . . ." But his words must have sounded meaningless. He was groping his way through emptiness as a blind man through thickly encumbered space. And then he had stopped before the hearth, staring, like one who has regained his sight, at the sculptured frieze.

Crackle of wood, furry rustle of crumbling logs as the flickering flame darted over rider and steed, drew from the shadows the tense, sharp molding of the straining

86

muscles, the clear-curved line of an arm shouldering javelin or spear—shoulder to shoulder, flank against flank.

"To go on like the riders . . ."

But, uncomprehending, the boy beside him no doubt
had seen only an empty hearth, a carving worn with age
and blackened with smoke.

"What on earth are they?" he had drawled. "They've
no armor except for their spears." And then his lips had
curved scornfully. "Was that how you used to ride out—
my mother told me—like Romans or the Greeks or
someone at their games? But he knighted you—didn't
he," he had added a little resentfully, "when you were still
a boy? Were you as young as I am?"

"Not quite."

(Dawn on the ramparts, only a wall's thickness away
and Trencavel's arms loosening their embrace. It had
taken him a long moment before he had realized it was
Trencavel's own sword that hung at his side. . . . "Keep
it—till I return.")

"You weren't a Cathar then?"

Receiving no answer, the boy had stood fidgeting, uncertain, while slowly the too-bright enamel of his eyes had
begun to cloud, almost in fear. "But he wasn't a heretic
. . . my father?"

"A heretic?" he had echoed, as if half hearing. "Not in
the sense you mean."

(Yet weren't they all heretics, they who had dreamed
of the break of the new day, the rebirth of society—a
brotherhood of men? Wasn't it in that very room they had
begun to plan it—that night Trencavel had returned out
of the storm? And they had sat before the hearth,
watching the firelight play upon the frieze. Suddenly a
gust of smoke had swirled across it. "War may come
. . ." Trencavel had said. But fevent, unthinking, the retort had sprung to his own lips: "Then won't that be a
beginning?" The beginning . . . oh God!)

"Is it true," the boy was saying, his forehead puckered
to a nervous frown as if he were formulating a thought
long hidden and suppressed, "they say he'd got some mad
idea about the citizens—that if it hadn't been for them he
would never have given himself up like a coward?"

"A coward—?" And then at last all the pent-up emotions of those days and weeks had broken from him uncontrollably. "A coward—" Trencavel, out there beyond the reeking fever-stricken palisades or at the giant machines, always foremost among them while all his heart had yearned to charge out through the gates to a last sally.

A coward? Smeared with grime and dirt he had come down from the battlements to meet the embassy of the Spanish king and with hardening lips ignored the pardon in Pedro of Aragon's outstretched hand. "Rather would I die than betray my people." And then at last that the citizens might go free . . .

All the while the boy had stood listening, staring at him, his insipidly pretty features contorted with bewilderment as no doubt he struggled to reconcile the image that was being held out to him as a symbol of heroism with what only could appear to him as plain subversion, an unforgivable betrayal of feudal right.

"It can't be true. You can't mean my father really felt himself one with them—the rabble who murdered my ancestor and his? He was a Trencavel—don't you know what that means?" He had drawn himself up to his full height, his slight shoulders twitching, his hands clenched against his thighs.

But even as anger and bitterness had sprung to deliver the retort, somehow his own voice had gone dead.

"No . . . perhaps I don't."

He hardly remembered what happened then till he had grown aware of steps sounding along the corridor outside. The next moment two Aragonese courtiers had stood on the threshold regarding the bare room, the evident agitation of its inmates, with curiosity and mistrust.

Had their young lord forgotten he was due to set out on a triumphal tour of the city? It was time to robe himself.

In a flash the torment had vanished from the boy's face. Glancing down at his tunic, he seemed already to envisage only his robes of state. "My cloak, the coronet . . . the sword."

Caught in the shaft of light, tremulous with dust motes,

88

the golden hilt shimmered in Wolf's hand. Slowly, inch by inch, he began to draw out the blade. . . . Had he dreamed for a moment that, after all, it was not broken sheer through? The failure had begun not even at Muret, but long before, centuries ago perhaps, when an older blade had shattered in Alaric's hand, when he and Trencavel had pitted a mad dream against Frenchmen or Franks or the world itself—it was all one.

With a sudden movement he thrust the sword back into the sheath.

He need but ride back to Carcassonne, lay it at the boy's feet, and return to Durban forever. There need be no further doubt, no more self-questioning.

Even now perhaps he was riding through the cobbled streets of the town, to the shouts of the citizens, the acclamations of the crowd . . . Which of them really remembered?

"Kings must die for the people."

Beside the blazing hearth Trencavel was leaning forward, a strange, haunted look in his feverish eyes. But he, Wolf, had not asked what that look might mean, nor apprehended the burden of heritage upon a spirit born in advance of his time.

The boy had not launched his thrust in vain. What had he really known of his friend, let alone of his race?

Had he after all returned to Carcassonne to seek for a lost dream and to lead this boy into a new fatality?

"To go on like the riders . . ."

But to what goal?

Above the flickering flames the ghost of Trencavel seemed once more to bend forward, his eyes fixed upon the frieze. "The rhythm of the earth, the unity of men."

"The unity of the realm, world empire." But the voice that had spoken last belonged to the face of a boy, desperate and attenuated with hunger, staring at Wolf, his jailer, in mingled arrogance and scorn. And between the two lay the horrors of interminable war. Where for each of them had their vision ended? For Trencavel in the fetid reeking dungeons of Carcassonne, for Berengar in the swirling waters of the Ariège.

And who had sent them there—kindling or nourishing those fatal dreams?

Another voice was speaking now, the voice of an old man, gazing at him with clear and penetrating gaze out of the cavern in the Sabarthez.

"Whatever else had happened, in the end between you, it was bound to fail, if only for this, that all the time it was not Berengar you saw, any more than Trencavel, but a fictitious image projected out of yourself."

Had not young Raimon-Roger accused him of the same?

The minutes passed. Perhaps they were hours. Stooped forward, Wolf stared into the dusk. He never heard the light step on the stairs or rightly realized that the door had opened.

Even when he recognized the tall straight figure looming out of the dusky light, he felt almost no surprise. Slowly he got to his feet.

It was Honoria who spoke. "Are you returning there at once?" Her voice was calm, tempered as the steel in his hand.

"Returning where?"

He could scarcely discern the play of her features as she stood by the door, but her body seemed to stiffen.

"I presume to Carcassonne."

"To Carcassonne?" he echoed.

"Where else?"

For the answer he had let the sword slip slowly onto the chest. "I never intended to remain. Didn't you get the letter I sent on my return from Catalonia to Foix?"

"Yes—" her voice remained intransigently cold.

She had not believed him. Why should she? he thought. Had he in the end ever believed himself? But a fearful weariness had come over him. He could not think.

Her eyes were fixed on the chest.

"It was the mute," she said, "who made me guess you were here. He kept on pointing to the path. Is that what you came to fetch?" she hardly deigned to indicate the weapon. "As you are not going yourself, I presume you will send it to young Trencavel."

"No." He spoke softly, but with a decision that almost amazed himself.

"Then you will destroy it?"

He made no reply.

For a moment her body seemed to tremble as though struggling violently with some unseen power, and then, suddenly, her voice broke out strange and almost shrill.

"Do what you like, go where you like—but in the end you will always return, for God will drag you back."

The next instant the door had closed behind her and she was gone.

Wolf had sunk back onto the chest. God, he thought through a maze of weariness, would God care, at all, where he came or went?

Long ago there had been a time, as a boy at the monastery when he had wrestled to find God's love, but he had sought in vain among the scholastic sophistries of the priests, and to the question how could God who made this world of sorrows and sin nonetheless be the spirit of omnipotence and love, even their hair-thin subleties had found no answer. And once again, in the shadows of the Sabarthez, he had offered himself in a frenzy of despair and submission to a God whose undivided attribute, the Cathars said, was absolute love. Yet he had been turned away.

Where then should he go on seeking? Would he ever find again the power, the yearning, that overwhelming thirst for possession and for surrender for what he scarcely remembered till dimly he saw himself in memory when, as a boy lost on the mountains, he saw for the first time, born out of the dissolving mists, the towered peak of Montségur?

"To go on—" Could Trencavel or anyone demand it of him still, could God himself? To go on—though he had lost sight of the quest, though the sword had been turned into the plowshare and he must drive it across a barren waste.

How much longer he remained rapt in his brooding he hardly knew. At last, with an infinite effort, he rose and, locking the sword once more in the chest, descended the stairs and made his way down to the farm.

THE NORMAN APPLE

L'eau des bois se perdait sur des sables vierges,
Le vent, du ciel, jetait des glaçons aux mares . . .
Or! tel qu'un pêcheur d'or ou de coquillages,
Dire que je n'ai pas eu souci de boire!

(RIMBAUD: Larmes)

Mox complexantur, complexaque copulantur,
Per se solvantur, per se quoque conficiantur,
Ut duo qui fuerant, unum quasi corpore fiant.

(MERCULINUS)

THROUGHOUT LANGUEDOC, THE RESTORATION OF CARCAS-
sonne had appeared to all except the Cathars and Wolf of
Foix as the ultimate symbol of peace and prosperity
restored.

After the long, unending years of ruin and defeat, even
the sudden turn of fortune on the battlefield, the subsequent victories, the slow but persistent evacuation of the
French from stronghold upon stronghold had not seemed
so unequivocal a sign of liberation from the foreign yoke
as the restoration of the city whose fall over a decade ago
had heralded the holocaust of the Albigensian Crusade.
With its capitulation had set in, it seemed, the doom that
for over a decade had not stayed its course till the whole
face of Languedoc, once the heart of the free, emancipated, pleasure-loving South, had changed to a desert of
pillaged castles, of burned-out hamlets and fields laid
waste.

With its restoration, one imagined, civilization had been
reborn.

The shafts of the spring sun shot down upon Toulouse,
kindling the unmellowed brick of the rebuilt ramparts to a
flaming ring. Even inside the walls, in the narrow streets
between the jostling houses, the light, temporarily
eclipsed, flared up again at every turn of a corner, at each
reluctant admission of space, as though it would mock the
avidity of burgher rivalry even as it had withstood the
vicissitudes of centuries, the ravages of repeated wars. For

still an aura of pagan insouciance hung over the city, pervading even the cathedral square. Unfinished, as though the hand of the craftsman had striven in vain to fashion a memorial to a God of pain and suffering, the grim deformed façade crouched on the site of a forgotten temple, while here and there between the carved and gabled palaces of merchants and town councillors, between the sagging timbers of the workers' dens, incongruous yet imperishably indigenous, a marble column stood, the fragment of some crumbling peristyle, mirroring even in mutilation the spirit of the absolute, invoked Apolo.

Suddenly disgorged from the shadows of the narrow alley that threatened the Faubourg of St. Cyprien, Peire-Roger of Mirepoix reined in his horse and, gazing at the city rising from the further side of the bridge, blinked in the scintillating light that shot up from the Garonne.

Sun-spangled, gilded cataracts of ice, thawed crystal spurted from Pyrenean summits, wind-wooed by the African breeze, they had gushed, tumbling and swelling, past Saltat and Las Bordas, past the disastrous banks of Muret to sweep across the plain of Languedoc to the uttermost limits of a land set free.

Freedom from the foreign yoke, freedom from domestic tyranny, Peire-Roger sang to himself as, drinking in the freshening breeze, he crossed the bridge and rode along the quay toward his accustomed hostelry.

Still, so far, he was forced to admit, he had hardly been chafed too sorely by his matrimonial bonds. If anything, he had become the slave of his house rather than its housekeeper, and the architectural enthusiasm he had developed once he had put his mind to the task of restoring the glories of Mirepoix had, for the moment at least, eclipsed all other ambitions, even those loftier fantasies enveloping the image of Montségur. For *they* verged on the realm of the absolute, demanding a subtlety of concept and execution to which, caught as he was in the throes of more mundane exigencies, he could at the moment not possibly do justice. Sufficient, for the start, that the myth-enshrouded edifice should be built on a firm foundation—in this case his marriage and the re-establishment of his estates. The result had been that eventually he

93

had felt a certain ironic amusement in seeing himself installed in the ancestral seat, while even Ramon of Pérelha had been forced to admit that his ubiquitous son-in-law had at last shown a sign of curbing his restlessness.

Yes, really, Peire-Roger pondered as he proceeded on his way, in spite of Villemur's prognostications he might almost be said to have proved an exemplary model of matrimonial dutifulness. Philippa had no cause to complain. Had he not shown himself considerate and solicitous to the utmost degree? For his part, he had discovered, there was after all a saving grace to be found in every situation, viewed objectively, and he had even derived some amusement from the task of educating a pupil so eager to learn. Not that poor Philippa would ever be likely to develop taste! But her docility, her unshakable faith in his arbitration, her readiness to carry out to the minutest detail his every command, would strengthen the chance of the old castle of Mirepoix becoming an aesthetic feature between the Olmes and the Ariège, the paragon of all that the combined forces of mason and craftsman could achieve—provided he had the means. But even on that point he had few doubts. The idealistic caprice that had inspired his betrothal had after all been founded on no airy base. Philippa's dowry, though not spectacular, was of sterling worth. Old Pérelha, in refusing to contribute any lump sum for his spendthrift son-in-law to squander, had actually done him a boon, for the lands from which he and Philippa were to derive an annual profit would, under Ramon's thrifty guidance, only increase in value year by year. A superior farmer, Villemur might mock; still Peire-Roger had seen with satisfaction that where Ramon of Pérelha ruled not an inch of soil would be put to waste. Moreover, he had been careful to extract a share in the weaving sheds at Lavelanet. Another chance for Villemur to gibe he had missed his vocation. Well, when all was said and done, wasn't the glory of Languedoc mainly attributable to its merchants? Besides, however material the roots, Peire-Roger smiled to himself, he could always be counted on to sublimate them. Even as he had weighed the output of the looms at Lavelanet, his fancy, carrying him far above the level of the grossly material, had conjured up the glory of Byzantine textiles, while there rose before him the possibility of introducing into Languedoc those tiny miraculous spinners of silken tissues that, it was rumored, had lately been imported to the valley of the Rhône.

The glories of the East—and no less its vices. . . . Before the war both had been equally at home in Toulouse, and young Ramonet, it seemed, according to recent accounts, was actually having a bid at reviving them. Hardly with the inborn genius of his father, Mirepoix considered skeptically.

He had reached La Daurade, the very church within whose gilded aisles that incorrigible old pagan Raymond VI had made, it was said, a last-minute attempt to be reconciled to his Savior; and for a second Peire-Roger paused, while his eyes wandered through the open door as if they must even now detect in the uncertain gloom beneath that burnished tunnel of mosaic the obese, decrepit figure dribbling its mimicry of prayer. Yet was it after all mere mummery? Might not the old hedonist, in fixing his failing eyes upon those marbled columns, those relics of a pagan past, have restored them to their original environment? Had he perhaps, even while the priest droned his monotonous liturgy, seen in his mind's eye another libation poured upon the altar stone, and, as the monstrance flashed its wheeling rays, might he not have experienced, in an access of militant fervor never vouchsafed to his pampered flesh, an echo of the mysteries of Mithras? Perhaps after all, diplomatist to the last, he had played his game and won. For even while, as the priests maintained, a God-sent paralysis choked his sinful lips, might he not dumbly have rejoiced that the intransigent abbot refused the excommunicate the right of Christian burial? Possibly even now, from some clearer vantage point in the Beyond, he was enjoying with something of his old amused skepticism the sight of his own bones rejected by the bigoted gloom of the ancestral charnel house, bleaching in the radiant glare of the Toulousan sun.

"Possibly—" The eternal question mark. But therein, Peire-Roger mused, lay, after all, the tragedy *and* the simultaneous charm of human existence. For when it came to it, who would have the strength to face fact robbed of its last illusion? Certainly not Ramonet, he considered, as, some minutes later, he saw rising above the water the massive walls of the Castel Narbonnès.

Draw a veil over the Gorgon face of fact; clothe the putrefying corpse of reality with the balm of elegiac wistfulness—why not? Raymond VI had been a master hand at the game; Ramonet was evidently preparing to copy him—with this difference: that while the father had been fully aware he was only assuming the role of impresario in the great Mystery, Ramonet would more likely discover, too late, that he was only playing the puppet to other, all too human, strings. He was already playing it, some said, to Yolande de Montfort's tune. Peire-Roger gave a little laugh. If it were true, it was but another example of the ironical justice of the gods, for hadn't young Yolande, when still a small pigtailed child, been affianced to Ramonet, while his father had still considered it expedient to collaborate with the foe? Needless to say, the turn of diplomacy had soon ruptured the bond and she had been dispatched safely to the North, to be married off eventually to some French usurper in the Carcassès. Today, at twenty, she found herself a widow, and thanks to the liberation of Languedoc, all but penniless, her estates confiscated. Penniless but, according to all accounts, spirited enough, seeing she was determined to assail Ramonet with pleas for compensation in regard to her lost lands. Banking on tender memories of that ephemeral affiance? Peire-Roger shrugged, wondering with amusement whether she would prove as irresistible in her female strategy as had her father, Simon de Montfort, in his military assaults. Well, within the next few days he might see for himself.

He was destined to see even sooner than he had imagined when, a few hours later, bathed and refreshed, he presented himself at the Castel Narbonnès.

Ramonet was holding a party that evening, he had been informed by the squire who had announced his arrival in the city, and hoped that Peire-Roger of Mirepoix would be one of his guests.

He had accepted with alacrity, but purposely timed his arrival late, determined that his visit, after so long an absence, should prove a spectacle to the whole assembly. At any rate, he thought as, clad in his most elegant attire, he followed the page beneath horseshoe arches of checkered marble, no one could say that matrimony and rural seclusion had left him incognizant of the latest fashions at court.

The party, it appeared, was of an intimate nature, for silence reigned between the mosaic-encrusted walls of the great hall, though only recently, he had heard, its Moorish splendors had provided a fitting background to scenes unwitnessed since old Raymond's days—a performance by a prize troupe of belly dancers sent as token of some Syrian emir's admiration of "the young victor and upholder of the Peace," or, more accurately, Mirepoix privately commented, of that Eastern potentate's prospects regarding frontiers and trade. Whatever his motives, the virtuosity of his delegates' plastic eurhythmics had roused the bishop to a tirade against such blatant backsliding on the part of the young count, and Ramonet, it seemed, had been forced to hold penitential vigil while, through the long watches of a chill March night, his sinful eyes sought purification in the lapidary writhings of ascetic ecstasy graven on the sepulchral vaults beneath the cathedral choir.

The ordeal, however, had hardly proved too stringent, Peire-Roger reflected a few minutes later as he entered an adjoining door held open by the page. The boy, knowing the visitor was expected and instructed not to disturb the gathering, had already turned, leaving him on the threshold, and for a moment even Mirepoix's customary insouciance was shaken by the sight that confronted him.

If the bishop's scruples had forced Ramonet to sacrifice the luxuriance of true Oriental orgies, he was apparently managing to find sufficient compensation in a travesty of the original—or such, at least, Peire-Roger took to be the aim of the sinuous anatomical gyrations being enacted that moment by the veiled figure weaving its way in and out of the circle of men and women stretched in various stages of abandonment upon low couches or cushions spread on the tessellated floor. Squatting cross-legged on a small carpet, a fair-haired youth thrummed a monotonous accompaniment on one string of a guitar while wisps of aromatic smoke rose from the braziers obscuring the contours, but in the light of chain-suspended Persian lamps Mirepoix, with the eyes of the connoisseur, registered at once those too vigorously swaying hips, the milk-white ankles peeping between the embroidered slippers and trousers of turquoise silk.

For a moment he stood watching, his presence evidently unnoticed; then with a dramatic gesture stepped forward into the ring.

"Heavens, Peire—" Propping herself on her elbow, a woman, whose dress likewise betrayed an impromptu Orientalization but lacked the mysterious nuance of the dancer's yashmak, welcomed him effusively. "We all thought matrimony had buried you alive like the poor Cathars—and there you are risen from the grave."

"Evidently—" he returned laughing. "If so, it seems I've happily landed in the realms of the blessed. Or is it only an illusion—have I partaken of hasheesh? If so, the Old Man of the Mountains could hardly have staged things better. But what neat little work of assassination shall I be expected to carry out as a result—that of our friend the bishop perhaps?" He bowed in the direction of a young man in a saffron turban, stretched upon a particularly sumptuous couch.

Ramonet of Toulouse's answer was accompanied by a light wave of the hand and a slightly falsetto laugh.

"I think really we ought rather to send him special thanks. After all, but for his Reverence we should have hardly hit on the idea. . . ." As if waiting for applause, his eyes roved from the dancer to his assembled guests.

An approving murmur rose from close at hand. Drowsed by wine and fumes of incense or deep in conversation, the remainder seemed already half lost to the existing world. Between them the dancer, a hallucination or herself half hypnotized, twined her serpentine path.

"Exquisite—if only I had known . . . ?" Mirepoix cast a rueful glance at his clothes which only a few minutes past had caused him such satisfaction.

"There was hardly time to warn you. In any case," Ramonet smiled, "I thought it would be a little surprise." He did not disclose the fact that he had purposely kept it so, knowing too well that any masque assumed by Peire-Roger would certainly outstrip his own.

In the meantime the dancer, who had seemed oblivious or careless of the newcomer, had gradually but inevitably woven her way toward them. Now, however, either in honor of her host or aware that she was the focus of his guest's attention, the impetus of her dance suddenly increased. As though in dervish ecstasy she twirled, spun, gyrated, a whirling diaphanous cloud. Then suddenly the image cracked, disintegrated, and, swaying backward, collapsed into Mirepoix's rescuing arms.

For a moment she rested there, with eyes closed and panting breath. A pair of captive doves, he thought, as the small taut breasts shuddered in his cupped hands. But even as, struggling to free herself, she lifted her eyelids above the concealing veil, Ramonet sprang from his couch and with easy grace Peire-Roger let her straightening body glide into the other's arm and beneath a thunder of applause be drawn toward the couch of state.

"Ravishing," Ramonet murmured, letting himself down on a pile of cushions at her feet. "So much more piquant than the original—don't you agree?" He turned toward Mirepoix, his momentary jealousy already fading in a sense of triumph.

"Absolutely." Narrowing, Peire-Roger's gaze rested quizzically on the blue eyes, the clear white forehead flushed with exertion above the Mohammedan veil. "What dusky enchantress could ever rival that damask rose?"

Under the saffron turban, pierced with its diamond aigrette, Ramonet's somewhat indecisive eyebrows contracted, then relaxed again, as from beneath the yashmak the girl's high voice, with an unmistakable French intonation, flashed back in repartee, "But the damask rose—surely it, too, comes from the East?"

"The eglantiné then." Mirepoix smiled, unruffled, "The

glory of the English hedgerows and of France." It was a bold venture but he was ready to take the risk.

"England?" the girl retorted in the same rippling staccato. "You must ask my brother—Simon, Earl of Leicester. He is there. Montfort l'Amaury was not enough for him. So he sailed over the sea to claim his rights. And now they say he would claim rights for England itself—against the king. For what they call . . ." she shrugged, turning to her audience for the word.

"Parliament—" gulped an elderly guest who appeared to be struggling with the intricacies of a hookah.

"Parl—ia—ment . . ." The yashmak quivered under a long-drawn yawn. "What a lot of talking they must do."

"Even worse than our dear consuls," Mirepoix remarked, dropping down on a spare couch.

"Much. If Simon's among them, I think he will keep the king silent." She laughed, turning toward Ramonet. "Are you not glad you do not stand in Henry's shoes?"

"He who vanquished the lion would hardly fail to conquer the whelp." The words fell acrid and biting from the lips of a hard-faced, suavely elegant female at Peire-Roger's side who had obviously been watching the scene with growing jealousy. But the sting was so obvious that it failed in its aim, for, dismissing the remark with an air that hardly dissimulated the secret gratification he felt at the flattery, Ramonet turned toward Yolande de Montfort in a gallant effort to heal the wound.

"If Louis Capet possessed a quarter of your father's valor, we should hardly be enjoying the fruits of peace. Shouldn't we enjoy them?" he added more softly. Stretching out his hand, he filled the goblet from a long-necked pitcher of enamel gold; then, bending toward her, unpinned the veil with his spare hand. "Aren't you dying of thirst? Heavens!" He tossed the yashmak on his knee, "Aren't you thankful you're not forced to walk enshrouded every day?"

"It's scarcely worse than the widow's wimple," the voice of Yolande's rival cut in once more.

"Or the nun's veil." Peire-Roger laughed, glossing over the thrust. "But possibly the discomfort is duly compensated by knowing the allurements doubled, especially when a woman is only too well aware of the treasure she's hiding beneath." Appreciatively his gaze summed up the flawless complexion, the clear, almost childlike oval of Yolande de Montfort's cheeks. "Maybe that's half the game in turning nun or Cathar."

"What—" the woman who had first greeted him wagged a knowing finger—"is poor Philippa already fleeing into the *bonshommes'* arms? If so, I fancy it's more likely to be from sheer despair."

"I should have thought," drawled the youth who had thrummed the accompaniment to the dance, "you'd supply enough troubadours to keep her from running into the Cathars' fold. Of course, if you have need of any more. . . ." Striking an attitude, he began to trill an amorous plaint.

"Thanks—but unfortunately, she refuses to accept all but the offerings of my own muse."

"She must keep you busy," Ramonet's abandoned favorite mocked, rousing herself to a half-hearted interest in Mirepoix.

"Exactly—for which reason I'm so exhausted as to be in dire need of refreshment." Heaving a mock sigh, he sank back on the cushions, drawing a little nearer.

"Are you really?" She leaned forward and, taking a sweetmeat from the platter, held it to his lips. As though relishing the fullness of relaxation after long-protracted strain, he abandoned himself to the luxury, lazily nibbling at the proffered fruit while now and then, between a bite, his darting tongue licked playfully at the fingers, which, withdrawn an instant, would as surely return a moment later in yet closer proximity.

Yet even while his attention seemed drowsily focused on that recurrent game, his eyes, under half-closed lids, were watching, amused, the increasing intimacy between Ramonet and Yolande de Montfort.

That the reckless, almost brazen abandon with which the offspring of Northern virtue was yielding to this atmosphere of Orientalized meridional decadence was to some extent a pose, he had no doubt. Yet exactly how much was due to calculation, how much merely to the fickleness of the cool, ineffably smooth skin? No doubt, like the rest

101

of her sex. Yolande de Montfort presented a synthesis of reactions complex enough yet capable of exact analysis—if he made the effort. But for the present, he considered, taking another nibble at the synthesis of human and candied sweetmeat, he was quite content to remain a passive observer.

"Good—isn't it?" Ramonet whispered as, refilling the goblet, he held it once more to Yolande's lips. "The secret recipe of the Raymonds of St. Gilles and Toulouse, distilled from nectar, spice, and oranges—oranges," he repeated with his slightly uncertain laugh. "Do you remember how your father raged? He wouldn't hear of them supplanting a Norman apple."

"Remember . . ." A little stab of pain pierced the narcotic vapor enveloping Yolande de Montfort's senses. Suddenly there flashed back on her memory the image of two rugged hands, seemingly incapable of handling anything less ponderous than sword and ax, peeling an apple for a child's delight till, in one long unbroken spiral, the tenuous crimson serpentine coil fell from the naked globe of the fruit.

What would he have thought of her now, she pondered—disporting herself in the enemy's midst, among these effete Southerners whom he had scorned and hated? She closed her eyes, trying to focus her memory on the far-off scene, the long stout oaken board in the great gaunt hall of Montfort l'Amaury; the cool Northern light filtering through the windows, glimmering palely on pewter and silver plate to gather suddenly in an exotic glory of pomegranate and orange some returning Crusader had brought back from the South. Already then, perhaps, she had dreamed of the glamour of that meridional fairyland. But was it her fault that it had grown to be a poison in her veins? Was it she who for the sake of diplomatic strategy had engineered a spurious affiance between a pig-tailed prattling child and a mere boy? Slight and pallid, little better than a hostage, she saw him still at the victor's banquet in Carcassonne, offering her an orange, the glowing spherical symbol of the South. . . .

But the aromatic scent of the wine was rising in her nostrils, pulsing through her veins. She opened her eyes

102

and found herself gazing into that same face, grown healthier-skinned and firmer-contoured now, a little arrogant even in its easy vanity, yet with a strangely conflicting weakness about the too small mouth, the almost pleading eyes.

Ramonet, the betrothed of her childhood—son of the arch-opportunist, resurrected from shame and ignominy to a flashy victory, the self-satisfied ease of a spurious peace. A wave of mingled bitterness, pity, and terror rose within her. For what were they both but the dupes of political ambition tossing them like balls in a juggler's hands? To meet and part and meet again—she as the twenty-year-old widow of an aged and expropriated knight, he as the husband of a sickly creature who even now, somewhere in this huge gilded prison of the Castel Narbonnès, was recovering from the childbed that would remain her first and last. And all this time, Yolande pondered, might not Ramonet and she have been creating the scions of a united Languedoc and France? Instead, North and South lay irreconciled as ever, the toil and heroic labor of her father thrown to the winds, while the plighted troth of a diplomatic engagement had proved as brittle as the promise of a boy.

"Remember—" she echoed. "I think it is you who has forgotten."

"I—!" he murmured, concerned.

"But surely . . . you." Her eyes, unbearably blue with mockery, fixed laughing on his, but her fingers, plucking with sudden fierceness at the cushions, frayed the silken fringe. "Your orange—we were mere children at that feast. And you promised to show them to me growing on the tree down there in your other lands in Provence. You never did."

Ramonet winced and the color mounted to his cheeks. It had always been intolerable to his vanity to see himself unpopular or guilty of a social breach, but here, he was beginning to feel too well, deeper issues had been involved, an emotional experience that to his cost he had forfeited. And yet might it not be retrieved? The desires frustrated and repressed under the stricture of his wife's illness, the rebellious whim that had contrived to im-

103

provise the absurdities of tonight's party, all gathered now in the one wish to let fortune have its way. Besides, he never felt happier than when seeing himself the magnanimous dispenser of a boon.

For a moment he remained absorbed, irresolute, then looked up with the sudden quivering smile that, while it marked, only too often, his uncertainty, nevertheless won him all hearts.

"A small castle," he suggested, "set among pines and orange groves—somewhere between Beaucairn and the sea. Would it in some way compensate for the confiscated lands of the Sire de Melun?" She did not answer at once, seeing, in a flash, the turreted house set in the grove above the Mediterranean shores and beside it, pacing the crenelated terrace, she herself, waiting, watching the black metallic shadow of the leaves out on the white and crumbling stucco of the walls, watching till from the night-dark boscage, hung with its burning globes of fruit, would bound with careless grace upon his caracoling steed, Ramonet— She checked herself and a throttled sound, half laugh, half cry, broke from her throat. Ramonet—alias Raymond VII, Count of Toulouse and St. Gilles—enemy of France, suspect of the Church, the self-same man who had chased Amaury, her brother, out of Languedoc, killed her husband, and by ruse instigated the tree down there in other lands in Provence. You what? That she, Yolande, great Simon de Montfort's daughter, might lie as Ramonet's leman under the languors of those Southern skies?

Perhaps, she went on thinking bitterly, if the South had not been held up through her childhood as the epitome of all fleshly lust, it would never have appeared to her the devil's lure. The South—the dreamland of her childhood—that she had learned to know at last under the holocaust of fire and sword, from which she had only gathered the tarnished spoils of a land laid waste. But now that, after all, the gates of that closed fairyland were opening, was she to turn away from the price, be driven back on the very threshold of fulfillment?

"Et Franc en France dulce terre retornent." Among all the heroic glories of the song of Roland, that line, she be-

104

lieved, had been the one her father had most loved. Yet he, who had yearned so much for his home, had never let himself return to the North except for a brief moment. For the sake of France he had stayed on, fighting against uncountable odds in the land he hated and loathed. For the sake of France. . . . Suddenly an idea stirred in her brain with lightning-like rapidity.

Had Ramonet, gazing so rapturously upon her, at that moment possessed greater divining powers, he might have recognized in the pouting mouth, the round determined chin, something of the obstinacy of the old Simon, and in those starry eyes something of Alys de Montmorency's cool and steely gleam.

"For the sake of France. . . ." Enmeshed in curling fumes of incense, the words echoed in her brain, circling pattern on pattern. What if vice, she persuaded herself, could be turned into virtue, the traitress become her country's savior! And gradually, with every repetition of the phrase, as if under the influence of self-hypnosis, the image of her father grew with such strange compulsion that she yearned toward him with something of the secret adoration she had possessed for him as a self-willed child. "Like father, like daughter—the devil's own. . . ." The words of the old physician echoed in her ear and now, as then, she felt the old triumph.

Laughing, she stretched out the cup. "Compensate? Who knows—till I see it—your castle—or must you build it first?"

The half-mocking tone was challenge enough. Refilling the goblet, Ramonet bent toward her.

"Suppose it already exists? If I were to order a little hunting expedition down to Provence—"

She gave a low soft laugh.

"And would you also order the white stag to lead us into the magic wood?"

He hesitated, seeking the words already mirrored in his eyes. He was unaware that the door had opened, unaware of the page who, threading his way through the chaos of Orientalized debauchery, was standing at his side.

"The Countess—" the boy was persisting, "the Countess desires your presence—"

For a long moment Ramonet answered with a vacant stare. Then, as memory flashed home, he turned to him in anger. "What does she want? Is the condition of the Countess worse?" He controlled himself with an effort.

The page shrugged. "She is troubled with fears and dreams."

"Dreams—" A laugh came from Ramonet's abandoned favorite. "It is little wonder—"

Somewhat bashfully the boy bowed in her direction. "It is also the Countess's wish that the Lady of Niort—if she were found—might attend her."

"I?" Making no attempt to move, she settled herself with more blatant intimacy to her preoccupation with Mirepoix. "Didn't the Countess," she called over her shoulder, "also request the pleasure of my Lady of Montfort's company?"

The boy looked from one to the other, uncomprehending.

"My Lady of Melun then—" Alys of Niort mocked.

Bewildered, the page's eyes followed hers to the couch. But Ramonet had risen. Already his inherent weakness, his fear to offend, to be found lacking in social amenities, was impelling him to curb even his violent desires.

For a moment he still lingered, then, bending, kissed Yolande's hand.

"I shall not forget," he murmured.

"What?" she prompted. "The compensatory castle?" Her voice rang clear as a child's in triumph, nailing him down that all might hear. "As price for the dance?"

"For the dance," he echoed and turned to follow the page. A touch was laid upon his arm.

"Since it is the wish of the Countess that you should escort me. . . ." Alys of Niort lay, half suspended against the cushions, as if the effort to rise unaided were too much. It was Peire-Roger who helped her. Ramonet bowed stiffly, offering her his arm. She leaned upon it with the full voluptuousness of her weight. "It seems that by some, at any rate, our names are still coupled together," she added bitingly as he led her to the door.

He stopped, drawing away his arm under the pretext of removing his turban. "We can hardly appear like this," he
106

evaded. "Escort the Lady Alys to the robing room," he commanded the page. Then, with a return of his old graciousness, he made a deep bow. "We shall meet at the Countess's apartment." The tremulous, almost apologetic, smile that accompanied his words caused even Alys of Niort to wonder whether after all the words had been meant ironically.

As though the disappearance of Ramonet of Toulouse formed but part of the improbable dream sequence of the last hours, Yolande de Montfort lay for a little time with eyes shut, abandoned so completely to the images she had created that the voice which intruded on those fantasies seemed almost a part of a mythical world.

"And the towers were all entangled in roses—"

She hardly cared what the words meant. Perhaps they were not even spoken. And still they climbed—creamy petaled, silken, tenuous, and mingled here and there with crimson. But suddenly the red splashed over, ran, not from the hidden heart of the flower, but from her hand. The thorns hooked deep. She started with a stifled cry and found herself looking into the green quizzical gaze of Mirepoix.

"Of what do you speak?" she asked, almost in defense. He had slipped onto Ramonet's deserted couch.

"I was only offering a suggestion."

"A suggestion about what?" With a desperate effort she tried to penetrate through the labyrinth of briers to what lay behind.

Peire-Roger gave a little laugh.

"The compensatory castle. And naturally it must be embowered in roses. The question is—damask or eglantine."

But the impudence of his raillery only stung her to greater boldness. "Neither. Oranges."

"So . . . ?" The monosyllable seemed to draw out, merge, crystallize into that emerald-green, hypnotic gaze. What, she attempted to think, was he driving at, what did he know? It didn't matter. She had won, as, in the end, the Montforts always did—first the father, then the uncle, then the brother, and when they failed the woman would

107

take on—a flaxen pig-tailed child—oranges. But even as she tried to conjure up that glowing vision of some minutes past, the image paled, the bright globed torches of the fruit grew dim; and everywhere, meshing the dark interstices of that metallic grove, the briers ran rampant guarding within secret castle, invisible fortress, heart of France, hidden, inviolable, secure amid the exotic wildness.

Of what was the man really speaking—building, decorating, furnishing castles? He seemed a consummate arbiter of the arts. God knew. She let the voice flow on, content to float on its mellifluousness, so infinite a relief after Ramonet's strained and nervous eagerness, for she was utterly and deliciously tired with the lassitude of strong young limbs after exertion, with the consciousness of a first battle fought and won. She had come to take part in a private skirmish and it had turned out a major victory. "For the sake of France . . ."

In the blonde small head of Simon de Montfort's daughter, inebriated by fumes of incense and spiced wine, an idea was germinating that might wreck a princedom and consolidate a realm, and all for the sake of an orange; or—she was no longer sure—was it a rose?

ROSA MYSTICA

*Thus I who set out to find my ideal, came back rejoicing
that I had lost my shadow.*

(MACDONALD: *Phantastes*)

I know but one freedom and that is freedom of the mind.

THE ROSE . . .

In the course of the days that followed, the mind of
Peire-Roger of Mirepoix, mercurial as ever, gripped by
the image, had started off tracing a thousand possibilities.

The first and most obvious, however, offered the least
allure. Ready as he had been to abandon himself to the
pleasures of the city and confident enough that, if he
wished, Yolande de Montfort could prove but another of
his countless conquests, her charms had provoked him,
for the moment at any rate, to subtler tactics than a
frontal attack on her feminine frailty, let alone on that
core of crystal-cold intransigence which, he suspected, un-
derlay her apparent surrender to the profligacies of the
South. Might not more lie behind it than coquetry—a
characteristic Montfortian tenacity, a perverse desire to
hold on to those rights of a shattered betrothal even as
she did to her confiscated lands? He was not sure, but to
watch the amorous liaison evidently unfolding itself between her and Ramonet offered more promise of amusement than an attempt to rupture the harmonies of the
duet or extend it to the necessarily vulgar dissonance of a
trio. For did not expectation always produce a rapture
greater than fulfillment? In the meantime Ramonet's court
could offer a variety of amusements to satisfy the senses,
even if they could not offer that same damascene texture
of skin.

Damascene. . . . Stretched on his couch and taking a

short siesta between the diversions that crowded to over-flowing every hour of his sojourn in the city, his eyes rested on the rosebush standing in an antique terra-cotta vase at his side.

An Eastern species that might have grown on the terraced garden of Semiramis he had discovered it in the courtyard of a Levantine trader who, dealing in every article of Oriental fabrication from silks and tissues to carpets, ivories, and hasheesh, was supplying him with certain of those objects that were to invest the ancient stronghold of Mirepoix with the aura of civilization.

Rose of Sharon, Rosa Mystica, Rosa Crucis—the names rose on his lips like an incantation.

Palely waxen in the shuttered light, the five petals formed a shimmering chalice from which the stamens thrust like nails studded with gold—the instruments of the Passion, it struck him, juxtaposed to the tenuous vulnerability of the concupiscent flesh. The agony, the lust for destruction were already implicit within the blossom itself. What need of the crude symbol of the thorns? Wasn't suggestion always more compelling than statement? For that matter, did not the spendthrift pollen itself scatter the first seeds of disintegration? With a flick of his fingers he blew a shower of gold dust over the silken petals of the rose. Too mortal Danae smothered in the god's embrace—the smooth, taunt texture of the shimmering skin stretched on the rack of parturition, withered to the sagging dugs of a penitent Magdalene. Death lurking within the bud, death within life. . . . That from ensuing death—*mortificatio*—may rise . . . but what. . . .? A face old with the wisdom of ages was lifted from the bubbling crucible . . . "the imperishable secret, the divine quintessence . . . the Stone."

Three years ago in Toledo he had stood perhaps on the very verge of initiation, would have reached there by now, if the cause of Liberty had not called him back. The Stone—*lapis exilis*, or whatever Esclarmonde of Foix's hapless minstrel had called it—the Grail itself.

After all, one might consider staging the grand mystery at Montségur as a respite from domestic languor. But in the meantime, he remembered suddenly, he must really

110

retrieve that little library Cousin Batalha had salvaged for him from the ravages of the French. Alchemy and the Grail. No fear that that hardened sportsman would want to hang on to the prize. Evidently he had even offered it to Wolf or Foix and his ill-starred prisoner to while away the tedium of their gloomy fort. But all its esoteric wisdom, he reflected, had evidently failed to bring young Parzival any nearer Montsalvat than the hermitage on the brink of the Waste Land. And if, according to Roger, even the restitution of Carcassonne had not restored Wolf to reason or to the world, he was still, it seemed, no nearer attaining to the *Visio Dei*.

Poor Wolf! he mused. How much happier he might be if instead of glooming in his Cathar purgatories, he could have cultivated the symbol of the rose—*"Rosa Mystica, rose of Sharon"*—the words re-echoed through his brain—"A garden inclosed is my sister, my spouse, a spring shut up, a fountain sealed." But the Wolfling had scarcely found the magic formula with which to break into that not so dissimilar Oriental pleasance of his. He smiled, recalling the mask of chiseled ivory out of which, long ago, the heavy-lidded eyes of Miriam Caravita had fixed them both with their half-mocking, questioning gaze. Ivory, he went on thinking, shell-pink, blush-rose, sun-burnished bronze, yes, if one would (why not?), the sculptured luster of jet-black limbs (Solomon had evidently shared his opinion). Even within the manifold categories how infinite was the range, how intricate the art of sampling their ever-varying texture. As if half consciously demonstrating his thoughts, he had stretched out his hand, while delicately, ever so delicately, his fingertips, relishing in advance the damascene softness of Yolande de Montfort's skin, glided in lingering caress over the pearly petals of the rose.

If the symbol of the rose had conjured up before Peire-Roger of Mirepoix an unending vista of fantasies, at least quasiintellectual, those it aroused in his wife Philippa were on a purely emotional plane. Incapable of comprehending any abstruse symbolism, she would have thought the thorns alone emblematic of the injuries to

111

which she had been exposed. Not only the secret fear of her newly wed husband's infidelity but the fact that on his visit to so long-coveted a goal as Toulouse, he should have left her behind, had wounded her to the quick. For what, at the root of her circumscribed being, Philippa had desired of marriage as fully as erotic fulfillment itself was the chance it promised of entering the grand world. Toulouse, inaccessible during the war, and vetoed in any case by parental authority as the pit of destruction, had hitherto appeared to her as an unreachable fairyland. Now, she had fondly imagined, the ban would be lifted. But instead, mustering a thousand plausible excuses—the illness of the countess, the suspension of all public gaieties—Peire-Roger had ridden off alone. Impossible that he could share her father's hidebound morals. Did then the standards he applied to his wife differ from those with which he approached life in general, or was he perhaps ashamed of her rusticity, she reflected in an agony of shame, remembering the quizzical and incalculable look with which he had greeted some new dress of which she had been inordinately proud, or how, with a slight twist of those long sinuous fingers, he had managed to give an undreamed-of slant of elegance to her linen coif.

Why, then, if he was ashamed of her, had he married her? a still small voice would whisper in secret, to be immediately silenced under the blandishment of his gallantries. Never had she quite ceased in the first months of her marriage to believe that after all it was a dream. Sometimes in fact, wandering through the rooms that under the hand of the mason or artisan transformed themselves day by day from the grim fastness of a dingy fort into the halls of an enchanted palace, she wondered whether they did in fact exist, and to reassure herself, her hand would fearfully explore the thick soft pile of Persian velvet, the glossy intricacies of Indian chessmen, the wiry scales of an enameled vase. Soon, within a month perhaps, he had promised, those exotic luxuries would form the setting of continued galas, music and dancing— a symposium of the poets. Reviewing all her knowledge of romantic literature, she prepared to fit herself for her role. For must she not be ready to accept or reject a troubadour's worship and find herself the center of those reputed courts of love? Only her husband's homage she must not receive. True passion, the fashionable world dictated, must never be defiled by the intimacies of the marriage bed. Had she then lost his already, she asked herself in sudden fear? In the silence of his absence it became a certainty. Even the thought of what vengeance she would take on his callousness failed to quell the secret thought that no troubadour's adulations could replace Peire-Roger of Mirepoix's allures.

And then one day the messenger had come, bearing with him that miracle of horticultural art. A token of fidelity, or repentance? The thorns seemed eloquent enough. But already, bent above the shimmering coronet of petals, inhaling their intoxicating perfume, the sting had faded, doubt flew to the winds. For how could she not help seeing in the emblem of the rose the manifest revival of the first rapturous promise of his love?

Even so her exultation fell short of the silent ecstacy with which young Esclarmonde, her sister, on a visit to the castle of Mirepoix, had stood contemplating the rose.

For this then, the child had apprehended with overwhelming wonder, was the mystery shut within the casket, this budding, burgeoning, blossoming resurgence of a withered flower; this the unfolding of the secret so darkly hid within the unfathomable recesses of Philippa's and Peire-Roger's hearts. The miracle had happened—yet wasn't it her magic that had brought it about?

It was a few days later that Ramon of Pérelha, returning from an inspection of his weaving sheds, was reminded by his wife that he had promised to supply some bales of linen for the new hostel at Durban. The building, she had heard, had been completed at last and the dormitories were to be opened this spring.

He might send over a load by one of the muleteers in the coming week, Ramon considered. In any case he had some business to settle with a landowner in the Plantaurel. Possibly he might even go on to Durban via the Mas d'Azil himself.

Durban—the Mas d'Azil. Esclarmonde, sitting on a

113

stool at Corba's knee winding a skein of worsted, had let her hands fall into her lap.

"You promised to take me—"

"Where?"

"The Mas d'Azil."

"What, that murky tunnel?" he answered gruffly. But jumping to her feet so that the ball of yarn rolled across the room, she crossed to his side.

"Wasn't it there they waylaid the French?" Her eyes were fixed on his with such passionate intensity that he had to laugh.

"And what could that mean to a chit of a girl? One would almost think you'd have liked to take part in that exploit yourself."

"I would."

"You'd do much better to attend to your spinning," her mother's voice broke in, "than to be aping boys' ways. And much use you'd be in any case, mooning half the day in the treetops. There, I knew it." Jumping up from her work, she bustled across the room to retrieve her infant son who was chasing kitten-like after the ball that Esclarmonde in her excitement had dropped, and now wrestled frantically to free himself on the one hand from the restriction of his mother's embrace, on the other from the entangling threads.

"It might do you good," Corba turned on her daughter exasperated, "if you were to take the linen to Durban— and stay there for a while. Honoria, by what I know of her, may have more success in imposing discipline on you than I." She sighed and, shaking out her skirts under which the boy, to make up for his curtailed pleasures, was playing hide and seek, settled once more to her spinning.

Honoria —At the name a shadow had dimmed the light in Esclarmonde's face. Mechanically she picked up the ball and, starting to disentangle and rewind it, sat down without a word upon her stool.

Corba, surprised at her sudden docility, could only attribute it to the effect of her threats, having gathered already that at the banquet at Foix, the mistress of Durban had exerted some chastening influence on her daughter's waywardness. Aware of her own shortcomings as a disci-

114

plinarian, she shook her head in helpless renunciation, too flustered, as usual, by the burden of housekeeping to give further thought to the problem.

Perhaps because her mother's threat had robbed the proposed excursion of its initial glamour, fate, with its usual contrariness, caused it to materialize even sooner than she expected. Nevertheless, when, in the week that followed, Esclarmonde actually found herself setting out with her father and a small caravan of mules bound for the Plantaurel, the exhilaration of the ride and the keenness of the fresh spring air soon dispelled the ghost of Honoria, and by the time Ramon had done with his proposed visits and they were at last approaching the Mas d'Azil, the excursion had regained for her all its original promise of adventure and excitement.

Her father was in an unusually benign mood. Often during the war, after their estates had been burned and pillaged, he had ridden out with her in the saddle before him foraging for provender in the Sabarthez, but he had been too busy of late and today's expedition was like a holiday for them both.

They had left the muleteers and their beasts of burden behind them. In front the road wound on toward a barrier of rock that, to all appearances, cut off the higher part of the valley beyond. But, absorbed in the task of drawing from her somewhat laconic father a detailed description of how Count Roger and his brother had waylaid the French, she hardly noticed that they were fast approaching the face of the cliff. All of a sudden, with a catch of breath, the last question died on her lips, for suddenly the sky was obliterated. Shutting them in by walls of rock, the tunnel was closing in on them like a vault. They were riding into the mountain itself.

In a few moments it had grown quite dark. Bending sideways, she could see nothing but a last patch of the road swallowed up by the shadows and somewhere far below on her right a gleam of white spume from the torrent hurtling and churning in the depths. Even the horse had grown restless. She could feel it chafing at the bit. Involuntarily she clung faster to her father's arm.

115

"It was there in the caverns they waited," he was saying. His voice was almost drowned by the roar of the water, but with beating heart she tried to follow his pointing hand to where the walls of rock seemed to recede, sucked into yet more terrifying depths of darkness. Caves, she thought, slippery, bottomless crevasses leading into the black belly of the hill. She tried to picture how it felt, crouching behind the boulders, taking aim from behind an invisible spur of rocks, hand clasped on dagger or javelin, ready to spring. And it seemed to her that the suspense, all that unendurable waiting, was upon her—the waiting, not of seconds, minutes, hours, but years. Suddenly she felt them there in the dark, all around her, men savage with hate, hunger, and fear, beasts tracked to their last hiding place or dragging the mauled prey to their lair. But somehow they belonged not only to the past but to the future—centuries, aeons of hunting of man and animal, pursuing and pursued.

Perhaps her father felt her terror, for with a sharp pull on the bridle he was urging on his horse. A minute or two later they were safe in the open.

"Well," he laughed, "are you still so eager to take part in an ambush?" And as she failed to reply, he began to describe how Gui de Montfort's horsemen had fled helter-skelter down the valley before them right into the open jaws of the trap. But her eagerness to know every detail of the skirmish had abated a little. It was as though she knew far more than ever her father could tell. Besides, she was still quite dazed, coming out suddenly into the sunshine, into the valley lying all green and open between two low ridges of wooded hill. And how, she thought, could it be the same river, rippling past, quite friendly now, while a bird sat chirping on the brake? Had she been dreaming or was she dreaming now? Then which, something within her cried aloud in sudden fear, which was real? That terror or this peace?

They had ridden on a mile or two. The valley was narrowing now, the trees were drawing close to the road, till at a bend the river bed widened again for a moment,

116

forming a kind of amphitheater before it was once more all but closed by an outthrusting mass of forest and hill.

"It was from here that Palhers came thundering down on Gui," her father pointed to where, above the trees, the walls of a castle glimmered gray.

"Is that Durban?" she asked.

"Yes—no one lives there now," Ramon said. But she knew that. Hadn't Wolf told her? And there, she went on thinking, were the trees, just as he'd said. They crowded everywhere—trunk on trunk, tier upon tier, thrust against the sky. Even riding down here on the road, it was as though one had to cut a way through.

But they were out at last, for the trees had been felled on the scarp above them; beyond the scrub, the newly plowed fields stretched away between them and the farther woods.

"They've plowed up a lot of land," Ramon continued, "since last I was here." Reining in his horse, he cast his gaze with the experienced eye of the landowner over the adjoining hills. "Using every bit of soil for what it's worth," he commented to himself approvingly.

Half mechanically his eye followed a figure striding, its back toward them, to the crest of the ridge.

The child was watching it too, arrested by something about it that seemed both familiar and strange. She had seen a peasant sowing the seed on their farm so often, it struck her, had noticed that rhythmic, swinging gait as at every few steps his arm flung out, scattering the seed. Yet it hadn't been like that. She stared more sharply at the figure moving solitary high up on the horizon's edge—as though he were sowing the whole earth, she thought, and then suddenly her heartbeat quickened.

"The man's left-handed," her father remarked laconically, as if something that had puzzled him too had been explained. But even before he spoke Esclarmonde was slipping down from the saddle and scrambling up the adjoining slope. If only she could get across that bit of scrub before he turned, she considered. She'd hide behind those bushes, on the edge of the field, and then when he came back she'd jump right out on him. He'd think she'd fallen from the sky.

He was out of sight now. Panting, she ran on and just managed to throw herself behind a clump of gorse bushes before he appeared once more over the horizon's edge. Stretched flat on her belly she waited, regaining her breath. He was almost level with her now. Another moment and she had jumped from her hiding place right into his path.

He halted, utterly taken aback. She was leaping around him, diving her hands into the bag slung from his shoulder.

"How on earth . . . ?" he stammered at last. But for answer she only tossed a handful of seed into the air. It fell in a shower upon him, smothering his eyes and mouth. Even while, half-blinded, he brushed the grain from his face, she had emptied a good portion of the seed into her looped-up skirt and, laughingly, run off across the field.

Still too bewildered to move, he stood, rooted to the spot. She had slackened her pace now and, swaying a little from side to side, was scattering the seed on the wind.

She dances over the earth: Proserpina . . . it flashed through his mind, or was it Ceres—Ceres as a child—if ever she was one? he thought confused.

She was coming back again, skipping, leaping over the furrows in a cloud of waving arms and hair. But as she reached him, her hand dropped to her side.

"Do you want more?" he asked half ruefully. She'd probably spoiled his field.

She shook her head, her face sobered. "I can't do it— properly. Will you teach me?"

"You'd better ask one of the villagers," he gave a little laugh. "They're far better at it than I."

She shook her head again. "I can get one of our men at Lavelanet to show me, any day I want. But won't you? You must, you *must*," she pleaded vehemently. "Up there—" Catching hold of the bag, she made an attempt to drag him along. "It's as if . . ."

But he was turning in the direction of the scrub from which Ramon of Pérelha was riding toward them.

"Is it your father?" he asked.

But if he only knew the chief of the Pérelhas vaguely by sight, Ramon had soon recognized him.

"I'm afraid," he began, pulling at his horse at the edge of the furrows, "you'll think this scamp of a daughter of mine's been brought up without respect of man's property or the soil. What do you mean by it," he turned toward her, frowning, "wasting the seed and trampling on the furrows? Will you apologize?" As she remained silent, looking from one to the other with her puzzled enigmatic expression, he added with rising anger, "Do you realize with whom you've been jesting?"

And then suddenly her face broke into open laughter. "Of course."

"Why, do you know each other?" her father asked surprised.

"We've met once or twice—at Foix, at the assembly," Wolf made an attempt to explain.

"Hm. Still, there's no reason for her to go spoiling your fields."

"Did I really spoil them?" she asked, looking up at Wolf with an expression half wistful, half whimsical.

He gave a little laugh, thinking once more of Ceres—field on field of ripening corn. "We'll have to wait till harvest to see."

"I reckon you'll be claiming reparation," Ramon retorted, and went on to explain the reason for their visit.

Turning to where, at the foot of the hill, the pack mules were slowly winding their way along the road, Wolf returned thanks. "I'll walk down with you to the hostel."

Ramon, aware of a certain deadening in the other's tone and taking it for reluctance to leave his work—an attitude with which he thoroughly sympathized—urged him to finish. Wolf, however, professing it could wait, made as though to lift the child into the saddle, but she resisted, considering it best to let her father, who was still eying her with reproach, first recover his temper, while she herself, in hardly chastened mood, sped off across the grass.

She had been right. Glancing back after a little while she saw that the two men, Wolf of Foix walking at the horse's head, were evidently so deeply in their talk she might have been forgotten.

She was contented enough, skipping along, sniffing the cool, urgent scents of the spring. And then suddenly at a turn of the road, beyond a group of older buildings nestling among the trees, she saw the hostel, or rather she guessed at once what the gray rectangular building of fresh-quarried stone must be, cold, gaunt, and dreary—like Honoria herself, she thought, and shivered a little.

She shivered still more when, a little later, the mistress of Durban greeted them in person.

Honoria had evidently been occupied in one of the wards, for the sister who had met them in the hall went to fetch her.

As she appeared in the frame of the further door, Wolf moved swiftly toward her.

"The senhor of Pérelha has come to bring you the promised linen," she heard him say. There was an almost pleading eagerness in his voice, as if he were anxious to share her expected pleasure, but the expression of her face scarcely changed as, almost ignoring her husband, she thanked Ramon in words that seemed to account his favor a matter-of-course duty in the name of humanity. A moment later, without inquiring as to whether her guests were in need of rest or refreshment, she was leading them on a tour of the hostel, and with feet that flagged as no amount of exercise made them, Esclarmonde dragged behind while close-lipped Honoria, delivering her homily on the aims of the hostel, guided them from corridor to corridor opening on the same vista of bare or empty-bedded rooms.

In the refectory it was worse. She dared hardly speak, let alone laugh, in that chapel-like hall where to eat seemed almost a sacrilege. Perhaps, she realized desperately as she stood at the long table, wedged between one of the Cathar sisters and the file of cronies who had come hobbling into the hall, it might never come to more than the breaking of the bread.

She was well acquainted with that ceremony, which many a Cathar elder had performed when receiving hospitality at Lavelanet. But somehow their presence had usually exerted a benign influence on her father's stern rule or her mother's flustered distraction and none of the *bons-*

120

hommes had ever made them wait in silence so long as this. She glanced surreptitiously at the stark, rigid figure of Honoria standing motionless at the head of the board. Supposing she never moved at all, supposing those bowls were never filled, she thought in sudden terror, while hunger began to gnaw viciously at her entrails?

"Give us this day our heavenly bread." But it might have been years ago the words had been spoken. And in the meantime all of them, everyone, everything here had perhaps been turned to stone. As if she must make sure she was still alive she moved her feet a little. It was like breaking the silence in a vault of the dead. And then, suddenly, she felt again the sense of fevered, unendurable waiting she had experienced in the tunnel of the Mas d'Azil. So strong was it that, when at last she found herself seated, her pent-up feelings burst out in an uncontrollable necessity to break the silence.

"We came through the tunnel of the Mas d'Azil."

To mitigate the violent explosiveness of so apparently disconnected a statement, Ramon of Pérelha hastily attempted an explanation. "She was bent on seeing the scene of the great exploits. She's wishing herself a boy. But I fancy," he added laughing, "she was half cured of her brazenness in that Stygian gloom."

"I wasn't." The belittlement had roused all her powers of resistance. "It was only the waiting—" she blurted out, and realized suddenly she didn't know rightly to what she referred: her hunger, the silence, or her strange, tormented feelings in the tunnel—all that inexplicable burden of suspense. In a desperate attempt to get clear somewhere she called down the table to Wolf, "I mean—could you bear it—waiting all that time—to pounce on them?"

His answer, if he was about to give one, was cut short by Honoria. "We don't discuss such subjects at Durban or harbor their memory either. Isn't it a pity," she turned to Pérelha, "that the child should be brought up on tales of bloodshed and murder?"

She could not catch her father's answer and Wolf was half hidden by the figures sitting between them. He seemed to be muttering something about it being long ago. But all she knew was that she'd only managed to

121

spoil everything again. She remembered how his face had darkened when she talked of the ambush, that day at Foix; and she had imagined he was offended because she hadn't guessed, till then, he was the hero of the tale. But instead, she realized now, it was all quite different and just as that sinister stranger had hinted, Wolf cared nothing for his knightly prowess. And it was quite true that he had turned Cathar and refused to fight. But he wasn't a coward, she admitted to herself—he had proved that on the rampart walls—and besides, he had scaled the mountain. Why, she thought angrily, if he could climb to the skies and look down on the whole earth, why ever did he go and bury himself in this tomb of a place?

For it would never come alive, she was certain, this gaunt gray hollow prison of a hostel, even when the rows of beds and benches were filled to overflowing with old cracked, whining men and women, and long-faced Cathar sisters dressed in gray—worse than the rows of nuns with whom Cousin Forneria had gone to live after she had been converted by the Dominican brothers. For there, she reflected, even the poor in the almshouses had been quite jolly, while these—she glanced at the handful of pensioners sipping furtively from their bowls as if they were ashamed of showing an appetite. Even her own was gone now. Fretfully she picked and dug at the stew of vegetables in her bowl.

Honoria's eyes were upon her. She could feel their gray, withering light upon her, on Wolf, on everything in this cold naked room.

And then she knew what it was. Honoria was casting an enchantment on them all, withering, shriveling them up till in the end they'd become as thin and gray and cold as the bare-washed walls, the spindly pointed rafters, the ghostly windowpanes. But it should never happen, she thought impulsively, for she would weave her counter-spells. Honoria would have no power. With sudden determination she fixed her eyes on the bowl while with her spoon, slowly but with intense and fearful concentration, she began to draw patterns in the mash, circle on circle, till at last she knew herself secure, encompassed by a magical ring.

Somewhere, on its periphery, Wolf of Foix was talking to her father—talking, she was sure, about landlords and peasants and the freeing of the serf. But all that was happening in another world to that in which she had entrenched herself against Honoria and her deadly wiles. She had withdrawn, invisible, like a snail into its shell, into the fastness of her secret world. If she wanted, she could make Wolf walk into it too. But she didn't really want to—now.

Perhaps she had really become invisible, it dawned on her, for all of a sudden she realized that everyone but herself was moving. And there were her father and Wolf of Foix walking past her, out of the door, as though she did not exist.

Bewildered, she watched them for a moment, silhouetted against the splash of sunlight outside. Then, as if rediscovering her senses, she jumped to her feet. But the hand of the Cathar sister beside her drew her back. "They have merely gone to inspect the farm." Perhaps, the sister went on to suggest, she would like to accompany her on her round and help her feed some of the poor bedridden patients in the upper ward.

At a little distance Honoria was giving one of the women instructions about dressing an injured plowman's wounds. Suddenly it dawned on Esclarmonde that they might want her to help, like the little princess people talked about who washed the lepers' wounds—somewhere far away in Germany or Hungary, she'd forgotten which—or the girl who had sacrificed herself in order that the poor knight could be healed of his fearful sickness. Yet had she not healed Wolf? But that was by magic, she reflected. Had he not said so himself—by the snakes and the enchanted water and her witches' dance down by the lake?

The sister who had spoken to her had been called away by the others. Honoria, still giving orders, was moving down the far end of the room. Seizing her chance, Esclarmonde slipped in among the crowd that was slowly gravitating toward the door. Before anyone had noticed, she had escaped into the open.

Wolf and her father were already out of sight. She had

best not try and follow them, it struck her, or they might send her back. Making for a gap in the fence she found herself in the meadows. Running on, she scrambled up a slope and in a minute was safe among the trees.

An hour or so later she ventured out. By now, she considered, her father might have returned to the hostel and be ready to start home. But it might be best not to hurry, she went on thinking, and decided to go back by way of the farm. They might still be there and if not, they could easily find her if they wanted. Satisfied, she made her way in the direction of the older buildings at the other end of the field.

There seemed to be no one about, however, except for a knock-kneed figure shambling across the yard who, eying her with a vacant stare, disappeared into an adjoining hut.

In no hurry to return to the hostel she loitered, curious. There was a good reassuring smell of dung and animals about the place. So much better, she thought, than soap and bandages. And in one byre there were great white, sleek oxen tethered to their stalls and snuffing the hay with their muzzles breathing out slow clouds of steaming breath. But why were there no milch cows, she wondered, and remembered that the Cathars didn't even allow milk—or eggs, of course, so that there weren't any fowls either, but pigeons . . . why, they were everywhere, fluttering to and fro between the roof and the eaves of the stable, pecking at remnants of straw, strutting and preening themselves with white, fanned tails. Turning toward the cornstack under which she was standing, she pulled out a few stalks of grain, then, drawing her fingers along them, scattered the corn.

In an instant they were there, crowds of them. Wheeling, circling, tentatively alighting and veering again, till the ground was a heavy sea of gray, white-crested waves.

She watched spellbound, while her fingers tore ear on ear from the stack and hurled them one after another into the fluctuant sea. How long she continued she didn't know, till suddenly the surface was broken by a surging

124

uprush of wings. In a moment the courtyard was empty but for a few brazen stragglers stalking, as though unperturbed, under the very feet of the intruder.

Wolf of Foix was standing at her side. "So you *are* here. But where were you hiding all the time? Sister Agnes thought you'd followed us, so they didn't worry, but when we came back without you . . ."

She shook her head. "I ran off to the forest."

"What—playing hide and seek? We might never have found you."

"You wouldn't—unless I'd wanted you to."

There was such gravity in her look and her voice that he answered abashed, "You mean—you *didn't?*"

She stood regarding him doubtfully. "I don't know."

"Anyhow," he gave a little laugh, "you're found. I went on with your father to the rye fields. The men are working down there today. He wanted to see how it all works," he continued. There was a curious light in his face, she noticed suddenly, something that hadn't been in it before, as if almost he had awakened from a long sleep and didn't quite know where he was. At any rate, he seemed quite oblivious to the litter of empty corn ears around him. "It's time for you to be riding home," he added.

"Already?" she pouted, quite forgetting that only an hour or two ago, inside the hostel, it had been her one desire to be off. And suddenly she realized she was desperately hungry. "I've hardly eaten anything," she said.

"Why?" he asked surprised. "Didn't you eat anything at dinner?"

She shook her head. "Hardly—I didn't feel like it—in there."

Rummaging in his pocket, he extracted a hunk of brown bread. "I've usually a bit with me. It's rather stale, I'm afraid."

Wondering whether he, too, lost his appetite in that gray, dim room and had to fortify himself against ensuing hunger, she gnawed eagerly at the crust; then having allayed hers for a moment, she threw a few crumbs to the remaining birds. Only then did he seem to become aware of the waste of straw at his feet. His gaze swerved to the stacks.

"So that's what you've been up to." But in spite of his admonishing looks, he seemed almost to be laughing. "If you give them a chance, they'll eat up the whole stack." Walking across, he made an attempt to repair the damage.

"How many are there?" she asked.

"Hundreds. As we never kill them, they go on increasing. When they're too many they fly off to the forest."

Her eyes traveled back to the great scarp of trees crowned by the crenelated towers. "Why don't you live up there yourself?"

"We used to. We have no use for it now. Your father will be waiting," he added abruptly, turning to go.

Realizing only too well what would be the consequences of her father's impatience, she followed reluctantly, but a few seconds later she halted once more, gazing up at the gray squat tower of the pigeon house. "Can I look in?"

He hesitated. "If you don't frighten them," he said, pushing open the door.

She slipped in under his arm, catching her breath as the pungent darkness rose up to meet her. It was a moment before her eyes, accustomed to the brilliant sunlight outside, could distinguish anything. But above her the air seemed to divide as in a sudden commotion the birds rose to the dusky bell of the roof.

She stood quite still, afraid to move, almost to breathe, aware that Wolf, shutting the door behind him, was standing beside her. Gradually the hubbub subsided. High above, against the light filtering through the checkered holes in the masonry, a wing flashed into existence, or the azure pinpoint of sky was extinguished as an alighting body blocked the opening. But from all around, as she listened, sound on sound was borne in on her ear—rustle and ruffle of feathers, pitter-patter of innumerable feet, and beneath, enveloping them all, the dim, incessant throb of cooing, till she wondered whether it came out of the darkness or from the depths of her body itself. Perhaps, it struck her, she had already been turned into a bird. But the very thought broke the illusion. And, as she stood trying to decipher those rows of huddled, feathery shapes, she seemed to become aware of the myriad beady

126

eyes fixing her with their own—a world of down and feathers and of sharp fastidious claws and pecking beaks—an otherness in which she and her companion had no part. Awestruck, she stretched out her hand, groping for Wolf's.

Once again in the sunlight, the whole landscape had for them both a strange, diluted look, as if, suddenly cast out from that fearful concentration of identity, they found themselves in a world too full of irrelevance to have substance and meaning. Perhaps, Esclarmonde thought as she approached the gray, stark house, even the hostel didn't really exist. They would walk on and through it. But into what? In the pigeon tower she had experienced an apprehension of life that she had never known before. Yet they hadn't belonged to it, neither she nor Wolf. Half unconsciously, feeling the need of solidarity between them, she still clung to his hand, as if together they must fortify themselves against emptiness. . . .

In the courtyard Ramon of Pérelha's horse stood ready saddled. He was pacing the hall, the constraint he felt in the presence of Honoria did not improve his temper. "Where have you been?" he rated the child as she came into sight.

"Feeding the pigeons." It was Wolf who answered.

"I reckon," her father put in, "she's been up to some mischief."

"Isn't it in the nature of elves?" Wolf gave a little laugh, but Ramon turned to Honoria, frowning.

"If it weren't that I see good signs of your husband spoiling her, I'd have a mind to ask you to undertake her training. What with the troubles of the last years, her education, I'm afraid, was sadly neglected."

"The warmongers don't think of that," Honoria retorted acridly.

But her face as, calling to one of the sisters for a towel and comb, she made an attempt to repair the child's disheveled appearance, knew nothing of pity or understanding. And when Esclarmonde, escaping from Honoria, let Wolf lift her into the saddle, it was almost with relief that she felt herself rescued from the violently conflicting emotions of the last few hours into unequivocal security.

"Well," Ramon asked gruffly when they had ridden a little way, "would you have liked me to leave you to Honoria's training?"

She made no reply except for a violent shake of the head. His answering laugh, and the fact that he made no further attempt to take her to task, reassured her that he himself had evidently not felt too much at home at the hostel or with its mistress. But as they rode, Ramon of Pérelha's thoughts soon moved from the memory of Honoria to his discussion with Wolf, while he weighed in his mind the pros and cons of the young man's wild notions regarding the abolishment of serfdom and the communal working and profit sharing of his lands. True, it wasn't the first time he had come across them. The Cathar elders, when all was said and done, preached much the same. Still, they hardly expected a man to put their ideas into practice—Christian in principle, no doubt, but the world was too rotten. You'd need a kingdom of saints to carry it through. The free farmers would start making a fine fuss. As if there wasn't enough trouble already. Down here, maybe, it might work in a pinch. The serfs had already been more or less trained to freedom in Mabilia of Durban's day—a saintly little woman, he remembered, if ever there was one, not like her daughter. For all her piety and the pother she made about nonviolence, Honoria was a first-rate slave driver, he reckoned. She'd crush the very spirit out of her husband if she could—or what was left of it. The war had dealt pretty hard with him—body and soul. No doubt with all her talk about peace and brotherhood she'd managed to work on his sentiments. He had always, by all accounts, let things touch him too deep—that business about an escaped prisoner. And long before that his adoration of Trencavel—adolescent madness. But maybe, after all, his reforms derived more from that quarter than from her Cathar sermons. Wolf had soon found out there was no chance of their materializing in the Carcassonne of today. And so, as a last hope, he had fallen back on the farm. Quite pathetic, the way he had

128

seemed to brighten up while he talked about it. Seemed grateful for the least bit of sympathy for his plans.

Still, Ramon reflected, he'd rather deal with *his* type of madness than that of Peire-Roger of Mirepoix. God, how it galled him that he had given in and let Roger of Foix badger him into selling Philippa to that libertine fop. For all the signs he'd shown of temporarily settling down, rumor had not been silent as to his recent adventures at Toulouse. Nonetheless, even now Ramon failed to see what other course he could have taken. If he had refused, Count Roger would have shown his displeasure and he'd have lost all chance of keeping Montségur; might even have seen it fall to Jordan of the Isle. Once again, as in the presence of the young Count of Foix, he felt himself bated. Never would he forget the promise he had given to Esclarmonde of Foix to guard the land for her sake, even if the citadel fell. Oh, they knew well enough it was the one point through which they could work on him. Mirepoix had buttressed himself well with Roger's support. When it came to it, a vassal wasn't much better in relation to his landlord than a serf. Embittered at the memory of his private wrongs, Ramon of Pérelha rode on, while the thought almost made him feel a growing sympathy for Wolf's revolutionary dreams. Heavens, of the two, he'd rather see the Bastard fathering Philippa's children than that perfumed fop. Incidentally, Honoria, he reflected, probably refused the man her bed for fear of propagating Satan's breed. Catharism, drawn to its last conclusion, would deprive a man of his very guts. But so would the Church if it honestly followed Augustine. And the good *bonshommes* were less exacting, when all was said and done, on the weakness of their fleshly brethren than the monks, in their penances, at least, and less of a drag on the purse. With a sense of having reasserted his own freedom against the tryant, whether ecclesiastical or temporal, he spurred on his horse.

When at nightfall he again reached the valley of the Olmes and saw the moon-bathed cone of Montségur rise above the woods of Lavelanet, he knew that it was inseparable from his own lands as the heart's blood from his own flesh. For was it not the core of his honor, his fealty, and his freedom that he would defend to his last breath? But still the giant held sway over them all, Esclarmonde would have added, had she not already been fast asleep in her father's arms.

In the meantime Wolf had returned to the field without reentering the hostel. Honoria, he knew, would have enough on her hands, cutting and hemming the linen. Another step in the attainment of her wish had been fulfilled, even if she had grudged admitting it when he greeted her with the news.

He had half expected she would repulse him as if he had no right to share in her feelings. Since she had given way to that one emotional outburst on the eve of his return from Carcassonne, her attitude reflected what he could only take for complete disillusionment and contempt. He did not blame her, realizing that in her eyes his action in escorting young Trencavel could only seem a betrayal of the Cathar faith. Explanations, he knew, would be useless. She had abandoned him, he well believed, even as she had cried in desperation that day to the hand of God—the God of Light or Darkness, he would reflect at times. In her Manichaean intransigence that recognized no intermediary between an absolute of heaven and hell it might well be the latter. Alone, beset only by that trait of stubbornness which forced the strange unintegrated counterpart of his impressionable idealism, he persisted in the way he had set himself, without hope of grace. Perhaps she had even found consolation in seeing him arrived at last beyond the tempestuous tides of spiritual violence, beyond desire and despair, like a ship fog-bound in icy seas.

Yet this evening, as he made his way back to the fields, his footsteps had an unaccustomed resilience. Was it due to his recent encounter with the child or her father? He couldn't tell, and now they were gone he was almost unable to believe the discussion he had had with Ramon of Pérelha had really taken place.

He had long ago given up the idea of broaching his plans for agricultural reforms to the neighboring landowners, yet today he had somehow been led to unburden

130

himself. Pérelha, for his part, had shown little more faith in their ultimate success than had the others, but he had at least not broken out in fury at what they would doubtless have considered a heinous offense against their feudal rights. What was more, he had even admitted that under certain circumstances it might be worth giving the plan a trial—at Durban, for instance, where the tenants had for generations been impregnated with the Cathar doctrine of dispossessiveness. It might work among the poorer villeins, those who had nothing to lose, Pérelha had conceded skeptically, though doubtless there would be enough grumbles behind his back and the more ambitious or industrious among them would think they'd been cheated out of the profit. Probably he was right, and yet . . .

Wolf halted. Turning in the direction of the lower fields shelving gently toward the village, long ridges of soil sliced into countless strips, many of them indifferently tilled. Soon the seeds of some weed-grown plot would have spoiled its neighbor; burr and thistle run riot through the corn, where instead might stretch a sea of unbroken rippling gold. And from its store, he went on thinking, each man would draw his equal share when autumn came, fearless that in winter cold his family would be reduced to penury and starvation.

"Material benefits," Honoria would mock, "could not enrich the spirit." And yet, weren't they the basis of all spiritual liberty? Might there not be among men some who would work for a communal aim, the vision of a fuller, completer existence with a solidarity that had united the younger members of the City Guard at Carcassonne? He caught himself up sharply. Was he once more being led astray into blank ideals—for what had been the end? And yet, if the goal had been other than war? If Trencavel had lived today—if before *them* had spread the hope of peace . . . ?

He had reached the spot where earlier that day he had sowed the corn. In the evening light the furrowed slope loomed bigger, darker, almost threatening in its potential power—a vast curving arch spanned between the receding woods. Unconsciously he stooped down and gathered a handful of soil. . . .

"The earth," Trencavel had cried as together they galloped over the frost-bound plain. "The earth, isn't it enough?" Clouded in dreams, Wolf had hardly known what Trencavel meant. But now . . . he gazed out across the dark ridges of soil swinging out into infinity, converging on what invisible goal?

Suddenly, as he watched, two birds wheeled out of the twilight and, almost brushing his cheek, passed like a flash of white silver into the woods beyond. But even in the moment in which they had dipped toward him and risen again, it had seemed to him as if they had been cast up from his land. Flight of feathers or spray of seed? Venus dove-charioted or Demeter spreading fecundity over the earth?

Yet the same dove, he remembered darkly, that had dropped the fructifying seed on the Manichaean stone had brooded over the blood sacrifice of Mithra—the emblem of murder, or the symbol of peace?

He stood gazing at the place where the two birds had vanished into the forest. Baffled but shaken by an overwhelming emotion, he stared into the falling twilight, battling in vain to solve the old paradox, the duality of all being that had haunted him as a boy. What if, he felt with sudden fear, the answer were not unequivocal after all? But he suppressed the thought. For to what end had he then followed the path he had trodden the last two years, if it had not brought him to recognition at least of that one truth—the gospel of nonviolence? For a moment longer he stood motionless, then with an abrupt movement he turned and strode through the falling dusk back to the hostel.

AMBITION AND DESTINY

*Our task is to stamp this provisional, perishing earth
into ourselves so deeply, so painfully and passionately,
that its being may rise again, "invisibly," in us.*

(RILKE in a letter to Witold von Hulewicz)

IF EVEN FOR WOLF OF FOIX THE DUAL CONCEPTS OF WAR
and peace threatened for a moment to appear, in the
metaphysical sense, ambiguous, they certainly proved so,
during the next few years, in the world of fact.

To be sure, peace had to all events and purposes returned to Languedoc. The castles were rebuilt, music and
merriment once more echoed in the halls of the nobles
and burghers. And yet the ease, the spontaneity, that had
belonged to a culture old enough for its barbaric origins
to have long since been merged in the remnants of classic
civilization, and sufficiently sensitive to imbibe the exotic
culture of Arab Spain, had somehow vanished. The tone,
even if it was gayer, more reckless than before, had about
it at times a quality almost hectic, as if people were but
too well aware that the regained liberty they boasted was
ephemeral, was perhaps even a mask. That trouble was
indeed brewing, that behind the scenes politics were
weaving an ever more inextricable net, seemed if anything
to increase the general insouciance, as if those dangers at
which one could still point a finger only veiled the inevita-
bility of the greater disaster hidden beneath—the underlying consciousness of irredeemable decadence. If Trencavel
in his day had already despaired at his countrymen's refusal to realize impending disaster, he would have seen
them now without will to act through fatalistic certainty
of their doom. What he, had he lived, would have apprehended in anguish, France and the Roman Church

watched with ever-growing satisfaction and joy. The prize was sure. All that remained was to see how it should be divided. Languedoc was, in fact, reduced to the role of a pawn in their diplomatic game, a game in which, as the powers vied for supremacy, Ramonet was protected now by the Pope, now by Louis VIII. But subtly, silently, the net was drawn closer till the young Count of Toulouse found not only himself excommunicated but his territories once again invaded by the French troops.

It was not, however, against the towns of Languedoc that they launched their first attack, but on his possessions in Provence, marching on Avignon and Beaucaire—Beaucaire that had witnessed the phenomenal victory of young Ramonet, Beaucaire the miraculous turning point in the unending pageant of shame and defeat. The very memory might have been enough to instill courage and certainty of success. Ramonet indeed had no doubt as to the fact and was immediately spurred to action. Yet when, affecting as usual a carefree arrogance, he called his feudatories to resistance, he was dumfounded at the lack of response. Some desultorily rallied to the colors. But already Beaucaire had submitted. Avignon was surrounded. At the last minute the town decided to make a show of defense. In vain; with the advance of the French army toward the city, one after another of the Languedocien nobles seceded. Within three months, Béziers, Belpech, Pamiers had yielded, while Jordan of the Isle, even Comminges himself, had paid allegiance to the French king. Young Trencavel, making little attempt in the general panic to prove by personal experience whether after all his father merited the name of hero or of coward, found himself fleeing from Carcassonne.

Farther removed from immediate peril, Foix alone stood firm guarding the redoubt of the Pyrenees.

It must be the noise of the portcullis rising.

Yolande de Montfort started up from the pillows, gazing at the arched oblong of gray twilight opposite her bed. Beyond, she could hear the shuffling stamp of horses treading the cobbles, a brief command and then the clatter of hoofs, sharp and urgent, then dulling as they faded into the distance. Still she listened, raised on her elbow, only half believing—but no, the voice had clearly spoken in French. She was in territory no longer held by Toulouse but by the victorious armies of Louis VIII, King of France, pitched outside Avignon and already masters of Beaucaire.

Not only that. She drew in her breath, struggling to gather in a flash the happenings of the last night and convince herself that it was really Thibaut, Count of Champagne, who had just ridden out of the gates.

When, a few days before, after the surrender of the district, she had sent him her invitation, she had scarcely dared to hope that, in spite of his reputed indifference to the present campaign and his rancor against King Louis, he would leave the field the moment he had served his quadraginta and forfeit the chance of spoil. Even if he did so, it was questionable whether he would deign to make a detour from the direct route on his return to his own lands. What, after all, should entice him to accept so mysterious or at least unexpected an invitation—respect for her father, a condescending acquaintanceship with her brother Amaury? What, he must have argued, could she possibly want with him? To plead perhaps—depending on his quarrel with Louis—for the wretched Count of Toulouse? Doubtless rumors had not failed to inform him she was Ramonet's strumpet. In the darkness her cheeks flushed with anger and shame. She threw herself on the pillows, but soon a wave of pride and assurance swept over her. With whatever thoughts Thibaut might have come, she was certain that he had departed with the knowledge that Simon of Montfort's daughter was as devoted to the cause of her native land as ever her father was, as devoted and as patient. Braced by the thought, she stretched her limbs and turned once more on her back. How long had she waited since first there had dawned on her the possibility of her action? She stared at the graying light of the window and in the cold, stealthy, yet ever expanding haze, the immensity of her project suddenly struck her with the appalling weight of its significance. Had she that night when, under the spell of incense and drugged wine, the idea had first awakened in her brain, imagined it might really materialize—that she, Yolande de Montfort, held in her hands not only the heart of a weak, heedless youth, but the fate of two nations?

As if the thought made idleness impossible, she rose from the bed and, throwing a wrap around her shoulders, moved to the window.

The courtyard was empty. The porter, having once more lowered the portcullis, had evidently retired again to his lodge. Had she been dreaming after all? There had been other dawns—more than she could ever count— when she had looked down from the window just as now. She leaned forward. From far below, as from the bottom of a well, the flagstones of the yard swam up to meet her, milk-white, blotched here and there with the black, humped heaps of recently dropped horse dung. The smell rose faint but pungent in her nostrils.

But no, the last time of Ramonet's parting—three weeks ago, even less—she had stood not here but out beyond the walls in the shadow of the orange grove, hemmed in by the iron lattice of the boughs. She could remember how the sharp glazed edge of the leaves had lashed her skin as the branch swung back against her when at last she freed herself from his embrace. Involuntarily, as though she felt them cutting her even now, she winced, shutting her eyes to ward off the memory. How every minute, every second had impressed itself on her consciousness, interminably, while with anguished hands and lips he struggled to hold her prisoner. Yet all the time her brain had been registering, as on another plane, the chances of the future, of this very day. Even so, had she ever dreamed while she murmured words of flattery and comfort in his ear that within a mere three weeks she would receive his enemy within these very gates, would invite him to a tryst that might have power to redeem her name from all the shame that Ramonet had brought, was even then bringing upon it, yes, cause it one day to be blazoned abroad as that of a savior of France? Savior—Toulouse's paramour. Could that stain ever be wiped out? Would even her father, who had sacrificed his every pleasure and his own life that victory might be achieved, have not counted *that* price too great? For the sake of France . . . how often during the last months and years she had taken refuge in the phrase, while in ever-growing ennui and sick revulsion at herself she had counted each caress an anguish, a thorn in the flesh to goad on her passion—not for Ramonet, but for the wish-fantasies she had spun round his lands.

Did she deserve a worse censure because at first the ultimate goal had seemed so phantasmagorical that she had scarcely troubled to think how the end was to be achieved? How, when it far transcended her father's notions of conquests, perhaps even the ambitions of Philippe Auguste himself? Languedoc, the whole South incorporated in the French realm, as it once had been, as it once again should be, but this time forever, an integral part of the Empire of Charlemagne. Incredulous, she tried to conjure up the vision—the fulfillment of the Capets' dream, of all her father had striven for in vain, to be achieved this time not by force of arms but through the machinations of the feminine mind. "Women's wiles," Simon would doubtless have mocked, even without knowing what the price itself might be. Yet, she thought with a sudden burst of pride, what if they had achieved more than bloodshed and massacre had ever done? If they could save from ultimate destruction the land she had loved with a passion greater than she had ever felt for her lover's flesh? She stretched her bare arms a little, letting them rest upon the window frame as if to receive the warm and breathless air's caress. If ever she had felt drawn to Ramonet, she impressed on herself once again, it could only have been for the sake of achieving that one end. Already at the banquet as a child, what but the burning potent symbol of the orange had linked her to that fragile, indecisive boy—until, through the long unending passage of the years, the fulfillment of her whims had grown to an utter necessity, not for herself (she was

137

sure of that now) but to achieve the secret purpose of destiny? How, otherwise, would she have been ready to risk all for the sake of a worthless estate, quasi castle, quasi hunting lodge, hidden among the orange groves of Provence that, thanks to Ramonet's jealousy, had already grown to be little more than a prison, scarce better than some eunuch-guarded harem of the East? How could she have borne it had the South not already come to mean as much as it did for Ramonet, as much as it meant for France? Her passion was theirs—the coveted price of two nations, hers to squander yet hers to save. In betraying Ramonet, was she not saving what was most his?

Ramonet . . . suddenly her own thoughts, the occurrences of the last days, seemed so fantastic that she grasped at his image as though it alone had reality.

She saw him again as he had come to her during the last months, tormented and bewildered, torn between his ambition to preserve his name as victor and liberator and his insuperable desire to remain popular in the eyes of all—a circumstance utilized to the utmost by the rival powers. She had despised him then till she had almost hated him in his weakness. Yet when at last things had come to a head, when Louis of France, set on restoring the triumphs of Philippe Auguste's reign, had marched on Beaucaire, when, stung to recapture the glory of his boyhood's fame, Ramonet, transfigured, had conjured in her ears almost an epic of heroic resistance, had she not warmed to him as never before, feeling perhaps well up within her the thought of all that might have been? If their betrothal had never been broken, if Ramonet and she had been man and wife, if, all those years ago, the unity of the realms had been consolidated, what need would there have been for a generation of wars, let alone this new onslaught that could end, this time, only in the ultimate ruin of the South?

No, after all, she comforted herself, she was not so utterly pitiless as she seemed. While he lay locked in her arms that for him had become the one security from perpetual uncertainty, from all the sham and subterfuge of his existence, had she not shuddered a little, thinking how

138

even then Louis was marching southward, marching on Avignon and Beaucaire, prompted perhaps by the information she had not failed to give in intermittent letters to her brother Amaury? Then, in a sudden transport of pitying tenderness, lauding his bravery, deriding his vassals' treachery, she had tightened her embrace.

A week, two weeks, a month . . . fief on fief had already seceded to the French. Louis' troops stood posted outside Avignon. The city's doom was sealed.

He had come to her for the last time. Cajoling, wrestling with his despair, she had urged him to surrender, at least to hold back from the fight himself, that in the end, she had argued, perfectly sincere, he might win a greater victory. Preservation, not destruction, was his goal.

Even as, half feverish in his zeal and anguish, he had refused to listen, a strange fierce love had for a moment sprung up within her and suddenly she had known she could not bear to surrender him to Louis' cold intransigence.

Union with France! Though she could not tell him, it was their goal, their destiny, the one objective that could redeem them both from falsehood and shame. And he should reach it through his own will, not through defeat of arms and political disgrace. Let him return to Foix, she argued; Louis had had enough triumphs for the present. He would not risk an immediate march upon the mountain fastnesses. In the meantime, in the meantime, what . . . ?

But almost immediately, as by a miracle, the answer had come. The answer was Thibaut IV of Champagne.

From all she knew of rumor concerning this most powerful, perhaps, of all counts of France, she well believed that the brilliant young nobleman, already famed as poet and lover of the arts, would set more store by a peaceful conquest of the remnants of southern civilization than by their inevitable destruction. Added to which, his pique at having recently been refused the commandership of the French troops had so incensed him against Louis that he was said to have joined with some of the most important peers of the realm in vetoing the supremacy of royal power. Whatever the case might be, Thibaut, it was said, having all but completed his forty days' service with the besieging armies outside Avignon, was threatening to strike camp and prepare to return to France.

She had summed up the situation with all the sharpness of feminine wit and instinct against which her father had so fondly railed. (Hadn't he known in his heart his daughter was worth ten of the sluggard Amaury?) For all his present success, Louis, she reflected, would soon find himself in such difficulties with his chief feudatories that, to re-establish his power in his own country, he would have to loosen his military hold on Languedoc. The Southerners, consequently, recovering from their present intimidation, would rebel and the long struggle begin again without hope of end, while French arms and valor were sacrificed and a civilization bled to death. Yet if one of the peers of France could be brought to see what Louis would never realize, if a man with vision and insight and finesse, a man bent on making an art of existence, applied his genius to fashioning peace even as he was said to fashion verses, if, in short, Thibaut of Champagne . . . ?

But how to get hold of him? Again fate seemed to play into her hands. During the next few days the little castle hidden in the depths of the fruit groves was taken by the French. The leader of the troops, an old friend of her father, treated her with courtesy and respect and even conceded to her request to have a letter carried to Count Thibaut of Champagne.

She had acted in a flash, out of pure instinct. If she had given herself time to think, let alone reflect, it would have been too late. As it was, her action seemed to her fantastic. Yet, in contempt of all rational likelihood, Thibaut had accepted her invitation and come. Coolly courteous and, far more than any other Northerner of her acquaintance, the polished, incalculable diplomat, he had listened to the prattle of an exiled daughter of fair France, so sweetly wistful to start with, so full of nostalgic reminiscences of a northern childhood, till gradually, almost imperceptibly, the innocent scene was punctured here and there to let in phantasmagorical flashes of strange undreamed-of possibilities. And still he had listened with gracious yet half-mocking seriousness, smiled, knit his brows, smiled again, and departed.

If the vista of stupendous horizons she had so subtly yet so incisively opened up before him had roused in him amazement, not to speak of curiosity, he had not shown it. Should he ever reach the goal she had tried to conjure up before him, he was never likely, she well knew, to own that the germ of his greatest triumph had been sown in a small, if exquisitely furnished, hunting lodge in the vanquished South, in a conversation with a woman of dubious repute, and lasting deep into the hours of an August night.

Now it was dawn. . . .

Yolande of Montfort stretched, drew herself to her full height. If she had dreamed, she had certainly now awakened. On the bench in the embrasure of the window lay a small volume bearing on the cover the arms of Champagne—a modest token of Count Thibaud's appreciation of a night's hospitality.

For he had really come, come and departed, paying her the homage that he would have tendered to any woman of rank—no more, and yet, if her unerring instinct, her knowledge of men did not deceive her, if ambition and destiny conspired, as she hoped, to set Thibaut of Champagne's foot on the ladder of glory. . . . Her heart throbbed with wild excitement and an almost visionary certainty of success, and then slowly relaxed its beat. For how long would she have to wait, how long? Yet had she not grown used to waiting, here, shut away in this castle of the sleeping beauty, waiting, week in, week out, for the lover whose consuming jealousy gave him alone the right to penetrate the labyrinthine thicket of thorns. Thorns . . . ? There were no thorns in orange groves. Roses . . . ? She took a deep breath, as if she divined their scent drifting up toward her from the depths, but she could catch only the aromatic smell of myrtle shrubs, of lavender rock-bound and desiccated by the blinding sun. Down by the wall a small brief wind stirred in the laurels. But behind the ramparts of Montfort l'Amaury, the poplars had kept up their perpetual quivering, showering down their rain of pale autumnal gold, or in summer, roses—she could smell their cool clear fragrance, cascades of shimmering petals blown on the crinkling ripples of the moat, pale-petaled boats of rose leaves, a fairy fleet launched by a small, fair pig-tailed child on the dank dark perilous waters by the mill. Roses . . . or had they only existed on the lips of that strange foppish sycophant of Ramonet's court, in those velvet somniferous accents perforating the mosaic-gilded, incense-laden atmosphere of the palace at Toulouse?

She struggled for breath, but even the air of dawn was lifeless with the heat of yesterday or with the latent fiercer heat of the day to come, and the puffs of wind that blew little eddying gusts across the laurels had the prickly hot aroma of African sands.

AND THEY SHALL BEAT
THEIR SWORDS INTO
PLOWSHARES

*What we call evil is the only and best shape, which, for the
person and his condition at the time, could be assumed
by the best good.*

WHETHER SET IN MOTION BY THE SCHEMES OF YOLANDE
de Montfort or not, the ball of fortune began to roll in a
curiously similar direction to that envisaged by her
erotic-political dreams, and within a shorter space of time
than she had ever imagined possible, Thibaut of
Champagne had climbed to heights that must not only
have satisfied his ambitious temperament but that actually
assigned him a chief role in shaping the destiny of Languedoc.

For Louis VIII's triumph proved more evanescent than
even his enemies would have dared hope. Enervated by
the southern summer, stricken with fever, he decided to
turn homeward, only to be overtaken by death before either Toulouse had fallen or Paris had been reached. And
yet, even this sudden chastening (as though by act of
Providence) of the conquering hand had little or no
power to rouse the spirit of the South. The almost undis-
puted advance of the king's army, the systematic soil-
scorching policy of the royal officers left in charge of the
conquered domains, had gripped the whole country in a
clutch that, if it lacked the fanatical religious zeal of Simon de Montfort, yet inevitably outrivaled it in lasting efficiency through the possession of unlimited resources and
the irrefutable authority of royal power. What difference
could the death of the reigning monarch make, since that
authority must needs pass on to the next of line, for what

Capet would ever relax the inherited craving to restore the disrupted Frankish realm?

True, the heir to the throne, young Louis IX, was a mere boy and already showed signs of uncommon piety, while his mother, Blanche of Castile, might scarcely hold her own against the league of rebellious feudatories who were not failing to grasp their chance. If, for a moment, hope made a halfhearted attempt to break through the general inertia of despair, it was short-lived. Whether by means of feminine guile on the part of Blanche or whether due to Thibaut's sheer capacity for calculating the issues, that chief recreant was by hook or by crook persuaded to become the adoring vassal of the widowed queen and faithful defender of the royal cause. However scandal might interpret the case, it certainly did nothing to lessen his power either in temporal or spiritual eyes, and the brilliant speculative brain that till lately had lent itself to such dangerous acts of subversion was already being deflected to a constructive enterprise of far more momentous significance. Before long, indeed, Thibaut, Count of Champagne, appeared in the role of chief mediator in the treaty by which that excommunicate and renegade prince, Ramonet of Toulouse, agreed to pledge himself subservient to France and to Holy Church.

The conference was held in Thibaut's own territories, at Meaux, in the midst of a bleak northern winter. By the time the catkins were drifting along the wind-rippled waters of the Seine, Raymond VII, Count of St. Gilles and Toulouse, Duke of Narbonne, was kneeling prostrate at the iron-barred door of Notre-Dame de Paris. The visionary perspicacity that had defied the feeble body of Philippe Auguste had achieved its goal at last. The fantasies that had risen years ago before that rheumy eye weakly blinking through the sharp spring sunlight from the palace window by the Seine had become flesh and blood: Toulouse, whose realm dared flaunt its accursed pride in the face of the rightful heir of Charlemagne; Toulouse, who had mocked the authority of Holy Church, lay humbled in the dust. Not as before, when Raymond

VI, his father, had managed with a flick of his flaccid hand to annul every treaty he had made.

Today the net had been drawn close. Ramonet, almost of his own accord, had walked into the trap and every loophole of escape was closed. Or not quite—the very brilliance of the strategy lay in the fact that, despite the general rigor of the terms, the treaty offered not only an immediate sop but gave the victim an illusory hope of ultimately throwing off the yoke.

True, Ramonet was to hand over a number of his castles, surrender the duchy of Narbonne, dismantle the walls of Toulouse, suffer the appointment of French seneschals at the key points of the whole realm; but for the span of his lifetime his lands were to remain his. Afterward they would pass to his only child, the little daughter whose formal marriage to the king's brother formed part and parcel of the treaty. Thus, through natural ties and the blessed bond of matrimony, Languedoc, so long the hapless cause of rivalry and bloodshed, would be at last incorporated in the realm of France.

At last—but what might not happen in the interim? Therein lay the subtle bait at which Ramonet was rightly expected to nibble. He was still young and death appeared a shadowy concept. Above all, since Sancie of Aragon, sickly as she was, would surely fail to bear him further issue, he harbored no doubts as to his right to divorce. A carefully chosen mate would more than likely provide him with male offspring who would annul his daughter's inheritance and thus make void the French claim. Involuntarily his thoughts flew to the hidden hunting lodge near Beaucaire. Even now his passion rose irrepressibly and flooded the anger and shame that told him repeatedly it was Yolande de Montfort, Yolande with her smooth cool limbs, her eyes of laughing azure mockery and wistful reproach, who had urged him more even than the hopeless inertia of his vassals to sign the treaty of Meaux. Christ, was not she the root and cause of his shame? Yet before a week had passed, while still virtually a prisoner behind the walls of the Louvre, he had sent her a messenger with a token from her native land. What, he asked himself, worn out with the farce of little Jeanne's marriage celebrations, while unconsciously his malleable ease-loving nature was already responding to the flattery of the French court, what has Yolande to gain from the Capets' triumph—or even their ultimate befooling? In neither case could she be his. The promise of consummation that love had once held out for them had been jettisoned on the diplomatic gaming tables long ago. What remained for them both was only to play in the brief space of snatched and secret moments a children's game of make-believe.

If Ramonet clung to a last illusion of cheating the Capet of his price, his vassals, with a few exceptions, were completely indifferent. All that Languedoc, worn out by years of war and intermittent truces, craved for was a lasting peace. Only a handful of Pyrenean barons, safely ensconced in the natural fortress of their mountain home, showed any inclination to resist. Roger of Foix, reared in the wilds of Andorra, was at their head. What should they, to whom the suzerainty of Toulouse had meant little more than a name, care for Ramonet's debacle? None but the fanatical Montfort had ever managed to penetrate the Olmes in one of his sporadic raids. Nevertheless Roger was well aware that the majority of his barons whose lands lay exposed toward the plain took a very different view. He had made it plain to Toulouse that whatever came of it, Foix would resist.

In vain Ramonet sent messengers from Paris threatening to enforce the law of the treaty by which the French commanded him to bring his recalcitrant vassals to heel. Roger, stubborn as a peasant, only ordered his feudatories to arm to the teeth. The Frenchies were indulging in mere bluff, he persisted. They'd be in no mood to send an army to smoke out the Ariège. At the worst there was plenty of time to prepare for a stiff resistance. The general attitude of dissension he met with roused him to such fury that it demanded the necessity of a whipping boy. He was found easily enough in the person of his illegitimate brother.

Summoned to Foix, Wolf guessed well enough that he

146

would be presented with an ultimatum—fortify Durban or hand over the estates. If Ramonet's troops advanced on the Ariège, they might well try attacking by way of the Mas d'Azil. The heights of Durban would in that case furnish a key point of resistance. To sacrifice the natural advantages of the old fort would be little short of a crime. From the military point of view Roger's attitude needed no excuse. Indeed, as Wolf rode toward Foix he could not help recalling the time when he himself had leveled almost identical arguments against Honoria. His fury at her refusal then had formed the prelude to the tragedy that caused him to stand where he stood today as the uncompromising upholder of nonviolence. All Roger's bullying would prove useless to move him, he reflected calmly. Even Honoria seemed convinced of that at last. Looking back and remembering her fears and distrust, it struck him almost with surprise how much in the course of the last years their relationship had changed. Somehow, though neither betrayed it in word or emotion, they had achieved a kind of passive understanding. No doubt the firm stand he had taken at the new outbreak of hostilities had convinced her at last of his conversion. Feeling a genuine urge to do all in his power to resist the encroaching tide of violence, he had worked the farm at double rate to provide food and clothing for the refugees who on the fall of Avignon flocked to the hostel on the Arise. The agricultural reforms that he had envisaged and that he had begun slowly to convert to reality were nipped in the bud. Honoria's house of mercy had grown to be a center of refuge in Languedoc. In any case, Ramonet, while still bent on resistance and excommunication, had shut an eye to a Cathar nucleus in the lands of his one remaining ally.

But today all that had changed. The field of battle threatened to shift to the domains of Foix, the bourn of peace and nonviolence to become a snare and pitfall to the belligerents. Durban must be rearmed, if not by the will of its owners, then by force. For Wolf and Honoria the situation was unequivocal. Passive resistance, they well knew, must needs prove useless in the face of the garrison Roger had sent over to man the castle on the

147

heights. If Wolf refused to take over the command, the captain of the troops had been authorized to do so himself. Already they were building the dismantled ramparts. Seemingly impassive, stony-faced, Honoria continued to nurse and succor her flock in the rooms not yet appropriated by the soldiers. She would continue, undeterred, unhesitating, until they turned her out. And that, as Wolf knew, might happen any moment. Had there not been a day on which he had flung in her face the fact that the unfortified building of the hostel would jeopardize the whole valley? The wheel had turned full circle on himself.

Arrived at Foix, he was conducted without ceremony to the audience chamber—the same room, for good or evil, it flashed through his mind, in which on the day of assembly he had been faced with that shattering choice. There could be no question today.

"So he's become the playboy of the prelates and that middle-aged bitch of Castile."

Bracing himself to present to Roger the calm intransigent front he intended, Wolf was scarcely aware for the minute that the words were not addressed to him.

"Your epithets," answered a voice from the embrasure of the window, "hardly become the brother of a budding saint—or possibly they do. Nature's readjustment."

No need to look at the speaker to identify him. That low ambiguous laugh, the very paradox of the words themselves, could only belong to Peire-Roger of Mirepoix. As if stung, Wolf started back as if to withdraw. "I didn't know," he addressed his brother, "your squire didn't tell me you were engaged."

But Roger had swung round toward him flourishing a scroll of parchment. "Stop. Since you're forever preaching holiness, maybe you're more fit than I to interpret the mission of a saint—especially when it's accompanied by an army of thirty thousand."

Baffled, Wolf unrolled the parchment Roger had thrust in his hands, swiftly scanning the lines.

It was an ultimatum signed by Ramonet but obviously dictated by the French crown, stating that if the terms of

148

the treaty herewith tendered for the third time were not immediately and fully concluded, the troops of Count Raymond of Toulouse, backed by a French army of thirty thousand to reinforce them, would advance on the Ariège without further delay.

"The vanguard already stands on the borders," Roger bawled, "as a symbol of Christian good will, led by the papal legate Piero de Collemezzo."

"Already—?" was all Wolf was capable of muttering.

"Already. Even Ramonet," Mirepoix interjected, "is forgetting his good manners at the Louvre. By tonight, if they don't receive your words of humble appreciation, they'll be sitting comfortably in Saverdun."

"Never. They won't advance a step. They'll meet with resistance at every turn." The very fact that in his heart Roger was more than uncertain made his boast more arrogant while he vented his hidden doubts on his half brother. "Have you rebuilt the walls?" he shouted. "The arquebuses should be posted to the northeast—the long bows on the upper bridge."

"Your soldiers," Wolf drew a deep breath, "are doubtless carrying out your orders to the letter."

"Mine? Do you mean you're really sitting back and leaving them the run of the place?"

"There was hardly an alternative."

"Christ, so you don't mind them mocking the hero of the Mas d'Azil turned swineherd to supply the troops of Foix with backside and gammon?"

"I have no intention to supply provender for any troops," Wolf replied quietly.

"But naturally," Mirepoix threw in lightly, "they don't go in for pigsticking at Durban." Rising with an air of easy nonchalance, almost of friendliness, he approached Wolf, who visibly stiffened. Peire-Roger only smiled. "You'd best impress on your belligerent brother that, except for the possibility of a last redoubt in the Sabarthez, resistance is hopeless. And even that would mean sheer waste—at least for the present. After all, the offer is not so intransigent, even if we've to sacrifice a few estates— Mirepoix, for instance—" He gave a little sigh. "A pity,

149

especially after all the work I've put into it. I only hope Lévis will appreciate the fact that they'll get one of the finest gems in Languedoc."

"The Lévis," Roger swung round. "Do you mean you sat there in the Louvre listening calmly to how they intend parceling out your estates?"

Mirepoix shrugged. "Swordplay would hardly have bettered matters. As it is, I haven't come off too badly. They might have suggested handing the place over to some Vandal."

"They haven't got it yet," Roger shouted. "If you let them—"

"There may be no other way. We'll see. If it comes to the worst, even Mirepoix isn't the last resort. One might climb even higher—" he smiled enigmatically, raising his eyebrows as if amused by a question self-imposed.

Exasperated by his insouciant gabble, Wolf had turned aside and picked up a second scroll that lay on the table. It was the treaty itself. Swiftly his eyes ran down the page gauging the main issues:

"Direct dependence of the lands of Foix on the French crown. Partial recompense for estates commandeered by the royal seneschals posted at given points throughout the land, in so far as the disappropriated owners swore allegiance to the King and were neither proven heretics or harborers of the same. Systematic extermination of all heretics and those who failed to conform with the teaching of Holy Church. . . . That the sword of dissension be buried, brother cease to spill the blood of brother and Christ's reign extend unviolated throughout the realm of France—"

Almost unconsciously Wolf had read the last words aloud.

"France—" Roger, head thrust forward, hands clasped behind his back, had begun to pace up and down the room. "France—since when did the Ariège owe allegiance to a Capet?"

"Possibly never—except to Charlemagne—" Mirepoix suggested. "And he, after all, was scarcely a barbarian."

150

"And now? Do you mean you're going to kowtow to those marauding ruffians—those—"

Peire-Roger interrupted the inevitable string of clichés. "You'd probably find some of them too civilized for your taste, Roger. Thibaut de Champagne, for instance. . . ." Sinking into a chair, he attempted to brush a patch of dust from his cloak.

"Thibaut—that cunning fox," Roger retorted, "so it's he who wound you all round his little finger—gulled you as he gulled the Capet. They say he cuckolded the ghost of Louis so he could govern the realm himself."

"You're generous to call it only the ghost," Mirepoix laughed. "They're already making rhymes:

> *'Maintes paroles en dit en*
> *Comme d'Iseult et de Tristan.'*

Only that Tristan and Iseult weren't so fortunate, or so accomplished in the gentle art of poisoning, as to manage to dispose of King Marc. Still, I'd rather have Tristan's share of the bargain than Thibaut's—at least in bed."

"Do you mean there's really something in the poisoning business?" Roger muttered.

"Unlikely—but since he's won renown for mixing paints, it's not such a far call to poison-mixing—at any rate in the eyes of the uninitiated."

"Paints—what the hell are you talking of?"

"He paints the walls of his chateaux—with his own verses—they're quite accomplished—" Peire-Roger smiled condescendingly.

"So that's how he inveigled you. Christ! If Rabat or Verdun had done the talking—"

"They wouldn't have," Mirepoix replied amiably, "and the terms would have been the worse."

"You mean you discussed those conditions with Thibaut yourself?"

"Not at all. If you want to know—we discussed roses."

"Roses?"

"Exactly. It seems he collects them."

"God—is that all you came for?" Roger turned his

151

back on him furiously and for once Wolf felt a solidarity with his brother. He was still standing by the table, the treaty in his hand.

"That the sword of dissension be buried—brother cease to spill the blood of brother—" All he had struggled and prayed for. . . .

He looked up. Roger was staring out of the window. With a sudden resolution, Wolf crossed over to his side. "Couldn't you," he attempted, "at least meet them as they suggest?" He glanced once more at the parchment. "At the Church of St. John by the Pas de la Barre—you might be able to offer—"

"Offer?" Roger lifted his head. The flush mounted from his thick neck over cheek and temple. "If I offer anything it will be the edge of my sword." But the boast sounded strangely hollow for his usually resonant bass.

Mirepoix had risen to his feet. The flippancy seemed somehow suddenly to have vanished from his features, leaving them unfamiliar and strange. "You're a madman if you don't accept. Are we to lose everything? By signing we might at least gain—"

"What?"

"—what we have never possessed before," Wolf completed, and wondered at his own eloquence. "The chance of building a real peace—an understanding between the nations."

"Peace—" Roger blurted. "Peace—haven't we had it often enough before? And what came of it?"

"It was only marking time—waiting for retribution—for vengeance—"

"Do you think," Roger cried, "if I ever have to buckle under to them, every second of my life won't be spent waiting for vengeance?"

"That is—" Mirepoix, toying with his sword, drew the blade a few inches from its scabbard—"until His Holiness the Pope deigns to grant Ramonet a divorce and provide the possibility of male progeny."

"Little likelihood." Roger laughed. "The papal weathercock veers with every fresh wind. But not the

152

French. Once the Capet plants himself in our strongholds—"

Mirepoix answered with a shrug. "We got rid of them before. In any case, 'sufficient unto the day is the evil thereof.' "

"It's more than sufficient."

"Exactly," Mirepoix replied. "For the sake of which, see reason and sign the treaty. After all, it's only a conciliatory measure—temporary as everything in this world."

"Temporary—" It was Wolf who broke in. "Is it to be the same all over again? Are you going to undermine the peace even before it's built?"

But his impassioned earnestness only caused Roger's anger to flare up doubly.

"Undermining—Christ, do you imagine that your blessed kingdom of saints won't be the first to be undermined and blasted to the ground once the Frenchies or Ramonet's heretic-hunters cross the border? And you twaddle about peace—you, who will lose everything—"

"I was aware that I would lose it anyway," Wolf retorted.

"And so it doesn't matter. But to us—to Foix—to your country—"

"If it means lasting peace . . ." The thought of the cause Wolf was defending had already possessed him so completely that Durban had almost lost its reality.

Roger had turned his back on him in disgust. "Christ! I rejoice to say the rest of my vassals don't possess your sluggishness."

"I am inclined to think they do," Mirepoix interjected, "only more completely, since they lack even the backbone of conviction. And you know it."

Roger knew it only too well. But it needed another half hour's persuasion before he conceded. There was no time even to consult his vassals, but he knew that when it came to it, even the most truculent would have taken Mirepoix's advice. What, after all, had they to lose? Even the French seneschals had no wish, as Peire-Roger assured him, to penetrate to the heart of the Sabarthez. Yet

153

his pride would have suffered less if the avowal could have come from them.

"You expect *me* to command them to—surrender?" His voice under the stress of combined emotion and strain broke suddenly on a strangely raucous note. Wolf was reminded of a bull in the arena, a bull who had received the death blow.

"If you like," he began tentatively, "I could take a message—"

"And make them think I've let myself be cajoled by a shirking bastard?"

"For God's sake," Mirepoix broke in, "come to your senses. It's the best possible solution. Send him along to Pérelha. I'd go myself, but I've got to get back. And anyhow, I always manage to set the old man on edge. He may not like the news, but he's got a hard enough head to realize you can't evade facts."

"But Lordat, Verdun, the Rabats," Roger persisted, "they'll never—"

"They're not likely to start a rebellion for your sake, Roger, and you know it. Even your mountain stalwarts prefer to sit tight and cozy in their eyries if they can. They know if they keep quiet the Frenchies aren't likely to show much eagerness to scale their slippery crags! You'd better ride off to Lavelanet at once," he added, turning to Wolf.

"He'll not find him there—" growled Roger. "Some of my vassals still think it worth their while to strengthen their forts. They're not all—" He took a step forward, his right hand clenched, and for a moment Wolf thought he was going to strike out at him, but Mirepoix stepped between.

"He'd best make straight for Roccafissada—"

But Roger had let his huge bulk drop into a chair. The crimson flush was fading from his cheeks, leaving them mottled and patched, but on the walls of his temples the purple veins stood out against his skin like the knotted creeping tendrils of some mural.

"Yes or no?" Mirepoix touched him on the arm, impatient. "I've got to be going. Every hour of delay will make things more difficult."

Roger lay half sprawled across the table. Impotently his clenched fists beat on the board. When at last he spoke, his voice had lost all its natural volume. "Let him ride, let him ride to hell . . ." He paused as though struggling to draw breath, but the sound that came from his throat was a harsh unnatural laugh. "The peacemaker—since—even our father—prophesied—" His voice trailed away unintelligibly. Then his head fell forward over his arms.

In sudden fear Wolf took a swift step forward, but the great heavy shoulders were heaving like those of a weeping child. Relieved, he followed Mirepoix's gesture to be gone. The sight of his bullying braggadocio brother, so changed and broken, filled him with a strange unbearable sense of shame.

SPECULATIONS

Possunt quia posse videntur.

      (VERGIL: *Aeneid*)

Ideas, however correct, will never prevail by themselves. There must be people who are prepared to stand or fall with them.

      (E. WILSON)

THE ROAD LAY UPSTREAM AT FIRST, SKIRTING THE RIVER until, at Montgaillard, a narrower track turned in among the hills. Beyond, the highroad continued a little, then it forked eastward toward the Sabarthez. It was a region that for the last years Wolf had avoided, too full as it was of memories. But today those dreaded images had little power to rise. Bewildered by the events of the past hour, he rode quickly, as though mechanically impelled by the mission the full significance of which he had as yet not even made clear to himself. This morning, starting from Durban, he had never thought it possible that he would become the emissary of peace. Till now he had given himself no time to think how Pérelha might accept the news, but rode as fast as he could, his mind fixed on the goal. In spite of the sympathy that had awakened between the two of them at the time of Ramon's visit, he had not seen him since. The shyness that since the tragedy in the Sabarthez had withheld him from contact with others, added to his doubts as to what might be Ramon's reaction to his attitude toward the renewal of the war, had kept him from following up the other's invitation to Lavelanet.

How then would he receive him today? Somehow all that seemed to matter were the tidings themselves—that Ramon, if anyone, should be made to understand their necessity. But though Mirepoix might testify to his father-in-law's common sense, Pérelha, in his quiet stern way, might prove as truculent as Roger himself. The man

156

was attached to his estates as the lichen to the rock. He would never brook interference from the French. Involuntarily Wolf raised his head and saw with surprise and relief that he had already ridden far along the track that branched off from the road leading toward the Sabarthez. He might already be in Pérelha's lands.

On either side, the valley slopes were clothed in the pale green of the young corn (Ramon obviously, he noted with an experienced eye, lived up to his reputation as a farmer), but far away above a dark belt of virgin forest, a turreted mass of rock rose so sharply fretted against the sky that it was difficult to conceive it was built by human hand. Yet it must be the fort. He recalled how once on the hunt, his father, hawk on hand, had pointed to what he called Pérelha's eagle's eyrie.

Suddenly the image of Ramon-Roger of Foix rose before him with overwhelming clarity—that gloriously self-confident figure, gazing scornfully from its imperious height upon the tongue-tied boy whose dreams and foibles he would wither in one single phrase of his eloquence. From the first they had been at logger-heads. The Sabarthez affair had only been, Wolf knew, the final blow he had dealt his father in a lifetime of disappointments. They had never met again until he had been called to the deathbed at Foix.

It was a mercy, Wolf reflected, he could not see him on his embassy today. And yet there was a time, it flashed on him ironically, when he himself had played Roger's part, inveighing furiously against his father's pusillanimity in making a treaty with Montfort and the Pope. Was he now to learn something of his suffering, to understand too late the man he had always fled? But their concept of peace, he thought bitterly, had nothing in common. What, by the way, could Roger have muttered about his father and peace? He remembered the day he had been called to his deathbed, so late that he had arrived only just in time to witness his parting breath. For a moment as he had stood, awkward and useless, beside his legitimate brother, it had seemed that his father's eyes had opened and been directed toward him, that his lips had even struggled to speak.

But Roger had bent between them. If words had really fallen from the dying lips, only his brother had heard them and for whom else could they have been meant? All his life there had been no understanding between them. Why should it be different in the end? The proud and silent countenance lying motionless upon the pillows had betrayed no sign that its last utterance had not been understood. When, tentatively, he had asked Roger what his words had been, his half brother had muttered, shrugging, "Delirium—he was worrying maybe about the peace. Afraid, no doubt, we'd give in before the Frenchies were really done for. Never got it off his liver he'd once been cheated by the devils, for all the vengeance he got."

Vengeance—no, of course, Wolf dispelled his momentary uncertainty—it was surely with that thought his father had breathed his last breath. Futile, he told himself, to imagine there could ever have been understanding between them. The consciousness that he himself had once been guilty of the same attitude only stiffened his intransigence. But today—the thought whipped him with a strange sort of exhilaration—it seemed to him almost that by this mission of peace on which he had been sent forth, he might redeem something in himself.

The last lap of the serpentine path was steep, so steep that even on that spring day his horse was drenched in sweat. And when at last he arrived at the summit, it was only to hear that Ramon Pérelha had ridden over to the other fort to see about some reinforcements. Little use to ride after him, one of the guards insisted, he might very likely return by the other road. Probably he'd be back within the hour, certainly before sunset.

Wolf hesitated. If he set out to meet him, he might well miss him. His horse was tired. Probably he could borrow another beast, but still the chances of meeting Pérelha were small. After some consideration he decided to wait and, handing his horse to the man, climbed the steps to the keep.

Inside, the place was cold and silent. All life was gathered on the towers, on the ramparts. He could hear them on all sides, hammering, chiseling, fixing the mortars and catapults in the slits. The noise fretted him like the incessant hum of some futile activity. Thinking, with relief, that it would soon be proved vain and useless, and anxious to collect and prepare himself for delivering his message, he decided to wait in the hall.

It appeared to be empty, except for some young squire or page sitting, his back toward him, in the embrasure of the window, cleaning a bit of armor and evidently so engrossed in his work that he did not even glance up. He had advanced desultorily some way across the floor before the figure turned, stared a moment, and then sprang so suddenly to its feet that the half-polished helmet fell clattering to the ground.

"Wolf—"

He had stopped short, smitten with confusion. The gleaming coppery hair was after all only looped into the collar of the hauberk.

"I thought," he stammered, "you were a boy—your brother perhaps—your hair—"

"But he's dark. Besides," she added with an air of self-importance, "he's only a child."

"And you?" he laughed, but, regarding the slim young figure before him, stopped short. The hauberk was two sizes too large, but from beneath it the small taut breasts molded the pliant mesh of steel. "You've grown a lot," he admitted.

"Luckily." She pulled herself to her full height. "Or I'd have found nothing to fit. Look," she cried, and lifting a sword that was lying on the window seat, swung it in both hands. "I've learned that too. You see," she ran on with confident frankness as though they were friends whose life-long companionship had only been interrupted for a time, "they sent me for a year to my aunt's on the Aude—to see whether she couldn't tame me and teach me manners, but it wasn't much use. I was fearfully bored till I made friends with an old armorer. He taught me all about swords and spears and arquebuses and even preparing the molten lead. I help them out there," she nodded toward the ramparts, "but then I thought I must get my own armor ready. He taught me to clean that too. By the way, he seemed to know you. He'd been Trencavel's armorer at Carcassonne. His name is Pons."

"Pons—" Wolf echoed, bewildered. "But of course—is he still alive?"

"Yes, only he's frightfully old—he wanted to go back to Carcassonne when the French cleared out, but the young viscount wouldn't even look at him. Just offered him a ducat through one of his courtiers. I believe it hurt him more than if he'd been hit in the face."

"He was proud, old Pons, even then," Wolf murmured, moved by a sharp fierce sympathy that he had not felt in the days when the armorer had scarcely managed to disguise his jealousy of Trencavel's young favorite. "I'm afraid he didn't care for me very much," he added regretfully.

She shrugged. "Oh, he just didn't like your games. All those new-fangled sports, he called them, you tried with Trencavel—throwing light javelins and wrestling—unarmed and the rest. But I think it must have been rather fun. Still, it's no use in war. And now they're going to attack us."

"I don't think they will," Wolf answered.

"You mean they won't get so far. But you can't be sure. They did before, you know. But we're all prepared. The ramparts are just bristling," she cried eagerly. "Count Roger asked us to see everything's in order. Is that what you came about?" she continued in one and the same breath. "If so, you can tell him. I'm in charge here till Father comes back," she explained. "He's ridden over to our other fort to see everything's being prepared all right there too."

"I don't think it'll be necessary," he repeated.

"Oh, the place is very strong," she explained, misunderstanding his meaning, "but Father wants to make sure. All of us are doing the same roundabout. From Lavelanet to Belcaire, and Montajon to the Sabarthez. We're not like those sluggards down in the valleys," she added proudly. "We'll make Toulouse sit up and even the French, if they venture. They never thought we'd resist since all the others deserted. It's rather grand being the only ones, isn't it?" There was such a light in her face that he waited before he spoke.

"He're not resisting," he said at last.

She gazed at him blankly. "You mean Count Ramonet's won over King Louis? They say he's generous. They're letting us keep our independence?" But there was almost a note of disappointment in her voice.

He shook his head. "We're making peace."

"Peace?" She stared at him, uncomprehending.

"Yes. We're meeting the French embassy at the Pas de la Barre—to sign the treaty." But the very quietness of his voice made it sound all the more unreal.

She took a step forward and halted. Standing there motionless, the sword planted before her, gripping the hilt in both hands, she fixed her eyes upon him, like a living indictment. "But it's impossible. Count Roger promised. He'd never give in."

"He saw in the end it was the only way."

"But why? Father said we could hold out for months . . ."

"Perhaps—right in here—in the mountains. But it would be useless in the end and only make things much worse for the rest. The more we resist, the worse the reprisals—Ramonet threatened—"

But her face lit up with renewed hope and scorn. "Count Ramonet—do you think we're afraid of him? Do you know what they call him?" she laughed aloud. "Do you think we'd listen a minute—you can ask Father . . ."

"Ask what?" A voice sounded from behind them. Ramon Pérelha stood framed in the doorway. The next second she was dashing and flinging herself upon her father's breast.

"He says—he came to tell you—but it's impossible—" Her voice was lost in angry sobbing.

Freeing himself gently from her clasp, Ramon of Pérelha stepped forward into the room.

"What's wrong? Has anything happened to Count Roger?" he began anxiously.

Wolf had stooped down, mechanically picking up the

sword that Esclarmonde had dropped unheeding in her despair. He shook his head. "I come from Foix—I was to tell you that there will be no resistance. We are signing the peace."

Ramon of Pérelha's expression hardly changed. Only his straight square figure grew perhaps still more upright. "You mean—it is Count Roger's wish?"

Wolf nodded.

"But it *can't* be." Esclarmonde turned to her father imploringly. "Count Roger promised." Suddenly her face contorted. "It's he," she cried wildly, gazing at Wolf in anguished hate, "he's talked him over—he doesn't believe in fighting and so he thinks that everyone else is a coward—"

"Be quiet," her father muttered. "You'd best go out on the ramparts while we talk it over," he commanded more sharply, as his daughter still stood staring before her, her hands and body quivering with misery and rage. "But say nothing as yet to the men." She seemed scarcely to hear. As if bracing herself to a great effort, she made suddenly for the door.

Mirepoix's prognostications as to his father-in-law's reactions proved, as Wolf discovered, not very far wrong. Indeed, he almost gained the impression that, so long as Peire-Roger himself was not acting as courier and emissary, Ramon of Pérelha needed few arguments to convince him of the hopelessness of the situation. Loyalty to Roger had been, after all, Pérelha's main incentive to resistance. True, his attitude toward Ramonet was one of impatience and scorn, and the thought of possible French vigilance being imposed in the district caused him for a moment to hesitate. Nonetheless he had spent too much time in restoring his estates during the last years not to feel thankful that they would be spared further ravages. His was, indeed, the slow, quiet philosophy that comes of age-long contact with the soil and recognizes the futility of useless resistance. All things, he had often enough forced himself to admit, have their appointed seasons, and temporary darkness did not exclude a new awakening.

That that awakening might necessarily herald in a better age he did not delude himself. Each time it might be for the better or for the worse—the cycle of life continued in repeated spirals. Wolf, confronted with his sober realism, found the fervent arguments with which he had been kindled by Roger's hotheaded pugilism and Mirepoix's flippancy gradually sounding somehow almost rhetorical.

It was dusk before he left, but he refused Pérelha's invitation to stay. He could count he had won a victory. Not only had Pérelha, though grudgingly, shown himself in favor of concluding the peace, but he was ready to wager that his opinion would be shared by nearly all his neighbors. He could promise that Roger's decision was unlikely to meet with real dissent. And yet Wolf, riding back the way he had come, was aware of a sense of failure. It was to the child that he should have presented those arguments, the meaning of peace, the foundation of a unity on which true peace could at last be built—something far beyond Roger's waiting for vengeance or Mirepoix's speculations on the subtle relationships of papal diplomacy and lust, beyond even Ramon's fatalistic acceptance of fact. But she had fled. He saw her again, standing before him in her boy's hauberk—the sharp small breasts quivering under the clear shining mail, her leaf-green eyes darkening with tears and scorn.

But at Durban, Honoria, when she heard the news, would turn to him with a look he had always hoped to see. He tried to figure it and couldn't. . . .

It was already dark. He had to ride warily through the woods. Beyond there was a house—the manor, he remembered vaguely. He had passed it as he rode up. Lights glowed under the eaves—a smell of dung and fodder and then, from the darker blur of the hedge, a fragrance. Roses . . . ?

A laugh like tinkling glass—behind the trellis of the pleasance in Carcassonne—and he had stood powerless to move, petrified as the hexagonal fount, the clipped symmetric beds of flowers, while Mirepoix's white fingers groped in the trailing folds of Agnes of Mont-

pellier's dress, unhooking the clinging brier. Roses—
Rosa mundi—was it the voice of Father Gregorius or
himself intoning the Marianic hymn among the choir-
boys of Bolbona? But if a rose is more than a rose? He
had posed the question himself, lying there with his
sprained ankle, listening to Sicard's minstrel friends. . . .

With a sudden effort he spurred on his horse. It was
still a fair way even to Foix. Roger, he trusted, would be
feeling too bitter to detain him long and then he would
ride straight on through the night to Durban.

Once more he tried to think with what a sense of triumph he would be able to confront Honoria. It was only
when he saw the crenelated ramparts of Foix towering
darkly above the river and thought of the violated hostel
on the Arise that he remembered once more that the
treaty would fail to spare Durban any more than had
Roger's soldiers, and that from the peace he had been
preaching with such fervor, Honoria and he would be
shut out.

RETRIBUTION

He thinks too much; such men are dangerous.

(SHAKESPEARE: Julius Caesar)

PEACE HAD COME TO LANGUEDOC AT LAST—A PEACE that promised not a mere cessation of hostilities, a temporary truce, but an enduring mercy through whose grace the truant and recreant vassal was at long last firmly clasped within the embrace of "douce France." If those maternal arms were of necessity encased in steel, they nevertheless gave to a country enervated by ceaseless strife what seemed a primal blessing—security. Security for the feudal vassal ready to swear allegiance to the crown instead of finding himself the playball of the shifting rivalries of Toulouse and Aragon; security for the peasant who, as long as he was not the serf of an overweening master, might at last feel freed from the incessant fear of seeing his hamlet ravaged by fire, his crops laid waste; security for the errant soul delivered through the certainties of infallible and orthodox dogma from the dark aberrations of metaphysical speculation and the terrible responsibility of choice.

Certainty—ultimate and absolute certainty. During the forty tormented years of his sojourn on earth, it had been the goal that Jordan of the Isle had craved in vain, the goal that even the tenets of his unshatterable faith had failed to give. Heaven or Hell—*they* were certain enough, inevitable as the threat of excommunication, the inevitable withholding of grace. Yet, even if his unerring loyalty to Holy Church found its ultimate reward, yes, even if salvation were extended to him, would grace itself have a power to redeem him from the all-obsessing horror?

Would not the question always remain, unanswerable beyond the redemptive power of chalice and Eucharist, beyond the grave and death itself, inscribed on the vast dome of the empyrean, making of Heaven a worse than Hell, the question so seemingly transparent and yet insoluble—the question of his mother's guilt?

For there was no reprieve from the doubt that had risen out of his earliest childhood, dogging his every step, inseparable as his own shadow, forcing him against the precipiced edge of that abyss of the spirit where he was condemned to walk sleeping or waking through and beyond what men called life.

Materially life had not treated him too badly. Such torment of the spirit as he had suffered did not leave much room (apart from somewhat indifferent health) for the lusts of the flesh, or the harrowing anxieties accompanying an ambition for power and wealth. Secure at any rate in the heritage of his father's patrimony, he had been content to uphold the undebatable tradition of a name that traced its genealogy to St. Bertrand of Comminges, the legendary tamer of dragons and the terror of heresy. His own unremitting orthodoxy having compelled him to espouse the cause of the Crusade, his estates had been mercifully preserved from the successive usurpations of the French, while, in those intermittent moments when Toulouse was gathered to the forgiving bosom of Holy Church, he was able with a clear conscience to return his allegiance to his terrestrial lord. If so apparently ambivalent an attitude had won him the scorn of many of his countrymen, they did him, perhaps, something of an injustice. For even if they were ready to admit that religious fanaticism rather than personal ambition incited him to play his double-faced game, who realized the ceaseless conflict waged behind the strange impassive mask of cold cynicism and haughtiness, between inherent racial pride and the craving to witness man's spirit subjected to a tyranny that should balance the dark bondages of his own soul?

Even now, as he rode along the highway from Pamiers to Mirepoix through the lands annexed by Guy de Lévis, self-styled Maréchal des Terres—in short, royal commander over all the lands between the Sabarthez and the Olmes—he felt an overpowering resentment. But, glancing back, he saw the towers of Pamiers looming behind him, the towers from which his mother, purging her guilt in asceticism and good works, had gazed toward the line of mountains and cloud-covered peaks, refiguring the visions that had sprung from the lips of a Eurasian bastard of a troubadour, the towers in which she had exhorted a runaway boy, another bastard, to materialize her frustrated dreams, nurturing in his eager, vulnerable spirit the flame of human compassion, the all-consuming fire of love—love that should speed, all-embracing, all-encompassing through the whole universe, from which he alone, the son of her own flesh, should be wiped out. After all, it surged over him in a wave of agony, if Languedoc were lost forever to the northern savages, if he had to forfeit even his inherited rights, there would be sufficient compensation if that dream could be wiped out forever.

It would never be wiped out, he knew darkly. Yet if he could poison it at the roots, in the heart that bore its legacy within it, poison it in each of those ever-changing forms in which it sprang up, despoilable yet irradicable in the heart of Wolf of Foix (even though the Bastard himself was too disillusioned to recognize it), the recompense would be enough.

There was no doubt, he reflected as, a little later, he came in sight of the castle of Mirepoix, that Peire-Roger had supplied the Maréchal with one of the choicest sites in Languedoc. Strange that Peire-Roger had not made a greater effort to keep it. Since he must have much in common with one of the most influential instigators of the treaty, Thibaut de Champagne, it was the more surprising. Another example of the man's waywardness. The moment he had attained his goal, it lost all interest for him. For Peire-Roger all lay in the desire, the achieving. The achievement was like a fruit that has lost its bloom—even if the prize were the Grail. If Peire-Roger, it entered his mind, were to reach that enchanted citadel, insatiable curiosity coupled with sheer grace of manners would ensure that he posed the fateful question. But the soldering of the sword, the responsibility, the work of consolidation and endurance he would leave to another, rejecting the kingship with a flick of his hand.

To another . . . it echoed through Jordan's mind . . . but to whom? The errant fool who, through his gaucherie, his single-minded blindness had forfeited the prize? Forfeited it surely—but forever? His thoughts, drawn once more into the fatal circle, caused the radiance of the summer day suddenly to darken as though it had been enveloped in a network of black gauze. Slowly the mesh widened, drawn out to a pattern of gray transparent veins along whose translucent channels black smudges swam, increased, diminished—circling particles, like the ever-moving particles in the stream of his blood.

For always the doubt would circle. Certainty lay only in fixation—the unequivocally envisaged vengeance for a hypothetical guilt that could never be proved, so that release could be found only in protracting that vengeance through the minutes, months—the years. Even if at moments he released his hold it would only be to tighten his grip more firmly. Then, if the interval was long, the fulfillment would be redoubled, trebled by the waiting. To wait with an infinity of patience, to preserve, in the seeming moment of consummation, one last dreg to be distilled, decanted, preserved for the hour that would once more come. *Must* come. For were not the life of his victim and his own bound as by invisible chains? In death alone Wolf of Foix might escape him; alive, he held him fast, to drag him with him even into the eternity of Hell.

Obsessed in his thoughts, Jordan became suddenly aware that he had reached the barbican. Without knowing it he must have answered to the guard's challenge, for the portcullis was being lifted and, a moment later, he was riding into the castle yard.

Specimens of the exotic embellishments with which Peire-Roger had transformed the old fort were evident even here. Sculptured slabs had been let into the masonry of the curtain walls, and a stone trough providing water for the horses was carved with figures and vine leaves like some ancient sarcophagus in the Roman cemetery of

Toulouse. As he dismounted, he caught sight through a small arched doorway of what might be a garden hidden by the perforated screens filling the interstices of a horseshoe arcade. Had Peire-Roger's plain-faced spouse, it flashed through his mind ironically, held court amid that Mauresque setting, or had it screened more devastating charms from eyes uninitiated to the subtleties of courtly love? Incidentally, had Mirepoix's choice in matrimony (he had asked himself the question somewhat incuriously before) been dictated by material reasons that were scarcely apparent or by the perversity of desire that, having tasted every possible nuance of the harmonious, sought to whet its spoiled appetite by the creation of the incongruous? Everything was possible to Peire-Roger's restless, mercurial brain as long as it moved forward carried on the flux of the evanescent moment. Only to be borne, Jordan reflected, on the stream of phenomena, instead of being bound inescapably on the dark inevitable circling of the blood. Once more he felt himself caught up in its remorseless gyration. If he could fix it, hold once and for all that ever-fleeing center. . . .

His speculations were cut short by the appearance of a squire who had come to conduct him into the presence of the Maréchal.

With whatever mixed feelings Jordan had recently contemplated the thought of the usurper, the appearance of Guy de Lévis reassured him that the report he had gathered at the See of Toulouse had not been too unreliable and that, whatever excellent qualities the marshal possessed, they were certainly not those of a religious zealot. To the bishop the fact was evidently a matter of regret, to himself it might in this instance prove only too advantageous.

Tall and erect of carriage, Guy de Lévis met him with an air of easy command that, if it betrayed unmistakable marks of ambition, was not lacking in a certain bonhomie and love of the good things of existence. The luxurious appointments of Mirepoix, Jordan reflected, were likely to find genuine, if somewhat crude appreciation, and Peire-Roger could comfort himself that the refinements he had spent so much trouble in producing would at any rate not be subject to the iconoclastic fury of a Simon de Montfort.

"Pretty little place," the marshal remarked with a condescension that, if it was intended to impress his visitor with the fact that the Lévis were used to the most massive and grandiose of the castles of Normandy and Northern France, did not fail to hide a sense of gratification.

Having received and cursorily investigated the ecclesiastical bulletins that ostensibly had provided the reason for Jordan's visit, he then invited him to a goblet of wine, it having already become his established policy to treat the conquered, where their rank permitted, as guests rather than victims—a measure by which he hoped and was indeed already beginning to achieve some success in winning favor among the more tractable landowners of the district, the more so as he showed an obvious unwillingness to copy the ruthlessness of the seneschal appointed to Carcassonne, or to tolerate the meddling intervention of the Church. His attitude toward his present guest might indeed have possessed an even greater cordiality if Jordan of the Isle had not been the emissary of the Bishop of Toulouse, and the letters he had brought had not contained an exhortation to yet more stringent persecution of the heretics, a procedure best designed to spoil Lévis' chances of establishing the position of benevolent tyranny he was bent on achieving.

"Pretty, though a bit finicky," he repeated, filling, for the sixth time, the thin-stemmed cup of aquamarine glass that shimmered palely in Jordan's bloodless hand, and feeling as he did so a compelling urge to shatter the man's strange impassive reserve that he ascribed to either religious bigotry or (with more sympathy) to racial pride. But even the heavy gold wine failed to bring color to the opaque ivory mask of the face; only the dropping lips pursed themselves slightly as, sipping from the cup, he ruminated cynically on the fact that the marshal's lavish hospitality was still conveniently dispensed at the cost of Peire-Roger's cellar.

"I'm afraid," Lévis placated as though reading the other's thoughts, "that the loss of so exquisite a little property must have been a great blow to the Sire de Luna." (For Peire-Roger the dispossession of his ancestral seat had entailed also the forfeiting of his name.) "He may rest assured that it has fallen into the hands of those who know how to appreciate it. My wife—I'm expecting her next month—will doubtless find it ravishing, particularly the pleasance. I'm keeping it as a surprise. Almost a bit of Spain, though what with roses, lilies, doves, she'll think she's landed in the garden of the Blessed Virgin herself." That the faint blasphemy, to judge by his companion's expression, had aroused disfavor only heightened his delight.

"I fear she may suffer a slight disillusionment when she discovers its function." Jordan's French was adequate, but he refused to use it in conversation with the usurper, and the almost insulting slowness in enunciating his own dialect, added to his natural lethargy, gave his words a peculiar suggestivity. "I mean," his lips actually curved to a parody of a smile, "that the pleasures of restrictions of a harem are somewhat unfamiliar to a northern lady's taste."

"A harem!" Guy de Lévis exclaimed, and even his self-assurance was slightly ruffled. "I was aware that the Sire de Luna was renowned for his—hm—gallantry. But I can hardly credit him—"

"—with emulating the morals of the emperor?" Jordan concluded the sentence for him. "Perhaps not with the same ostentation; the Pyrenees provide—in appearance—a better protection from the Moslem than the African sea. We are not quite Sicily. In Languedoc our titillations with the Orient may lack the august Frederick's frankness—which, however, hardly renders them more innocuous."

Had Guy de Lévis' interest lain in solving the problem of the individual psyche rather than creating for himself and his descendants an almost autochthonous position in this newly won corner of France, he might have been alive to the sudden quickening in the other's hitherto so impassive tone. As it was, he interpreted the

171

close-lipped censure to priest-ridden bigotry, a fact that only roused him to a generous defense of the dispossessed.

"I fancy you overrate the Sire de Luna's seriousness. He suggested to me rather a worshipper at the shrine of beauty than an addict to vice. Maybe he likes to affect the picturesque trappings of the East."

Jordan merely shrugged. "My remarks did not refer to him alone. The lusts of the flesh are perhaps relatively harmless when compared to the canker that Eastern idolatry breeds in the soul."

"You refer, I presume, to the Manichaean heresy?" Lévis retorted, the growing distaste he had felt for his visitor sharply increasing. Not content with their epistles, the ecclesiastical busy-bodies were evidently bent on plaguing him with dreary sermons.

"Your fears," he added sharply, "are doubtless not un-founded, but in my experience the Cathar heresy is in many cases a matter of politics, nothing more than a truc-ulent will for independence. Now they know the game's up, they'll forget their idolatry soon enough if they're given a chance. We'll be losing many a prospective loyal subject of King Louis if you go ferreting too deep into every man's soul."

"There are depths," Jordan muttered, "that we can never plumb."

"Doubtless," Lévis retorted, "and therefore I'm very willing to leave them to the care of the Church. I'm here to represent our sovereign, and since he has declared his readiness to extend pardon to those who prove loyal subjects, I consider it my duty to further and safeguard the interests of the Union and of France."

"I trust my countrymen appreciate such magnanim-ity." A light suddenly flickered in Jordan's eyes. "You have a momentous mission to fulfill and one that doubtless entails great difficulties—to distinguish, for in-stance, between those whom you may or may not trust."

The last words had been spoken with a strange and subtle emphasis. Was the man, it flashed through Lévis' mind, possibly an informer? The practice among the Lan-guedocians of denouncing a rival and so winning favor with the conqueror was becoming so pernicious that it was badly complicating the task of redistributing the confiscated lands. Assured of his ecclesiastic backing, he had very probably come with the hope of worming himself into good favor on the temporal level or pleading for some friend of his. Jordan's next words reinforced his suspicions.

"The matter is certainly double-sided. For even where the record as a faithful adherent of the Church is unblemished, the love of the conqueror is not perhaps sufficiently developed to cut out the possibility of future sedition and rebellion. There are, I fear, few who, as yet, regard the Union as a life ideal."

Sickened by the innuendo, Lévis cut him short. "One cannot expect too much at a start."

"Nevertheless," Jordan continued, "there may be a few."

"More than you possibly imagine," Lévis replied curtly, "and I trust there will soon be more."

"It must be particularly difficult," the other continued with quiet insistence, "in a district that borders on a territory so rugged as the Sabarthez. Men who for centuries have been for the most part little better than predatory bandits can hardly be expected to harbor a constructively peaceful ideal. Even their liege lord, the Count of Foix, is, I fancy, not likely to prove very helpful."

Lévis made no reply. The Count of Foix was indeed proving a bugbear in the furthering of good relations.

"A pity," the voice went on, strangely slurred. "Were it only his brother—"

"His brother?" the marshal echoed without interest. "I was not even aware he possessed one."

"Well—to be more exact—a half brother. One possibly of many." Jordan gave a little laugh. "The old Count of Foix was a great pursuer of the fair sex in his time. But the son in question hardly shares his promiscuity. He is indeed something of a recluse."

"A recluse?" Lévis echoed again. "I have heard, I believe, that a natural son of the count was a heretic."

"Hm—the point is debatable." Jordan had put down his glass. "His wife ran a hostel at Durban. Naturally the property was confiscated." He paused a moment. On the table his long knotted fingers resembled a species of insect performing a complicated dance. "It is known, I am confident, throughout Languedoc that I have always maintained the one salvation of this unhappy land to lie in the extirpation of heresy. Nevertheless, there may be circumstances in which a nearer investigation . . ."

Lévis pushed back his chair impatiently. So the man was coming to the point at last, though in a somewhat unexpected direction. "In the light of your previous arguments, I should have thought that heretical activities of so blatant a nature would of necessity merit their fate. You surely cannot imply that property used for such purposes should be returned."

Jordan stiffened. "Far from it. It is imperative that the smallest nucleus should be relentlessly combed out. In regard to any extenuating circumstances, I was referring only to the Bastard of Foix—not to his consort. There may be instances as you say yourself, where the incentive to religious nonconformity was merely of a political nature." He hesitated, putting his hand to his cheek to hide the muscle that had begun to twitch uncontrollably between nostril and lip. "In the case of Wolf of Foix I should suggest—paradoxical as it may sound—that his alleged heresy is actually but the result of his love for France."

"For France?" Lévis retorted almost angrily. Was the man gulling him or—he scrutinized the strange taut expression on his visitor's face—was he even in his right senses?

"I am aware that I must appear to talk in riddles," Jordan continued. "Nevertheless, as I alone, perhaps, possess an inside knowledge of the subject, I feel it my duty to acquaint you with the facts. They date from some years ago," he continued, leaning back and half shutting his eyelids. "The Bastard of Foix was at the time convalescent from serious wounds sustained at the siege of Toulouse. (The fact of his military prowess, incidentally, in itself proves he was anything but an adherent of the Cathar faith.) Debarred from playing an active part, he took on the custody of a French prisoner. Being of an undeniably idealistic nature and acti-

174

vated by feelings that, after all, can be called nothing but Christian, he showed perhaps an unusual clemency toward the captive (who, it must be remembered, was a mere boy). Through no fault of his own, but through the machinations of an unscrupulous warder, however, the prisoner unfortunately escaped, only to be tracked down by some fanatical pursuers and finally hunted to death. The Bastard of Foix was absent at the time, ironically enough, on the mission of procuring the prisoner's release by ransom. Discovering the tragedy on his return, the whole thing seems to have worked so disastrously on his imagination, always sensitive and rendered doubly vulnerable by pain and illness, that he was well-nigh on the brink of losing his reason. The one refuge open to him seemed naturally that offered by his wife, or, more precisely, her tenets of peace and brotherhood."

"In other words—Catharism," Lévis clinched the argument impatiently.

"So it might seem," Jordan gave a faintly acid smile. "And doubtless Honoria of Durban harbored strong hopes that he would become an ardent defender of her faith. Unfortunately he interpreted the Holy Word more literally. 'The sword shall be beaten into the plowshare,' and his conception of nonviolence rejected prayer meetings and charity in favor of agriculture. He appears to have proved a first-rate farmer." Jordan paused. A little smear of saliva had gathered at the corner of his lips. With the back of his hand he wiped it away. "It is unfortunate that such useful talents should be wasted, still more that he should forget the chance of materializing his dream—a true understanding between France and Languedoc. Since King Louis is showing such clemency, it would seem a pity, surely, that for the sake of a mere misunderstanding your sovereign should lose the allegiance of one who might well prove his sincerest supporter."

The marshal had half risen from his seat. "You infer that the case of the Bastard of Foix should be reconsidered. It appears to me out of the question. Even if there is doubt as to his being a heretic himself, he is linked with the Cathars by the closest ties."

Jordan made a negligent gesture with his hand. "It is not of importance. I was perhaps mistaken in acquainting you with the case. But since you had yourself criticized the intransigence of persecution, I thought it might interest you."

Lévis colored in rage. Had the fellow perhaps been sent by the priests to lead him into a trap? But Jordan was continuing suavely. "The ties, I fancy, are not so close as they appear. Marriage is, after all, usually a matter of feudal considerations and I can vouch for it that in the case of the Bastard of Foix and his spouse it was certainly not a matter of the heart. Were it not for the facts already mentioned, I fancy they would long have parted—they had, to tell the truth, as good as done so when the tragedy with the prisoner occurred. I am pretty sure that if opportunity were offered to him to practice his humanitarian idealism in a more realistic field, any heretical fantasies would soon be blown on the winds.

"One would require some better guarantee than that," the marshal replied skeptically.

Jordan smiled. "I do not think that would be very difficult to obtain. More than one serf will witness to the reproaches the Bastard won from his wife in preferring his farm work to her religious meetings. Many of his compatriots will vouch for the respect he harbored for the French on the occasion of the banquet in honor of the victories temporarily achieved by Languedoc, when he surprised if not outraged the patriotic sensibility of his fellow countrymen by his refusal to join in the toast of anathema and perdition hurled at the foe. Somewhat eccentric behavior, no doubt, but then, the Bastard always had moral scruples, which is less surprising, perhaps, when one considers he was brought up to be a monk."

"A monk?" So the Church, Lévis reflected, had her hand in the game after all. Bent maybe on bringing an erring sheep back to the fold and unwilling openly to support a semi-heretic, they were trying to employ a layman as agent. They would see they were mistaken. "I begin to understand," he said acridly. "You have come in the name of the bishop to plead his case."

"Hell, no—" As though to cover his embarrassment,

Jordan took another sip of the wine. "The Holy See can hardly be responsible for anyone with even an indirect relationship with heresy. Moreover, as a mere boy the Bastard of Foix escaped from the monastery where he was reared."

"He appears to have led a life of strange vicissitudes," Lévis commented, not without feeling a certain sympathy with this illegitimate scion of the house of Foix on the score of his escape from the cloister. Nevertheless it was still incomprehensible to him that his cause should be espoused by this apparent emissary of the priests.

"Am I then to understand," he inquired distrustfully, "that you have been sent to plead as an advocate by your friend?"

For a moment a spasm seemed to contort Jordan's face, but he controlled it and a second later his features had again resumed their cold enigmatic mask, except for the slight ticking of the nerve by his chin.

"The Bastard of Foix is unlikely to beg anyone to plead his cause—last of all my own person. The truth is that a grave misunderstanding about the tragedy to which I referred has caused him, I fear, ever since to look on me with disfavor. By an evil chance it happened it was my own henchmen who were instrumental in recapturing the fugitive. When I arrived on the scene, it was, alas, too late to stop what such crude natures as theirs considered a just punishment. I have by now given up the hope of ever convincing the Bastard of Foix that such retribution was not carried out at my command. Realizing that his mind was temporarily almost deranged by the horrible event, I cannot bear him a grudge. On the contrary, I still desire to do all in my power to make amends."

So that was the root of the matter, Lévis reflected, sardonically relieved. Retribution—a guilty conscience and, because heresy was involved, the man for all his bigotry could not take his trouble to the priests. If he had only come out with the truth directly instead of beating about the bush, But that, no doubt, was the result of belonging to a conquered people—Southerners into the bargain. Well, he ought to be getting used to their suavities by now. But the man's innuendoes were really too much. His

177

confessions did not make him any more prepossessing and the story sounded shady. He'd certainly better not get involved in the matter.

"The case is certainly moving," he evaded. "But you must surely see for yourself the difficulties are almost insurmountable." Pushing back his chair, he turned as if to terminate the conversation and took a few steps down the hall.

Jordan too had risen, murmuring apologies. "I fear I have trespassed seriously on your valuable time. However, all things considered, I felt it incumbent on me to recommend, for your own advantage as well as my own, one so likely to prove useful to your cause." He ceased abruptly, entering once more on the subject of his official mission. It was not until he took his leave a little later that he referred to Wolf of Foix again. "As to that other matter of which we were speaking, should circumstances by chance cause you to reconsider the case, it is imperative that there should be no mention of my name. If the Bastard of Foix were to dream for an instant that I had in any way been instrumental in achieving his pardon, he would doubtless refuse it straightway. One day perhaps," he sighed, "having regained a sufficiently objective attitude toward me, he might be told who was his benefactor. In the meantime, it will be reward enough to know that I have done my best to compensate him and at the same time helped a little in furthering the peace of the land. Incidentally," he added as a seeming afterthought, "the pardon of the half brother might pave the way to reconciling the Count of Foix."

SPOILING THE PICTURE

And everywhere the sad derision
That kills Today and says, Tomorrow never comes.
The mind as sharp as knives,
Tapped by his gang of hard facts, cuts his throat.

(D. J. ENRIGHT: *The Laughing Hyena*)

IT WAS ACTUALLY THAT CONCLUDING REMARK, AP-
parently so casually delivered, which, about a month
later, prompted Guy de Lévis to recall his conversation
with his somewhat uncongenial visitor. Jordan of the Isle
had indeed almost immediately been dismissed from his
mind and it was only the question of handling the Count
of Foix, and the necessity of employing diplomatic means
or military compulsion that caused the marshal to reflect
on the stranger's advice.

The Ariège was providing a knotty problem in any
case. The barons of the Sabarthez, realizing they had
nothing to gain by a resistance that, in the long run, was
bound to prove fruitless, had followed their liege lord in
swearing a reluctant allegiance to the French throne.
Nonetheless they were well aware of their power to prove,
from the vantage point of their eagle-eyries, a constant
thorn in the flesh. Lévis for his part had the sense to realize that the appointment of a French seneschal in their
midst would not only rouse their rancor but necessitate
the upkeep of considerably larger forces with which to
hold the peace, an intervention that would inevitably incense the Count of Foix.

If only he could win the support of that feudal
chieftain, the marshal reflected, his path would be
considerably eased. Of course one could always adopt the
ruthless measures of Montfort, but where had they ended?

With the loss of everything he had gained, his son chased from the land, his daughter a Southerner's harlot, and no more left to his credit than the reputation of having been the devil incarnate. No—Mirepoix, Lévis smiled to himself, was after all a little property worth keeping and he was determined to establish himself there, by hook or by crook, for all time. He had already, he pondered with gratification, made himself, all things considered, not too unpopular in the immediate district. But in the long run all depended on the taming of that truculent giant, licking his wounds like a beast in its liar, Roger, Count of Foix.

Could there be anything in Jordan of the Isle's seemingly fantastic suggestion? Ambition, a sense of humor, a certain weakness for the hazardous and the bizarre, perhaps, above all, the very thought of double-crossing the meddling priests, all conspired to prompt Lévis to make inquiries concerning the natural brother of the count. Rather to his surprise the evidence pretty well corroborated Jordan of the Isle's own statements. The wife, an intransigent heretic, was certainly a stumbling block, but the loss of Durban seemed to have unhinged her completely. It was rumored she was even dead. As for the Bastard himself, the worst he could gather about him was that he was an incorrigibly idealistic fool who had developed crazy scruples about fighting on account of a young prisoner's death. Carefully handled, Lévis considered, and decoyed with some grand slogan of Peace and Unity, he would soon be brought to toe the line. Naturally there could be no possibility of a restoration of Durban, nor would that suit his plans. But he could well devise a compensation. Was not King Louis himself recommending mercy and reimbursement to those ready to swear loyalty? As to Wolf of Foix's alleged heresy, it seemed he could easily find witnesses to disprove it. For that matter, many a Southerner who had listened to the sermons of those wandering anchorites was happily reinstalled in some nice little property today.

The net result of all these considerations was two little talks with the count. Intransigent and suspicious at first, even he began at last to nibble the bait.

It was with amazement, therefore, that Wolf of Foix, in the retreat of an abandoned farmhouse among the hills of the Mas d'Azil, received news from his brother that his appearance at Foix on a given day was not only imperative but might prove to his advantage. What surprised him even more was that the summons was accompanied by a letter of self-conduct and return from a certain inn on the highroad to Foix. It was sealed with the arms of the Maréchal des Terres.

He felt little inclination to respond, yet to refuse was, as he knew, to incur almost certain disaster. For himself he cared little. The future offered a hardly less hopeless vista than the past. But it entailed the fate of Honoria. He was constantly in search of a way to bring her into safety across the border, whence they might be able to reach one of the Cathar centers abroad. But the severe illness that had befallen her after the loss of Durban had made the journey at first impossible and had left her since in a state of fearful apathy, broken only by moments of visionary ecstasy in which she was convinced that direction would come from Above. All practical considerations, all attempts to spur her to action, proved fruitless. It was as though she who for years had worked with such ruthless efficiency, dominating all who came into contact with her by her relentless will, had suddenly been emptied of all initiative and felt only the terrible need to be led.

Should he tell her of the summons? Wolf considered and decided at last, no. Too well he remembered the occasions on which his absence from Durban had evoked in her those terrible tempests of the mind. Now she appeared almost too lethargic to care. Yet how could he read the dark, secret wanderings of her troubled mind?

The change in her character had had its repercussions upon him also. If in the course of her illness, her weakness and almost complete dependence upon him had drawn her inevitably into a closer proximity than she had ever allowed him, it brought home to him more clearly the depth of her physical aversion and with it his sense of initial responsibility and guilt.

It was at last with the excuse that he might be absent a whole day in search of provender and possible contact with some Cathar refugee center that Wolf set out for Foix.

He had been prepared for the strange, almost taciturn bitterness that had replaced his half brother's former patronizing bombast, but though he had gathered that Roger could not get over the humiliations of the peace treaty, he realized with a shock on his arrival at Foix how greatly his half brother had aged. They had not met since the day Mirepoix had arrived with the ultimatum, and Wolf had scarcely dreamed that the collapse he had witnessed then would have left so lasting an effect. Roger's tawny hair had lost its fiery glow and was even streaked with gray; he looked thinner, while his shoulders stooped a little as if his huge frame were not supported sufficiently by the diminished bulk. The gesture with which he introduced Wolf to the man sitting beside him had, in spite of its proud resentment, something of nervous anxiety and strain.

"My brother—"

The stranger rose, bowed with an air of easy arrogance, fixing his hazel eyes on the newcomer in a gaze of sharp and slightly humorous inquiry, devoid of malice or scorn.

"The Maréchal des Terres," Roger muttered as if he had difficulty in forcing the name over his lips, "has done you the honor of asking to make your acquaintance. He has, I gather, gained some—hm—not altogether unfavorable information concerning your person. I trust you will not disappoint his expectations." As he spoke, a shade of the old bantering condescension came into his voice, rousing in Wolf his habitual resentment, but the overtone of weariness that had accompanied the words caused him to swallow his chagrin. Returning the stranger's greeting, he replied with reserve, "I fear any reports that may circulate around my name are scarcely likely to ingratiate me in the eyes of the Maréchal."

Roger frowned, but Guy de Lévis advanced a step, unperturbed. "I have gathered," he began, "you are versed in the French tongue—"

"I can understand it," Wolf replied, "I am afraid my speech is far from perfect."

"You have had little practice," Lévis encouraged him, "at any rate in the last years? Perhaps you may now have better opportunities."

"If you have," Roger muttered to Wolf almost inaudibly, "let us hope the results will prove luckier than before. My brother," he turned to the marshal, "underestimates his linguistic talents. Having been brought up in the cloister, he's even an authority on Latin." He let his hand fall on Wolf's shoulders with something of the old half-patronizing, half-ironic recognition of his erudite accomplishments; then turned again to the Frenchman. "Actually, your tongue was almost his companion for the space of a whole winter—under somewhat unfortunate circumstances."

The marshal evidently understood the allusion, for he fixed his eyes on Wolf with a not unfriendly gravity. "I understand that during his imprisonment you showed exceptional kindness to a young member of His Majesty's forces. I should like to take the opportunity of thanking you." He paused a moment and, aware of the deepening pallor on the other's face, continued, "I have gathered also that the tragic outcome was due to no fault of yours, but to one of the inevitable brutalities that accompany war. Since the unhappy enmity between our two countries has been put to an end forever, we can comfort ourselves at least that such circumstances cannot arise again."

"Far worse is happening at the present time," Roger gave a bitter laugh. "You need only consider the reprisals being enacted daily."

Guy de Lévis' face darkened, but he attempted to meet the situation with diplomacy. "There have been and still are many misunderstandings between us. Nonetheless our king has expressed a fervent wish that all should be done to foster a spirit of good will and harmonious relationship, if the people of Languedoc are, for their part, equally willing to cooperate."

183

"By sitting mute while his officers strengthen their fortresses throughout our land, redouble the walls of Carcassonne, and set their seneschals to watch over us like jailers—" Roger expostulated, pacing up and down the room. "Not all possess your magnanimity," he growled, making a clumsy apology to the marshal who, passing over the count's outbreak with equanimity, had reseated himself.

"Some of my countrymen," he replied, "may resort to measures that seem perhaps unnecessarily harsh. I myself feel that only mutual trust can establish a lasting friendly relationship. It is time," he continued, "that we stopped thinking in terms of the past. The Union has put an end to strife and dissension. We are concerned with the building of one realm, one nation—France."

"France—that petty kingdom which by guile and subterfuge has managed to augment its paltry territories?" Roger's ungovernable temper was once more beginning to win mastery over all attempts at diplomacy or handling of the situation to his own benefit.

All the time Wolf had been standing silent, wondering confusedly to what purpose he had been called to Foix— to act as mediator in an argument? As through a veil he saw the color mount dangerously to Roger's temples, but with increasing emotion he had followed the marshal's words.

Suddenly he was listening to the sound of his own voice. "Perhaps even France alone is not large enough."

"Christ!" Roger swung round in fury. "Perhaps you would add to it Brittany, Flanders, Burgundy, half the lands of the Germans—in short, the blessed realm of Charlemagne? I was not wrong in assuring you, Sir Guy de Lévis," he laughed ironically, "that my brother would have more understanding for the schemes of your monarch than I."

The marshal might have been expected to silence by strong measures what he could only regard as a flaunting insult to the crown, but, as if ignoring the remark, his glance merely wandered from the enraged giant to the face of the slighter figure beside him. At first it had appeared to him worn, taciturn, and almost morose; now, under the scarred forehead, the eyes seemed to brighten, the lips part as though some deep-buried, half-forgotten emotion were stirring beneath the hardened surface.

"I fear," Wolf was saying, "I know little of the projects of King Louis. In any case, we are probably talking at cross-purposes. The realm I meant must embrace all mankind."

"God in heaven," Roger broke in, exasperated, "you're surely not going to start that tomfoolery again." But the marshal was regarding Wolf with skeptical amusement.

"Your plans sound somewhat ambitious. Wouldn't it be wise to limit them to a more attainable goal—let us say, the true consolidation of the Union?"

The shutter seemed to have closed on Wolf's features again.

"I am hardly in a position to do so as, since you are acquainted with my history, I gathered you must have understood."

Guy de Lévis smiled. "I have already said that the misfortunes of the past do not necessarily preclude a more auspicious future. The times are favorable to those who strive to build and maintain the peace. The king is anxious to support them."

Wolf bit his lip. "I only hope," he said quietly, "that you will find many ready to dedicate themselves to that cause."

"Amen. I fear however not all His Majesty's feudatories possess what the Count of Foix seems to consider a somewhat extravagant idealism. It would stand us all in good stead." The marshal paused and, as though absorbed in his thoughts, examined the signet ring on his finger. "With regret I gather you are forced to leave this country."

There was no reply.

"We may perhaps hope," the marshal suddenly looked up, regarding him with a little smile, "that you will return."

Wolf stiffened. "There must, I think, have been a misconception," he murmured, then turned to his half

185

brother with a look of accusation. "I thought the marshal was fully acquainted with the circumstances."

"He is," Roger growled, turned on his heel, then faced round again. "You may be surprised to hear that he has actually shown . . . the kindness . . . of trying to get your case reconsidered. I trust you will not prove yourself a fool."

Guy de Lévis had risen to his feet. "King Louis in his clemency is ready to examine the question of enforced exile in certain exceptions and extend his pardon to those who are ready to swear him fealty and allegiance."

Wolf took a deep breath. "It is clear to me that you cannot possibly understand the circumstances."

Clasping his hands in his sword belt, the Frenchman drew a step nearer. "You harbor possibly—hm—some doubts as to your power to fulfill your feudal duties. I do not think there is any need for you to worry on that score. First of all, the possibility of war within the realm is ended once and for all. For the rest, I gather you suffered serious disablement at the siege of Toulouse. Naturally that would be sufficient to excuse—"

"It is not a matter of physical ability," Wolf cut in abruptly, "but of principle. I can only thank you for your solicitude, but since you have obviously been misinformed, I have no right to waste your time in pursuing the question further."

The marshal gave a little shrug. Readjusting the cloak on his shoulders, he prepared without hurry to depart. Even now he did not seem to lose his equanimity, but turned once more toward Wolf.

"I can assure you," he said with a little smile, "that for my part I have counted our conversation no waste of time. It is not often my fortune to meet with a Southerner so well disposed toward our common cause. I should feel I had not only neglected my duty by failing to present your name to the king for the purpose of a just reconsideration of your exile, but deprived the realm of a staunch and invaluable supporter." He paused. "I can quite understand your perturbation, and that issues we have not touched upon—ties of a more intimate

186

nature—may be involved. It is doubtful whether such clemency as I would recommend in your case could be extended to your wife, unless she could be prevailed upon to renounce her heresy. Else a complete disassociation on your part from all her activities would naturally be inevitable. But those are considerations you naturally have to discuss between yourselves. There is no need to make any immediate decision. My suggestion has doubtless come as something of a shock. I can only hope that what may now appear to you as insuperable difficulties may, on reflection, dwindle to irrelevances in the light of what I well think your profound nobility of spirit must surely regard as a mission—a mission that, incidentally, might well provide a more promising field of activity than a heretic hostel." He paused again, adding with a smile, "One might consider possibly the governorship of the small town of Ax in the Sabarthez." He waited an instant, gazing at the man who stood before him apparently too dumfounded to reply, let alone offer his thanks; then, with a casual gesture of farewell, turned to the Count of Foix and in his company left the hall.

Wolf did not move.

He was still standing on the same spot, transfixed, unseeing, when, some minutes later, his half brother re-entered the room.

"Well, it's more than you ever expected, more, I must say, than you even deserve," Roger greeted him as he bore down on him from the door, the rancor he had striven vainly to repress in the presence of the hated victor breaking forth redoubled, now he was left alone with his brother. "If you miss your chance, I've done with you."

"I—?" Still half incapable of taking in the present, Wolf stared at him vacantly. "What on earth does it mean? What do you take me for?"

"For less of a fool, I hope, than you have proved hitherto—"

"But it's sheer impossibility—doesn't he know I'm a heretic?"

A laugh heartier than any he had uttered that day escaped from Roger's throat. "I don't fancy Guy de Lévis is much of a churchman—"

"Maybe. Even so—" Suddenly Wolf turned on his half brother in anger. "Was it perhaps your doing—one of your practical jokes?"

"Mine? Do you think I'd go pleading with a damned French usurper?"

"I shouldn't have thought so," Wolf muttered bitterly. But he remembered the mixture of insulting arrogance and servility with which Roger had treated the Frenchman. "You mean he approached *you?*"

"I met him a few weeks ago. He happened to mention you—quite casually, and, rather surprisingly, didn't seem ill-disposed toward you. Naturally, I didn't attempt to disillusion him. Do you think I'm going to lower the name of Foix in the eyes of that imposter?"

Wolf's face darkened. "You'd have done best to keep silent. What on earth did you tell him?"

"Little more than he knew already. He appeared to have your life's history pretty well at his fingertips—at any rate as far as your dear friend Berengar was concerned."

"So he did know even about that?" The blood had drained from Wolf's face as quickly as it had come.

"Evidently that's at the root of the matter," Roger's voice rang with scorn. "The tragic story of a young Southerner who loved his French foe."

"You might have spared me that mockery."

"I did. As I saw it, our one chance depended on it."

"Our chance?"

"What else? That's what it's come to." Roger flung himself into a chair. "One has to grasp at any straw they deign to hold out to us. God knows what Lévis really wants. He's out to make himself popular, I suppose, and show his power. He's not too good a friend of the priesthood and so, no doubt, he wants to ingratiate himself with us."

"Possibly." Wolf gave a shrug and sighed. "Anyhow, he seemed straightforward and generous enough. You've led him nicely up the path."

188

Roger looked up frowning. "You don't mean to say you're going to make difficulties?"

"I? But the whole thing's fantastic. Even if it weren't, do you think I could ever live in the Sabarthez?"

"Ax is at the far end. You'd probably never need to go near the blessed lake. In any case," Roger added, "I'd have thought you'd find it particularly fitting—quite symbolic, in fact—a memorial to peace and friendship."

"Be quiet." Wolf stood staring before him. Then he lifted his hand and passed it over his forehead. It was clammy with sweat. "It's no good discussing this further. I'm a heretic. That's enough."

"A heretic?" Roger leaned back, drumming his fingers on the table. "They've let off worse cases than yours—when it suits them. Besides, what's there to prove? That you were so crazed by the death of a wretched prisoner, you let yourself be cajoled into listening to the *bonshommes'* tirades against homicide? With Lévis that only stands in your favor. Further, that your wife ran a Cathar hostel? If we're to be responsible for all our wives' foibles, God knows where we'll end. Incidentally, you can bring enough witnesses to prove that she rated you often enough for your lack of zeal and for taking more interest in your earthly estates than your spiritual salvation."

Wolf turned aside.

"We'd best leave this, Roger. You know quite well I revere the Cathars."

His brother merely laughed. "Even some of the dear clergy do that. When all's said and done they can't deny the *bonshommes* provide a perfect model for their own Christian shibboleths. But evidently it was too galling a pill for you to swallow or you would have joined the brethren forever and aye."

A moment passed before Wolf murmured, "I wanted to. They wouldn't have me."

"So that's why you went back to Durban. Christ, did you really want to become one of the old soul-savers?" Roger scrutinized his half brother derisively.

"Yes."

"Good God." Roger rose heavily to his feet, took a few paces across the room, and turned abruptly. "And now?"

There was no reply.

"So you've come to your senses at last. You're sick of the whole affair. And you can't deny it. You care more for a square patch of soil and an ear of corn than a shower of manna from heaven. You can thank your stars the old brethren evidently knew you better than ever you did yourself."

"Can't you hold your tongue?"

"No." Roger had returned to Wolf's side. Gripping his shoulders, he stooped over him, the great, flushed muzzle of his face thrust close to him. "I've let you pursue your fool's paradise for years and though I gave you a fair chance of getting out of it long ago, you were too damned self-righteous. Then, for all I cared, you could go on playing the saint if it pleased you—a saint with the dung straw stuck in your hair in place of a halo. Taste's taste after all, and maybe the smell was more pleasant to your nostrils than the scent of young Trencavel's courtiers. God knows I'd not wish to see you a spittle-licking henchman of Carcassonne. But now when everything's at stake, do you think I'm going to let you betray Foix for the sake of your whims and all the cursed humbug in which you don't even believe?"

"You know I believe—"

"In what? In your damned self-conceit, your fear of owning up to your true feelings—of spoiling the smug, pious little picture you've made of yourself."

. . . Spoiling the picture . . . betraying the picture . . . the image. . . . Darkly the words echoed through the fevered confusion enveloping Wolf's brain, but he persisted.

"You know quite well I have accepted the faith, Roger."

"The faith of the Cathars?" Roger let go his grip and laughed aloud. "Then why did you wake like a man roused from the dead when you told Lévis of your blessed world empire? Why did you fill young Trencavel's ears with the mad dreams of his father?"

"They are not incompatible with the Cathar faith."

190

"No? I fancy your earthly paradise would hardly renounce all worldly ties sufficiently to please the *bonshommes*. Well then," he fired his parting shot, "why do you still keep Trencavel's sword instead of sending it back to the youngster? Surely the pious Honoria doesn't favor the keeping of such murderous weapons?"

"It's broken—"

"That doesn't say it cannot be mended."

"It's a symbol," Wolf muttered.

"Exactly. A symbol of what? You don't know? But I reckon I can tell you—a symbol of something more sacred to you than all your pious claptrap, a symbol of freedom and justice for which you were ready to fight, oh so gallantly, with Trencavel, but which, if there's a chance of retaining a last bit of it—"

"For God's sake—" Wolf confronted him trembling and wild-eyed. "Can't you stop it?"

"No—not until I get you to see the truth."

"The truth. What *is* truth?" Wolf cried hoarsely. "In any case," he added in despair. "I can't see what bearing all this has on the marshal's offer."

"You can't—of course. Well, then, to make it plain, you have the chance of getting a fiefdom in the Sabarthez. You're the only Foix they'd ever consider. If not, a Frenchy will have it—the last chance will be gone."

"The last chance—of what?" Suddenly Wolf turned on Roger with clenched hands. "You mean you want me to get it so that you can use the place as a center of rebellion and the starting point of a new war?"

"War—" Roger tossed back his head, but the action was like that of a wounded animal at bay. "War—you know yourself what chance there is for that. It's a matter of maintaining what you're always ranting about, the damned peace. You were eager enough for me to sign it, but now you won't lift a finger to make it bearable."

"Bearable—how?" Wolf gave a bitter laugh. "You mean, I suppose, I'm to act as mediator, playing a double game while all the time you're hatching your plots."

"Plots? You're optimistic." Roger had started again on his prowling but now he stopped short, leaning against a

191

chair, and once more, so when he had entered, Wolf realized how worn, even ill, his half brother looked.

"Can't we stop this?" he begged. "You know it's quite fruitless."

"Stop it? Of course you want me to stop it when it doesn't suit you to help, though I did everything to get you out of a fix when you persisted in your madness. I might have known," Roger added, leaning forward in the chair into which he had sunk as one in pain. "Have you ever caused anything but trouble since you ran away from the cloister where you'd have done a thousand times better to stop?" In spite of his anger his voice sounded so broken that, as on the day of defeat, Wolf's own wretchedness was transcended by the sense of shame he felt for the man before him.

"Why don't you leave me out of it, Roger?" he pleaded. "Why do you always interfere? Why didn't you let me go to the devil alone long ago and have done with it?"

"Why?" Roger echoed. Why indeed? he asked himself, and his wonder was honest. He scarcely understood what it was that drew him ever and again to the illegitimate brother he half good-humoredly scoffed at, half despised—pride, condescension, genuine affection, and, though he did not know it, a hidden envy, an instinctive need for something that, he realized blindly, he himself utterly lacked. "You made even our father despair," he cried as if to defend his own weakness.

"I know," Wolf answered dully. "But I suppose he got used to it so early he at least had no more illusions."

"Illusions—" Roger dragged up his great grizzled head as if with an effort. "Even on his deathbed he didn't give them up."

"On his deathbed?"

"His last words—you must have heard them," Roger muttered doggedly.

"You know I didn't—" Wolf drew a step nearer his brother. "I asked you—you said he was raving."

"Raving—doubtless he was. But his ravings were a

good prophecy—that is, if you'd turned out as he evidently hoped even then."

"How?" Wolf whispered. Through the numbing confusion of emotion that encompassed him his heart began to beat with fearful expectancy.

"As the peacemaker—as you're so fond of styling yourself. Because, in the end, he said only the way of peace would save Foix. And now when you've got the chance, you shirk it."

Minutes passed before Wolf answered. In the silence he could hear Roger's strange wheezing breath. "Why didn't you tell me before?"

"Would it have made a difference?"

"No. I suppose not. You wouldn't have wanted it then anyway."

Roger stumbled to his feet. "There's no use in thinking what might have been. The point is, what are you going to do about it now?"

Wolf turned away. "What's the use of asking? You know as well as I do that what you want is impossible. There's not only myself involved."

"You mean Honoria?" Roger gave a bitter laugh. "God, one would think you'd be grateful to find a valid excuse to throw off that blight. You'd have had one long before now if you'd possessed any guts—a wife who's no more than a nun. Has she given you children? Has she ever deigned to share your bed?"

"She's my wife. That's enough, Roger—do you understand? Incidentally," Wolf added, "in marrying her it was the one time, perhaps, that I came up to our father's expectations."

"Hm—he wasn't always infallible. Besides, he'd have been the last to make you keep to the bargain when it lost its point. Marriage for him was just a diplomatic game."

"I don't think you have any need to tell *me* that," Wolf gave a strained laugh. "After all, I owe my own existence to it."

The rebuff hit Roger on his weakest spot—the strange inexplicable sense of guilt that somehow had always haunted him in his relationship with his illegitimate brother.

193

"Have I ever made you feel it?" he muttered. "I've done my best."

"Maybe you've done a little too much—as I said before." Wolf had taken a step forward. "God knows I'm grateful. But the more you do, the more I've become entangled. The trees got too thick for the wood and there's no way out."

"God, can't you hack them down?"

Wolf gave a tired little smile. "I'd have to pull them out at the roots—and they're rooted in me. You may as well know," he muttered, "it wasn't to please our father I bound myself to Honoria, but to spite him. I took the responsibility on myself and so . . ."

Roger made no reply. He had reached a point where he could penetrate no further into an intransigence of spirit that, for all his own innate stubbornness, he could not understand.

"Thank the marshal for his solicitude," Wolf was saying, "but tell him—circumstances make it quite impossible."

"I shall tell him nothing," Roger mumbled. "If, when three days have passed, you haven't come to your senses, you can write and tell him yourself." But he did not raise his eyes from the floor and he was hardly aware of Wolf's farewell greeting or even that he had left.

PRIVATE AGONY

*Thou fool, that which thou sowest is not quickened,
except it die.*

(*Corinthians xv*)

HONORIA OF DURBAN STOOD IN THE SHADE OF A GROUP OF
pine trees that marked the limit of the abandoned farm,
gazing down on the road to Foix. It lay there coiling,
gleaming in the evening sun, like the belly of a snake. It
was empty. He would not come, must not come, she told
herself, till the sun was set. And still it had not touched
the rim of the hills.

Now she would close her eyes counting another three
hundred, then open them again. So she had gone on,
counting, waiting, for how many hours, for how many
days? She did not know, for all life was waiting—waiting
for his return. From Foix, from Carcassonne, from
Toulouse. Only night could end the waiting, but he had
always returned by day. Even that first evening after her
betrothal at Durban in the snow. Then twilight had even
fallen. A few more minutes and darkness would have enveloped her, muffled her in forever, shutting out sight,
sound, sense. But the day had mocked her, projecting,
protracting its false fickle light over the whiteness of the
snow. Before it had faded he had come. She had been
trapped. Her life of delusion had begun.

Two hundred . . . two hundred and fifty . . . ninety,
three hundred. . . . She turned her head.

The sun was touching the shoulder of the mountain,
striking sparks from the rock. Blinding, they shot through
space, singeing, searing, scorching the flesh. She put up
her hands as if to protect herself, and instinctively, as if to

195

ward off the evil, started counting again. She had counted and paused three times. The road was empty still, but in the west when she turned, the sun was a crimson sphere half sunk into the hollow of the hills. Even as she watched, it shrank to a semicircle, a quarter. And still she counted.

It was a battle between them now—between her and the glowing furnace in the west that even as it shrank grew fiercer, a well of consuming fire dragging, sucking her in.

One hundred, two hundred, two hundred and seventy-three. All now depended, she knew, on reaching three hundred at the moment the sun disappeared. It was a mere spot now, a bleeding scab blistering the outline of the hill, sucking her into its center, the festering, seething pinpoint of light. She could hardly see, blinded by its dazzle, those fiery daggers, piercing, burning to the heart. Two hundred and ninety-seven, ninety-eight, ninety-nine. In a last frenzy of anguish she closed her eyes—three hundred—and opened them again. Before her the curving hummock of the hill lay silhouetted darkly against a liquid sea. The fires were extinguished forever. Even as she gazed, the last faint glow of rose merged into apricot and gold, translucent greenness, curtains of blue falling from the wings of the night.

She sank on her knees, in the shadow of the pines, into the dank musty smell of bark and earth. For here the darkness would fall, fall unimpeded by the shadows, by the dun gray soil, the darkening grass spread round about, here where there was no snow.

Why were people afraid of the dark? But were they? They were only afraid of the dawn—the dawn that the troubadours dreaded in the songs Sicard had sung. Yet he'd seldom composed them himself. It was the light he had run after like a wanton insect dancing in the sun, like a young goat gamboling in the light-drenched hills. But she had saved him, from the fickle, dancing sunbeams, the vain deluding light of day. With her own hands she had bound his eyes, extinguished the bright glancing fires dancing in the brown depths of the pupils, bound them, lashed them, blinded them with the dark twining tendrils

196

of his hair. And now they were buried deep, scooped from the hollowed sockets, black gleaming pebbles entangled in the fibers of the roots.

So she too would be buried, blinded.

As if following her thoughts, her hands scraped among the fallen pine needles and earth and lifted them to her eyes. For no eyes, she repeated to herself, were needed to see the true light, and those who receive the baptism of the spirit are as those who have passed beyond death. She had already passed there, passed with the setting of the sun—or was it long ago, with the *bonshommes'* visit? How long ago? She did not know. For all her previous life was shut away behind it where she could not reach. Before her stretched only an infinite twilight, reaching into the darkness, reaching into the night. . . .

It was dark already. How many hours had she been here? she wondered suddenly. But why should she wonder, when all waiting, all counting had ceased? Nevertheless she rose to her feet. Around her the land shelved away into wave upon wave of darkness. Somewhere there had been a road. She had been waiting. But what matter? Roads were made to travel by, not that one should wait. And she had a long journey before her—tomorrow. There were no morrows or yesterdays when one was dead. Yet she was tired, so tired. Like one sleepwalking, she made her way back to the house.

"Where are you—where—Honoria?" The words broke over her head, senseless at first, jarring and always increasing, like a cracked bell, peal on peal.

All she could do was to draw back into the shadows.

"Honoria—" It clanged again, broke, ending in a short startled cry.

He had almost fallen over her where she sat huddled in the corner behind the hearth.

"Are you ill?" Wolf bent over her anxiously, but she edged away.

Groping, he found a candle and lit it in the smoldering ash. By its flicker he could see her crouching in the shadows, staring before her, and the soiled dress, the

197

loosened strands of hair, contrasting so strongly with her former efficiency, smote him with a pang.

"You should not sit waiting in the darkness," he said gently, blaming himself for having left her alone.

"I have ceased to wait."

He took her answer for complete hopelessness, the paralyzing inertia that was wont to attack her for ever-increasing periods since her illness.

"I do not think you will have to wait much longer," he said. Should he tell her at once? Perhaps it would rouse her better than anything else. "Roger will protect us no longer. As soon as you are able, we shall have to leave."

But the words seemed to arouse no surprise. She sat motionless, her eyes fixed on the distance beyond him, as if she were unaware of his presence. "I am leaving now."

He shook his head. "Not now, not immediately, tomorrow perhaps. We must find a way."

"It has been found. They have shown it me."

"Who?"

"The *bonshommes*," she answered. "Didn't I tell you they would come?"

She was suffering from one of her hallucinations, he thought at once. "They will come," he attempted to cajole her as though talking to a sick child.

"They have come." In her voice there was suddenly a note of almost malignant triumph. "They are here."

"Here?" he echoed incredulous, and mechanically his eyes followed hers to the table. It was laid for two—for him and for herself; he had taken it for granted. But now, looking more closely, he saw the dregs of wine in the cups, the remnants of a meal littering the board. "You have had visitors?" he asked perturbed.

"The *bonshommes*—the *perfecti*—" she insisted as though he failed to understand.

"But how did they come? Who sent them?"

"The deacon—Macart, or Marty?" She seemed baffled a moment. "What does it matter? I knew they must come."

"Did you know them?"

She shook her head. "They came in disguise as hucksters peddling their wares. But I knew the moment they

198

showed them—the cingulum—the holy girdle—" A strange light began to animate her face. "It lay there plain and unspoiled among all their gilded baubles and jewels."

"Peddlers—hucksters?" Wolf's face had darkened. "Didn't I tell you not to let anyone in?"

"Would you have me deny hospitality to two *perfecti*?" She drew herself erect.

"How could you be certain? There is always danger—"

"There is only one danger." Suddenly she rose to her feet. "That which blinds the spirit—the deluding day."

Had they really been here? Again he began to doubt it. She was obviously distraught. "But what did they want?" he persisted anxiously.

"To save us."

"But how?"

"By leading us to the light. The one true light that shines only through the darkness—the light hidden in the depths of death and of night."

She was beside herself. He was certain of it now.

"We will talk of it later, you are tired," he placated. "It was too much of a shock." He took a step toward her but she stretched out her hands as though to ward him off.

"Do not touch me."

He stopped short and turned aside. "You are worn out," he murmured. "Lie down and sleep."

But she remained standing motionless, her hands still held a little in front of her as though she were a priestess performing a sacred rite.

"I have slept long enough. For years I have slept blinded by sin. All these years I have lived in iniquity and my blindness grew day by day. But *they* revealed to me the depth of my delusion."

"Aren't we all deluded?" Wolf turned back to the table and his eye rested once more on the basket of loaves, the stained cups.

"They told you all that, sitting here?" he asked skeptically.

"They celebrated the breaking of the bread."

"And you partook of it?"

"Of the bread of the spirit."

She was staring before her once more as though he were bodiless, as though he were not there, and suddenly he was filled with a fierce jealousy of the intrusion. Why had they not come when he was there, that they might have discussed some possible action as to how to rescue her, instead of in his absence, to work on the overwrought senses of this poor sick woman?

"But didn't they tell you," he persisted, impatient now, "of some refuge? Didn't they tell you of a way of escape? We have need of it, Honoria."

"There is no escape," she answered, "but that which loosens us from the bond of flesh."

"It may be loosened for us any moment. Within three days our lives will be forfeit."

"What are our lives worth," she cried, "while daily we create our fetters?"

"What fetters?" he asked.

"The fetters of desire—of lust."

A moment passed before he answered. "I thought those fetters had been loosened long ago, Honoria, if ever they began to exist."

Her face, but for the eyes burning deep in their cadaverous sockets, was of stone. "On earth all partnership between man and woman must be sin."

Sin? He had not pretended to himself that, on his part, it had been otherwise, had not tried to justify in his own eyes the unthinking selfishness that had let him woo her for no other reason than that, by banking on her certain refusal, he might spite his father. Yet when he would have freed her, it was she who had held him to the bond.

"Was it I who bound you, Honoria?" he asked.

"No," she muttered. "Not you."

"Then why—why did you—?"

"That I might lead you to the light—or so I thought."

(That she might fetter his spirit, though she had abhorred his flesh. He had known it all along and accepted it as a just retribution.)

"But it was a delusion," she continued. "I cheated myself. All the time it was my desire I was fostering, my hidden yearnings, my lust."

"For what, Honoria?" Unbelievable as her words

seemed, they roused in him a strange emotion, a hope of what he scarcely knew. But already with her next utterance it had died.

"My love for Sicard—my sin, my wicked desire."

"Sicard . . . ?" he echoed, nonplused.

"Yes. Sicard," she repeated. Her voice had sunk to a mere whisper. "You never knew—I wished him dead—before he fell at Muret—so that he could not force me to return to the world."

"You wished him—dead—your brother?" Wolf was gazing at her in horror, but her face was rapt.

"Yes. Dead—dead—dead." She seemed held fast, gripped in some strange and terrible fascination. "But that was not my sin. The *bonshommes* made that clear. All these years I have been blinding myself in expiation for an imagined sin. For what sin is there in wishing another the one and only release?" She drew a deep breath and continued in a voice of almost hysterical hate. "I was destined for the life of the spirit. For Sicard's sake, I told myself, I returned to Durban, for Sicard's sake, I married you. But it was only to drag him back with me to earth, to the life for which in secret I lusted."

For Sicard's sake. . . . Through the mad confession of her world, the face of a brown-haired, tousled faun mocked at him with its satyr's grin. Had the fervent plea of a fey youth at the battle of Muret such powers that it could entangle itself in another's guilt, in the grudge of a bastard war-scourged son against his father, the distorted yearnings of an adolescent girl? And all, he reflected with bitter irony, might resolve itself, in the last issue, into the failure of a boy's caprice to rescue his sister from her Cathar school.

"We are all guilty, Honoria," he murmured, "all three of us—God knows."

"We are all blinded," she cried, 'blinded by the false rays of the deluding day. But the night is coming, the night in which all delusions will vanish." Her voice, which had risen almost ecstatically, subsided once more into a mysterious singsong. "They are coming for me at dawn—when the sky lightens, but it will not be the same sun. They are coming for me at the break of the true day—and it will be a beginning, not an end."

"A beginning . . . ?" he echoed to himself in agony. What beginning? He had no doubt now that she was raving.

But she was looking straight at him with a sly intensity, as if she were drawing him into a plot. "They are sending the sisters to fetch me—they have a secret house at Las Saltat. Later they will bring me to safety, and I shall found a greater hostel in another land. You don't believe me?" she added querulously.

"I believe you," he answered without conviction. But what, indeed, it struck him forcibly, could he believe after the events of this night and this day? If she was mad, so was he. "And I?" he asked with mockery.

"You—" She seemed like one returning from a long distance, trying to recall a message of importance with which she had been entrusted a long time since. "You—" And then suddenly she appeared to remember. "You, too, will receive the call. The *bonshommes* promised. Perhaps, they said, you might even have received it already. . . ."

Already? At Foix perhaps? If her *bonshommes* had really existed, he reflected with bitter irony, they might well have boasted the second sight with which many of the Cathars were credited. If he told her of that visit, it struck him suddenly, she might well be shaken out of her delusions and he would know whether she or he had any sanity left.

"Would you like to know what call I received today at Foix?"

"At Foix?" She was struggling to remember and slowly a look of fearful suspicion crept into her face. "At Foix—you have been there?"

Only ruthlessness alone, he knew, might save her now. "At Foix—Roger sent for me." In a few brief words he told her of his rencontre with Guy de Lévis.

Even while he was speaking, the lifeless mask of her face began gradually to disrupt under the stress of a dawning comprehension and fear.

Must he hurt her so to bring her to her senses?

"You . . . accepted?"

"You need not ask," he ended gently, "what my answer was."

Christ, he thought, watching that tortured convulsive face. What agonies must he have caused her in the past? "How can you doubt, Honoria, how for a moment could you ever imagine I could betray our faith?"

"Betray?" She raised her hand to her brow as if struggling to find clarity, wrestling with the conflicting emotions that raged in her poor benighted brain. And then suddenly the look of terror vanished and turned to an almost visionary ecstasy. "But don't you see," she cried in triumph, "it was the sign?"

"The sign?"

Had he not learned in all those years to know her? Since he had miscalculated so completely the day on which he had wooed her, he reflected afterward, he might well have been prepared now, when he believed her only half responsible for her words.

"The sign—" She stood, swaying a little on her feet. Her eyes were closed. She spoke as though without seeing or hearing, listening only to the voice within. "They said the sign would be given—that I might find it different from what I had thought—the ways of God are inscrutable. . . . But even Roger saw it."

"Roger?" He gave a short, harsh laugh. "What Roger figures is the chance of my furnishing him with a secret cell where he can plot and intrigue and lay the foundation of another war."

"No, no . . ." She still stood, her eyes shut, talking as though in a trance. "Roger is only the means—the instrument by which the will of God is fulfilled, that there may still be a secret place where the light may shine through darkness, a shrine where they will preserve the faith. And you, you have been chosen to defend it—you among all others—Wolf. . . ." She took a step forward and staggered. Before he could catch her she fell crumpled on the floor.

It must be near dawn now. Beyond the open door a first faint shimmer defined the contour of the hills. But to Wolf, keeping his long vigil, the promise it held out seemed as chimerical as the hallucinations of the woman lying in the bed.

She was sleeping now more calmly, perhaps, than on any night since she had fallen ill. When she woke, he persuaded himself at moments, she might even be cured. Cured of what—the insane delusions of the last night, the paralyzing inertia of the foregoing months, the fevered relentless intransigence of years of self-castigation and despair—a chain of which he could see no beginning or end but the flaw where he himself had soldered the link?

Yet she had existed before he stepped in her path, would exist beyond the moment where he trod out of it again, had existed with all the burden of her private agonies, her secret guilt, alone, separate from himself. That which he had thought insoluble could be broken after all, the fetters loosed.

Yet could they? Incredulous, he gazed at the worn, emaciated figure lying on the bed, that had lived by his side for all these years, yet that he had never embraced till tonight when she had lain in his arms unconscious.

There was a touch on his arm. Had he also for a brief moment slept?

Two women stood in the room—farmers' wives by their clothes, but under the wimple of one he recognized dimly the features of a sister who had served for a time in the hostel of Durban.

When they woke Honoria, she showed neither emotion nor surprise, but let herself be prepared for the voyage like a child, and what questions he himself asked of the women received answers so straightforward and simple that only his fears and doubts seemed unreal and unnatural.

When, a little time later, he stood at the top of the path gazing after the three figures riding away on their pack-laden mules into the uncertain light, it was as though he felt the anguish of one who has been emptied, drained of something he had never possessed.

DRIFTING

And you shall wake, from country sleep, this dawn and
each first dawn,
Your faith as deathless as the outcry of the ruled sun.

(DYLAN THOMAS: *Collected Poems*)

IT WAS THE LAST DOCUMENT. RUNNING HIS EYES OVER
master Gerald's meticulously written lines, Wolf of Foix
dipped the quill into the inkwell and scrawled his name at
the foot of the page; then, pushing it toward the scribe,
watched with weary fascination the movement of the thin,
punctilious fingers as they prepared the circle of gleaming
wax. Leaning forward, he imprinted his seal.

"You can go," he muttered mechanically.

But the clerk, stacking the parchments in a file, still
hesitated. He had become used to the fact that the governor of Ax, unlike his former masters, was not in the habit
of keeping him hanging about at his beck and call, nor
did he force him to ruin his eyesight hour upon hour deciphering barbarous script. Today, however, his voice had
sounded so preoccupied that he had his doubts.

True, it was the governor's habit to reread the more
important of the documents before they were dispatched
or their content put into effect, yet today there had
scarcely been one that refered to any but straightforward
matters. Surely he could spare himself such unnecessary
trouble and put more faith in his service. Master Gerald
reflected with mingled feelings of pique and puzzled respect. He'll wear himself out, he pondered, on the point
of suggesting that any necessary revision could be left to
him, but Wolf's next words nipped him in the bud.

"It's all right. You can go. I'll call you when I'm
ready."

Mumbling somewhat doubtful thanks, Master Gerald collected his tools.

For a few moments after he had gone, Wolf sat back in his chair gazing abstractedly into space; then with a visible effort he drew the topmost parchment toward him and, scanning the contents, pushed it aside, glanced at a couple of others, then returned them to the pile. A license for a traveling apothecary, two permits for Oriental merchants crossing the border from Spain, an authorization for the new building of the guildhouse on the market square, orders for a contingent of workmen from Andorra to improve the road over the pass. He had already interviewed the town clerk in regard to available funds. There was no necessity to reconsider the documents in question, scarcely any need to read them at all. He had learned in the course of a year that he could rely on Master Gerald well enough. And yet, as always, he was haunted by the fear that to show a minute's laxity, to let a single case of legislation pass without his endorsement, might spell disaster.

It was no doubt absurd, even a form of conceit. Had he, it struck him suddenly, come to lay such importance on his person, his very name? As though following the course of his thoughts, his eyes rested on his signature scrawled with such apparent abandonment at the foot of the page.

A few swift strokes, dragged obliquely upward and downward, a couple of loops and meanders sufficed, and there stood the magic formula that had power to judicate over a merchant's wares, the town's material prosperity, the penalty for some minor act of arson or theft; also, if it came to it, over a man's life or death.

It had not come to that yet, or, at least, the handful of more serious crimes that had occurred in the region of Ax—crimes that had involved the death penalty—he had been bound by fealty, after preliminary trial, to pass on to the courts of Mirepoix and Foix. Was he only evading the issue? he often asked himself. Did not the responsibility remain after all his own? How often he attempted to reassure himself that he had not made a single condemnation without inquiring into the circumstances, not only of the crime but of the criminal. A robber, a poacher, a cutthroat even—he had spent hours, days, nights in pursuing their history, with the result that many a wretch who before would surely have been seen dangling from the gallows had not only been set free but had received, into the bargain, the promise of work and a bundle of food and clothing for his starving family.

But was that much to boast of? he asked himself. What of those incorrigibles whom he had felt constrained to hand over to justice—such as it was called? Could he be sure he had investigated all the available evidence, let alone plumbed that secret depth of existence in which each man (had he not experienced it with horror in his own being?) is a stranger to himself?

And what of those sporadic cases of insurgency that had lately been cropping up more frequently in the surrounding hills—a brawl between a local farmer and one of Lévis' squires boasting at some wayside tavern of his master's prowess in battle, the failure of some stubborn baron to respond to the royal levies, the reputed insolence of a boy who had made mock of the French seneschal as he rode down the valley—those and a dozen far more trivial occurrences that scarcely merited serious punishment yet must be held in check or anywhere, any time the small flame of disorder might spread, grow to revolt, the peace be threatened, all the work of consolidation be undermined.

The peace . . . of which he was the acknowledged prop, the sworn upholder. Once more his eyes rested on the signature, the name that for years he had tried to disclaim as the hallmark of feudal prejudice, of perfidious compromise, and later of a bestial and revengeful war. How it had become a symbol of all that his ancestry had laughed to scorn. And yet, if Roger had been right, had not his father with his dying breath urged the very course he was himself following? But to what end—the old game of chicanery and diplomacy whose consummate master had been Raymond VI of Toulouse? He had never been able to convince himself that the peace his father envisaged had a different goal, and yet he knew well enough that to many of his countrymen he himself appeared probably no less despicable—the henchman of the aggrandizer, the pretended Cathar turning his doctrines of nonviolence to his own profitable ends.

There were moments when he himself had his doubts, if not of his mission itself, then of his power to fulfill it. And often he asked himself what actually had decided him to undertake it at all.

When, stunned by the shock of Honoria's departure, all responsibility had been so suddenly lifted from him that, scarcely aware what he was doing, he had surrendered his life to Roger, it had certainly been with no conscious thought of accepting Guy de Lévis' offer, nor, rather surprisingly, had his half brother shown any attempt to bring pressure upon him to do so. Instead, under the pretext of inspecting certain neglected estates, Roger had persuaded him to accompany him on a tour of the upper reaches of the Ariège. So he had found himself, for the first time since that day of horror, riding the same road through the Sabarthez, the road he had known only in rain and snow, white now with summer dust and shaded with forest, until, emerging from the trees, he had looked down on the fort with its three gray towers insubstantial as ghosts in the heat haze, faintly outlined against the shimmering silver of the lake. Were they really the same as those that had haunted his sleep, his waking dreams for years? Even if he had wanted to make sure, even if he had braced himself to ride down the narrow track, knock at that shut, too well-remembered door, Roger had not given him the chance. Talking, always talking of the arrogance of the French and grudgingly admitting that the one and only hope lay in maintaining the good will of Guy de Lévis, he had led on past the fort, past Lordat and across the Col into the higher valley of the Ariège.

By twilight they had reached Ax. Even as they rode through the narrow streets between the cramped, gray houses, crushed as though by guilt between the converging hills, even as they crossed the drawbridge to the governor's castle and his heart sickened at the sight of the churning water beneath, he had known it had to be. Only here, if he set his will to meet it, could the flood be dammed, only by the bulwark of peace and understanding that he would build could these seething waters be prevented from ever again carrying out their terrible work of destruction. "Quite symbolic—the memorial of a friendship"—but even Roger had ceased to mock.

Had it dawned on him then that the responsibility even for his half brother's actions rested with him, so that whatever might be Roger's ulterior motives, they might yet be led into better channels? Had he, swept off his feet by the sheer incredibility of it all, been plunged into a fit of self-exaltation? "Don't you see you are chosen . . . ?" Perhaps after all it was Honoria's poor distraught brain that had possessed the power to register those motives that lay beyond rational comprehension.

In how far had he been urged by will, by faith, by ambition or superhuman compulsion? He did not know even now, yet if faith played no part, he might as well give up. What counted, after all, was what he was achieving—little enough, God knew.

His own political power was worth next to nil. The most he could do was to try to hold Roger, who was always ready to kick against the pricks, in check, with wry amusement he reflected on the advantage he had won over his half brother who, terrified above all that Ax would be handed over to the French, had several times been enticed to follow his lead. Guy de Lévis, for his part, had on the whole proved reasonable, yet the horizon grew no lighter and out beyond the Ariège things were supposed to happen that made him quail to think he was accepting power from French hands. Yet, to cast the onus on the blameless was as good as inviting evil where it did not exist and, in his own small sphere, by struggling to maintain order, was he not in fact, Wolf persuaded himself, fostering the last hope of liberty of conscience and true peace? The marshal (whether merely to gain popularity or not) was averse to all religious persecution. As long as he did not actively foster or protect the heretics, Wolf knew that the Sabarthez might remain their safest refuge—as long as he kept silent, blind to what he apprehended and mute to all he heard whispered. Was he serving two masters? It struck him sometimes with disgust. Was he in fact playing less of a double game spiritually than Roger would have had him play politically, if he could? The Cathars knew well enough that they could receive no open support in Ax—that all traffic that passed through the town would be subjected rigorously to the strictest censor at the city gates. Yet they knew also that beyond the confines of the walls, no watch would be set on their tracks.

Skeptically his eye fell once more on the documents before him. They represented the chief field of his activity—trivial, material realities, while outside, the vast sum of evil piled ever higher.

With a movement of weary despair he pushed the parchments aside and, rising to his feet, crossed to the window.

Beyond the small tributary stream that emptied itself at the foot of the castle, the hills rose, terrace on terrace, on one side toward the unwieldy mass of the Tabor, on the other to the passes leading into the territory of the Aude. Obscured by the black felt of pine trees, the rock was visible only here and there—a stony ledge of soil gilded by the light of the late afternoon. How often he had longed to ride up there to the small estate of Ascou that he had received as fief. The village was poor and barren enough, perched on an edge of windswept cliff, and below, the meadows sloped too steeply to the brook lost amid thicket and scrub. Yet he had come to love the estate as he had never loved Durban, though there had been no time to spend on its development. Even if there were, he wondered, would he try to extend its limits into the forest that barred it to north and east? The woods of Durban had stood waiting, silent, inimical. Amid destruction they would still stand remote, inimical, and wait. But these? He was not sure. He had scarcely had a chance of exploring them yet. The peasants said that they were boundless, that they extended beyond Le Peire, beyond the Col di Chioula through the gorges under the Tabor, across the pass of Pradel. And if anyone ever reached the end he would find himself not in the territory of Ariège or Aude but in . . . who knows? They shook their heads in question, muttering something about the Selva encantada. Well, he smiled wearily, it was unlikely he would ever have time to penetrate its depths, let alone solve the mystery of its enchantment. Yet just today he was moved by an uncontrollable desire to venture into the unknown. And if he lost himself . . . all the better perhaps. Why not ride up to Ascou this very evening? As if the wish had already given birth to its fulfillment, footsteps were actually sounding along the corridor. Probably the clerk, guessing he must by now have finished, had returned to fetch the scrolls. Expectantly he turned toward the door, but when it opened a minute later, it was not to reveal the pinched and meager form of Master Gerald but the rugged weathered countenance of one of the guards from the Andorran Gate.

"Beg pardon, Senhor, but I thought it best to let you know at once."

"Yes—what?" Wolf's expression resolved itself once more into one of harassed weariness.

"As fine a bird as we're likely to catch in a twelve-month." The malignant triumph was so sharply reflected on the man's coarse but generally good-natured features that Wolf felt a qualm of terror.

"A Cathar?" he muttered.

"That's to be seen." Master Jehan was no brute, but the primitive lust for the successful man hunt apparently held him in thrall.

Wolf shuddered. He could still hardly hear of the tracking down of the meanest tramp without conjuring up the image of Berengar. "Have you got him here?" His voice sounded harsh with apprehension.

"Below." The man jerked his thumb downward. "A regular trickster. Says he's from Spain. But I reckon the place he comes from is blacker than any that vomited even their murky heathen souls. We've got him though," he added with renewed gusto, "for all his impudence and his box full of devils' tricks."

Some poor traveling juggler probably, toiling along from Andorra with a caseful of horoscopes and Moorish charms, it struck Wolf with a certain relief. "Didn't he tell you his trade?" he asked sharply.

"Trade—only the devil knows what trade *he's* in. But I know this much." The man glanced behind him apprehen-

211

sively. "Whatever it is and whatever he carries with him's not fit by his own telling for Christian folks to meddle with."

"But what does he want? Where is he bound for?" Wolf retorted.

"He's on his way to Toulouse—or so he says—" Master Jehan slapped his thigh in self-approval—"at the express invitation of the count."

"Toulouse—and what if he is?" Wolf was roused to anger now. "If he reports what treatment he received at the hands of the town guard of Ax, who will it be finds himself in custody then?"

"Little fear." With a knowing grin the man advanced a step into the room. "Trust me to know a bad 'un when I meet him and him down there's as dark and ugly a bird as ever was made, and foul-mouthed at that. It'll need three barrelfuls of holy water to wash the room clean behind him."

Master Jehan crossed himself. He laid stress on his orthodoxy, since his post depended upon it, and the profession of gatekeeper proved lucrative. "In any case—" as if to impart knowledge of a confidential nature he drew still nearer—"they won't dare make trouble. They say the Count of Toulouse was used from boyhood to unchristian ways. Maybe in the last years he's turned a pious face toward the clerics, but they don't trust him and if he's up to his tricks again they'll soon get wind of it. Him down there—" he lowered his thumb as before— "won't help him."

"You'd better bring him up," Wolf returned impatiently.

"And his pack?" The gatekeeper's look grew apprehensive.

"Wares and all—and be quick about it."

With a sigh Wolf turned once more to the window. Another delay, he reflected, and God knows where it would end. More investigations, more passes to be drawn up and signed. Was Ramonet, it struck him with a certain acrid amusement, toying once more with the charms of the East? What a chance he might have considered it once, to have spoiled the fun of a Toulouse. But the onus would probably only have fallen back on the poor wretch. Moreover, he'd most likely prove an impostor, in which case, if nothing worse could be brought against him, the best would be to let him go with a warning that he would be punished if he was found making mischief in the countryside. They were long enough bringing him up— taking their delight no doubt in tormenting the miserable creature and inciting him to new rogueries. But perhaps his sympathy was premature, Wolf mocked himself, hearing the volley of abuse that followed a crashing thud outside. Even if the words were uttered in Castilian, their meaning was easily deduced. At the same time Wolf wondered what it was in the tone of voice that made it vaguely familiar. The next moment the door was flung open.

"Take care!" The speaker had changed over now to the idiom of Languedoc.

Still turned to the window, Wolf was aware that the following words were addressed to him.

"If your henchmen won't respect my person, they would be advised at their own risk not to maltreat my wares."

Wolf swung slowly round. For a moment he stood staring blankly at the dark, travel-stained figure who stood under the arch of the doorway, gripped in the vice of two steel-clad arms.

The features that confronted him were doubtless at any time not likely to prove prepossessing; now, contorted with anger, they were probably at their worst. Even so, the mouth, pulled (by force of habit or nature) slightly sideways above the wedge-like jaw, suggested not so much fury as a loathing and disdain so intense that it created for its possessor a complete isolation from all human relationships. And yet, even as Wolf gazed at it with a peculiar horrified fascination, the sense of familiarity increased, till suddenly from under the incongruously fine molding of temple and brow, the eyes narrowed and the lips yielded to a sardonic grin.

"D'Alfaro! Let go!" he commanded, as the guards still hung on to their victim. "They never told me," he stammered, taking a step in the direction of the now liberated

213

prisoner. "Be off with you!" he cried as the men still loitered while the gatekeeper shot apprehensive glances at the two chests that he and a third guardsman had deposited on the floor. When they had departed, Wolf still stood, rooted to the spot.

The newcomer, on the other hand, as if already oblivious of his recent tormentors, advanced into the room with the nonchalance of a customary visitor entering familiar halls. "If I hadn't been promised a royal reception by the governor of Ax, I might have taken trouble to insure my goods."

"Promised—?" Somewhat recovered from his initial shock, Wolf, completely baffled by the last words but feeling he was somehow mysteriously implicated, attempted to express concern, but as though recoiling from any demonstration of human sympathy, his visitor turned aside and, pulling off his cloak, flung it on the chair Wolf had recently vacated.

"Merely one of Mirepoix's fantasies," he shrugged. "In his letter he advised me to travel over the Andorran pass. I could rest assured of a hearty welcome from the governor of Ax." He turned and fixed the other with a look of satirical scrutiny. "I never guessed it was you."

Mirepoix, Wolf was thinking. Who but he could have possessed the resilience to have wriggled so easily out of every compromising situation, to have made a joke of it and to his own advantage? But very probably his ephemeral conscience had long ago forgotten that it was due to d'Alfaro's brusque handling of his insouciant vagaries that a young fool of the name of Wolf of Foix had once owed his life.

Perhaps some of the same thoughts flitted through the Spaniard's mind as his gaze searched the features of the man before him, curious as to whether they revealed more of the marks of pathological hatred that had contorted the face of the boy from whom he had parted years ago—the face of a boy wounded to the quick by the death of Trencavel and Mirepoix's shattering of a first rhapsodic love, or that of the moonstruck lad who, in the preceding months, had so often been the target of his ironic sallies. But the scars of pain, disillusion, self-inflicted torment,

214

and sheer weariness had so blurred the expression of any defined emotion that he gave up the task and bent instead over the wooden chests which had caused Master Jehan such alarm.

"They've probably smashed the lot," he remarked ruefully, dropping onto the chair.

"But didn't you explain your business?" Wolf asked somewhat nervously. Even after all these years, the presence of the man whose iconoclastic destruction of every belief had, as a boy, so infuriated yet fascinated him, left him ill at ease.

"To judge from Peire-Roger's letter," d'Alfaro returned, "he'd arranged everything. I quite forgot I ought to have royal credentials before venturing into the territories of the Count of Toulouse. Well, after all, perhaps *you* can supply them." His glance, traveling round the room, caught the row of parchments spread on the table before him. "They would probably prove more valuable, in the long run, than the patronage of the defunct."

Were the words, it flashed through Wolf's mind, intended as a thrust at his position or were they merely those of the cynic intent on getting everything he could from a world he despised?

"Why on earth didn't you give them your name?" he evaded. "They would have told me—"

"I wasn't too sure of the effects, seeing how things had begun. One never knows what Peire-Roger's up to. Besides—" D'Alfaro gave a short truncated laugh—"a name's an imponderable quantity. One isn't always too certain where it's going to land you—that is, who's going to take the lead—you or it—at least if you've gone separate ways for the best part of your lifetime."

Before Wolf's mind flitted the memory of the renegade student ensconced in self-imposed penury in the slums of Narbonne, raging against eight hundred years of genealogical tyranny. "You mean—you've become reconciled to your ancestry at last?"

"No more than to anything else. But at times even the undesirable can prove useful." Leaning his elbow on the table, d'Alfaro flicked a fragment of sealing wax across the board. In so doing, his eye caught the repeated signa-

215

ture inscribed on the sheets of parchment. "You evidently have plenty of experience," he smiled wryly, "you might initiate me. 'Lupus de Fuxo, governor of Ax'—it sounds formidable enough."

The irony was incontestable now. But actually it was not of the present but the past that Hugo d'Alfaro was thinking. "So the monkling's turned into the wolf and lived up to his name after all." He laughed freely now, leaning back in the chair.

Wolf guessed well enough of what the other was thinking—the green young squire of Trencavel's court—the runaway novice whom everyone had teased on account of his absurdly inappropriate name. But through and above the shrill mocking chorus, one voice, strangely husky yet compelling, penetrated through all the rest. "Wolf—why ever did they call you that?" Out of the moonlit mask of white carved ivory, the dark enigmatic eyes of Miriam Caravita were turned on his. "Mind you live up to it and save us from the Franks." With a sudden movement Wolf thrust his foot against the nearer of the two chests.

"What have you got in there?" he asked abruptly.

"The way to eternal bliss—or blissful extinction. It's just a matter of how one looks at things." Drawing out a key, the Spaniard bent forward and fitted it into the lock.

Whatever he was after, Wolf reflected, it was evident that d'Alfaro hadn't yielded a jot of the paradoxical cynicism he had boasted in his student days at Narbonne. "Extinction or whatever you may like to call it," he retorted, stung to something like the rebelliousness that Hugo's cynicism had so often aroused in him years ago, "you managed right enough to instill the devil of terror into my poor men."

"Probably. Their idea of the Evil One just about equals the palpable image of their own ignorance."

"Which it's amusing but somewhat costly to gull," Wolf replied, perceiving, not without a mite of satisfaction, the havoc wrought among the bottles and jars revealed by the now open case. "Do you mean to say you deserted law in favor of alchemy?" he added, scanning the names inscribed on the labels.

D'Alfaro grinned. "I've dabbled in them both and even

inhaled a whiff of theology. On the whole I've come to the conclusion alchemy's infinitely superior to both—less redolent of human casuistry."

"But more of the infernal regions." Wolf made a face at the stench that escaped from the broken pots. "No wonder the poor fellows thought you'd bundled Satan into your baggage."

"Hm—in some ways they were nearer the truth than they imagined." Snatching at random a piece of parchment from the table, Hugo d'Alfaro rolled it up and whisked the crocks and scattered powders on to the floor. Then, thrusting aside the debris with his foot, he brooded gloomily over the unscathed remains. "There's stuff in there, or was, might make your Greek fire mere child's play by comparison. All your ramparts, your machicolated towers, your drawbridges and portcullises won't help you. Fly up in the air as so much dust."

Seeking refuge from the pungent odors emanating from the alchemical mystery box, Wolf had moved back to the window. Sounding from the depths of the room, the threat of mass annihilation uttered with almost sardonic glee contrasted so strangely with the beauty of the waning day that it seemed almost meaningless.

"Hasn't there been destruction enough without your fantasies?" he asked wearily.

Relocking the chest, Hugo d'Alfaro rose to his feet. "It's a matter of relative terms. The worst we've managed so far is probably a petty skirmish compared with what's to come. All the maraudings of Attila are missing so far—towns and cities reduced to a shambles—a vast human bonfire."

"We had Béziers," Wolf muttered grimly, "if that's what you want."

"Béziers? A dozen, a hundred Béziers all over the land, through the whole world, and not a sword stroke necessary—"

"It wasn't needed even there."

"Hm—thanks to the dear prelates' idea of civilian murder minus the sword. But the new weapon will render even armed defense effete and futile. The holocaust's complete. You may as well surrender at once. Actually," he added, "it may be the one way to bring people to their senses."

"You mean stop war through sheer terror?"

D'Alfaro made a questioning gesture and leaned against the chimney piece. "Nothing else is likely to be successful."

"Successful?" Wolf echoed dully. "What will fear create but more fear, hate and more hate unto eternity?"

"Inevitably. In short, the old vicious circle—Man will wreck himself anyway."

"And so the best fun you can get out of life is to hasten the process?" Wolf retorted, remembering how in the old days Hugo had goaded him to fury in the same way by his cynical refutation of all values. "Resistance for the sake of resistance." Now it was destruction for the sake of destruction. "Is that what you've been employed in down in Spain?" he asked bitterly.

"The invention of explosives?" D'Alfaro gave him a quizzical look, guessing his thoughts. "I'm not altogether unique in my diabolic propensities. They say they've possessed the secret for centuries away in the Far East, but their rulers won't allow its use except for festivities. Christ, what a show! Cascades of colored fire, whirlpools of spattering flame illuminating the night."

The tension on Wolf's face relaxed. After all, the majority of Hugo's statements had to be taken with a grain of salt.

"Do you intend enhancing Ramonet's galas with your fireworks?" he asked mockingly.

"Or explode the whole blessed Capet realm?" D'Alfaro shrugged. "The question is whether one rotten dynasty is worth the other. Even Ramonet, when it comes to it, would probably have his doubts; violent measures were never to his taste, unless he could play a decorative part on a caracoling steed. Gunpowder's far too anonymous. Anyhow," he paused, grinning as though he had held back the anticlimax to torment his hearer, "I'm not actually in the position to give him the chance—at least not yet. Old Abdul Hassan wouldn't let me into the secret. The ingredients *may* be in there—he left me the stuff on his deathbed, but he took care to destroy the formula. He belonged to the civilized—like the rulers of Cathay. Christ! Fancy having the chance of blowing your enemies to pieces and foregoing it. Or perhaps they're right. It would only add to the mess unless you destroyed the whole world."

"Or rather the universe," Wolf put in. "All the immeasurable space of the heavens, since some say we go journeying on to the stars."

"Isn't one tour of duty enough?" D'Alfaro's lips curled in an expression of utter disgust. "One would think even Satan would sicken of his experiment by the world's end."

"If so," Wolf retorted, "he might be ready to relinquish his hold and let the divine spark find its way back to its origin."

"To what—the Divine Intelligence perhaps? As well speak of law and order in this confounded world."

It was as in the old days at Carcassonne and Narbonne. They could go on arguing into the early hours of the morning, yet somehow, little as he would have relished the thought of d'Alfaro's visit had he known of it in advance, he was almost beginning to feel reconciled to his presence. Nevertheless, he realized with wistful irony that his projected visit to Ascou was once more vanishing into smoke, for even if he might find the intrusion of Hugo's anarchic cynicism a stimulus here in the gloomy restriction of the castle of Ax, it would be a different matter amid the magic of those woods. He turned to the other with slightly more than a half-hearted show of hospitality.

"You're staying the night? Ax is more like a guardroom than a palace, but it can provide a bed."

As Wolf had imagined, they talked late into the night till gradually his constraint lessened. There was no question, he soon realized, of d'Alfaro harboring the least suspicions regarding the post he held as governor of Ax. The scorn that, in the old days, he had hurled at the defunct civilization of Languedoc had not lessened with the years. If Wolf had then been uncertain as to how far the Spaniard's return to his own country had been activated by a genuine loathing of tyranny or merely by boredom, pique, and a refusal to brook any interference with his own will,

he had no illusions about his return. Acknowledging neither love nor respect for any but a few isolated individuals
(and those belonged to history or to a despised and
persecuted race), he was evidently left after the death of
his Arab teacher amid a vacuum that, for the moment at
least, he was ready to fill with any adventure and in the
service of the bidder who offered the highest price.

"After all," he laughed, "I haven't wandered so far
from the tracks of my ancestry—the unmentionable line
of course. I'm a mercenary to my fingertips—only an intellectual one."

That he expected the price for his services to be paid
likewise in intellectual currency Wolf surmised well
enough, but Hugo was still apparently as far from admitting to nobler motives as he was from confessing to any
tender emotion.

Suddenly Wolf was back again in the preposterously
opulent palace of the rabbi at Narbonne while Miriam
Caravita, stretched like some odalisque on her divan, dis-
sected the characters of her friends: "Hugo? He's too
much infatuated with his own personality ever to fall in
love." He tried to conceive her as d'Alfaro had depicted
her tonight—the fecund wife of a Jewish physician at
Montpellier. There was no connection between the image
(if he could conceive it at all) and that which inhabited
his memory, yet even the remembered image split and
shivered into two, the feline, seductive scion of an ancient,
skeptical race and the brilliant indefatigable champion of
enlightenment and emancipation. But when he tried to
weld them to an entity, he saw only a kaleidoscope of
ever-changing facets whose sharp shifting points had once
wounded him to the quick. Now only the pattern remained. He marveled himself that he had actually
managed to talk of her. One day, perhaps, he would be
able to conceive the present in the same way. At moments
already, the thought of Honoria had contracted to a
picture graven on his memory, gray on gray, so that with
an effort he had forced himself to conceive the woman
caged in her prison house of sick fantasies till he was
shot through with live pain. Only a year ago, it flashed
through his mind, he had been praying he might at last
220

attain to a state of true detachment. Did it consist only of two alternatives—that sense of shadowy remoteness or d'Alfaro's cynicism? Suddenly he felt a terrible need to strip him of what even now might possibly prove a pose. He leaned forward to replenish the other's goblet.

"Is your goal really Toulouse?"

"Goal?" Hugo returned, characteristically contemptuous. "Is there any such thing?" But the unexpectedness with which the question had been spoken, added to the sudden tenseness in Wolf's voice, caused him to look up. As he did so his eyes narrowed in ironic amusement. "Christ, you don't mean to say you're still on the quest?"

"Quest—what quest?" Wolf echoed, and the note of interrogation was as much a shield to the other's cynicism as it was to his own doubt.

"Galahad's—or was it Parzival's?" The heavy lips twisted in disdain while the eyes continued their ironic scrutiny.

Wolf was holding the wine jug in his right hand. Crimson drops splashed over the goblet's edge. The bronze ewer was heavy. He changed it to his left.

Life has done its best to cripple Wolf, body and spirit, it flashed through d'Alfaro's mind, and suddenly the numbed yet ineradicable look of hunger on the other's face roused him to sick fury against existence, as once long ago the sight of a boy's too eager, vulnerable face contorted by hatred and disillusion had stirred him to curse the very God his intellect refuted. But compassion was an emotion Hugo never allowed himself to indulge in, either at his own or another's expense.

"Hasn't the ship foundered yet?" he mocked with deliberate ruthlessness. "Centuries wrecked on the old delusion and still you go on inventing it afresh. Galahad, Parzival, Bors, Bran, and the rest of them. All setting out in search of the Isles of the Blesséd and the Grand Ideal. But the tragedy is," he added with diabolic zest, "not that you don't get there or that, getting there, it's only to die or never be seen again, but that the whole damned enterprise is just an illusion. No goal, no quest. You just drift. For a

221

moment, maybe, you clutch at a rotten spar and delude yourself into thinking it's a royal galleon sailing full speed ahead, but at best it's a raft without rudder and oars and you're no better than a bit of flotsam tossed about as the wind lists."

Wolf had turned away. Bent over the table while his fingers played with the scattered crumbs, his face was half hidden. "At that rate," he muttered, "you don't believe in free will."

"Will?" Hugo laughed aloud. "I've lived too long among Orientals for that. Allah, the stars, divine necessity—call it what you like. In the long run it'll get you where it wants."

"You mean you have no choice?"

"Fundamentally, no. You have the illusion, of course. Actually, you're bound to make the choice you do."

"In short, you're predestined—" Wolf stared unseeing at the crumbs in his fingers—"to Heaven or to Hell."

"If you like to call it that. For my part it smacks too much of punishment and reward. Man can't help imbuing God with his pigmy mentality."

"Agreed. Nonetheless—" suddenly Wolf raised his head and fixed the other's eyes as if in challenge—your argument reduces man's responsibility to nil. In other words, man is mere nothing."

D'Alfaro grimaced. "Rather less than nothing. Nothingness, after all, is an imposing concept, so imposing in fact as to be almost Satanic. In his own estimation man may be a Titan; in reality he's no more than a flea kicking in the void. A flea," he repeated, reveling in the bathos of his imagery, "a flea sucking at sheer nothingness and fancying it's a nice luscious thigh."

"And when he realizes it's only nothingness," Wolf queried, "does he cease to be a flea?"

"Let's hope," the other shrugged, "he's entered on the first step of initiation."

"Into what—his own sense of superiority, or extinction?"

D'Alfaro paused a moment before answering. The monkling, he reflected, had evidently grown up, but he advanced to his *pointe* undeterred. "The realization of complete futility."

There was a long silence. Suddenly Wolf got to his feet and took a few paces up and down the room. "Why go on then?"

"Exactly."

Why? To Wolf the question seemed to ring on into the shadows, gathering round his head, in ever-tightening circles, wave on wave. The cause for which he had fought, vainly enough in the past, the faith in which he had tried to find an anchor, the despised and perhaps hopeless task to which he had devoted himself in the last year—were they indeed, as d'Alfaro insisted, mere egoistic illusion? He had already believed so once, in those nightmare hours that had brought him to the verge of destruction in the Sabarthez. Through the grace of a small red-haired child he had returned to the world, believing if not, as once, in the triumph of absolute goodness or a reachable goal, then at least in man's power to choose a way. Did his renewed failures, the terrible irony of his relationship to Honoria, the seeming uselessness of his present work not prove d'Alfaro right? And yet the more his doubt found resonance, the more, for some inexplicable reason, did it seem to awaken in him a strange resistance. Suddenly a thought dawned on him—a mere pinpoint of light at the farthermost end of a tunnel, yet it seemed to cut through the meshes of d'Alfaro's argument like the point of a spear. He turned back to the table and as he spoke his voice held almost a note of triumph.

"Do you remember, Hugo, one day long ago you mocked in just the same way? 'Resist for the sake of honor. Resist for the sake of the Cause. Or merely for the sake of resisting.' I loathed you for it then. Well, perhaps you were right. The first two may prove an illusion. As to the third . . . after all, it may be worth something." He paused, catching his breath. "Resistance—even in the face of futility. Suppose, whatever you say, it's just that that makes us human?"

"Human?" Hugo d'Alfaro's voice seemed to express the acme of disgust, but the cynical thrust that had already sprung to his lips remained unspoken. Instead he opened his mouth in a wide yawn.

"Fool," he muttered a little later as he lay shifting his awkward limbs on the rough mattress. "Fool," he repeated to himself the following morning as he rode northward over the Col di Chioula. But his scorn, though he would not have admitted it, did not lack a touch of envy.

THE SERPENT

Time and the hour runs through the roughest day.

(SHAKESPEARE: *Macbeth*)

And, like a lobster boiled the morn
From black to red began to turn.

(BUTLER: *Hudibras*)

IN HIS LETTER URGING HIM TO TRAVEL VIA AX, MIREPOIX
had suggested that d'Alfaro should pick him up at the
Pérelhas, whence, if the heat was not insufferable, they
could set out together for Toulouse. He should find him
therefore at Lavelanet or Roccafissada. Probably at neither, Hugo demurred, fairly confident that Peire-Roger,
for all the sobering influence of matrimony, had not
changed his ubiquitous habits. "You'll be amused by my
worthy in-laws," Mirepoix had added in parenthesis.
Would he? The encouragement, for all he knew, might
entail another of those little jests of which he had lately
been the victim—not entirely to his regret, Hugo
conceded as, skeptically, he approached the manor of
Lavelanet.

As he had expected, it was only to be informed that the
Pérelhas were spending the summer season in their
mountain fortress. His inquiries concerning Peire-Roger
were received with a shrug. He had certainly accompanied
the family when they set out. Whether he had remained
was another question. Popular opinion apparently tallied
with his own. For the moment he hesitated, but
considering that in the blistering heat Toulouse nor the
journey across the treeless plain held much to recommend
them, he decided to leave his baggage at Lavelanet and
ride up into the hills. Somehow, whether it was due to his
meeting with Wolf, the return to the land he had so long
abandoned, the escape from years of intellectual incarcer-

ation, or merely to the effect of this wild forested country after the barren plateau of Castile, he was tempted to linger. Was there, after all, he asked himself wryly, some significance in experiences not plumbable by the intellect? But that was luxury—he was yielding to the deadly sin of *luxuria,* he grinned, recalling his acquaintance with the terms of theology. As if to put his thoughts into practice, he egged on his flagging mount. But the road was steep and the horse but an old nag that had served him all the way from Toledo. After a moment's effort it fell back into its lethargic pace. Indeed, it almost seemed as if the beast was laming. Cursing his lack of foresight in having failed to see to its shoeing, Hugo looked ahead up the road that, having just emerged from thick forest, appeared to spiral through a blazing track of mountain grass before it lost itself once more behind some trees. Above them the hill seemed suddenly to end in a shelf before it made the last spasmodic effort to reach the height where, planted on a pedestal of rock, Pérelha's fort certainly justified its name.

Hugo groaned aloud and, dismounting, inspected the horse's hoofs. As he had surmised, one of the irons had loosened itself. Without his weight the beast would probably be able to go on for a time—there might well be some sort of village at the foot of the castle crag. After all, the animal had served him well enough all these weeks, he reflected as, taking it by the bridle, he stoically plunged into the simmering cauldron of the white noonday heat.

It took him more than an hour to cross the blazing meadows. When at last the road reached the comparative shelter of a bank of beech and hazel, he stopped in relief, but after letting the animal graze a moment, he cajoled it on. Best get on to the bitter end, he muttered, digging it good-humoredly in the ribs. "You've no illusions about Paradise, but at least you'll get your earthly Elysium of grass."

Their progress became ever slower, for the road, growing appreciably steeper now, wound interminably on, little more than a track of wheel-scarred rock and loosened stone that in winter might well turn to a rushing stream. At last, turning abruptly, they were once more in the open, but beyond some few hundred meters of cultivated field, the sloping tiles of housetops shone red above patches of barley and a screen of trellised vines. Something to drink, he thought, licking his blistered lips, Mirepoix or no Mirepoix. All that mattered at the moment was a cup of wine. With a last effort he lured the reluctant beast along the broiling track that now led close to the edge of the abyss.

The village, if it was worthy of the name, consisted, it seemed, of a few shacks grouped so as to form three sides of a square, the front of which lay open to the precipiced shelf of rock on which it stood. The houses themselves consisted in point of fact of little more than a kind of appendage to the massive fort that towered above them, approachable by no path that was visible. It might, as far as Hugo cared, have remained as inaccessible as an enchanted castle of dream. He was going no farther. Someone in one or the other of those hovels could doubtless see to the horse; as for himself, he needn't even go as far. Shade, that was all that mattered; and water might, after all, do as well as wine. He stood staring half incredulous at the great tree that rose in the middle of the square, stretching its arms in a vast canopy while from its roots a spring of water jetted into a natural basin formed by the underhung rock. No wonder, he reflected wryly, that man, for all his transcendental illusions, had given them a sound enough symbol in the tree of life. As footsore almost as his horse, he limped across to the shade. "It will do equally for both of us," he laughed and, letting go the bridle, bent and, cupping his hands, splashed the water into his mouth; then, flinging himself on the bank, half closed his eyes. He won't wander far, he commented to himself drowsily, half aware of the beast lapping the water beneath his head.

It was still lapping, or no—had he perhaps slept? he thought, suddenly aware of a sharper sound—a human footstep, the chink of a vessel set down on stone. He rolled over on his elbow and lazily opened his eyes. A woman? A girl, to judge by the two loose braids of hair that fell down her back. Her face was hidden as she stood stooping low over the spring. Perhaps it was only his sudden reawakening to the light that made her hair dance before his eyes like threads of flame. He laughed aloud and so suddenly that the second pitcher she was filling almost dropped from her hand.

Startled, she had drawn back a little, but the face he now saw looking down on him showed nothing of fear.

It was not a beautiful face, at least not in the accepted sense of the word. Yet the strange intensity and frankness with which the dark leaf-green eyes were fixed on his, in wonder or curiosity (or was it a deep intuitive comprehension?), gave her a look he never remembered having encountered before in woman. He gave another sound, somewhere between a laugh and a grunt.

"Why are you laughing?" she asked, and her voice held neither pretended coyness nor coquetry. He made no attempt to move but met her gaze with his sardonic, almost impudent look.

"It's all too symbolic—"

"Symbolic—" she echoed uncomprehending, "—of what?"

"First of all—the elements: earth, water, air and . . . fire—" He had hesitated a moment, but in the shimmering atmosphere against which she now stood outlined, her hair really seemed an aureole of flame.

"And then the landscape—" he made a gesture in the direction of the stream, pointing to the thick branches twining above—"It only needed the snake—"

"The snake—" she murmured, and her gaze seemed suddenly to draw inward in a deep unfathomable look.

"The snake—the serpent—not only Eve's, though almost it might be that too."

But she answered as if bemused. "I used to play with them when I was a child."

"Play with them?" His gaze switched back to assess the slim girl's figure in the ankle-length skirt. Hardly a peasant, he concluded, but where among the sophisticated daughters of the nobility would one meet with that direct simplicity, the curious elfin smile of the perhaps too long mouth?

"Did you know what you were playing with? After all, it's pretty dangerous. The hydra and the fire dragon, the mercurial salamander—the snake of resurrection that bites into his own tail and rekindles life."

"Who told you?" Her leaf-green eyes kindled with a look of surprise.

"Books," he answered.

"Books—can one learn that in books?" But as though apprehending the presence of a fellow adept, she drew a step nearer.

"Much more," he vouchsafed. "All the mysteries of alchemy, the whole abracadabra of the occult sciences." He roused himself from his lethargy and sat up with his back against the tree trunk. "To discover the essence of things—the qualities of liquids, the properties of metals—and under what circumstances they will alter their nature. If, for instance, the baser can be changed into the nobler."

"Can they?" she asked, and the doubt in her voice seemed to have a secret significance of experience.

"Convert human clay into the stuff of angels?" He gave a mocking laugh. Scrabbling up a handful of earth, he tossed it in the palm of his hand. "Better aim at disintegrating the universe."

She had listened till now with a rapt attention, but as though ignoring the last sentence, she sat down on the roots of the tree and returned to her former theme. "Tell me more about the snakes," she said.

He regarded her amused. A child after all, he pondered, with a child's single-minded insistence on truth. "You might not like the rest," he warned her.

"What?" she persisted.

Well, then, she should have it. He would not even spare that innocence his coruscating skepticism. "The serpent," he retorted, "crucified on the tree of wisdom."

She raised her hand to her mouth as though to stifle a cry. He had pierced her now. But in a second she was facing him quite calmly.

"Are you sure?"

"Is one ever sure of anything?" he returned. "At best we invent hypotheses to hide our basic ignorance, for which nothing is more conveniently ambiguous than symbols—"

But she wasn't to be put off.

"Where did you learn it all?" she asked.

"In Spain—from the Arabs."

"Are you an Arab?" She scrutinized him doubtfully. He was dark and ugly except for his forehead—but he didn't resemble the few Arabs she had seen.

"Unfortunately not," he retorted. But his remark seemed to cause her little surprise. Since he had employed one of his customary ruses for provoking horror in his audience, he would ordinarily have felt her reaction an insult. As it was, he was only taken aback. "You don't think it matters?"

She shrugged. "What's the use. If you *are* one you can't change your skin—it's not your fault."

"A pity the ecclesiastics and our noble sovereigns don't share your opinion," he grunted, but she was obsessed with her own trend of thought.

"Have you come all the way from Spain?" she asked wondering.

"From Toledo."

"How?"

"On my horse." He nodded in the direction of the beast that was grazing at a little distance. "It lamed on me halfway up the hill. Where's the blacksmith?"

"He went down with Father to the manor."

"Is your father Ramon of Pérelha perhaps?"

"Of course. Why shouldn't he be?"

And why should he? What resemblance, Hugo wondered, had the reputedly so prosaic Pérelha to this incalculable child of his? Did she take after her mother? Or by what chance in the countless possibilities of the hereditary gamble had incompatibles combined to form such progeny? All of which thoughts he left unpronounced and, contenting himself instead with the one-sided pull of his mouth that served as a smile, said, "I've told you I wasn't sure whether you are reality or symbol."

"I'm quite real." Stretching out her hands, she lightly touched his fingers, laughing. "Feel—"

Her hands, from recently dabbling in the water, were deliciously cool.

"Have you come to see Father?" she asked him.

"Not exactly. Peire-Roger of Mirepoix (your brother-in-law, isn't he?) asked me to pick him up on my way to Toulouse."

"Toulouse?" At the name she frowned slightly.

"What's the matter?"

"Nothing—only . . . it makes my sister Philippa unhappy. He's so seldom at home."

"Is he at home now?"

"I believe so—he was going to ride out and then he said it was too hot. Perhaps you'd best come up to the castle—" she added reluctantly.

He laughed. "I'm waiting here till your father returns with the blacksmith. If Peire-Roger wants me," he added, "he can come and fetch me himself. Tell him I had my fill of gatekeepers at Ax."

"Ax?" She had gotten to her feet and stood looking down at him with dismay. "You came over at Ax? You mean," she added, as from bitter knowledge, "they tried to arrest you?"

"The town guards were a bit too assiduous in their duties. But it was all a mistake."

"A mistake?" Her voice grew husky with sudden anger. "Didn't you know that the governor—"

"—was an old acquaintance of mine?" he completed for her and laughed. "I didn't till I got there."

The elemental vivacity that had characterized her seemed to have departed. "He's a traitor."

"To what?" Quizzically Hugo's eyes rested on those darkening looks. The green iris of the eye had darkened to black. The lips, now they had lost their strange elfin smile, betrayed their excessive length. "After all," he commented, "you're not so tolerant as you led me to believe when you defended the Arabs."

"That's different. They're what they are, but he—"

"The Wolfling? I knew him years ago when he was practically a boy. He's grown up a bit but fundamentally he seems to me the same. Rather remarkably so, considering what he's gone through—still ensconced in a fool's paradise. Then it was Liberty and the New Order. Now it's the peace—"

"Peace—peace with the French?" Her face seemed to

231

come alive again but with a look of fearful incrimination. "How can it be the same?"

"Essentially it is—all part of the same disease—the search for the grand illusion—the quest—"

But she had picked up the two pitchers and, lifting one on her shoulder, had turned away. Without uttering another word, even a farewell, she went across the square of open ground and disappeared between the hovels. Evidently she had transposed the anger she felt against Wolf or the French to his own person, Hugo reflected, amused. There was fire in her veins as well as in her hair, he reckoned as, stretching himself on his back, he gazed musing into the hazy distances that lay beyond the precipiced shelf of rock. An unusual laziness had taken hold of him. The heat, the silence, broken only by faint sounds of domesticity intermittently heard from the cottages, a child or two appearing now and again at the door and staring dumbly, finger in mouth, at him or his grazing beast, all added to the strange lethargy that encompassed him. What on earth could Peire-Roger find to amuse him among these rustic surroundings? No wonder his wife had reason for complaint. His choice of a spouse incidentally remained a mystery, though certainly when his manor was confiscated it must have turned out a blessing. And, however limited Ramon of Pérelha proved, his young child at least might provide the relief of the fantastic in which Mirepoix reveled, though she was evidently quite capable of holding her own—passionate in her convictions—and, for all those qualities of the elemental, reimbursed with an intransigent code of moral virtues.

Involuntarily Hugo glanced down at his hand. Almost it seemed that the coolness that had emanated from those nereid fingers had left the skin somehow changed. Ridiculous. To allay such absurd superstition he touched the suspected zone with his other hand. It felt no different than the rest of the flesh and yet that curious sensation persisted, at once disturbing, yet strangely agreeable. Again Hugo laughed himself to scorn. It was long since he had felt the impress of a woman's touch upon his flesh—he had doubtless forgotten the feeling, if, indeed, he had ever allowed himself to indulge in such weakness or, more honestly, in any blandishment not repaid in coin. . . . His reverie was cut short by a step behind him.

"It *is* you." Peire-Roger was leaning against the bole of the tree, gazing at him with quizzical amusement. "I guessed by the description."

"So she told you, I see." D'Alfaro made no attempt to change his recumbent position. "Did she give you the rest of the message?"

"That I'd have to come down and fetch you myself? She doesn't varnish the truth, young Esclarmonde."

"So I gathered. Is *that* what she's called?" Hugo queried. "Is she going to take after her namesake and rank as seeress?"

"More like the nymph of the Egerian spring. Has she been instructing the venerable student of the occult sciences?" Peire-Roger bantered. "I trust she duly endowed you with the wisdom of Numa Pompilius."

"Anything but—" D'Alfaro stretched himself, unwilling to rise. "Far from extolling bloodless worship, she's been inveighing against the ignominy of nonviolence."

Mirepoix lifted an eyebrow. "What—apropos of the Wolfling? It's a sore point with her. The one spot in which you could be sure that she's human."

"*Are* you sure?" Hugo got to his feet at last and, brushing the dust from his clothes, found himself glancing once more involuntarily at his hand.

Mirepoix shrugged. "Not altogether. Time and again you'd almost say she was super—or sub—it's impossible to say which. She penetrates too deep, except in the case of the Wolfling. Get her on that topic and she's just a patriotic little virago."

"So I gathered. Tolerance is blown to the winds," Hugo grunted. "But, then, what *is* tolerance?" he added, moving in the direction of his horse. "Half the time it's just the lack of courage to face the fact that the world is a vile cesspool and human beings a mass of maggots wallowing in the filth."

"As bad as idealism?" Mirepoix laughed, walking beside him. "Still tilting against the Grand Delusion? But, after all, *in*tolerance, which is the obvious alternative, may very quickly result from harboring ideals."

"Or seeing them shattered."

"Well, then, what remains?"

"The golden mean."

"What ho?" Mirepoix swung lightly at his side. "You've been won over to the classics?"

"Aristotle—through the Arabs."

"I hope they prove more reliable than your horse," Mirepoix mocked, looking at the jaded beast.

"She's carried me all the way across the inferno of Castile." Patting the horse's crop, Hugo took it by the bridle.

"Good for you. Well," Peire-Roger yawned, "I suppose she can hobble as far as the smithy. Didn't you bring the stuff?" He glanced round anxiously for baggage.

"Left it at Lavelanet—what remains of it. God, if I'd known what a trick you'd play on me with your Ax."

"What, surely the Wolfling hasn't been so assiduous in exercising his censorship as to confiscate your property?"

"No—" Hugo grunted. "But that doesn't say his cursed satellites are able to show an appreciation of the sciences."

"You expect too much. An idealist after all," Mirepoix laughed. "Anyhow, let's hope you've still got paraphernalia enough to amuse Ramonet. He needs it. He's never been the same since the fiasco at Paris. Still, even the treaty left him a loophole and all these years he's been comforting himself with the thought he might still trick the Capet. Divorce—marry and beget a son and the whole question of the French succession would fall to pieces. But the Pope's intransigent. Even if Ramonet managed to wheedle him as did Innocent at the Lateran council (the victim lamb paying for the sins of his father), the bishops have always proved too much for him. Fulk of Marseilles never forgave him or old Ramon for cheating him out of his coveted palace of the arts. And to give him his due, our erst-time troubadour—merchant's son or not—was the better artist. He's at the end of his tether now. They say he hasn't another three months to live. Well, he can comfort himself that even if the pastoral crook of his successor doesn't prove as efficient, the scourge of the Dominicans will. They say they've made a terror house at Albi. Well," he concluded with his usual insouciance, "it'll take them a bit of time yet to install themselves down here—and if they do . . ."

While he spoke Peire-Roger had led the way between the huts where Esclarmonde of Pérelah had disappeared, and they had by now climbed halfway up the path that led to the castle itself. Pausing in the midst of his sentence, Mirepoix halted and pointed over the platform of rock on which the huts seemed perched like a nest of beehives, to the valley far below. In the midst of the heat haze it might have been a vast lake broken by darkening waves of forest and hill. But from that uncertain groundwork a tusk of rock rose, dominating the whole landscape and even the almost chimerical silhouette of the Pyrènees.

"If things take a turn for the worse again, there's always Montségur as a last refuge."

Hugo stared into the distance. "So that's your famous citadel of the Holy Spirit," he mocked. "Looks like the Castle of the Grail."

"Exactly—" Peire-Roger poked his elegantly shod foot in the dust, "and maybe it will still become one."

"Hm. Even the Paraclete will have a job to stand up against the holocaust—" Hugo muttered.

Mirepoix laughed. "If Montfort didn't manage to take it, who will?"

"No one." Hugo cut his most derisive grimace. "That's just it—the individual won't count for anything. Your victor will amount to the biggest arsenal of chemical powders, and the myth of heroism will explode with the rest."

Peire-Roger's green eyes, which hardly flinched under the sun's direct beams, regarded his friend quizzically. "Did you manage to discover the formula?" he asked. "Ramonet will be mightily intrigued."

"No," Hugo growled. "And the likelihood's less now you've destroyed half the stuff with your pranks. "Possibly—if your Ramonet's willing to give me a sinecure for research—"

"We'll probably wheedle him," Mirepoix returned gaily.

"I can't vouch that the results will be to his liking," Alfaro demurred, "nor to yours—my knight of the Grail—"

"You needn't mock," Peire-Roger retorted, "at any rate not before you've discovered your prodigious invention, and even then—man's power to rise from the ashes is almost insuperable."

"Yours may be, certainly," Hugo agreed wryly, "but whether the resulting panorama will provide a fitting foil to your ideas of existence, I have my doubts."

"One can recreate it," Mirepoix answered unperturbed. "The whole point of life lies in fashioning it—artistically."

"Possibly—as far as you're concerned—" Hugo made another attempt to egg on his horse, "—but I'm afraid your aesthetic world will be the first to crumble; and ash and rubble and starvation aren't the best materials for building it anew."

"No doubt." Mirepoix ambled easily at his side. "But the flaw in your diagnosis, my friend, is its complete materialism. After all, when everything has been destroyed, there is still the imagination."

"It remains to be seen how well, under such circumstances, your blessed imagination manages to work. For that matter, have you tried even in a dungeon, bedded in the muck of your own feces—"

"God," Mirepoix wrinkled his nose, "must your brain always confine itself to the drains? If you'd only cultivate the heights." Turning his head, he waved in the direction of Montségur, but Hugo was not to be confounded.

"It's all part of the same thing—the compensatory illusion for the truth you don't dare face. The more highflown your fantasy, the deeper your unacknowledged avowal that life is a hell."

"At that rate," Mirepoix laughed, "I've at least a plus to the general score of nullity."

"You're welcome to it. You and the Wolfling—" Hugo suddenly broke into a guffaw of laughter—"you're always at loggerheads and yet, actually, you're pilgrims on the same fools' errand."

"The grand ideal—beauty or truth?" Peire-Roger parried. "I'm surprised, Hugo, you put them on the same footing."

"I don't necessarily. All I say is they're aspects of the same illusion."

"Well," Mirepoix shrugged, "if you're content with the cesspool."

"I never said I was," Hugo muttered. "Still, I don't let its stench make the hell of my existence that the spiritual vapors inflict on a man."

"The Wolfling? Still no hope of grace descending?"

"Grace?" Hugo swore. "Even the Cathars have sense enough to see through that swindle."

"Human grace then," Peire-Roger returned laughing. "But whence?"

"Hm. He seems to have cut himself off from it pretty thoroughly. The usual result of too much love of Humanity with a big H. What happened to the wife?"

"Landed herself in a madhouse after having maddened him and everyone else. Poor Wolfling! All the curses of Cain seem to have descended upon him. One might have set a last hope in young Esclarmonde's redeeming him, but he's done for himself in her eyes. Can't forgive him his truck with the French. Still, I believe she almost worshiped him—the hero of the Mas d'Azil and all that. You should have seen him at the banquet at Foix. (She was a mere child.) Yet he posed as a Cathar even then."

"Posed—exactly," Hugo grunted. "Maybe she had the intellect to see through him—sees through a good deal more than most of us with those eyes of hers—".

Mirepoix regarded him quizzically. "What! Has she bewitched even you? Be careful! Luckily you can protect yourself with your occult arts. For my part, I'd leave well alone."

"Do you ever?" Hugo retorted. To himself he commented that Peire-Roger had evidently for once suffered a rebuff in the tilting field of love. But they had reached the entrance of the castle. It certainly lived up to its name for, at a first glance, at any rate, it was difficult to discern how many of those crenelated walls and towers were built of masonry, how many carved from the rock itself. Won't help them, Hugo considered with wry satisfaction, when the day comes; won't help them any more than two thousand feet of precipice will. Save the phantasmagorical Montségur. Tumbled remnants of rubble and stone, they'd stand there for future generations to mock the ambitious follies of man. Emblems of feudal hegemony or projections of man's wish-fantasies in which he boasted of outstripping his carnal self, they would both prove nonetheless reducible, in the last issue, to what they were—heaps of so much lapidary dust. *"Memento quia pulvis es et in pulverem reverteris."* The sooner man woke to the realization, the better, Hugo reflected.

He was further convinced of the necessity when, some hours later, the master of the house having returned, the whole family sat foregathered in the hall and abruptly and with a matter-of-factness that evidently matched his reputation, Ramon of Pérelha, who had appeared preoccupied with some problems relating to the sale of his sheep, suddenly vouchsafed a piece of shattering news. A group of Dominicans headed by Guillaume Arnaud, leader of the Inquisition into heresy, who was subjecting the whole of the Lauragais and the Razes to his researches with a zeal that doubtless surpassed the fervor of the founder of their order, had met lately with growing signs of resistance that had ended in open revolt, ambush, and actual murder. The reprisals would doubtless far exceed anything known heretofore.

"Worse than the burnings at Moissac?" Corba of Pérelha raised her head from behind the vast coverlet that she and Philippa were stuffing with down.

"Three hundred *perfecti* and believers—and all of them, they say, went singing to the stake."

"Two hundred and ten," Philippa's dry, small voice corrected primly. In the course of the last years the fabric of her world of romance had been so torn and tattered that one of her few consolations was to belittle willfully and systematically the exaggerations of others.

"Christ, why drag in arithmetic to weaken the grand effect?" Peire-Roger threw in, irritated as usual by his wife's clipped tone. "Two hundred and ten, two hundred and eleven, or two hundred and thirteen—what's in a number?"

"Everything," d'Alfaro retorted, "if you happen to be one of them."

"You can thank God you are not." Pérelha threw a scathing glance at his son-in-law. "Or perhaps your glib tongue will answer their conundrums when they have you up for trial."

Mirepoix laughed. "I've started studying dialectic. Doubtless it will prove more profitable than poetry."

Pérelha only ignored him. "As if their tongue-twisting weren't enough. A man doesn't even know who informed against him—his worst enemy or his friend."

"Even his children," Corba lamented. "They say that at Moissac the baker's own little son told the tribunal his father had hidden one of the *bonshommes* in the great oven. To think one could never be sure that one's own blood. . . ." She sighed so deeply that a flock of feathers was wafted upward like a little cloud of incense, to land and disperse on Philippa's coif.

The younger woman brushed them impatiently aside. "Not merely the quick but the dead," she pronounced succinctly but sententiously. When opportunity offered, she could still claim the right to outbid the others in a macabre tale, as long as she could hope Peire-Roger wouldn't make a fool of her, but this story he had told himself.

"If they can prove your grandfather was a heretic they dig up his bones and excommunicate them, so they can rob you of lands and goods."

"The sins of the fathers visited on their children unto the third generation," d'Alfaro growled, inwardly commenting on the utter lack of attraction of Mirepoix's spouse. "The Scriptures offer the best excuse and the resulting revenue is more profitable than the burnings."

Ramon of Pérelha rose to his feet and, crossing the room, stood looking down abstractedly on his wife's work. "A man is no more safe within the boards of his coffin than inside his four walls. Soon they'll be starting their tribunals down here. It's just a question which will be first—the Ariège or the upper Aude."

"They're more likely to choose Tarascon," Philippa spoke with unusual authority, gratified that d'Alfaro by his latest remark had taken notice of her and blissfully

239

unaware of his private thoughts. "They must know the *bonshommes* have a refuge in the caves of the Sabarthez."

"If they do, they'll find it still more uncomfortable than Narbonne or Albi," her father replied sarcastically. "Among all those fortresses—Lordat, Castel Verdun, Vicdessos—they would pounce on them like so many hawks."

"Unless," Mirepoix shrugged, "they manage to get the backing of royal troops. They've threatened long enough—"

"It might not even be necessary—" it was the voice of Esclarmonde that broke in from where during the whole evening she had sat crouched in the window seat, gazing out into the now fast-gathering twilight, "if they apply for a list of suspects to the governor of Ax." Only Hugo d'Alfaro caught the sharp note of anguish underlying those derisive tones, for Peire-Roger was expounding, with a seriousness unusual to him, the difficulties that would face even Lordat and Roccafissada if the Inquisition really won the support of the French troops.

"If the seneschal of Carcassonne were to get it into his head . . ." He began to paint an ominous picture of the strategic brilliance of the seneschal's commanders.

Bored by such military technicalities, d'Alfaro rose to his feet and, after a moment's aimless wandering, took up his stand in front of the girl.

"And if the Holy Inquisition *should* apply to the governor of Ax?" he queried, fixing her with his look of brutal mockery, "do you realize what the result will be?"

"Why do you ask," she returned his gaze unflinchingly, "after your own experiences?"

"Exactly—after my own." He made no attempt to explain the enigma. If they wanted, those eyes could read his meaning well enough. If they didn't, well. . . .

"And he himself—" he thrust the words at her, "have you thought about that?"

She did not answer.

"—will land himself where he habitually does," he concluded for her.

She shook her head and, rising to her feet, ran from the room.

The rest were too absorbed in their own conversation to take note of her, for Peire-Roger, as though moved by a sudden inspiration, had embarked on the project of restoring the citadel of Montségur. His arguments lasted well into the night. But by the early hours of the morning even Ramon of Pérelha, to his own disgust, had yielded to his son-in-law's plausibilities.

THE SECRET GIRDLE

Tantum religio potuit suadere malorum.
Such an enormity of evil has religion been able to instigate.

(LUCRETIUS)

IF PEIRE-ROGER'S PROJECTS INCURRED THE ANGER OF Ramon of Pérelha, they had a still more devastating effect on the mind of Jordan of the Isle.

The news of the resuscitation of Montségur had on him less the effect of a stunning blow than of a peculiar and insidious influence, as if the stream of his blood, sluggish at the best of times, were gradually brought to a complete standstill. It was the very slowness of realization that gave the experience its sickening character: a feeling that the knowledge had been present all the time, not without but within him, was indeed inextricable from his own being, the curse from which he could never be freed. How could he? Since he was part of his mother's flesh, was he not also part of her guilt? Even if he had tried to force Roger's hand and laid claim to the castle as his natural heritage, it would have availed nothing, since the contamination was in him as well as in those stones.

But no, he need not fear, he persuaded himself. Though Pérelha, Mirepoix, and the rest of the exiled barons might do all in their power to protect their heretic eyrie, the cause of the Cathars was doomed. Sooner or later the citadel would fall, the last heretic be squeezed in the vice of the Inquisition.

Yet the knowledge brought no comfort, no quickening of his sagging pulse. What was the Cathar heresy against that deeper unexpurgatable sin of the flesh? The flesh— But even that might be redeemed. Was there not a satisfaction in the thought of Peire-Roger of Mirepoix's sensual frivolities making a mockery of her passion? But he knew too well and, at the thought, the blood seemed to stand still in his arteries. The center of the problem was left untouched. The sins of the flesh, the aberrations of the spirit—they were categories too easy. For where was the dividing line, where could he ever lay his finger on the cankered spot?

As long as he lived he would not know, but would carry the burden of her unsolved, insoluble secret alone. No, not alone—his blood seemed to spring forward in a sudden pulse—for there was one who could share it— share the agony of his doubt: he who had shared her dreams, an unwitting boy, he whom she had loved as a son, he and no other.

Dream upon dream he had watched born in the mind of the Bastard of Foix, dream upon dream he had watched shatter.

So he had dogged Wolf's footsteps through the years, through his adolescent passion for Trencavel, his friendship with the prisoner, his retributive Catharism and dreams of peace, to watch, even in these last months, through the reports of his informers, the agonized struggle between conflicting loyalties waged in the heart of the governor of Ax. Oh, he had known well enough, that day when he had recommended the Bastard to the French seneschal, where Wolf of Foix would end. His duties at Ax would soon become intolerable. Any time he would resign and then . . . what would stand between him and Montségur? He had not realized it then.

Doubt, doubt and disillusion— No, there was no fear, Jordan reassured himself, as long as Mirepoix ruled the roost. But what if the Bastard flee over the border, evade, escape where he could not follow him? The blood seemed to ebb from his veins. However much he might hate him, his power over Wolf of Foix was the pivot of his own existence, the one stimulus that gave life reason and purpose and even faith.

For a couple of hours he sat buried in his thoughts, then, suddenly rousing himself, called for parchment and quill. That same night his henchmen delivered at

Toulouse a letter addressed to the Most Holy Inquisition.

One afternoon, a few weeks later, Wolf stood face to face with Guy de Lévis in a small room of Peire-Roger's confiscated castle at Mirepoix.

It was not the first time he had paid a visit to the seneschal. As far as Guy was concerned, he would gladly have seen him there more often, but Wolf had proved perfunctory in accepting his hospitality, and his visits had been confined to little more than the delivery of reports or brief discussions on jurisdictional matters concerning the upper Ariège and Ax. Today, however, Wolf's presence was the result of a definite command—more pressing yet more personal than hitherto.

On each occasion of such an interview, the French seneschal had made an attempt to probe the character and intentions of the man before him; always he had found himself landing against a dead wall. Was he after all being duped? he would ask himself, perturbed. Was the Bastard of Foix, behind all that rigorous sense of duty, that indefatigable, almost feverish industry of his, playing, as had been intimated, a double game? But the letter he had received from the Inquisitional Tribunal of Toulouse a few days before had, though it strengthened his doubts as to Wolf of Foix's orthodoxy, if anything turned the scales in his favor. What did he care about the man's religious scruples? He had proved loyal enough to the crown, more loyal indeed than many a French official who had managed to turn a good part of the revenue to his own needs. And as far as he himself was concerned, Lévis reflected, Wolf of Foix had served him well, far better in fact than he had dreamed the day on which, through the guile of that enigmatic ambassador of the Church, or through sheer instinct, he had been led to offer him the governorship of Ax. He could not say that the venture had turned out a failure. The Sabarthez might have proved a thorn in the flesh and his pretty little domain less worth the keeping if the fear of a dagger in his back had haunted his every ride through his domains. But the barons of this wilderness cared little enough who was their overlord—France, Aragon, or Toulouse—as long as they were left their rough and ready freedom. The

244

Bastard was certainly the last to prove a tyrant unless it was to force them to a greater leniency toward their serfs—tactics which, incidentally, Lévis recalled with amusement, had caused them to come running to the French seneschal for protection. Yes, he had done well, he deliberated, and the damned religious business had been cut right out. No doubt a few of those salad-munching heretics had still flitted about the district, living, for all he cared, like half-entombed ghosts in the caverns of the mountainside, but they'd find little response among those predatory mountain lords. He didn't blame them. Have as little truck with soul-savers as possible, whatever their brand.

But now the situation had changed. Since the cursed Inquisition had been legalized by papal authority and had set up its machinery in every quarter of Languedoc, harrying the land with its burnings and tortures, the whole country would soon be a wasps' nest. Not that it could do more than buzz. It was no longer as in Montfort's time. The royal seneschals had fixed themselves too firmly in key positions for that; but it could spoil a man's nights and his digestion, and why not live in good companionable terms with one's fellow creatures if one could? A plague on those meddling monks! They hadn't done much more than warn and pester till recently, but now they were setting to work in earnest. Excommunication? It wouldn't worry him much, but his wife—it would break her heart. His mind reverted once more to the threats in that letter. Heretics, it was maintained by the Inquisitorial Commission, were known to be passed regularly across the border. The existence of a chain system of protectors and refuges was more than probable, conveniently screened, no doubt, by the continous flow of merchants whose persons and wares were evidently not submitted to a sufficiently strict censoring by the authorities. Strong suspicion fell on the area of Ax, whose governor, it had been ascertained, had in the past displayed marked sympathy with the Cathars. It was therefore the duty of the seneschal of Mirepoix to inquire immediately into the facts and to do all in his power to extirpate with merciless rigor every symptom of heresy and every possibility of its development in the countryside. Failure to do so within fourteen days would have disastrous results not only for the governor of Ax but invoke the ban upon the person and household of the seneschal himself.

They were evidently forcing him into taking action, Lévis reflected, but he was not going to be compelled so easily into giving up a prize. There was nothing for it but to summon the Bastard to Mirepoix and sound him out thoroughly. Not so easy when it came to it. He had little talent for subtle investigation, and the least lack of tact might result in the man resigning his post.

"In regard to the—hm—merchandise that passes through Ax," he had fixed his eyes upon Wolf of Foix, "I presume you have submitted it to the prescribed inspection?"

"I have enforced all regulations according to the royal decree."

Guy de Lévis drummed with his fingers on the board. "You have no reason to believe that wares of a—let us say—less commercial value are being passed across the border?"

"No—." Even as he spoke there flitted through Wolf's mind the memory of d'Alfaro and his instrument of hypothetical cataclysm. Had he, after all, discovered the formula and set about exploding the Capet realm? But the thought was so fantastic that, after the initial shock, he recovered himself immediately. "I do not know," he evaded, "what you mean."

Didn't he? The momentary hesitation had not escaped the seneschal's notice.

"Human wares—heretics—" Lévis came to the point impatiently, angered less by the fact that the Inquisiton might prove right than by a realization of the complications that would inevitably face his own future and rule in the Sabarthez.

"To my knowledge, no." As he spoke, Wolf's eyes rested directly on the seneschal's, and once more Lévis felt that his suspicions were perhaps, after all, unwarranted.

"You are sure you have taken all necessary precautions?"

Wolf did not flinch.

"When I took up the post of governor it was with the understanding that my duties were of a purely temporal kind."

"Hm." Lévis frowned. The very words were enough to convict their speaker. Nevertheless, he had to admit that the stipulation had been made as much to his own advantage as to that of the man before him. He cleared his throat.

"Circumstances have, alas, somewhat changed. Owing to the zeal of our—hm—orthodox friends, the situation has made it imperative to impose measures of extreme rigor."

Wolf had visibly stiffened. "You are asking me," his voice sounded suddenly low and hoarse, "to inflict punishment on the heretics?"

"Not punishment—" Lévis quickly interposed. "That is the concern of the Church and the Inquisitorial Court. They would doubtless be content if they were satisfied that any sign of heresy were brought to their notice."

Wolf's face darkened. "Are you asking me to turn informer?"

"No, no—" Lévis attempted to reassure him. "But your officers—were you to give them instructions—"

"To spy on the people, to ferret out their houses?" The pent-up fears, the doubt and self-searchings of the last months were on the point of breaking through Wolf's self-inforced calm and then he controlled himself. "When you first offered me the post, I refused it, explaining—"

"That you had ties with those of a different persuasion. I understood that they were broken." As Wolf did not answer, Lévis continued more sternly, "You are still in touch with your wife?"

"I have from time to time received news regarding her condition."

"Ah—" The seneschal frowned. "She is, I believe, in some—hm—heretic hostel in Andorra."

"Yes."

"You realize it is accounted a crime to hold converse with, let alone harbor, a professing Cathar?"

Again Lévis' query was met with that mute "Yes."

247

"How then," the seneschal continued, "did you, according to your own admission, receive the news?"

"It concerned only her health—a brief note written on a traveling apothecary's bill."

"Your wife is ailing?"

"Yes—in spirit—rather than body." The words were wrung from Wolf's lips with difficulty.

Damned sensitive, Lévis commented to himself. Probably, when it came to it, the grounds for the whole accusation could be traced to a domestic tragedy.

"Religious phobia?" he grunted sympathetically.

"Perhaps." But the shutter did not lift from the other's face.

"You hardly have cause to thank the heretics," Lévis remarked.

Wolf did not answer.

Christ, the seneschal reflected impatiently, the man was deep. Still he was somehow convinced of his loyalty. Too honest, and for the sake of his wretched scruples he was about to wreck himself and him. "It would be a source of regret to me," he attempted, "were you to believe that I, for my part, cast upon your conduct the least—hm—suspicion, but it is my duty—for your own sake—to warn you." As he spoke his hand stretched out toward a roll of parchment on the table. Opening it, he handed it to him.

For a long time, as though he could not take in their content, Wolf's eyes rested on the cramped words. Then quietly he laid the letter upon the table. To Lévis' surprise his face, when he raised it again, had almost a look of relief. "I appreciate your forethought, but I think there is no need to say more. For my part, I only regret, more deeply than I can express, the trouble I have caused you, and can only hope to spare your future anxiety by tendering you my resignation."

As though they were spoken by another, the words fell on Wolf's ears while their pomposity filled him with loathing. And yet, in part at least, they were no different than those he had trained himself to utter during the past months. Spoken at any time before, it struck him, they might have worn the quality of a heroic gesture, a noble sacrifice. Now to the Frenchman no doubt they sounded no more than wounded pride.

"I had feared," Lévis was indeed in the act of saying, "I had feared you might take my words in that light—whereas in fact it is in my very eagerness to prevent such an impasse that I summoned you to this—hm—discussion. It would pain me exceedingly to think you imagined I was unappreciative of the excellent services you have rendered not only me but—I was going to say *my*—I hope I may confidently use the word—*our*—country."

Was he being ironical, Wolf thought bitterly? But the seneschal continued, "I may indeed say that I attribute the prosperous and peaceful conditions which have been maintained in this part of Languedoc mainly to your ready co-operation. It would seem to me a tragedy were such a felicitous state of things to be wrecked on the rock of a mere irrelevancy."

"Irrelevancy?" Wolf echoed. "I cannot consider freedom of conscience as unimportant."

"I do not think we shall quarrel on that point," Lévis retorted. "Yet I had almost believed you would agree with me that understanding and good will between human beings should not be jeopardized by dogmatic zealots, whether Catholic or heretic."

"It is not a case of dogmas or fanaticism," Wolf retorted, "but of human rights."

"Exactly," the seneschal returned. "And I would have you consider what is likely to happen to those rights if I am forced to install at Ax a governor to conform with the notions of the Inquisition. Your resignation would set me an insuperable problem."

"I am not indispensable," Wolf replied tersely. "There must be others who would be ready to accept the task."

"Probably—" Lévis gave a sarcastic smile. "For the sake of their own advancement." He paused, regarding him fixedly. "It had always appeared to me that you regarded your post not in that light but as the fulfillment of—hm—an ideal."

For the first time that afternoon it seemed to the seneschal that the rigid mask of the man standing before him broke beneath the stress of an intense and painful emotion. The Seneschal arose but the other's face was already hardening once more into dumb intransigency.

"What you ask of me is impossible."

"It is equally impossible," Lévis retorted, "for me to accept your resignation at such short notice. The commission allowed a respite of fourteen days. Seven are still left. I trust that within that time we may, between us, have devised a plan that will make nil of their efforts to destroy what we have built."

What he had built . . . the words echoed vaguely through Wolf's mind while mechanically his eyes registered the carved moldings, the elaborate tracery that spun itself over wall and window and ceiling of the room.

What he had built . . . they echoed still as, some moments later, he made his way back through the rooms and passages through which he had passed as by habit during the last few years. Today was the last time, he realized dully, and simultaneously he wondered whether those years had really existed. Had they not ended where they had begun, with the same terms of an ultimatum he had no thought of fulfilling? Perhaps what fell between had never really come to pass. Already they seemed to have grown meaningless—those endless hours of uncertainty, of doubt and self-questioning, arising from the insuperable struggle between conflicting loyalties—meaningless as the sculptured vaults, the traceried arcades through which he was passing, the ghostly filigree of Mirepoix's spurious caprice.

Curious that later, when he tried to recall that last interview, he could scarcely visualize either the French marshal or even the room itself. Yet, from that shadow labyrinth of forms, one image would inconsequently detach itself—a sculptured boss on the ribbing of the vault at whose apex were carved, as on the arms of a cross, the five crisped petals of a rose.

That sense of unreality continued all the way back to Ax, until he had crossed the pass of Chioula and his gaze rested for a second on the rooftops of Ascou reflected in the glimmer of the evening sun. Suddenly it struck him that of all this territory over which he had held sway, this alone had reality. Because he had never had time to get to

250

know it? A sickening suspicion penetrated even his despair—a suspicion that all we prize and believe in is that which we have not and cannot possess. After all, wasn't it the old burden of the troubadours against which Sicard had once rebelled in vain? Was the achievement then futile, yes, not only the achievement, but—in spite of his boasting that day to d'Alfaro—all striving, all action itself?·

It was quite dark by the time he had reached Ax, and he was terribly tired. With what dread of the burdens and decisions that awaited him he had ridden over the draw-bridge during the last months. He could hardly take it in that he could count the days, even the hours, after which the last of them would have ceased to exist.

When the porter informed him that some traveling merchants had been waiting since the afternoon, insisting they must personally show him their wares, he felt no surprise, and as he went wearily to meet them, it seemed to him that what he was experiencing now had happened to him long ago.

His servants had evidently carried out his command to supply the needy with sustenance, for the table showed signs of a recent repast and the goblets still stood half filled before the two shabbily dressed figures sitting at the board. Peddlers or hawkers rather than well-to-do traders, and somehow familiar; but where could he possibly have met them before, it flashed through his mind, for, as they turned and rose deferentially to greet him, he realized their features were utterly unknown to him.

As if they were themselves aware of his predicament, one of them stepped forward a pace or two and bowed. "We should not have ventured to intrude thus on your hospitality, were this not the last time we are likely to travel this road. Therefore we felt it incumbent upon us to express to you personally our sincere thanks for the great generosity with which you have regularly rewarded our humble services."

"Services?" Wolf echoed, nonplused.

"But surely—" The man, whose eyes till now had rested on the ground, raised them in the direction of his

251

comrade. "Is it not so? Have we not in return for a very small service rendered always been handsomely repaid?"

"Indeed—indeed—" his companion, who had been occupied in unstrapping a coffer that stood by his side, acquiesced with repeated nods.

"As it is beyond the power of such poor hawkers as ourselves ever to repay such kindness," the first speaker continued, "we can only offer you a choice of our wares—wares so modest that we hardly dare display them before your eyes."

Probably, it entered Wolf's mind, they were a couple of miserable wretches he had saved from the gallows, but the whining, self-abasing tone worked on his overwrought senses, filling him with disgust.

"If I have assisted you in any way, you can rest assured it was through a sense of your deserts. There is no need whatever. . ." he retorted, anxious only to be rid of them, but the second hawker had already opened the lid of the box.

"If you would but deign to look—"

As if the voice were but part of the hypnotic trance in which he seemed to move, Wolf's eyes turned involuntarily toward the coffer. Uppermost lay a shallow tray containing no more than a collection of trinkets, hair snoods, pendants and amulets that belonged to the usual stock of trade they represented.

"I thank you—" he muttered, "but—"

"No, no," the first speaker interposed quickly, "not these—such baubles are too worthless, we should not dream of offering *them*." He made a derogatory gesture toward his partner, as though blaming him for their display. "Even these," he continued, as the other man exposed the lower compartment, "must appear by far too humble. Yet if you perhaps treasure things not alone by their mercenary value but by good faith—"

Mechanically, Wolf's mind registered the peculiar insinuating tone, even as it took note of the objects newly displayed—a couple of boxwood caskets, crudely carved, some indifferent example of Hispano-Moorish pottery, an ivory plaque of mediocre workmanship and, in their midst, as though strayed there by accident, a length of cord. A spare coil of rope, no doubt used for tying up their chests, and yet the incongruity troubled him, so that his eyes rested more attentively upon it. No, it struck him, the cording was too fine to serve such a purpose; for tying a sack then, he concluded, and wondered at the same time why so obviously possible a use could not convince him, why, in fact, he was certain that he knew or had known what it really was.

As if following the focus of his eyes, the first peddler, while recommending apologetically the comparative virtues of the plaque, stretched his hand toward the cord as though to brush it aside but instead, at the last moment, flicked it into a yet more prominent position.

"If this small carving of ivory would give any pleasure," he wheedled, "it is the best we have."

"I have no use for ornaments," Wolf murmured abstracted.

"No?" The man's eyes glanced half pityingly, half comprehendingly at the barren walls. "But I should have known at once. Beauty—the life of the senses—has no interest for the governor of Ax."

Was he mocking? Yet even as he uttered the words, the tone of the man's voice seemed to change to a fearful, hushed intensity. "But perhaps the life of the spirit—"

Suddenly Wolf remembered—the disguised hawkers, the mythical peddlers of Honoria's deranged and wandering mind. Were these men the same—and these their wares? Had she not insisted she recognized the cingulum—the secret girdle worn by the Cathar initiates?

So the accusations of the Tribunal of Toulouse, it dawned on him through the haze of his bewildered senses, had been justified, and all the time, without knowing it, he must have supported their activities—how, God knew. Now they were come to offer him their reward—for what? The deeds he had not performed, except unwittingly, while he kept faith with the duty to which he had sworn himself. Duty to whom? Once more he saw the strange light dawn on Honoria's distraught countenance— "Don't you see you are chosen?" Perhaps he had exalted himself so far as to imagine himself chosen, himself—first to be the creator of peace and justice in the wide world and, when that proved impossible, in this small territory of the Ariège.

Because he had failed, as he had always failed, was he to seek refuge in what even the hermit had proved to him was but a form of escape? What the alternative was he knew—even Lévis' good will could not save him now if he wished. Ironically it struck him that, on the contrary, the seneschal, too, were he ever to hear of this meeting, would think him a double-dealer who had only repudiated the Cathars out of fear.

"I do not know you," he muttered. "You must be mistaken. I have never set eyes upon you—" and even as he spoke the truth, it seemed to him he lied—"myself," he added under his breath.

"It is enough."

Suddenly, Wolf was aware that another voice was speaking. He had failed to notice the figure hidden in the deep recess of the farther window and that was now coming toward them across the room. Tall and spare, his arms folded under his cloak, he too wore the garb of a traveling merchant, but under the close-fitting hood, the eyes fixed Wolf with a piercing intelligence.

"It is enough if the governor of Ax recognizes the gift that you have brought." So saying, he pointed to the loop of cord.

"I have never set eyes on it," Wolf answered, and again something constrained him to add the word—"myself."

"Yourself— But perhaps it was seen by someone who was dear to you," the first merchant began once more, and his voice had regained its old tone of whining insinuation.

"Also that is irrelevant," the newcomer answered. "For, if he will reflect a little, I fancy that the governor of Ax might revise his memory of a day long past. If not, I think I can remind him." As he spoke he took from his garment a book and, opening it, pointed to seven words inscribed upon one side of a page.

"*Lupus de Fuxo in spulga Ornolaco haereticavit.*" Then, closing the book, he brushed back the hood, revealing his tonsured head. "On the charge of heresy I arrest you, Wolf of Foix, in the name of the Holy Inquisition."

Wolf hardly heard the last words. His mind was groping feverishly, struggling to unravel the confusion of his thoughts. "But I saw it—they bound him with cords—" (And above the supposed victim, the knife, the sacred weapon of the Mythrian sacrifice.) "It was only the initiate," the hermit's voice sought to comfort him—"they were belting him with the holy girdle—the vestment of light."

"I have no doubt," the Inquisitor was saying, "that if your memory still fails you, the Tribunal will find means of refreshing it."

But Wolf's tormented consciousness was already gripped in the vise of a sudden and more terrifying realization. "My wife—" he cried, turning to the mock merchants. "Was it not you—?"

"He does not deny that—" The peddler shot a triumphant glance at the monk, but the latter curbed him with a look of cold reserve. "The governor of Ax will remember everything, even as he remembers this, when the time comes. Regarding your wife," he turned to Wolf, "you need have no fear. She is well cared for. In our houses of contrition we find it unnecessary to correct the minds of those whom God has already visited with His scourge."

They were bound for the Lauragais, for Sorèze, where the next tribunal was to be held.

But they did not travel via the Sabarthez, perhaps in order that they might avoid Foix, perhaps because, for reasons of his own, the Inquisitor preferred the longer route across the pass of Chioula and through the narrow gorges of the Frau.

As at last they emerged from the winding ravine, the mountains seemed suddenly to retreat, opening on a semicircle of lower hills, but to the left, at a little distance, they consolidated themselves to a greater bulk from whose hulking shoulder a spur of rock shot up, its summit obscured in the wandering mists.

Mechanically Wolf pulled in the bridle and lifted his head. Somewhere invisible among those clouds must rise the citadel of Montségur. There his dreams had begun, only to peter out in nothingness upon nothingness, chimerical as those nonexistent towers—a wraith dragging all he had cared for into betrayal and death.

Yet up there—Peire-Roger of Mirepoix . . . Involuntarily he jerked on the reins; the horse increased its speed. But that momentary reaction had not escaped the attention of the Dominican whose eyes, following Wolf's glance, seemed to pierce through the mists.

One of the merchants riding up close beside him muttered something with a little laugh. But the monk showed little response.

"That, too," he replied, "will be brought before the Holy Tribunal when the time comes."

A MONTFORT

We will bend down and loosen our hair over you,
That it may drop faint perfume, and be heavy with dew,
Lilies of death-pale hope, roses of passionate dream.

(W. B. YEATS)

THE STORM RAGED OVER THE LAURAGAIS AS IF THE WIN-
ter had gathered its spent forces in jealous fury against
the spring, strengthened by the knowledge that its
flaunting greenness would itself soon yield to the stagnant
maturity of an overblown summer.

Peire-Roger of Mirepoix, battling on horseback the
driving, icy rain, consoled himself for the havoc it was
working on his clothes and person by the thought of the
dramatic color with which the fury of the elements was so
appropriately endowing his fateful enterprise—a night in
advance, it was true. But then violence, like most actions,
was only fully satisfying in the imagination. Its realization
would inevitably introduce the elements of practical
necessity—brute force and bestiality, jealous wrangling
and fear, in short, all the qualities of the vulgar and the
squalid. The deed of liberation would be reduced to the
level of a brawl in a tavern and the savior from the holy
citadel to the leader of a rabble mob.

As he struggled to cover himself more efficiently with
his cloak, there flashed before him an image of himself in
a billowing white mantle emblazoned with the silver emblem of a dove, offering Esclarmonde of Foix his services
as champion of her dreams. Would she have preferred
him now? he pondered sardonically, since what she had
probably termed aesthetic conceits had been reduced to
grim earnestness. Too grim; the impending conspiracy
would never have met with her sanction. But, her saint-

liness apart, she had belonged to the age of civilization, like old Raymond—Raymond, who had tried to rescue the culture of the South by means of diplomacy and finesse. Today Ramonet, his son, had to resort to the staff and cudgel methods of outlawry. But then, Raymond VI had had to deal with Bishop Fulk (and although the son of a merchant, Fulk, it must be admitted, had done credit to the Southern tradition in the gaya scienzia and art) while poor Ramonet was faced with clerical chicanery and torture chambers of the Inquisition. Heavens, if the springs of inspiration were not already sapped dry, the troubadours had best desert the groves of the muse for the schools of dialectic and try to rival the Dominicans in their verbal casuistry—the alternative being the thumb-screws and the rack. What a boon, he reflected, gratified, he had been blessed with a mercurial tongue. He might even hold his own on the inquisitorial bench. Still, he'd rather not run the risk. . . . For that matter, it struck him, as for the hundredth time he brushed the rain-sod-den curls from his face, muteness too could have its advantages, though not to him who was afflicted with it. If, for instance, Wolf of Foix at his trial, instead of keeping mum, had taken the chance of repaying an old score and informed against him. For all his saintliness, the Wolfling, he guessed, had never forgiven his robbing him of the fair Miriam. What a story he could have invented—good enough to divert the attention of that delver in secret heresies, the most learned leader of the Inquisition, Friar Guillaume Arnaud, to a subject so intensely rewarding: the esoteric cults preached by Peire-Roger of Mirepoix, lord of that mystery temple of vice and iniquity, Montségur. But put to the question, the simpleton had held his tongue and paid the penalty. Poor Wolfling—but then, if he hadn't the imagination. . . . Anyhow, Peire-Roger quietened his conscience and brushed aside the disquieting images of physical torture, he was doing what he could to show his gratitude. If they succeeded Wolf would be free, or at least avenged.

Ought he not have let d'Alfaro into the secret, considering the plot was to be carried out in his own domain and as a consequence he was bound to lose his sinecure? Never mind, he'd provide him with plenty of interest at Montségur, interpreting those Arab texts. It wouldn't hurt Hugo to desert practice for theory a while. In any case he was hardly appreciative of Ramonet's gifts. A castle at his disposal, yet he chose to spend all his time in that murky alchemist's kitchen of his in some wretched old hut down by the stream. Luckily it would keep him well out of the way till the whole affair was over. God knew, for all his vaunted ruthlessness, Hugo possessed a peculiar code of honor all his own and might make difficulties. No, Mirepoix reassured himself once more, it would have been too risky to let him into the business.

His thoughts were interrupted by a shout from his squire who, riding a short distance before him, had just rounded a bend in the road. They must, it struck him, be nearing the bridge, but the night was so dark that the river was invisible. The next instant as, turning the corner, he caught up with the man, he dragged back his horse. Almost at their feet a black stream of fluid metal swept past them into the darkness. The road seemed to lead straight into its midst—against its shadowy sheen a wreckage of the bridge thrust dimly out of the flood, a jumble of black truncated timbers.

Their way was cut off. Useless to try to ford higher upstream, and in the infernal hurricane a boat might be almost unmanageable. Return to Avignonet? Unwise to be seen too long in the district, God knew whether the old gatekeeper would manage to keep his mouth shut between him and Hugo. Besides which, if he didn't get to the meeting place at the appointed time, the rest of the conspirators would probably take it for granted the plan had failed and consequently lose nerve and disperse. At whatever cost, he must get a boat. He glanced around, trying to pierce the gloom. About a hundred yards back the road, he remembered, had forked, leading to a house built on the higher ground to insure its safety from what were possibly customary inundations. Some ramshackle tavern or other, he seemed to recall from former journeys. A faint glow came from the windows and the sound of what might well be roistering was blown fitfully toward them on the gust. It was a risk, but what else could be done,

259

and as yet, thanks to the Wolfling, the Inquisition had no proof against him and would scarcely yet be on his tracks. Accordingly, with a word to his squire, they retraced their steps.

As they approached, the door was torn open and a figure came lurching toward them.

"What," it cried, swaying perceptibly under the influence of drink, "another couple of dandies. If they don't parcel them off amd make two pretty pairs!" He laughed and staggered off into the darkness.

"Want to get across?" A second fellow, having followed, stood in the porch peering at the newcomers. "If so, you'll have to grow fins."

"Is there no chance of a ferry?" Peire-Roger shouted into the blast. "I'll make it worth your while."

"You'd have to get St. Peter himself to do the ferrying for you," the man retorted. "I've no mind to become fish food yet. Best pass the night snug and warm in there." He jerked back his thumb over his shoulder. "There's good company," he sniggered and shambled after his companion.

"The hell!" muttered Mirepoix. But to follow the man's suggestion seemed almost inevitable. Besides, now that he was sitting still, his sodden clothes sent the shivers up his spine. Better wait and catch your chill of death after the fell deed was done, he reflected, and called to his squire to report on the situation.

The man reappeared almost as soon as he had gone. "Company's rough enough on the whole, but they're more likely to be afraid of us than we are of them," he remarked encouragingly, obviously fortified by the thought of a stomach-warmer himself. "No one you'd know except the couple the fellow spoke of. As for them—" he broke off insinuatingly.

"Who the devil?" Mirepoix swore. "As long as it isn't any of the bald-pated brothers," he added, though after a draught of mulled wine, he privately commented, he'd probably be able to tackle even them.

The man's grin was invisible in the darkness. "Ladies—and if I'm not mistaken they'll appreciate your company."

"See to the horses!" Descending from the saddle with as much of a swagger than his stiffened limbs would allow, Peire-Roger brushed back the hood of his cloak and pushed open the door.

His adventures in the realm of Venus had certainly not lacked, on several occasions, an element of the unexpected, yet even so he could hardly manage to restrain a cry of surprise.

In an alcove beside the hearth a young woman half hidden from his sight was, by the strategy of wit and a babbling tongue whose accents seemed to Mirepoix somehow familiar, evidently struggling to withhold the encroachments of a circle of yokels to whose all too palpable admiration her serving woman had already succumbed. Under the shock, however, of the nobleman's unexpected entry, her captor momentarily loosened his hold and, with a little scream, the girl, wriggling from his wine-sotted blandishments, darted to her mistress's side and, falling at her feet, buried her head in her lap.

"Oh God, oh holy St. Denis," she cried in the Northern tongue. But either from a lack of sympathy, or merely in the sudden reaction of seeing deliverance at hand, the other seemed hardly aware of the girl's action.

"*Donna*—if you will permit me to offer my protection—" Advancing a step or two into the room, Peire-Roger had bowed in her direction but, chivalrously giving her time to collect herself, he turned to the red-faced and corpulent landlord who was hastening to detach himself somewhat sheepishly from his fellow revelers.

"The room is somewhat small," Mirepoix continued, "not to mention—" He supplied the rest of the comment by an expressive sniff.

The yokels retreated a step or two, facing him with half-surly, half-sheepish looks. "It's no time to be choosy on a night like this."

Throwing off his cloak, Peire-Roger negligently but significantly readjusted his sword belt. "My squire will not lessen the numbers." He gave a light shrug in the direction of the door. "There is doubtless a kitchen, my good fellows, where you can regale yourselves at my expense."

261

Drawing a piece of silver from the pouch at his belt, he flung it on the board.

As if the coin and the richly chiseled sword sheath were indeed potent with magic, the peasants under the now urgent gestures of the landlord were beating a slow but steady retreat toward a door in the farther wall.

Crossing to the hearth, Mirepoix stretched his hand to the blaze. "Food," he called over his shoulder. "You'll hardly tell me you can't boast at any rate a gammon and a stoup of mulled wine."

Hurrying forward to spread the cloak before the blaze, the host broke into effusive apologies, plaintively informing his distinguished guest of the best his poor larder could offer.

When he too had retired to the kitchen, Peire-Roger, having brushed back his weather-beaten locks, turned with smiling curiosity in the direction of the object of his chivalrous deliverance and repeated his obeisance.

"*Donna*—I fancy it is not the first time we have met—" It was the blush that suffused the pale cheeks bringing back something of their former damask that had enabled him after a moment's incredulity to identify their owner, while he questioned skeptically whether it was merely the exhausting effects of her recent ordeal or the disillusionments of her liaison with Ramonet that had brushed the bloom from Yolande of Montfort's Northern freshness.

But, recovering from the shock, she was already mastering the new situation. "Ah—the authority on the arts and the aesthetic embellishments of castles—was it not? I did not know you also made a profession of rescuing ladies—" Her eyes, no less blue for all the slight puckering of the skin, held almost a note of mockery.

"Why not? What, after all," he asked, bending over her proffered hand, "could prove more rewarding?"

"That depends . . . . But from where on earth—"

He gave a little laugh. "The question in such cases should perhaps not be confined to terrestrial limits. Nevertheless," he lifted his forefinger to his lips, "it might be wisest not to ask. Remember, curiosity proved fatal to Elsa of Brabant."

She gave a sigh that suggested something between

renunciation of that reputedly feminine frailty and relief or gratitude. "I should seem foolish indeed to risk losing my rescuer." Glancing at her maid who had retreated shamefacedly to a corner, she explained that when the storm fell after they had left Toulouse, a fallen branch had caused one of their horses to trip and break its leg, with the result that she had been forced to take refuge in this miserable hovel while their man had ridden on to the next hostelry to obtain a new mount. But hours had passed and she began to fear he must have met with some accident, so that it almost seemed they would be stranded till dawn.

Gallantly ignoring the painful situation in which he had found her, Peire-Roger cleared his throat so that his voice resumed its customary mellifluousness. "Fortune, it seems," he smiled, "has mercifully contrived to mitigate adverse circumstances to our mutual advantage that we may be spared the only really intolerable situation in which a human being can find himself—utter boredom." That even the baiting of yokels might seem preferable to that condition was a thought he tactfully kept to himself. Instead, seeing his squire already in the doorway, he called to him to spur on the meal. "See that he doesn't serve up the pig's swill as soup." Then to Yolande of Montfort, "You will forgive me if I attempt to rid myself of the impression that I have suffered a sea change into a seal."

But even the events of this night had not deprived her of her power of repartee.

"Why confuse the images?" she parried. "I imagined my Lohengrin had only tumbled out of his swan."

If in the course of that night Yolande of Montfort did not succeed in discovering what chance had really brought Peire-Roger of Mirepoix to her rescue, neither did he find out the real reason for her journey. And yet with the sensitiveness of an insect's antennae, each played exquisitely with the other's sensibility, as a butterfly dallies around the aromatic petals of a flower.

As if indeed life had no further purpose than to arrange such ephemeral meetings, each drew the utmost from the moment, secure in the knowledge that all earthly existence is but a play of semblances. Once upon a time ambition and a stubbornness that had promised to rival her father's had caused Yolande of Montfort to embark on an enterprise the most expert statesman would have quailed at. Yet success of which she had scarcely dreamed had left her with the realization of a hollow void. For the flaw of which Simon had already warned his pig-tailed flaxen-haired child, the sensuousness that had been unable to resist the glow of an orange, had invaded her whole being, undermining its tense resilience with an indolence that seemed even now to unwrap her invisibly in the breathless beat of the Provençal night. As if she guessed that Peire-Roger of Mirepoix must inevitably compare their last meeting with today's, she decided at last on a challenge.

"You haven't asked," she yawned, "whether I took your advice."

"Advice? I never give any—"

He was leaning easily on his elbows, his legs stretched to the blazing logs. From time to time his squire had thrown on the brands till at last, crouching there cross-legged by the hearth, he had fallen asleep.

"So?" Yolande echoed. On a bench at the far side of the room the serving woman had sunk into exhausted slumber. "You must have felt very altruistic that night. All the more," she added, "since I always get my own way."

"A Montfort," he commented succinctly.

She wondered whether he was being ironical. "After all," she pouted, and her mouth had still something of the spoiled child's—"I'd only wanted the oranges. It was you who talked of—roses."

His eyes rested on her cheek where the coif gathered the skin into little folds. Damask-sheened no longer, he thought, but the neck ran soft as eider to her breast.

"Roses have spines," she reminded him.

"Definitely." He gave a low laugh. Ramonet, he thought to himself, had been well hung on their hooks. The briers had thickened, but there was no tearing himself free. And she'd kept her oranges in the bargain—her little castle in Provence. She'd made Thibaut see to that in the treaty.

"Does the Count of Champagne still collect roses?" he asked suddenly.

"How should I know?" The words sprang to her lips, but he would have despised her for so weak a deception. "After all," she parried, "you found conversation could be quite entertaining even in the Louvre."

Who, he wondered, had told her? Ramonet or the Frenchman?

"He writes good verses," he yawned, and turned a little so that his head, coming to rest against the inpost of the fireplace, almost touched her elbow. As he moved, exposing a patch of damp clothing, a little cloud of steam rose from his shoulder and hair.

Outside the storm had abated—only now and again a last laggard wind rustled in leaf or bush. Peire-Roger chanted:

Nus hons ne puet ami reconforter
Se cele non ou il a son cuer mis.

They must be Thibaut's verse, yet never, she believed, had the texture of the words sounded so sonorous and rich. The candle flickered. A log crumbled and fell. The squire did not wake to replenish it. And still that voice continued groping through the shadows, tendril on tendril entwining ear and sense—

Por bien amer ai sovent esmaiance
A dire voir!

"From true love often have I learned distress. . . ." The briers grew, spiral on spiral winding her round, but between the spines the fruits hung like glowing spheres.

Dame, merci! Donez moi esperance
De joie avoir!

It was a little time before she realized that the voice

265

had ceased and that the rhythmic solace caressing her ears had been replaced by the regular impress of Peire-Roger's fingers gently beating their somnolent iambics on the inside of her wrist.

An hour before dawn her servant returned with the fresh horse. As to a ferry, he informed Mirepoix, he had seen a boat five miles downstream further west.

"Great Count Thibaut—" Peire-Roger smiled as in parting he lifted his lips from Yolande's hand. "One day perhaps I shall send him a rose that was brought back on the Crusades. I reckon he hasn't got it." He laughed to himself, thinking that now he would make Philippa foster them even on Montségur—under glass. "And in exchange—but that we can arrange when the time comes—"

A moment later he was in the saddle. He had missed the first bloom, he considered, remembering his soliloquy on damascene textures when first they had met, but he had used time to good advantage and stored even his sensualities against a worsening day.

"The feeble mouse, against the winter's cold
Garners the nuts and grain within his cell,
While man goes groping without sense to tell
Where to seek refuge against growing old. . . ."

He sang the words into the cold light of dawn. And then he realized that he was quoting Thibaut's own verses again.

THE INQUISITORS

*A maggior forza e a miglior natura
liberi soggiacete, e quella cria
la mente in voi, che il ciel non ha in sua cura . . .
Ye lie subject in your freedom, to a great power and to
a better nature; and that creates in you* mind *which the
heavens have not in their charge.*

(DANTE: "Purgatorio," tr. by T. OAKEY)

THE MAY MORNING THAT FOLLOWED BROKE RESPLENDENT
with a bright translucency, as though the powers of evil
had been vanquished with the storms of the preceding
days and the whole land purged in that clean luminous
fluid of pristine light. At least to the members of the Holy
Inquisition just departing from Sorèze and proceeding to
their next session in the Lauragais the change of weather
seemed almost symbolic and, with the intention of giving
humble voice to his appreciation of the Divine
Providence, Etienne de Saint Thibery, of the Order of the
Franciscans, turned with a smile of complacent self-satis-
faction to the Dominican prelate riding beside him.

"The legions of Satan were foregathered, but once
more we have triumphed over the powers of darkness. It
seems," his plump hand gesticulated in the direction of
the cloudless sky, "the heavens themselves vouchsafe to
smile on our work."

Friar Guillaume Arnaud made no answer. Ever since
they had left Sorèze he had remained immersed in a
brown study, oblivious, it appeared, of the good spirits of
his companions as of the radiant scene around him.

"The Evil One spreads his nets with ever greater
cunning to catch us. He failed as usual to confound us,"
The Franciscan began again, but as if the latter's op-
timism only aggravated his own preoccupation, the leader
of the Toulousan Inquisition muttered something between
thin, blue-shaven lips while his eyes fixed themselves once
more on the crop of his palfrey. It was not, however, the
fine curve of the Arab's neck (and a fastidiousness re-

garding the equine race was the one luxury Guillaume permitted himself) that absorbed his attention today, but another image that contrasted so violently with the clear beauty of the morning.

Torture . . . Had he not warned incessantly against its indiscriminate use? And if the man should die as a result. . . . True, no member of the Inquisition could be said to be more hardened to the task of drawing from the accused a confession that branded him with irrevocable guilt, none of his colleagues had proved himself such a past master in probing in their depths the incalculable regions of the spirit and laying bare the secret, yet, perhaps only, potential canker of which the victim himself had till then been hardly aware.

An authority on dogma, famed for his scholarship, he inspired through the brilliance of his dialectic almost as much terror in his own colleagues as in the heretics themselves. To an intellect of his capacity, the need to apply measures of physical violence seemed almost an insult to his mental powers. Indeed, it was a method which, fortunately, he was practically never constrained to use. For the most part, the higher strata of the *perfecti* were only too ready in their Satanic obstinacy to confess proudly to their belief, in which, should they attempt to defend it by argument, his own analysis had never yet failed to reveal the fatal flaw. Not that it was always easy. For what, after all, he admitted to himself, was the Cathar creed of world negation but the Augustinian duality drawn to its utterly logical conclusion? But even logic, except in the use of dialectic to the glory of God and Holy Church, must be safely held within the pale of the golden mean. Not only for the sake of maintaining authority and power. In justice to Guillaume Arnaud it must be admitted that his fanatic zeal was born of the sincere belief that to rend from man the garment of the flesh was to shatter the ineffable equilibrium of the divine architecture. For was not God's creation as complex a synthesis of the tangible and spiritual as the cathedrals of Northern France? Tier on tier, pinnacle on pinnacle, its disembodied masonry reared itself into the skies to pierce the limitlessness of heaven, but the fundament rested on earth, was rooted in the solid

rock of being itself. Likewise to deny man his carnal validity was to rob him of his place in that divine order of
creation and to pitch him headlong into the abyss of nothingness. Fortunately, few but a small minority, blinded by
misery and ecstatic delusion, were lured irrevocably into
those unnavigable seas. Fear, ambition, the weaknesses of
the flesh proved too strong. Could, then, Satan himself
prove an unwitting aid of salvation? The first time that in-
credible paradox had raised its insidious head Friar Guillaume had striven to close his mind to the full implication
of so dangerous an ambivalance, but the exercise of his
intellect won the day, for after due meditation it had become clear to him that to deny the divine power to
change evil into good was the greatest sin of all, the sin
that was the prerogative of Lucifer—deadly pride. Yes, if
man came to recognize his very frailty as part of the
divine order, might he not by grace of humility transcend
his very weakness and change it into strength?

By such and similar arguments through which he led
man to realize his mission on earth, Friar Guillaume had
managed, on countless occasions, to guide the straying
lamb back to the fold, for in the end who did not rejoice
to find beneath him the unshatterable rock of Holy Fact?
"But water is stronger than rock." How insistently, during
the last months, that phrase echoed in the depths of his
own consciousness, in the flow of the river, the patter of
the rain, let alone the wild orgies of last night's storm.
Water—gushing from the unsealed mouth, brimming over
the porphyry lip of the moss-green fountain, till drip by
drip it wore away the hollowed basin of stone. Water . . .

The fountain of life—the ancient symbolism was orthodox enough, transmuted into the blood of the Lamb. But
in what garden had those paradisiac rivers their orgin?
What the breath that blew through those groves? "It appears now as bird, now as a creature swimming or diving
. . . it causes the streams to gush from the springs . . ."
The breath of the divine radiance, the depersonalized
God. From what dark corner of his vast, so well-tabulated
store of learning did the memory rise? Guillaume Arnaud
gave a sharp tug at the reins while his eyes fixed themselves yet more sharply on his horse's crop, as if in that

tense curve of muscle they beheld an irrefutable proof of the plastic surety of the divine works, of the Supreme Master Himself—*"Il miglio fabbro."*

Should he, after all, his thoughts wandered off at a tangent, have allowed that worldly comparison to fall uncriticized from the dying lips of the bishop of Toulouse? For all his zeal as pastor of an ungrateful and recalcitrant flock, the deceased prelate, as all the world knew, had never quite overcome his pride at having once been esteemed the best troubadour in Marseilles. Till the very end, indeed, it had been through the golden gate, Friar Guillaume suspected, that Bishop Fulk had sought to transcend carnal desire, while before him rose the image of an alabaster madonna who from her niche in the plain whitewashed walls had gazed down on the hard pallet in the cell of the abbey of Fontefroide where the pampered bishop, in somewhat belated humility, had chosen to end his days. Himself proof against charms that held for him so much less appeal than the finely molded flanks of some aristocratic member of the equine breed, the friar's ever-watchful eyes had not failed to register the air of exquisite grace, almost of coquetry that emanated from the sculptured fold of that star-enwrought cloak. The work, most certainly, of some *miglio fabbro* in the sculptor's craft, he reflected skeptically. No doubt disillusion had driven the converted troubadour to seek consolation in works of art—the mirror of that divine beauty often so lamentably distorted in the human form. Ah, not in the body alone. For the mind could prove a more dangerous tempter, Friar Guillaume pondered, than even the flesh. Yes, though it might appear pellucid as crystal, had he not seen what it contained in its depths, scented the rot gnawing at man's very soul? At first, long ago, he had recoiled in horror. Yet if he did not know the nature of each sin, each temptation, how could he tear it out? In those perilous descents into the dark subterranean passages of the human mind, one thing only could be his guide—knowledge. To that end he had acquainted himself with every possible aberration of man's spirit, explored the root of every heresy brought to his ken. Was he not considered the greatest authority, not only on the

270

Manichaean, but Paulician, the Docetist, the Bogomile heresies; nay, how many more of these secret cults and mysteries that misled the feeble intellect of man? Yet the last rumors brought to his notice he had still not fathomed. And defeat was a concept that, in the realm of knowledge, Friar Guillaume refused to accept.

When the dying bishop of Toulouse had hinted at the mystery encompassing the citadel of Montségur, he had at first believed that the prelate's concern had been born rather of a last hope of wrecking his archenemy, Ramonet, than of any genuine desire to stop the resuscitation of the Cathar fort. How much, indeed, of the late bishop's zeal could not be attributed to his uneradicable jealousy and to a lifelong rivalry for power between him and the dynasty of Toulouse whose luxuries he had so coveted? If he could prove that the ancient citadel had once more been installed as a chief center of the Cathar heresy and Ramonet made no attempt to interfere, Fulk would have won another point toward the count's excommunication. But Montségur was impregnable. It would need a considerable army and a year-long siege to reduce the fort that, it was said, Peire-Roger of Mirepoix had armed to the teeth. Besides which any serious association of that reputed gallant with the Cathar faith seemed hardly convincing. If in the days of Esclarmonde of Foix he had sometimes played an evanescent decorative role as courier, it had only been to the outspoken annoyance of the heretic bishop Guihalbert of Castres, who had made Montségur his refuge during the wars. Moreover, it appeared that Ramon of Pérelha, who, if only for political reasons, was a strong supporter of the Cathars, had evidently resented handing over a half share of the fief of Montségur to his son-in-law as part of his daughter's dowry.

Were then those dark rumors of a forbidden cult said to be practiced behind the walls of that impregnable fort after all more than a ruse by which the wily bishop had tried to capture his confessor's interest in order to wreck the Count of Toulouse? Or were they but a hallucination possessing the diseased brain of that warped and hapless creature to whom he had referred him as testimony?

Jordan of the Isle—the embittered, self-torturing son of a cuckold father betrayed by a woman revered as a Cathar saint. To Friar Guillaume Arnaud the man's character was readable enough. Nevertheless, the more he considered the whole question the more he asked himself what actually had been the mortal sin hidden behind the alleged heresy of Esclarmonde of Foix. Merely the adulterous passion for a Eurasian troubadour of which the dark insinuations of her own son accused her? A passion nevertheless that, inflaming the spirit more than the flesh, was therefore only the deadlier? For what had been the burden of that minstrel's song—the Grail?

Holy Church had not been blind to the dangers lurking in those symbols of a pagan cult, but with her usual perspicacity she had known how to direct them into safe channels. Cup and spear—how astutely those carnal emblems of the creative act had been sublimated to symbols of the divine sacrifice.

But *this* grail, they whispered, was no cup. What then—a stone, a jewel, an all-sufficing radiance, a star buried in the fathomless waters of a well? Even now he saw them rise and, gathering to an ever-growing stream, inundate the whole world. "Water is stronger than rock—" What if at last it undermine even the foundations of the Holy Church?

He must stop these destructive waters at their source, seal forever that hidden·spring—if he could find it. But where—among the Cathars? Why, they abhorred the blessed water of baptism itself. Where then? Through Peire-Roger of Mirepoix—or the wretched man whose lips he had failed to unseal? Obsessed by his meditation, Friar Guillaume had so slackened the reins that the Franciscan, edging close in order to avoid a puddle, almost jostled him into the ditch.

Spangled with dew, a branch of honeysuckle thrust itself from the hedgerow, brushing his face. A shower of fragrant coolness suffused his nostrils, but he smelled only the reek of the charcoal brazier, saw only the sweat of agony upon the tortured man's blotched skin.

"*Lupus de Fuxo in spulga Ornolaco haereticavit.*" That was the chief clause in the conviction. Well and good.

There were things that it was best even for the majority of the Inquisitorial Commission not to know. Enough that Cathar initiations had taken place at Ornolac. And yet he was convinced the governor of Ax had not lied when he refused to admit he had been accepted into the Cathar faith. The man had probably never been more than a sympathizer, yet he was sure he was not trying to avoid a heavier penalty, for he had made no attempt to defend himself, had indeed appeared to foil any attempt on his interlocutor's part to minimize his relations with acknowledged heretics. Was it to screen that deeper guilt, his connection with the secret of Montségur, since Jordan of the Isle insisted that as a boy the Bastard had enjoyed the confidence of Esclarmonde of Foix? That in spite of it he had played no part in the earlier defense of Montségur could be convincingly explained by his duties as squire to Trencavel. But since . . . Was there some connection between the ceremony in the caves of Ornolac and the secret cult at Montségur. Why then was he playing no part in the resuscitation of the fort? Merely because he harbored an old grudge against the fop who, it was said, had once cheated him of his earlier love or because he regarded the practices that Mirepoix was indulging in at Montségur as a travesty of the true faith?

Peire-Roger of Mirepoix. After careful consideration Friar Guillaume had come to the conclusion that on that name depended his main hope of extracting from the prisoner the information he was seeking. However strong was Wolf of Foix's sense of loyalty and power of endurance, once he was sufficiently worn down, the chance of exposing his old rival or, still more, he fancied, of avenging a violated ideal would make him speak. But the trump card must be reserved for the right moment, must come with the shock of surprise.

Thus through hours, days, weeks of repeated questioning in which (according to the rules of a well-tried technique) the prisoner was left as much as possible in the dark as to the goal of the questionnaire to which he was being submitted, Friar Guillaume had approached the subject step by step, till suddenly, almost casually, he had sprung the surprise upon him. Did he know what was the nature of the cult Peire-Roger of Mirepoix was practicing at Montségur?

For a second it had seemed to him that a spark kindled in the bleared eyes swollen with sleeplessness. Now or never. Friar Guillaume had waited, certain of success. Had not experience taught him that to go one step too far was to run the danger of extracting mere lies? Let his fellow commissioners be content with extorted confessions—what mattered to him now, more intensely than ever before in his life, was to know the *truth*.

But even as he waited, and the second drew itself out into eternity, the shutter closed again over the prisoner's face. "No."

Was it anger or an exhaustion that almost matched the prisoner's own that drove him to acquiesce at last in the use of the means he most despised? Yet as he watched that writhing body tauten like a bow to meet the onslaught of pain, he almost found himself praying the man would not speak, knowing what those contorted, bitten lips would cry would never be the truth.

It was almost in triumph that he had seen the angry disappointment on the faces of the jailers as they loosened the screws from the violated limbs that had passed beyond consciousness of pain. Tortune was not permitted a second time for one and the same offense. They would have to rake up new evidence for a further conviction. The governor of Ax had incriminated himself sufficiently as an alleged sympathizer of the Cathar cause. It was enough to keep him a prisoner but not (Guillaume Arnaud had seen to that) to warrant his being handed over as yet to the Civil Law. In the meantime, he had consoled himself, he could give the case further study while Wolf of Foix's physique, evidently never robust at the best, would be worn down past resistance. But supposing it failed to survive the effects of incarceration before the secret was revealed?

The same night, while the winds had howled around the towers of Soréze, and the river, swollen by the melting snows, swept through the valley, it seemed to Friar Guillaume that the elements themselves echoed his obsessing dread. What if the secret waters rose, even like those floods, and undermined the whole edifice of the Church itself?

Robbed of sleep, racked by the thought of failure, he rose from his bed and descended to the dungeons. A dull mutter, mingled with the sound of stertorous breathing, reached him through the walls of the common prison. But since his ordeal in the torture chamber, the prisoner, for the sake of private interrogation, had been put in a cell by himself. Might he not yet discover by subtle persuasion what no one could extort from Wolf by force? In a sudden hope he pushed open the door, but, raising the candle as its slanting light widened across the muddy floor, he experienced a sickening terror that the figure flung, seemingly like a half-filled sack, on the heap of filthy straw was dead. He moved forward, but a wet gust, blowing through the grating, almost extinguished the flame. Shielding it with his hand, he carefully brought the light nearer the prisoner's face. It looked so bloodless that he thought his suspicions confirmed. It was a little time before he was sure that the changing shadows that seemed to pass across the wan lineaments were due not to the vagrant play of the candle nor to his imagining.

The eyes were shut. Yet, under the sweat-dewed skin, thought or the torment of spirit itself seemed to keep up a restless monologue. Was he delirious? A sudden overwhelming hope took hold of the friar. What if the unconscious prisoner should confess the secret that even torture could not wring from him? Intent, scarcely daring to breathe, he followed every quiver, every tremor of the prostrate features until it seemed that his own unappeasable craving for truth had entered into an unspoken dialogue with the restless, hounded images haunting that fevered brain.

Even now as he looked back out of the clear light of day and reason upon the experiences of last night, Friar Guillaume was not sure whether he had really framed his question aloud or whether the apparent answer had been but the anguished articulation of the dreamer's thoughts.

"I do not know." It was no more than a whisper, a mere spasmodic contortion of the lips, as though even in sleep their slightest movement caused unbearable agony to the torn and swollen limbs. But of one thing Friar Guillaume, leader of the Inquisition of Toulouse, was certain: that whether the prisoner spoke consciously or in delirium, the confession was made not in fear or in any attempt to save himself but in the anguish of spirit that belongs to one who knows he has lost his goal.

And as for some minutes still he bent above him watching, like a bird of prey, the fluctuating shadow play of the unsleeping brain, he knew that not the subtlest cross-questioning or the most ruthless torture of body and mind would avail to disclose the last secrets of the human soul, and that all inquisition was in the last issue fruitless unless it had power to penetrate into the hidden world of dream.

THE SEAL

Pity is a mental illness induced by the spectacle of other people's miseries.

(SENECA)

If lecherous goats, if serpents envious
cannot be damned, Alas! why should I be?
Why should intent or reason, born in me
make sins, else equal, in me more heinous?
. . . But who am I, that dare dispute with thee,
o God?

(JOHN DONNE)

WAS THE STORM RISING AGAIN?

Hugo d'Alfaro paused a moment and raised his head from the aludel, but apart from the bubbling in the vessel all was silent. Perhaps it had only been the sound of a door slammed to . . . the Holy Brothers were not so subtle in their physical movements as in their machinations to trap men's souls.

Christ! They had made enough hubbub riding in at the yard and calling for servants—especially the fat Franciscan. To which he had replied that even the philosophers' stone had not as yet boasted of turning lumps of lead into an array of retainers. They'd as likely as not have considered charging him straightway with heresy had not the Dominican archmaster of spiritual inquiry displayed so keen an interest in alchemy, for which, after all, there was some precedent, seeing the most learned doctor of his order, Master Albertus Magnus, was known to be steeping himself in the occult sciences at Cologne. Probably Friar Guillaume would keep to his word and engage him in long conversations tomorrow; would have tonight if his clerks, luckily, hadn't overwhelmed him with documents. The man was intelligent, whatever else he was, d'Alfaro reflected, remembering the vulture-like certainty with which his eye had fastened on some evidently vital point in the argument and discarded the rest—a fanatic, yet rather, he suspected, in his seeking than in any preconception of the truth. The truth—Christ, when would man give up destroying himself and others for the sake of a mythic absolute and be content to realize that his thoughts were as predetermined as his bodily secretions—through Allah's will?

But almost he could have sworn those were footsteps—or was that the sound of the postern closing?

Must he, after all, go to see whether the watchman was regaling his exalted guests with sufficient wine? Cursing the disturbance, Hugo left his post by the furnace and opened the door, but outside the court was empty and silent and the babble of the stream that furnished him with water for his experiments flowed on uninterrupted through the night. Up in the keep the windows were dark except for a flicker in the direction of the hall. Was Friar Guillaume still poring over his dossiers, Hugo thought, and wondered whether they included that of Wolf of Foix. (He had not been so far out in his reckoning when he had warned Pérelha's child.) Jordan's doing, Mirepoix had surmised. The man had evidently been tracking the wretched Wolfling for years. Jealousy of the blessed Esclarmonde—or the Grail? Hugo bent closer to the aludel, watching the pigment deepen from silver to yellow and thence to gold. . . .

"Since all that is, is but as you see it," he heard old Abdul Aziz mutter sad-eyed and grave, "man will ever remain content to cheat himself with semblances." Hm—could one hope to transcend reality by that philosophy in a dungeon? How far was the Wolfling's fate determined by his own actions or by the stars? Or, for that matter, Hugo considered, what hidden powers had moved Ramonet to present him with this sinecure—in order that he might provide him with the illusory hope of destroying the Capet?

And if he did not—if, as Mirepoix had warned him, Ramonet tired of waiting? Was it perhaps as a threat that the Count of Toulouse had foisted this visitation upon him or merely because he knew that none of his blessed vassals would stomach the Inquisitorial Commission in their house? They weren't so willing to retire to the outhouse, he laughed. What did he care for a barracks of a castle, even if it *had* been furnished as lavishly as a

278

palace? He had accepted it, grinning; since Ramonet wanted a caretaker, he might as well appoint him. After all, he was earning his bread, tonight at any rate. As for the rest, the blessed Count of Toulouse, the whole blessed world, for that matter, could judge for themselves—if he chose to let them. . . .

Crossing to the desk he opened a book and, with the proud satisfaction a parent might feel for its successful progeny, his eyes rested almost incredulous on the formula scribbled on one of the leaves. Since twelve hours ago, could he not count himself the king of the earth? In those few scrawled letters and numbers lay the fate of nations—yes, in his hands rested the destiny of the world. And in how many others' besides? His skepticism supplied the necessary curb to vanity. How many might not reveal the most astounding discoveries, if the cursed Church did not threaten the freedom of the intellect with the flames? The intellect and the conscience. His eyes turned toward a flask standing innocently among a row of others on the shelf. Ten times the quantity and the most holy conclave gathered out there at a distance of a few hundred feet would be reduced to little more than powder in the glass—but neither Wolf of Foix nor freedom itself would be saved. For even if ecclesiastical tyranny were overthrown, humanity would manage to destroy itself. Well, if there were satisfaction in hastening the process. . . .

His speculations were checked by a sound—unmistakable now—of approaching footsteps. Had that mine of intellectual curiosity, Guillaume Arnaud, got it into his head to wile away sleeplessness with a discourse on alchemical mysteries after all? Or was his servant finding it hard to stomach the necessity of waiting on the inquisitional Conclave? He had actually been surprised at the old man's readiness (considering his professed hatred of the clerics) to open the gates to them. But the disturber of the peace, whoever it was, had sprung up the steps and was already knocking impatiently at the door.

"Are you there, Hugo?" The voice, for all its unusual stress, could be none other than Peire-Roger of Mirepoix's. Hardly knowing whether he felt relief or increased aggravation, d'Alfaro unmoved by the urgent tone, reluctantly crossed the room and raised the latch.

"What on earth do you want at this time of night?" he began, but Mirepoix, shutting the door behind him, glanced swiftly around the room.

"You'd best get out of here—as quick as possible! If there's anything you want to take with you for heaven's sake, hurry!"

"Get out?" Hugo echoed, turning back to the aludel. Was this another instance of Peire-Roger's whimsies, it flashed through his mind, or was Ramonet giving way to his querulous impatience, trying to frighten him—or worse? "If this is your or your blessed Count of Toulouse's idea of compelling me," he began. But Peire-Roger's customary nonchalance seemed to have deserted him.

"For God's sake, collect the stuff. The horses are down by the copse. We'll be safe at Montségur before day-break."

"I'll be where I please—"

"I'm afraid not," Mirepoix gave an impatient laugh. "Probably no one will be out till sunrise. But once they've raised the hue and cry—"

"After whom—me?" d'Alfaro retorted cynically, and then, lifting his eyes, stopped dead.

Peire-Roger had crossed to the table and dipped his hands in a bowl of water. With a look of fastidious disgust he was wiping them against his cloak. His clothes were bespattered with blood.

"Messy. If you'd made your grand discovery, perhaps you'd have managed things better with your wholesale reduction to dust. As you didn't—"

"What the hell have you been doing?"

"Annihilating the tyrant."

With an obvious effort to recover his usual swagger, Peire-Roger affected a tone of dramatic pathos.

"A somewhat vast undertaking," Hugo scoffed, and then slowly the possibility began to dawn on him. "You mean the Inquisitor—Guillaume Arnaud?"

"The whole lot of them. We were thorough while we were about it—count on Rabat for that. If you don't believe me," Mirepoix added, "you can look for yourself—though I don't advise you to."

D'Alfaro had made an involuntary movement toward the door, then turned as though not crediting Peire-Roger's story.

"How did you get in?" he challenged.

"The postern was open—as arranged," Peire-Roger returned with something like his old charming insolence. "A loyal adherent of the cause of liberty—your watchman."

"My own watchman? Christ, do you mean you plotted the whole thing behind my back?"

"It was the safest way," Mirepoix made an attempt to placate him. "I wanted to tell you, but with you one never knows. In spite of your damned cynicism—"

"Didn't it enter your minds I was responsible?"

"Precisely. That's why I came to the rescue."

"Thanks. Since you have deprived me of my post, to say the least—"

"I'm afraid you'd have lost it in any case. I've warned you before. Ramonet was getting tired of waiting—"

D'Alfaro gave a faint smile and his glance roved to the book on the desk. "A pity," he muttered. "And what will he say to this?" he added sardonically.

"He'll be delighted."

"So he knew of it too and I was the catspaw? I never dreamed Ramonet was so consummate an intriguer," Hugo laughed bitterly.

"He isn't, I'm afraid. I needed subtler and tougher work than he's capable of. In short, more fantasy and guts."

"Fantasy, no doubt." Hugo mocked. "Because you've butchered a handful of inquisitors you think you've freed the land of tyranny. It doesn't strike you that you've plunged it up to the neck in blood?"

"We've removed the real danger—Guillaume Arnaud."

"So because the dragon has lost its head you think the rump rendered impotent—a torso devoid of intelligence. It's more likely you'll find the *monstrum humanum* has only begun to be let loose—"

"At any rate we'll be left a moment's respite till your monster has grown a new head."

"You mean as far as you yourself are concerned and your blessed citadel."

"Isn't it worthwhile?" Mirepoix had evidently recovered his old insouciance. "If you have doubts as to my own person, at any rate you can comfort yourself with the thought that Wolf of Foix is avenged."

"Avenged—is he set free?"

"Unfortunately not. But one had to try and do something—considering what he's evidently gone through for my sake. I had meant to use a little persuasive argument and force the Inquisitor's hand. But there wasn't time. Young Rabat is quick at his work and he had finished with Friar Guillaume before I'd got a word in. That's the worst of zealous ruffians. Said he'd promised himself he'd present me with his skull as a holy relic for—"

"Your grail perhaps?" Hugo jeered.

For a moment Mirepoix's face actually darkened, but the next it had broken once more into a persuasive smile. "Wait with your mockery until you get to Montségur. Incidentally, there's enough work for you there, better than Ramonet could offer—deciphering Arabic texts. I need your advice. For God's sake," he urged, seeing that d'Alfaro had still made no attempt to collect his belongings, "hurry—"

"I'm afraid you'll have to go without me."

Peire-Roger stared at him bewildered. "But you can't stay here. Don't you realize the charge you're facing?"

"Completely."

"Then why?"

"Why anything?" There was a moment's pause. "Nevertheless, if any profit is to be derived from your damned enterprise, I intend to get it."

"Profit?"

"That remains to be seen. You'd better make haste and be gone."

"I *am* going." Peire-Roger's hand was already on the latch, but he turned once more. "I'm sending your henchman up to Pérelha to tell him the plot's a success. A pity about the Wolfling. If I'd rescued him, the child might even have rewarded me with a kiss. You're really not coming?"

Unhearing, d'Alfaro had gone back to his aludel. For a second Mirepoix hesitated. But he knew Hugo too well. The next minute he was gone.

For several moments Hugo remained staring abstractedly at his experiment. When at last he stirred, his movements were of an unhurried but strangely systematic precision. Lifting the matrix from the furnace, he quenched the fire. Then, taking the bottle from the shelf, he emptied the contents into a small bag, tied its neck, and, crossing to his desk, tore the page with the formula from the book. Fetching his cloak, he thrust the objects into a pocket in the lining, flung it around his shoulders, and, extinguishing the light, left the building.

Outside all was silent as before except for the murmuring of the brook. Only very faintly, when he strained his ears, he seemed to detect the sound of galloping horses. Then they too were silenced.

Beyond the paddock the bulk of the keep still loomed palpable but now the lights had disappeared from the upper window, as if even the last watcher had gone to rest. Such stillness reigned that for a moment he wondered whether Mirepoix's story, his whole visit, had not been a fantasy.

The courtyard lay in utter silence, at peace as on any other night, so that once more d'Alfaro had the feeling all had been imagination. But as he passed the kennels he became aware that the silence had deepened to an unnatural vacuum. He stopped, then with quickening footsteps crossed the yard. Under the faint light of the stars he could make out an animal's bulk stretched on the stone slabs. He bent down. The body was already cold. His hand encountered the half-dried slobber round the mouth. The way had been prepared thoroughly and in good time, he reflected acridly.

Under the arch by the porter's lodge the torch had been left burning, no doubt to give an appearance of normality. He took it from the bracket. They had probably not used the main door and it would be barred within, his mind registered with the impassivity that characterized all his present actions. But it was probable the porter had not locked the door that connected with the lodge and that he was in the habit of leaving open for his use. As he had surmised, it gave under his push. Torch in hand, he began to mount the narrow stairs. Once only he paused. The silence was unbroken, deeper even than outside. Once he started, imagining he heard a whisper, but it was only the sharpened intake of his own breath. On the walls of the curved vault his shadow threw a huge distorted image. It struck him that he was moving in a nightmare, wandering through an empty labyrinth of stair and vault, and then as suddenly he became aware of an object on the ground. The light of the torch caught the glint of silver breviary, the glow of carbuncle and amethyst set in the chiseled cover. It was only then, with the horrified yet dispassionate observation of the dreamer, that he realized it was clutched in the fingers of a truncated hand.

A little farther on lay the body, stretched face downward, wedged in a half-open door through which the mutilated man, turning on his own track, had evidently tried to rescue himself.

After all, he was awake, d'Alfaro told himself, and yet, a moment later, standing on the threshold of the hall, he recoiled in doubt. Were they not merely asleep, lulled into somnolence after their exploitations of the cellar—the tonsured head sunk on folded arms upon the table, the lean, beaked nose hooked forward, stabbing the narrow chest? Beside it, slumped in self-complacency upon his chair, the bloated Franciscan seemed to stare at him in bland surprise as though half roused from slumber.

Drugged—d'Alfaro reflected—like the beast in the yard. What if they waked? And then he became aware of that steady drip-drip-drip upon the floor.

Gripping the torch, he moved forward. A few of the monks, having drunk less heavily perhaps, had evidently made an attempt to defend themselves. Chairs were overturned, another piled on a chest to act as barricade. Sprawled half across it, the cowled figure of a Minorite still brandished in its right hand a bronze candlestick.

At the far end of the room in the alcove where he had left him, the black-and-white robed figure of the Chief Inquisitor sat stooped forward over his manuscripts. Round about him the floor was littered with parchments and books. Still perched at his desk, the little scribe had fallen asleep over his registers. Someone had amused himself by pinning to the open page with his dagger the hand that still held the quill pen.

Thrusting the torch into a bracket on the wall, d'Alfaro began to search through the scattered scrolls.

A blank order of release or, failing that, a clean page of parchment. It would take longer, but at a pinch— Suddenly he paused, satisfied. Lighting the rush light on the desk he gathered together the necessary writing materials and carried them and the light to the table. Slowly, in a scribe's meticulous hand, he inserted on the order to render up the prisoner to the bearer the name of Wolf of Foix. Then he set himself to prepare the wax.

While with systematic, almost automatic precision, he carried out each of his actions, he wondered whether he had really planned them standing over the aludel or even long before—whether, in fact, Mirepoix's arbitrary plot had not been determined by his own still dormant will— his own or Allah's? As though, after all, he were the victim of illusion, he glanced swiftly round. Free or not, one acted—how or why? Bracing himself, he approached the figure sitting in the alcove. With a swift movement he threw the cowl over the severed neck. The fingers were already stiffening and the joints were enlarged, but after a prolonged struggle he had drawn off the ring. Returning to the table he melted the wax and imprinted the seal; then, seemingly as methodically, he pushed the ring back on the damp cold hand. Throughout this and the former operation, he had fixed his gaze on the manuscript that had so closely compelled the attention of the Chief Inquisitor of Toulouse; yet though, in those protracted minutes, the retina had received the impression of every word, his mind had failed to take in their import. Had it done so, it would have learned that what so fascinated Friar Guillaume was the esoteric wisdom transmitted through the mystery of the Grail, and that against the name of Parzival of Waleys the Chief Inquisitor had inscribed, as if for idle pastime, the letters W. F.

A quarter of an hour later, Hugo d'Alfaro was riding through the darkness bearing the order for Wolf's release. Until now he had not settled clearly on any further plan. It was not yet midnight and it was probable that the murder would not be discovered before daybreak. Days might pass before the news that Wolf of Foix had been fetched from his prison might be connected with the Inquisitor's death. At first he had thought of fetching Wolf himself and taking him to Montségur, but it was doubtful if Wolf would be in a state to stand the journey, at any rate at the necessary speed, for in the meantime the full responsibility for the crime would have devolved upon himself, and if Wolf were found anywhere in his company the guilt would fall on him too. Moreover, he had his doubts as to how far, especially in Wolf's present state of mind, the proximity of Peire-Roger would prove salubrious. And then suddenly, perhaps through the association of Mirepoix's parting words, his course seemed obvious. Not that he'd stand much chance of receiving the suggested reward.

Before day had begun to break he reached Roccafissada.

Ramon of Pérelha was easily aroused. Few at the castle had found sleep that night, and less than an hour ago d'Alfaro's henchman had arrived with Mirepoix's message. Peire-Roger had deemed it as unwise to let his father-in-law into his project as he had to share it with Hugo, and all Pérelha had gathered was that Mirepoix had hopes of some plan for liberating Wolf of Foix. The news of the murder and the thought of the repercussions it would arouse, without even achieving any benefit to the man for whom Pérelha had always harbored a quiet affection, had not predisposed him toward d'Alfaro, whose skepticism had from the first repelled him and whom he could not but consider the secret instigator of the plot. As a result he came to meet him with obvious rancor. Hugo's henchman, on the other hand, dreading his master's anger, was all deference. He need not have feared.

There was neither time to give nor receive explanations. Sweating and breathless from the ride, Hugo ad-

286

vanced toward Pérelha and handed him the scroll. Scarcely glancing at the bearer, Ramon scanned the lines, then lifting his head, scrutinized him with a mixture of emotion and doubt. "How did you get it?" And seeing the strange expression on the other's face: "A forgery?" he concluded.

Hugo gave an indefinable sound. "The seal's valid. I presume your watchmen can hold their tongues. No one needs to know I've been here. You'd best get along to Montségur," he addressed his own henchman. "Tell Peire-Roger of Mirepoix I've completed the job for him and as I trust to some profit—he'll know what I mean. The more haste you make the more likely you'll save your own skin. If they'll have you, you'd better stay up there."

The man made an attempt to renew his excuses, but d'Alfaro waved him to be gone. He needed no second bidding.

Alone with Pérelha, Hugo briefly told him his plan. "If you can get him up here he'll be safe enough for the present."

"And Mirepoix?" Pérelha queried acridly.

"They'll scarcely suspect *him*—as yet. He's doubtless well covered his track." Hugo gave a queer contorted laugh. "I fancy I'm sufficient target. Within an hour or two I'll be far away from here. You needn't worry. I'm traveling by foot—less noticeable."

But Ramon was regarding him now with genuine concern. "Where are you going—Montségur?" he added, frowning. The citadel was still a sore point with him.

"Hardly. I'm afraid I'm not cut out for the higher vision."

"You're probably best in Spain," Pérelha muttered, but he was already preoccupied with the work ahead of him. "My wife shall give you food before you go. I'll set off at once and take a couple of men I can trust. They won't be known at Sorèze. They'll get him out. God grant we're successful." He turned to go, then feeling perhaps he had let his natural dislike of the man override his appreciation of his action, he paused. "I'll tell him, of course, to whom he owes this—not Mirepoix," he added, half audibly and with secret satisfaction.

As he reached the door a hand was laid on his arm.

"Let me come too."

Hugo knew it at once. That limpid cool voice so curiously sharpened by emotional stress. Had she been standing there all the time in the shadows, he wondered?

"Impossible. Are you mad, child?" Pérelha was saying. "There's enough to do helping your mother prepare herbal baths and salves and medicaments—he'll need it," and as she continued to plead, he threw her gently off. "Get back to bed—you're worn out." She evidently knew the uselessness of gainsaying her father, for she was silent. Still for a moment she seemed to hesitate while his footsteps gradually faded. Then with a catch in her breath she turned again to the room and took a step or two forward and stopped. It struck d'Alfaro that her face, but for its look of wild desperation, had grown white and wan.

"Do you really think it will save him?"

"It ought to."

She shook her head doubtfully. "Mirepoix sent a message—it was impossible."

"He wasn't referring to this part of the problem."

"The man said you weren't in the plot, and yet you managed it?" she murmured unbelieving.

"Things probably manage themselves," he retorted.

"But it is really valid?" she persisted.

"The order of release?"

She nodded. "The seal. I don't understand. How did you get it?"

"From Friar Guillaume Arnaud himself."

She stared at him, still uncomprehending. "You mean before they murdered him?"

"Hardly." He gave a short unnatural laugh.

"Then how? You mean——?" the dark, dilated pupils seemed to have robbed her eyes of their green. "You mean—when he was dead?"

He did not answer.

She continued her strange half-horrified, half-fascinated gaze. "The man said it was like a charnel house. Yet you—you walked among them—a stranger——" Her voice, dwindling almost to a whisper, seemed to echo on the last word, giving it a weird and ambiguous meaning. To re-lieve the tension he rescued himself by one of his strident tags.

"Death's only a variation on the general theme of corruption." But she seemed not to hear.

"Did you do it for him?"

"Does one ever know why one does anything? One may think one does—actually one just has to, thanks to the secretion of one's liver—" Even as he spoke, it struck him forcibly with what consummate ease Mirepoix would have managed to draw profit from her words.

But her eyes, still fixed upon him, had regained something of their old light.

"One has to act as one does because one is—oneself—" Again there was that curious stress on the last word. "In the end one has to be oneself, though half the time one tries to deny it."

He could guess of whom she was thinking. "You said something of the same the first time we met—yet you refused to admit—"

A little spasm passed across her face. It was sufficient revenge.

"I've got to be gone," he said abruptly and turned away.

He had almost reached the door when she made a sudden movement to stop him.

"Not yet—"

He shook his head. "It's not safe—"

She glanced around her as if seeking some reason to keep him. Very faintly in the arch of the farthest window the sky seemed to have lightened. "It will be safer here during daylight."

He laughed. "I'm not the one to be considered."

"But stay—stay at least till he comes—" Suddenly there was fear, almost pleading, in her voice.

Did she want him to defend her against her own fear, her sense of shame? he thought.

"No, my dear." He shook his head. "There are moments when not only one's presence but the setting itself becomes superfluous,"

She made a vague movement as if to protest, but he

289

had reached the door and without looking round was gone.

Already she had half forgotten him. Standing there in the middle of the dark hall she could hear the sound of hoofs clattering away into the night—her father and his men. When they returned, she thought, it might once more be evening, but the hours that lay between them seemed to loom up and grow like a huge and ever broadening wedge driven deeper and deeper into the very sinews of her being.

Look at the world, Hugo was accustomed to mock, look at your mistress, beauty, love itself in the denuding light of dawn and you will be cured of your illusions. The humped heaps of the hills that rose out of the dawn to meet him on every side seemed to provide the ultimate proof of his dictum.

He remembered the place from his long and arduous ride in last summer's heat—an old disused mill half hidden by a cluster of trees. Then, however, the stream had been reduced to a mere trickle; now he could hear the roar of the water even from afar.

It was evidently quite forsaken, for what must once have been a path was overgrown by brambles. He made in fact no attempt at using it but, clinging to branches and roots, groped his way down the slippery bank. Dimly at the bottom he could discern the bulk of the half-ruined walls. A little later he had reached them. An empty shell, the home of no more than night birds and vermin and bats, offering a momentary shelter to a shepherd in a thunderstorm or a cooler shade for some rustic love tryst than a sweltering heat of the summer hills. Now it seemed an emblem of desolation and waste. As if to heighten that sense of human transience, the wheel, started on its old momentum again by the onrush of the melted snow, was working. Through the tumbled wall he could hear the clatter of the broken slats as it cranked and turned. Climbing over the stones he could see it a few feet beyond the foaming trough, a sinister and obdurate grinding away in unending revolutions of futility. Whatever was caught in that seething cauldron would be churned and mangled

290

to be sufficiently unrecognizable before the summer's drought had laid bare those stones again.

Carefully from his cloak he drew out the page of manuscript and the little bag. For a moment he stood as though weighing the latter in his hand. Then with a sudden movement he hurled it in the trough. Slowly, deliberately he began to tear the parchment into shreds. Bit by bit he watched it vanish into the churning rift, the object of Ramonet's reward, the work of months, of years, decimated, reduced in a few moments to utter futility. And curiously with every rip he was filled almost with zest at the thought of the opportunities lost. What if on the day of his discovery he had sent a message to Toulouse, what if by hook or crook, in secret, in disguise he had reached the city even now, instead— He laughed aloud. A dozen, a hundred possibilities thrown to the winds, since Allah alias Necessity willed it so, even as they determined that now he should be stepping forward balancing carefully, gingerly across the wet, slippery stone? Still there was a last fragment in his fingers. He stretched them out and a bit of spume, blown from the churning water beneath, touched the back of his hand. Why was he troubling to wipe it away—or was that long ago? he thought.

"Feel—" The coolness was still there—a nereid's touch upon his hand. Yes, what if after all, it flashed through his mind, he had accepted her invitation to stay? What if he had followed Peire-Roger of Mirepoix's parting hint? But all questioning was already drowned in the deafening roar of one gigantic evergrowing interrogation mark as, deliberately, cocking a last triumphant snook at the only god he affirmed, he leaned across the few feet dividing him from the wheel and plunged forward into the vortex of whitening foam and pitchy murk below.

THE FOREST

*Love seeks no cause beyond itself and no fruit;
it is its own fruit.*

(ST. BERNARD)

THE FOREST, THEY SAID, WENT ON FOREVER ABOVE THE
ravine of the Larset, through the endless winding gorges
of the Frau, southward to the Col di Chioula, eastward
toward the Aude, and even then, they said. . . .

Esclarmonde of Pérelha halted in fear. Supposing after
all she had lost her way, supposing she had penetrated the
enchanted forest—*las silvas encantadas*—from which
there was no way out? She shuddered, glancing round, for
truly it seemed there might be no escape from the trees,
from these pines that would not let through one pure gold
dancing sunbeam but wove out of the filtered rags their
own dim cobweb film of twilight—an alien element in
which familiar things themselves grew strange and lost
their solidity, dwarfed by the great tall tree trunks, so
black, so relentlessly sheer, yet, when you raised your
head to find whether they ever ended, shifting suddenly
out of focus into a leaning world of tapering masts, a sea
forest upon whose sunken bottom she moved and all was
only a semblance of things that might have been, that
never were.

What if indeed they were not, it struck her with terror,
what if these were not the woods she had ridden through
with her father to bring provisions to Wolf when he had
lain in hiding in the deserted forester's hut higher up the
gorge only a month before, and then again, a couple of
weeks ago? But already it seemed to her that no living
soul had ever trodden these ways. Fearfully she peered

round her, but only the pillared trees rose, seemingly rootless, out of the penumbral haze, sunk in their carpet of pine needles, centuries deep. She thought, they who have walked here have long passed into another world.

Or was it she who had left the world of men and walked straight into her childhood's magic, into the forest perilous whose dark impenetrable mazes she heaped around a rock of crystal out of a myriad pine needles in her secret grove of Lavelanet? For to reach Monmur one must penetrate the labyrinth of the enchanted forest. But not alone. Together in the legend Esclarmonde and Huon of Bordeaux set out on their journey to fairyland and together they had braved the perils of territories never known to man.

Yet Wolf of Foix, Wolf, for all the promise he had given her that day in the Sabarthez, had gone on alone, climbing higher and higher toward his inaccessible peaks.

"Monmur—" she almost cried the name aloud as if she would force him to wait, or let him know that she was struggling after. Monmur—the name was lost among the labyrinth of boughs. Was it only the reverberation of the gorge that caused its echoing to add that other syllable, Monmur—Montségur?

For it was Montségur to which he had sworn himself, for which he had suffered agony and torture and almost death.

Montségur—though he had tried to avoid speaking of it, though he had even denied shielding Peire-Roger and concealing his secrets. Then why? Almost she did not believe he knew himself. Yet in those weeks of his convalescence she had grown even more convinced that the strange detachment, almost indifference, in which he seemed wrapped as in an invisible cocoon was not born merely of physical pain or weakness or even of his anxiety about Honoria but of his dedication to a secret of which he himself was scarce aware. She had guessed it the very evening they had brought him up to Roccafissada, after that endlessly dragging journey whose hours had closed her in, even as did this forest, and yet when at last she had heard the slow careful clatter of hoofs in the court she had fled in fear and shame.

It was not till she heard that he slept that she had dared go near him and take her turn watching by his side.

They had left no candle burning and the moon lay on the farther side of the tower, but a faint radiance filled the room, reflected from the shimmering landscape outside. Shutting the door behind her, she had crept on tiptoe to the stool beside the bed. She had not dared to stir, scarcely to look up. In the dusk the body under the bed-clothes, bolstered with soft down pillows, had no shape. Only the arms lay straight, too straight, upon the coverlets, and the wrists terminated in the two hummocks of the poulticed, bandaged hands.

She had sat there crouched forward, her mouth smothered in her sleeves for fear she should cry out. Beside her the breathing of that motionless form had seemed to possess its own terrifying life till under the influence of the opiates they had given him it had gradually quietened or, growing used to it, she had at last been drawn into its rhythm. Had she even slept? Had he spoken? She had turned fearful, expectant. The room seemed lighter than before. He must have moved his head a little and, for a moment in fear and shame, thinking he saw her, she had shrunk back into the shadows. But his eyes retained the same focus, fixed across the room to the arched space of the window. And, following his rapt gaze, for her, too, the walls had seemed to fade away and she had seen only the shimmering contour of hill between the fluctuating darkness of forest and sky, and rising from their midst, poised as though floating above a black crater of shadow, a tusk of rock, spectral in the light of the moon. . . .

Montségur—

She had strained every nerve to hear the muttered words—some unintelligible rigmarole about masons, a mule, and then (she had held her breath) her name—Esclarmonde. But the next second she had known—remembering how as a runaway boy he had been lost in the mountains near Montségur and how (they said) it was Esclarmonde of Foix, her own godmother, who had saved him from being sent back to his monastery school. A fearful jealousy had sprung up in her heart, as in her childhood she had rebelled against the reiteration of that

294

saintly name. Perhaps even then she had apprehended that the ghost of Esclarmonde of Foix would thrust itself between them, as that battlemented rock to which he was dedicated in the secret realms of his being. For did she not know only too well that that secret world counted for more than the everyday world of men? Yet into his she had no entry, though it lay on the border of her own—

Mont-ségur—Mon-mur—. It needed only the change of a syllable to make their boundaries dissolve.

And here where all things lost their identity, merged in perennial twilight, might it not be possible? Clasping the bundle she was carrying, she plunged with renewed desperation between the trees.

Forest enclosed her. The silence seemed the more profound bcause there was practically no undergrowth, no hiding place for bird or scurrying beast. Only here and there at the roots of the trees or in the shadow of some moss-grown boulder or cluster of toadstools, beetles, and crawling insects plied their indefatigable logical-illogical trade. The gray diaphanous wings of a moth brushed against her face, so soft it might have been a momentary stirring of the air itself. Almost it seemed to her that if she touched one of the trees, its scabrous lichen bark would crumble under her hand.

And then suddenly she knew that, after all, she was not lost. Those three boulders of rock, and springing from their base as though they formed a monumental fountain, hidden in a tangle of grass and fern so that all that was visible was a damp dark oozing path of soil, the spring.

That was why they had once built the hut here. It was where Wolf would fetch his water daily. If she waited now he might even come and, though it might give him a shock for the moment, soon he would think it quite natural, for hadn't he called her a naiad long ago? Long ago and in all time to come. That was as good as timeless, but here and now, she caught herself up sharply, each hour, each minute counted, and supposing he had already fetched his water for today, or supposing he had gone out far on the hunt for good, yes, supposing . . . the dread that haunted her always and had been held in check by

295

the excitement of her excursion suddenly renewed itself so strongly that she knew she could never wait.

Should she then give the signal? She pursed her lips to utter the long-drawn note of the quail that she had practiced so long and that had brought him out of his hiding when she had come with her father, but then she hesitated, seized by the desire that he should be taken unawares, as at the first time of their meeting by the lake and once again in Durban.

Carefully she followed the almost invisible track so that she wondered whether in fact it was ever used.

She crept forward and parted the branches. The hut looked so little changed from the derelict appearance it had worn when first they had brought him there that once more for a moment she felt it was forsaken. Hesitating a moment, she pushed the door. It gave under her hand. She waited a second to see whether there would be any result, but as the silence remained unbroken, she pushed harder.

The single room was empty, but almost at once she realized it had been quite recently inhabited. A jug of water stood on the rough table and beside it the remnants of a meal—some bits of fibrous, indescribable vegetable or root, a half of the barley bread that the shepherd, who had been let into the secret of his hiding, brought him every week. And she remembered that if anything had befallen Wolf, the man would have let them know. She had tried to reassure herself on that point so often, but what might not happen from week to week, from hour to hour? Her eyes fell on the tumbled bed—no more than a rude pallet half covered with a heap of skins. She drew a little nearer. The impress of his body was still discernible hollowed out of the mattress of straw.

In blessed relief she sat down on the edge and half laughing, half weeping looked around the room, the dirty hearth, the broken plate, the stained iron pot over the burned-out logs—evidence of masculine inefficiency. After a moment she got to her feet and with an alacrity that would have made Corba of Pérelha reconsider her opinions of her daughter's housewifery ability she smoothed out the bed, cleared the débris from the table and hearth, repiled the logs, and emptied the unpalatable contents of the cauldron outside the door. Then, unpacking her bundle, she set the contents on the table as though she had been preparing a feast. He can come now, she thought with pride, and, exhausted, sank down on a stool. How hot it was and silent! Was it the forest, the proximity of the trees that made the silence bear down on the hut like a leaden weight? Beyond the half-open door the tiny patch of clearing burned in a jewel-like concentration of light. She was too sleepy to move. . . .

Suddenly she was wide awake. The bending of a bough—a twig cracking underfoot? Yes, surely these were footsteps. She sprang to her feet and pressed herself against the wall in the angle behind the open door. So at least she would see him first. But if it were not he? The footsteps had paused abruptly. He must have noticed the open door—believed perhaps he was betrayed. Almost she had come out of hiding when the sound of the steps was renewed. Straight and firm they came toward the door. It was thrust open so sharply that she was almost crushed against the wall.

He advanced into the middle of the room and stopped abruptly, staring at the table, the tidied hearth, the bed. Then slowly he turned.

She did not know what she had expected—amazement, incredulity, fear, the hunted look of an animal at bay? But all she saw as the momentary expression of shock faded from his features was the look of utter weariness. The effect was almost of disappointment as his body slackened with the realization that it had been a false alarm.

The laughter that had quickened in joyful expectancy on her lips ebbed away as speedily as it had come.

"I'm sorry. Did I frighten you?" she asked lamely and knew the answer vain.

"Frighten?" he echoed vaguely.

And turned with the same blunted, indifferent look toward the door.

"Is your father outside?" he muttered.

She shook her head. For a moment he continued wrapped, it seemed, in his uncaring torpor and then a dark uneasy light kindled in his eyes. "Has anything happened?"

"Nothing," she answered. "Nothing except—" She paused and a look of mystification spread over her features, half smile, half desperate pleading. "I came through the forest perilous," she said.

"The forest—?" he echoed uncomprehending. "Alone?" he added suddenly, as if the realization of some remote numbed fright had penetrated.

She nodded. "Yes. At one time I thought I had lost the way and that I would never get here—or out. Does one?" she added. She was standing leaning with her back against the door that she had almost closed behind her as if she would never let him escape.

"I haven't tried—" he murmured, and his voice was as devoid of hope as his looks. But to Esclarmonde he was only as once long ago in the Sabarthez.

He hadn't tried, she thought to herself, and suddenly she was full of hope, for if he hadn't, there was still time. She had caught him up. But when she spoke it was of the everyday world.

"Father's gone to Toulouse," she said, "about selling his linen—and I thought—if you needed anything—"

He shook his head. "The shepherd brings me barley cake every few days. There are enough toadstools in the woods—"

She wrinkled her nose in the direction of the iron pot over the burned-out logs. "I thought you'd like a change of fare and—the place was in a horrible mess—"

He glanced without interest around the hut. "You've cleared up—you shouldn't have troubled—"

She shook her head. "There's no need to live in squalor, just like a woodman." Her eyes rested on the torn peasant's tunic, the unkempt hair, the bronzed skin covered by the already considerable beard. "*They* wouldn't know you. Even in prison. . . ." But a secret light of recognition was in her eyes and she drew nearer. "And yet—you weren't so different—long ago in the Sabarthez. Come and eat," she persuaded, and as he still stood unmoving she crossed to the table. Pouring out the wine she cut the pasty into bits. At last he too sat down

298

and began to eat, reluctantly at first but with increasing appetite. As he put the food to his lips she saw that his fingers were still discolored, but that they had almost regained their natural shape. He hardly spoke and she began to talk about her father, the growing danger, the threats, the new ban of excommunication they had laid on Ramonet because of the murder of Avignonet. "No one's heard any more of d'Alfaro," she said. "If only he reached Spain—" And desperately, to wake him from his lethargy, she added, "I believe, whatever he said, he risked it for you—"

"For me?" he muttered and gave a bitter incredulous laugh. Getting to his feet, he crossed to the door.

He stood with his back toward her, looking out. It was only then she noticed that the brilliant oblong of sunlight had changed to a dull incandescent hue. It was stiflingly hot. Sometimes, she remembered, as though only now aware of the fact, a low rumbling as of distant thunder had broken the silence between her desperate efforts to make him talk. As he stood there gazing out she wondered did he stand there every day looking out, waiting, wondering how he could escape beyond the forest?

Why had he refused to go to Spain, as Hugo d'Alfaro had done? She knew the answer, though she would not have spoken it. He would have thought it escape while Honoria lived. Lived? Had she ever known what real life was? Had she ever done anything besides make it a blight for others as for herself? Never had she been able truthfully to muster up pity for the sick woman, thinking of what Honoria had done to him, curbing his ardor at every turn—he who had dreamed of his mad new world with Trencavel, he who had been the hero of the Mas d'Azil— And if it hadn't been for her would he have gone and squandered himself at Ax for the sake of a cold and impossible ideal? Already at Carcassonne people had mocked. But there his dreams had been warmed with friendship. She tried to think of them as she had heard them described, those young men in their light tunics, bare-armed, barefooted, wrestling, hurling their javelins, racing across the plain with Trencavel.

"Your tunic's torn to pieces," she merely said. "Take it

off, I'll mend it. I've brought needle and thread." Rummaging in the bundle she thought, "How practical I've become."

He only muttered something about its being too filthy and stepped into the open. Rising to her feet, she followed.

It was hotter even than in the hut. Strange was the light, as though it did not come from the sky but was reflected from the dark, ominous pall of cloud that hung motionless over the trees. Gleaming with a strange metallic hue, their branches seemed to have been cast in metal. Even the blades of grass stood rigid, brittle as glass. Around them the forest waited.

Wolf was looking up at the sky. "There are storms close on the Tabor nearly every evening," he said. "It's early today."

"It can't be far past noon," she said. "If only it would begin."

The air was stifling. She took a step forward in the direction of the trees.

"Take care," he said. "They're dangerous. They come suddenly once they begin."

"I'm not afraid of storms," she laughed. "At Roccafissada—"

"It's different here—the trees—"

But she stood undaunted, her hands behind her, face tilted backward as if awaiting the lightning's flash, but it did not come. Instead great drops of rain began to fall, single, reluctant, measuring the interminable hush, and once more ceased. The treetops seemed fused with the cloud to an invisible pall. Somewhere above it the thunder rolled.

And then suddenly the tent of solid air was ripped open—white, incandescent, a pathway blazed between the trees. She stretched her arms exultant, but at the same moment she felt herself wrenched back into the hut.

"Are you mad?" he asked, thrusting her to the farther corner so that she sank upon the bed.

He took up his stand by the door. She was trembling, not with fear but with angry excitement, caring now only that it should break, break right into the hut, into the heart of the forest, and set them free. But the peal of thunder grew more distant. Intermittently the narrow walls expanded in a pale incandescence. On its periphery the silhouette of Wolf now loomed, now receded. If only, she thought, that rending flash would come.

The rain began to descend in a steady vertical stream. They were caught, imprisoned not in that rending dreamed-of cove of light but by the rain's flashing monotony.

And suddenly she realized the water was flowing all around them, not only out there in the forest, but in the hut, dripping, pouring through roof and smoke hole, flowing in runnels down the log walls, squelching in the mud floor under their feet.

"Is it often like this?" she asked aghast, waking to the world of fact.

"Hardly—"

"But you said there are storms every evening."

"Not like this. It doesn't usually come to rain—in summer at least."

Had he, she wondered, brooded over what it might be like in winter? Or had he lost the sense of time? In the forest time itself had ceased.

"Your tunic," she said. "I'm going to mend it now." And when he still resisted: "I'll sew it on you, then." Reluctantly he dragged it off. As she prodded the needle in and out of the coarse crash, it seemed to her that at each stitch she struggled vainly to pierce the impermeable curtain of rain.

When, having finished, she looked up, Wolf was no longer standing in the doorway. She jumped to her feet.

And then she saw that the rain had ceased.

Beyond the door, the grass was a glittering spangle of light. Tags of cloud still drifted across the tops of the pines as though they would sweep away the treetops themselves.

"Wolf—" she almost cried. But then she saw him. He had climbed up on a stack of logs and was examining the roof. Hearing her, he turned and clambered down. "You'd better set out at once," he said, "in case it starts again. I'll take you part of the way."

She shook her head. "I'll see your roof mended first—" And before he could stop her she had run over to a great pile of furze on the other side of the hut. Gathering up a pile in her arms, she said, "I've seen the cowherds mend their roofs often enough." She was already climbing the logs. "Come, I'll help you." He was powerless to resist. Soon she was reaching up tufts of turf and bracken to stuff in the rifts. "You must be off now," he urged anxiously, but leaning forward she stretched her hands, trying to help his own to twist the strands of bracken in between the spliced branches. The bits of chipped bark and furze clung to her wet fingers. Her nostrils were bathed in the scent of the damp-sodden turf—she felt a fierce longing to plunge her arms, her whole self into the earth as if into the forest's bottom.

Suddenly Wolf had swung himself from the roof. "It's good enough to keep out hail and snow," he vouchsafed and standing by her side looked at their work. As he did so a pool of water collected in the uneven thatching was loosened and descended, an icy miniature cascade upon their upturned faces. Blindly their hands, trying to brush off the water, entangled. When at last they had shaken themselves free and stood panting, the breathless laughter upon her lips quivered an instant and passed to his own.

She wondered with a strange little spasm almost of pain when last, when ever before, she had seen him laugh? "Come—" For some reason incomprehensible now to herself she was urging him to make haste. "Your tunic's on the bed," she cried.

They hardly spoke on their way through the woods and when they parted where the track led on to the farm she hardly stayed to bid him farewell. "I'll come again soon," she called over her shoulder as she ran down the path, nor did she turn.

He thought of their parting long ago in the Sabarthez.

When it came to it, many weeks were actually to pass before she was to repeat her visit—alone at least. On the few occasions on which she accompanied her father there was little chance of their talking or continuing that deeper silence of understanding where they had left off. Guessing that in earlier years she might not have acquainted

Ramon of Pérelha with her caprices, Wolf made no reference to their last meeting; but if Esclarmonde had kept it secret she was unconscious and indeed innocent of duplicity, for even now, as in her childhood, where could one draw a clear distinction between outward existence and that secret world in which she had as habitually lived? What relationship was there for all its terrible actuality between Wolf of Foix's hiding in these immense yet terrestrial forests and their meeting in the enchanted territories on the threshold of a second yet no less palpable world? His world or hers—Monmur or Montségur?

She listened as her father told Wolf of the latest developments—how the Church, infuriated by the murder of the Inquisitors, was inciting the French overlords to a desperate attempt to destroy the last heretic fortress and that as a consequence, Hugues d'Arcis, the relentless seneschal of Carcassonne, was gathering an armed force with which to besiege the citadel of Montségur.

They would have their work cut out, Ramon was saying, what with the impregnable position and the tenacity of its defenders. Peire-Roger, he grudgingly admitted, possessed the flair for seeing that its walls were manned by those who abounded in the qualities in which he, Mirepoix, was deficient. Nonetheless Ramon could not overcome his misgivings.

To Esclarmonde, listening, it was evident that her father was expressing the hidden wish that Wolf should join the defenders. If for a moment she had felt a qualm that his answer would be anything but impartially negative, her eyes lay on his with secret recognition when it came, for what, she thought, had her Montségur to do with Mirepoix's spurious fantasies, what even with the refuge of a cold, bleak Cathar asceticism?

And to the one question that was ever unspoken on Wolf's lips Ramon of Pérelha had no answer.

It was she who eventually brought it up. With the utmost care to avoid suspicion they had made inquiries as to Honoria of Durban's whereabouts, but in vain. And then one day while her father was absent on a journey, her mother had returned in a state of high excitement from a visit to the nunnery in which there was one of her cousins who had been reconverted to the Catholic faith. The sisters had been full of news that in the previous week they had had consigned to their care a number of sick Cathar incorrigibles and among them a woman of noble birth but unsound mind. When Corba, struggling to check her twittering curiosity, had managed to draw a description from the gossipy nuns, she had been left with little doubt that the tall, cadaverously handsome woman whom they had in their care was Honoria, though the state of will-less, beatified content in which she was alleged to find herself seemed to have little or nothing in common with the harrowed, unremitting energy of the woman she had known.

We must let Wolf know as soon as Father returns, Esclarmonde had said when her mother came back, but her heart was already beating with a plan.

THE TARN (SYNOPSIS)*

*You exist not alone. You cannot stay unchanging in a
world that all around is changing.*

RAMON OF PÉRELHA AND ESCLARMONDE FETCH WOLF
and hide him in Roccafissada to recuperate.

The shadow of Honoria's madness, which is almost
complete, mars their idyll.

Esclarmonde hears that the hermit has appeared in the
Ariège. Together they go in search of him. The hermit
shows them the caves and initiates them into the mystery
of the world of crystal and stone. In the darkness something of the "otherness" they experienced in the pigeon
house overcomes them. Esclarmonde reaches for Wolf's
hand, but it trembles under her touch. The hermit speaks
of the hard, imprisoned, self-centered, fixed light of the
minerals and crystals compared to the fluctuating light of
sun and moon. The flux of the eternal spring—fire and
water—light in water whose symbol is the pearl. When
they ask him to teach them, the hermit tells them they
can teach each other far more than he.

On the way back, Esclarmonde suddenly darts away
from Wolf. He follows in her track, coming out from the
trees. All is mist; at last he catches a glimpse of her hair
like flames flowing through smoke. It seems to him that
he has to dash into the heart of fire to reach her.

Arrived home, they find Honoria in strange excitement
though apparently saner. While Wolf is away Honoria
shows Esclarmonde the serpent fillet that Jordan of the
Isle has just given her on a visit during Esclarmonde's and
Wolf's absence as proof of their adulterous passion.

* This synopsis was written by the author, who died at forty-seven
before she was able to complete her novel or to go over the manuscript for final revisions.

Further tyranny and persecution of the Cathars. Mirepoix undertakes defense of Montségur as last refuge. Philippa accompanies him with Corba to superintend the refugee camp and the wounded. Esclarmonde tells Wolf of the discovery of Honoria and that she has decided to accompany her family to Montségur.

Jordan's interview with Hugues d'Arcis and plan for final destruction of Montségur. On his way Jordan is attacked by the heretical faedits. Found in darkness by Wolf, who saves his unconscious body and in the dawn recognizes it as Jordan. After terrible moral struggle does not kill him.

Hugues d'Arcis marches on Montségur to exterminate it. The ring tightens round the citadel—a whole year passes. Promised help fails to materialize. The garrison is more and more depleted. Wolf, tormented by his useless existence, thoughts of the vengeance missed, and hardly a word from Esclarmonde, hears of the faedits' plan to break through the French ring. The suspicion that he wants to join the guerrillas causes the death of Honoria. But when he hears them start out on their expedition at night, he takes Trencavel's sword from its hiding place and follows them.

They are overcome in the skirmish that ensues—arms and men captured and many flee in the darkness, but Wolf finds himself on the hither side of Montségur. He reaches the village and is hidden by the villagers. A shepherd who is in the habit of acting messenger to the citadel by a goat path up the seemingly unscalable precipice offers to take him up the following night. The dizzy climb in the darkness.

He arrives to find the citadel in extremis. Ramon of Pérelha seems reconciled to inevitable disaster. Only Mirepoix retorts with seeming bravado and welcomes the long-lost champion of the Grail.

Esclarmonde appears in the midst and so distracts Wolf from Mirepoix's raillery, but she cannot remain and has to return to her post of nursing the wounded.

But the passions awakened by the fight in the valley and by seeing Esclarmonde have roused all the demons that Wolf had for years struggled to quell. Fanned by

306

Mirepoix's jests, a sickening hatred of all Montségur embodies takes hold of him, as he sees his dream truly shattered. He is filled only with the desire to rescue Esclarmonde. Mad ideas of escape take hold of him. Mechanically he looks for the shepherd and sees him speak to Mirepoix and then disappear.

It is evening before he can see Esclarmonde alone, but she can be kept only a few moments from the side of her dying brother. He manages to tell her of Honoria's death. Then comes out with his plan to flee. Even if it were possible, she insists she cannot leave Montségur.

He realizes his madness, overcome by her bravery, and swears that he will remain to defend Montségur to the last. But she who had once incited him to arms is now troubled by this decision in him.

Suddenly the castle is aroused by cries of treachery.

The French have broken in.

Mirepoix gives the sign of surrender. Wolf, crying that Mirepoix has betrayed them, wants to fall on him but Pérehla holds him back. The French arrive with conditions of free transit for Mirepoix and his treasures. The castle is to be handed over the following dawn.

The final day passes—apathy and reaction and memories of Carcassonne.

Ramon Pérehla is hardly to be roused from his complete exhaustion.

At night Wolf makes his way to Mirepoix's room, the naked sword in his hand. In the passage he is waylaid by Esclarmonde. She draws him into an adjoining vault.

There, wrestling against his hatred of Mirepoix and the unworthy suspicion that her defense arouses in Wolf, she pleads their common guilt—the arguments that he once used. But he refuses to allow her to be implicated. He even implores her to dissociate herself from the Cathar faith. But she is determined to stand by Philippa and confesses her own guilt as a child, which brought the whole disaster on Philippa and Montségur— Overwhelmed, the fevered madness falls from Wolf and he remembers how he had failed Esclarmonde of Foix more than Mirepoix. He had confessed it once to the hermit. Now he truly realizes that he has failed.

He drops the sword.

Esclarmonde tells him what he can do to retrieve his boyish vow.

Four men are to be let down ropes and take the message of the Grail into the world. Three Cathari have been chosen: he is to be the fourth. He can hardly take in what she is saying; when he realizes it at last the agonized knowledge of what he is leaving her to overcomes him utterly. Then she reminds him of his promise to take her to the top of the Tabor. "If you go, you will take me with you," she says.

Hopelessly he regards the sword at his feet. Even if for her sake he agreed, how could he be one of the chosen— "You see what I am," he muttered.

"That which you were a moment past?" she asked. "And this also," she added.

And even I was near denying it, she thought troubled. And once, long ago, on the ramparts of Foix—

And yet I knew he hadn't changed, at the root of him.

Love—to look on another not as we would have him but as he is. The holiness of the fact.

"If I do not shrink from you, why should you shrink from yourself?"

And he remembered the hermit's words: "At root we are all one, in our depth as in our height."

A step sounded in their rear, but he did not hear it till the shadow of Bertran Marty fell across them.

"He has consented," she said. She was bending over him. He felt her hair across his face, but it was the elder's hand that lay on his shoulder. "They are ready," he said.

Wasn't it Trencavel who had spoken those words? But it was Wolf himself now who was going. The sword lay on the ground—

I have given it back, he thought, and wondered what he meant. Where she had stood there was only a pool of moonlight on the stones.

"We must not keep them," Marty said. As one who walks in his sleep he followed the old man through what seemed a labyrinth of stone.

The night air blew cold upon him.

He was the fourth.

On the third day—two of the elders had taken the path via Ax—he and his companions had emerged into the height of Vicdessos. "We had best rest awhile," the other said.

Now anguish sweeps over him. Radiance of sun-edged cloud, beauty *and* anguish. Why?—the question swells like a gigantic interrogation mark between the unfathomable depth of water and the infinite height of the sky.

Wolf by the Tarn. He realized that Esclarmonde had taken to her the whole of himself and with it the whole of his loves and hates. But in that sense of liberation there seemed to flow in upon him the fullness of all outside himself. His hand had picked up a stone. He was wondering where he had seen it before—of that very shape.

And then he began to remember his dream of the hermit. "You spent years in quest of the unreachable and all the time you were blind to the treasure that lay at your feet." He lifted his eyes to the Pyrenean chain —They were still there—unmitigable as when he was a child, humped with gray rock, shadowed with forest, towering under the silence of those eternal snows. Yet whatever darkness he had yet to penetrate, whatever summit he yet might reach, even though the mists might descend and swallow him up, he knew that it was only into the fastness of his spirit he need look to discover the light of Montségur.

Still holding the stone in his hand, he climbs on toward the pass.

Yet only when we have stopped seeking do we at last tread the path to the goal.

AUTHOR'S HISTORICAL NOTES

During recent years the Albigensian, or Cathar, heresy has aroused considerable interest both among scholars and writers, many of whom have come to believe that it exercised an important influence on medieval poetry and legend.

Based on Manichaean belief and the doctrine of the heretic sect known as the Paulicians, it appears to be impregnated with Gnostic ideas and concepts that remind one rather of Buddhism and the philosophy of the Far East. Its essential quality, however, seems to be in the emphasis it laid on the spiritual, inward side of religion, a fact that unites it with mysticism and that Perennial Philosophy that has continued to find expression from age to age among the most varied races.

Most of our knowledge of the Cathar heresy has, alas, been gathered from the annals of the Inquisition, and, being based on confessions extracted by physical and mental torture or from the mouths of the illiterate, must necessarily suffer from distortion.

The Manichaean dualism of which the Cathars have been accused appears to have been not always so extreme as is often suggested, and though a certain number may have insisted on an absolute cleavage between spirit and flesh, the majority seem rather to have believed in an incessant struggle between Good and Evil, light and darkness, in which, however, even Evil will ultimately be drawn into triumphant Good. Stress was nonetheless laid to such a degree on spiritual values that even the Incarnation of Christ was rejected, the Crucifixion being regarded as a semblance. In the same way all earthly things were only too easily relegated to the province of a mirage-like delusion effected by Satan, the creator of the apparent world.

Thus, for the Cathars, all man's striving must be direct-
ed to the one goal—to liberate the Divine spark from its
earthly prison, human creatures being regarded as fallen
angels incarcerated in the darkness of the flesh. This,
however, could be achieved as a rule only in the course of
countless rebirths in which the spirit migrates not only
from body to body and age to age, but from star to star.
The process might, it is true, be hastened by the
consolamentum, "the laying on of hands," but even this
ritual, which is described in an extant medieval
manuscript, betrays many orthodox characteristics and ac-
tually also makes mention of baptism by water, though
the Cathars in their belief and practice, even if they did
not reject the material element completely, certainly ap-
pear to have laid all the stress on baptism by the Spirit.
The consolamentum, which indeed stands for the reinte-
gration of the true Self with its divine angelic origin, was
moreover used as the rite of ordination, through which the
Cathar postulant became one of the true "perfecti." In a
few cases the "consoled," having transcended the things
of the earth, now proceeded to throw off the last shackle
by committing suicide, or "endura"; others seemed to
have entered on a hermit- or yogi-like existence, but the
majority became the elders of the Cathar Church, volun-
tarily continuing their earthly tie in order to lead others to
the Light through example and teaching.

The many apparent contradictions in the Cathar faith
can perhaps be explained by the likelihood that they laid
far less stress on actual dogma than on a way of life—the
attempt to return to the unadulterated faith of the Early
Christians, and indeed even the worst enemies of the
Cathars have praised their exemplary asceticism. In this
connection it may be mentioned that in their attitude to
life, in their vegetarianism and pacificism they foreshadow
the Quakers and other sects, while socially they strove to
realize the ideal of Christian communism. Nevertheless,
rigorous as the perfecti or elders were in regard to their
own rule of life, their tolerance towards others, even
towards the "Believers," was unlimited. This in itself may
have given an opportunity for the distortion of the pursuit
doctrine of love into those concepts that characterize the

311

cult of Courtly Love professed by the troubadour, though the latter is more likely to be a parallel movement deriving much from Arab influence and Persian mystic thought, a fact that, however, provides another link with the Perennial Philosophy. In the same way the lack of a rigid dogma may have made possible the infiltration of Eastern philosophy and legend, and even inspired, among lay sympathizers, a cult of the Grail. It is significant that the German medieval poet Wolfram von Eschenbach, in the "Parzival," maintains that he was inspired by a mysterious "Provençal" of the name of Kyot, whose unknown work some scholars have connected with Manichaean and Persian legends of the East.

Towards the end of the twelfth century the Cathari (Cathars) or Pure, as they were called, had become so important a sect in the South of France that the Roman Catholic Church, seeing its authority undermined, determined to put an end to the heresy, at first by the gentle method of persuasion. But the luxury and pomp of the papal legates and ecclesiastic missionaries only aroused the derision and scorn of the heretics. Domingo di Guzman (St. Dominic), realizing that the respect enjoyed by the Cathar elders was indeed largely due to the contrast their ascetic life afforded to that of the corrupt clergy, persuaded the missionaries to emulate the Christian simplicity of their rivals. But even his indefatigable zeal and asceticism were unable to make any lasting impression on the inhabitants of Languedoc, to whom heresy and the tolerance of the Cathar elders gave a chance of indulging a traditional love of freedom, emancipation from Rome, and moral licence that combined the remnants of pagan hedonism with a cultural refinement far in advance of the time.

Compelled at last to resort to force, Pope Innocent III proclaimed a Crusade, inciting the princes to take up arms against Raymond VI, Count of Toulouse, and all his vassals who professed the heretic faith or protected its adherents. The promise of adventure and booty without having to encounter the dangers of the East, coupled in some cases no doubt with religious sincerity, brought a quick response, and vast numbers, including the most *powerful barones of Burgundy and Flanders, flocked to join the Crusade, though Philippe Auguste, King of France, occupied by his quarrel with England, refused to weaken himself by an expedition to Languedoc.*

Nothing, however, could have been more in keeping with his dream of re-establishing the glory of France (so pitiably reduced since the days of Charlemagne) than the ultimate conquest of the powerful territories of the Count of Toulouse, and at the moment he could rely on his aims being fully safeguarded by the crusading zeal of his vassal Simon de Montfort (father to the "English" Montfort of Parliamentary fame).

The so-called religious crusade that swept over Languedoc in the year 1209 was, in fact, soon unmasked as a war of aggrandizement in which the greed of the Northern barons devoured the wealth and possessions of the expropriated nobility and powerful bourgeoisie of the South, for in Languedoc and Provence the cities and its foremost burghers, maintaining Roman tradition, enjoyed privileges unknown at that date in the feudal North. Actually, within a few years, the territory that had given birth to one of the most significant literary movements—the lyric poetry of the troubadours—was reduced to a waste over which the intrepid but ruthless Simon de Montfort exercised a rule of terror.

At the same time the Church was hardly less rigorous in its work of extermination, and month by month hundreds of heretics were led to the stake. Under the auspices of Domingo de Guzman a "court of inquiry" traveled the country and, quartered now in one district, now in another, invited the inhabitants, during what was termed a period of Grace, to confess not only their own heresy but to inform on that of their neighbors—proceedings which inevitably led to the institution of the Inquisition and to horrors of which its founder St. Dominic certainly never dreamed.

During the earlier years of the Albigensian Crusade, Toulouse itself, by virtue of the vacillating cat-and-mouse policy of its sovereign Raymond, was spared the holocaust, but in the end even the patience of this possibly

313

*far-sighted opportunist was exhausted and he was drawn
into the mêlée.*

*[It is at approximately this point in history that Wolf
of Foix—protagonist of Hannah Closs's trilogy—made his
appearance on the scene. As some time has passed since
the publication of the first two novels about him, readers
may wish to reacquaint themselves with the substance of
these stories, though doing so is not essential to an understanding of the present book. Synopses of the earlier
novel thus appear on the following pages.]*

Throughout the trilogy that closes with The Silent Tarn
*historical dates and intervals of time have been consci-
ously modified in the course of the narrative.*

*As to Wolf, bastard of Foix, apart from a legendary
anecdote regarding his birth and a couple of references in
the "Chanson de la Croisade contre les Albigeois," and
the annals of the Inquisition, practically nothing is known
of his character.*

*Montségur lies in a remote valley of the Pyrenees, not
far from Foix.*

*The Sabarthez is the part of the Ariège valley that ex-
tends from Tarascon to Ax-les-Thermes and lies between
Foix and Andorra. The lake, which existed till the
eighteenth century, has dwindled to the breadth of the
river itself, but the grottoes and fortified caverns or spul-
gas are still there, as is the natural tunnel in the Mas
d'Azil. In the summer of 1947 I was able to explore the
district at leisure.*

Synopsis of HIGH ARE THE MOUNTAINS

As a boy, Wolf, bastard of the house of Foix, runs away from his monastery school, his sensitive and inquiring spirit no more able to find, in monastic seclusion, an answer to the questions that perplex it, than in the military career alternatively offered him by his father. In the Pyrenees he encounters a hunter whose insinuating cynicism and spirit of pure negation utterly mar for him the profound experience roused a moment before by the stillness of a mountain tarn. Fleeing in horror, he loses his way and is put on the right path by an old man whom he subsequently imagines to be an elder of the Cathar faith. Spending the night near the ruin of Montségur which is being restored as a Cathar citadel by his aunt, Esclarmonde of Foix, he sees himself already its chosen champion and, mounted on a pitifully unheroic mule, rides to Pamiers to bring her a message from the masons, only to encounter his father.

The situation is saved by Esclarmonde who effects the boy's removal to Carcassonne to train as squire under the young and idealistic Viscount Trencavel. Here, falling under the spell of the emancipated daughter of Trencavel's Jewish financier and her circle of intellectuals and aesthetes, Wolf, tormented by adolescent passion, once more attempts to learn more of the Cathar faith. A harrowing sermon by the Cathar bishop, Guilhalbert of Castres, and Wolf's subsequent stay at Durban, the home of one of his fellow squires, enables him to do so, but his enthusiasm fades under the more powerful emotion of his friendship with Trencavel, during which his dream of a Universal Brotherhood of Montségur gradually suffers a transmutation into an amalgam of pagan athleticism and social reform. But the ideals which he and Trencavel attempt to materialize by the formation of the New Guard, in which citizen and noble are bound together in comradeship, are shattered by the onslaught of the Crusade, and his father compels him to return to Foix where he meets again with Esclarmonde.

She, whom a personal tragedy had years ago caused to embrace the Cathar faith, had been moved by the wild enthusiasm of the runaway boy, whom she now hopes to enroll in the Guard of Montségur, but her dreams are frustrated by the jealousy of her son, in whom Wolf recognizes the hunter by the tarn. Hearing from him that Raymond of Toulouse has yielded to the Crusaders and that the Northern armies are marching on Béziers, Wolf has only one goal—to return to Trencavel. Reaching Carcassonne only just in time, he helps Trencavel stimulate the New Guard to a heroic resistance that is broken only by drought and the consequent outbreak of fever.

When the Crusaders invite the Viscount and his vassals to negotiate, Trencavel, haunted all his life by the brutalities of his forebears towards the citizens, decides at last to offer himself as hostage on condition that the citizens may go free. But the Northerners violate their promise of safe conduct. The nobles are held back as prisoners and the citizens are allowed only to escape with their lives while their property is confiscated. Montfort, entering Carcassonne in triumph, throws Trencavel into the dungeons of his own castle, while the old hedonist, Raymond of Toulouse, enjoying the fruits of his opportunist policy, shares the banquet and aesthetic spoils of the victor. In the meantime Wolf of Foix has managed to escape with Miriam to Narbonne where her father attempts to achieve the viscount's ransom. Once more Wolf falls under Miriam's spell, but wearying of his idealism, she tries to analyze his enthusiasm for the workers as a sense of inferiority resulting from his bastardy and the false supposition that his mother was a peasant.

The disillusionment which he long refuses to admit is effected at last by the appearance of Peire-Roger of Mirepoix, his brilliant rival who, forever toying with some new aesthetic cult, has planned a pseudo Order of the Grail for Montségur and who now arrives in Narbonne *with the news of Trencavel's death. Completely shattered, Wolf is borne back by the nihilist student, Hugo d'Alfaro, to Foix, obsessed only with the promise made to Trencavel to fight on, and his resolve to avenge him.*

Synopsis of DEEP ARE THE VALLEYS

The story ranges from scenes of battle and guerrilla warfare to the quiet endurance and martyrdom of the Cathar believers; from the frivolities of an effete aestheticism to the search for truth in the alchemists' dens of Spain; from the vegetarian puritanism of the sectarians to memories of pagan ritual amongst the caverns of the Pyrenees, while the meeting of the hero with the child Esclarmonde of Pérelha affords one of the most poignant and unforgettable incidents in a book whose realism is transfused with poetry and spiritual significance.

For the exciting outward action is a mirror of the inner life of the characters: above all, of Wolf of Foix, and the dark Nemesis that pursues him.

Embittered by the death of his friend Trencavel at the hands of Simon de Montfort, he is haunted by one obsession—to avenge him, and so is flung into warfare from whose brutalities he actually shrinks. But the uncompromising pacifism of his wife Honoria drives him back from exile to join the citizens' insurrection in Toulouse. Victory, the almost accidental death of Montfort and the reinstallation of the opportunist ruler, Count Raymond, leave him with a sense of utter frustration. Maimed in body and spirit, he lands himself in circumstances so disastrous that he can only be healed by a complete reintegration of his being.

At the same time, his own struggles are but threads in the mesh interweaving a variety of characters which reflect the author's deep understanding of human nature, while here realization of the power of Evil has a psychological and metaphysical significance for our "existential" age.

FROM THE LAST LETTERS WRITTEN
BY HANNAH CLOSS

The dim Lethal stream is but a figment, and through winter and December the plains of Enna and the flowers and the winds and the gamboling lambs and calves and goats are the reality and the surety of their return.

All vision is really the apprehension of an infinite Rhythm, whether one calls it Spirit or Hvarnah or the music of the pipes of Pan.

If there is any immortality I shall be content to think of it as our becoming part of that Rhythmic being. . . .

Do we not really hanker after knowledge and understanding it all—which (at least to our earthly experience) seems to demand the survival of the ego—but the ego is integrated at last. . . .

I can get no further than this earth, and there I am bewildered, but of one thing at least I am sure, and this faith, too, is an aspect of that Rhythmic idea—that we have in us the power of infinite renewal—of being born anew in the imagination on the earth. Perhaps that is the nearest we can really come to our idea of immortality.

ALL TIME BESTSELLERS
FROM POPULAR LIBRARY

☐	THE BERLIN CONNECTION—Simmel	08607-6	1.95
☐	THE BEST PEOPLE—Van Slyke	08456-1	1.95
☐	A BRIDGE TOO FAR—Ryan	08373-5	2.50
☐	THE CAESAR CODE—Simmel	08413-8	1.95
☐	DO BLACK PATENT LEATHER SHOES REALLY REFLECT UP?—Powers	08490-1	1.75
☐	ELIZABETH—Hamilton	04013-0	1.75
☐	THE FURY—Farris	08620-3	2.25
☐	THE HAB THEORY—Eckert	08597-5	2.50
☐	HARDACRE—Skelton	04026-2	2.25
☐	THE HEART LISTENS—Van Slyke	08520-7	1.95
☐	TO KILL A MOCKINGBIRD—Lee	08376-X	1.75
☐	THE LAST BATTLE—Ryan	08381-6	2.25
☐	THE LAST CATHOLIC IN AMERICA—Powers	08523-2	1.50
☐	THE LONGEST DAY—Ryan	08380-8	1.95
☐	LOVE'S WILD DESIRE—Blake	08616-5	1.95
☐	THE MIXED BLESSING—Van Slyke	08491-X	1.95
☐	MORWENNA—Goring	08604-1	1.95
☐	THE RICH AND THE RIGHTEOUS —Van Slyke	08585-1	1.95

Buy them at your local bookstores or use this handy coupon for ordering:

Popular Library, P.O. Box C730, 524 Myrtle Avenue, Pratt Station Brooklyn, N.Y. 11205

Please send me the books I have checked above. Orders for less than 5 books must include 60¢ for the first book and 25¢ for each additional book to cover mailing and handling. Postage is FREE for orders of 5 books or more. Check or money order only. Please include sales tax.

Name_____   Books $_____
Address_____   Postage _____
                                        Sales Tax _____
City_____State/Zip_____   Total $_____

Please allow 4 to 5 weeks for delivery